Praise for

THE OLD RELIGION

'Waites brings all his storytelling talent and experience to this chilling tale, with results so spectacular I might never go to Cornwall again. Superb'

LEE CHILD

'Waites is one of the very best crime writers we have, simple as that. I'd been looking forward to this book for a long time and, boy, it was worth waiting for. I don't know if I devoured IT or IT devoured ME . . .'

MARK BILLINGHAM

'Martyn has written another raw, deftly-plotted thriller with a dark heart and a real emotional punch'

SIMON KERNICK

'Authentically spooky, thrillingly atmospheric and unnervingly relevant. It reads like *The Wicker Man* for the Brexit era'

CHRIS BROOKMYRE

'Reading Martyn Waites is a guaranteed thrill-ride. His characters sing off the page, his plots keep you guessing until the end, and I always read his books in a day. So grab *The Old Religion* and make Martyn Waites your new religion!'

SARAH PINBOROUGH

'A joyous new series with an adorable hero. Waites has come thundering back with all his talent intact'

ALEX MARWOOD

'A chilling slice of country noir. Great stuff'

MICK HERRON

'One of those books you start reading and feel it envelope you like a second skin, meaning you can't put it down. Deliciously creepy, with a startling evocation of that scary old village with hidden secrets vibe. I loved it. Every word. Superbly written, creepy as hell, and chilling to the bone. I can't recommend it highly enough!'

LUCA VESTE

'A superbly atmospheric book full of menace and secrets'

TOM WOOD

'*The Old Religion* is Martyn Waites at his dark and chilling best, a landmark work of rural noir which tears apart the countryside idyll and exposes just how twisted its bones really are'

EVA DOLAN

'The master of sinister. Prepare to be creeped out'

ANGELA CLARKE

'Martyn Waites is already crime fiction royalty. With *The Old Religion* he has delved into the fears and hearts of disillusioned Britain. Tom Killgannon is one of the best new characters in modern fiction. I bloody loved this book'

STEVE CAVANAGH

'An excellently woven crime novel, with a captivating setting and a brilliant lead character, from master storyteller Martyn Waites'

RAGNAR JONASSON

'A compulsive and creepy crime novel, *The Old Religion* is brilliantly atmospheric and original. It's one of those books you keep saying to yourself – just one more chapter – and then realise you've been up all night. One of the best books I've read this year'

STAV SHEREZ

'Deeply unsettling and hauntingly realistic, *The Old Religion* takes all the things I love in a book and smashes them together – hard'

SUSI HOLLIDAY

'This is a great read – dark and disturbing, like *The Wicker Man* reinvented for our own troubled times. This is the side of Cornwall you'd rather not see – full of sinister undercurrents – but the result is a novel that's gripping from the first page to its incredibly satisfying climax'

KEVIN WIGNALL, AUTHOR OF *A DEATH IN SWEDEN*

'*The Old Religion* is crime noir at its finest. Gritty, claustrophobically tense and deeply emotive – unputdownable!'

STEPH BROADRIBB, AUTHOR OF *DEEP BLUE TROUBLE*

'I LOVED *The Old Religion*. I adored the tense, taut prose punctuated with lyricism; the dark and twisting plot; the dance between the main characters'

A. K. BENEDICT, AUTHOR OF *THE EVIDENCE OF GHOSTS*

'A twisting, atmospheric, scary tale that delves into Cornwall's dark side – ancient *and* modern – to introduce a terrific new character in troubled cop-in-hiding Tom Killgannon. You won't be finding this one on the Cornish Tourist Board's reading list . . .'

ANYA LIPSKA, AUTHOR OF *THE KISZKA & KERSHAW SERIES*

Martyn Waites was born in Newcastle Upon Tyne. He trained at the Birmingham School of Speech and Drama and worked as an actor for many years before becoming a writer. His novels include the critically acclaimed Joe Donovan series, set in the north-east of England, and *The White Room*, which was a *Guardian* book of the year. In 2013 he was chosen to write *Angel of Death*, the official sequel to Susan Hill's *Woman in Black*, and in 2014 won the Grand Prix du Roman Noir for *Born Under Punches*. He has been nominated for every major British crime fiction award and has also enjoyed international commercial success with eight novels written under the name Tania Carver.

THE OLD RELIGION

RELIGION

Martyn Waites

ZAFFRE

First published in Great Britain in 2018 by
ZAFFRE PUBLISHING
80-81 Wimpole St, London W1G 9RE
www.zaffrebooks.co.uk

A CIP catalogue record for this book is
available from the British Library.

Trade paperback ISBN: 978–1–78576–414–1
Hardback ISBN: 978–1–78576–431–8

also available as an ebook

1 3 5 7 9 10 8 6 4 2

Typeset by IDSUK (Data Connection) Ltd

Printed and bound by Clays Ltd, St Ives Plc

Zaffre Publishing is an imprint of Bonnier Zaffre,
a Bonnier Publishing company
www.bonnierzaffre.co.uk
www.bonnierpublishing.co.uk

To Jamie,
Turns out it's just like The Black Keys said

PART ONE

1

Kyle Tanner opened his eyes. Peering out from the back of a deep, dark cave. Breathing jagged and heavy, body not his own, head not his own. He was walking. Staggering.

Where . . .? Why . . .?

Memory came back in fragments. Globs of paint dropped on a canvas, forming only an incomplete picture. His two mates. A campsite. Then there was a girl. Small, pretty. Nice smile. And some kind of spliff. Strong. Nauseatingly, sickeningly strong. Felt the smoke in his lungs, the heat prickling, stinging, head spinning . . . And then . . .

Nothing.

He kept walking, stumbling. Going nowhere. Waiting for more paint to fall, fill in the landscape. Then he heard something. A voice. Someone was talking to him. He turned, trying to trace the source.

'I said, d'you want a lift?'

It was the girl. With the smile and the spliff. Lily? Lila? Leaning out of the window on the passenger side of a VW camper van.

'My mates . . .'

'Went back ages ago,' she said. 'Come on, get in.'

He did so. Grateful not to have to walk.

The van pulled away.

And Kyle Tanner was never seen alive again.

2

The waves roiled and pushed towards the bay, dragging with them the threat of danger and violence, to a rising accompaniment of white noise. Some didn't make the shore, crashing against the lumpen rock outliers, breaking on the cliff faces, bursting upwards and outwards, all white spume and foam, a crescendoing explosion of static. Sheer, primal power. Whatever was left made it through to the shore, curling and unfolding, then lying down flat. Thin and spent. Their threat, their power, gone. Then the sea clawed them back once more, starting the whole process all over again.

Tom Killgannon watched from a cliff top. Hooded, bundled. His bad-weather gear was supposed to keep him insulated, impassive to the elements. But it didn't, even with the hood of his waterproof pulled over his head. The rain stung his exposed features, hurled into his face by gales threatening to uproot trees and upend people, icy needles shattering against his skin. He wished he could be as impervious to the elements as the rocks below were to the waves. But he wasn't. Nowhere near.

The clouds were low, dark and heavy. They leached the colour from the surrounding landscape, rendered the world a perpetual twilight. Black birds wheeled, caught in the airstream, cawing, a murder of angry dots. Tom weathered the elements, stood his ground. Watched the bay below.

Some desperate surfers had got themselves into wetsuits and were running down over the shingle towards the sea, racing each other to be the furthest out, fastest in. Idiots, he thought. Why would they want to court life-altering injuries, or even death, by hurling themselves against nature at its angriest? What did they have to prove, to themselves or anyone else? What was lacking in their lives that drove them to do that? He didn't know, didn't want to speculate. Just knew that these people hadn't faced real horror in their lives, real danger. If they had, the last thing they would do was actively seek it out.

He checked his watch, turned away from the cliff face, the surfers and their stupid death wishes dismissed.

Time to go to work.

The Sail Makers pub was all but empty. Sunday quiet. No roasts, no specials. No tourists ventured this way, especially out of season, so no point. Just the few daytime regulars, scattered and disparate, who would brave more than the storm outside to get their usual seat, their usual drink.

Tom came through the front door, closed it behind him, thankful that the fire had already been built up. The regulars all looked at him. Some nodded, some went back to nursing their ales. He was still relatively new here. He understood that. St Petroc, to put it mildly, wasn't the kind of community that was immediately accommodating to those who weren't just passing through and spending money, but had decided to remain and settle amongst them. He didn't mind. Welcome brought with it enquiry and interference and he didn't want either. That was one of the main reasons he had chosen the place.

Hardly anyone came to St Petroc who didn't live there. And hardly anyone came to live there. It wasn't the kind of place where TV crews would make period or heart-warming drama. It had no celebrity chef taking over all the restaurants and bars in the village, of which there were scant few anyway, to tempt Londoners down for the weekend. No hippy capitalists had based an organic confectionery business there. No Eden Project. Very few holiday cottages, no second homers.

He had come down the cliff path, walked through the town to get to the pub. Even in sunlight it looked bleak and depressing, on a day like this more than doubly so. It was a dying little village, shrinking all the time. Shopfronts were boarded up and locked, dusty flyers and bills stacked up and yellowing behind dirt- and rust-encrusted letter boxes. Buildings weren't maintained, stone slab frontage green with mildew and algae, busted drainpipes and guttering giving heavy localised showers. Where nearby villages had turned amenity stores into tourist gift and craft shops, St Petroc had nothing. Old businesses were selling up and getting out, new businesses never lasted long. The hardware store became, optimistically, an artisanal bakery, the family butcher's a coffee shop. Now they were nothing. As abandoned as the rest. About the only business remaining was the village grocery store, its shelves virtually bare, a pre-Glasnost supermarket in miniature. The church stood lonely and weed-choked, its pews almost empty come Sunday, its spire pointing towards the sky like a raised middle finger.

The bar of the Sail Makers was dark, all old wooden beams, low ceilings, uneven floors. It was getting on for three hundred years old and no one really wanted to update it. The owners were holding their breath, hoping that tourists would think themselves the first to discover a cosy old hidden gem of an inn, and the locals just didn't like change on principle. It was supposed to have an authentic smugglers tunnel leading from behind the bar down to one of the caves in the cliff face on the seafront. Tom couldn't testify whether that was real or an attempt at myth-making, but there was definitely some kind of hole in the wall behind the bar. Too small for anyone but a child to get through though.

He crossed to the fire, took off his coat, water dripping off it. He shivered before the heat.

'You walked here?'

He turned. Pearl had heard the door, had come through from the back room to behind the bar. Curious to see who would turn up in this weather.

He shook out his coat one last time, dropped it on the floor. Began warming his hands. 'Yeah. Didn't think it would be so bad. Came along the cliffs.'

She laughed, turned away. Back to what she had been doing.

He knew what she was thinking. What all those in the bar were thinking. *City boy. Northerner. Doesn't know anything.*

Let them think that.

Warmed through, he picked his coat up, went round to the other side of the bar, lifting the heavy wooden flap to do so. This was his job. Bar work. He hung his coat on one of the pegs reserved for staff. Checked the sealed inside pocket before he did so, made sure the coat was within sight all the time he was on the bar. His wallet was there. It held more than just money, it held his whole Tom Killgannon identity. And it was too precious to leave anywhere else. So, like hiding a tree in a forest, he knew it would be safest in his coat. Pearl was waiting for him.

'You're early,' she said.

'Yeah. Not much to do today.'

She laughed. 'Or any day, round here.'

He liked it when she laughed. Even the gloomy back bar of the pub seemed to light up when she did that.

She wasn't a stereotypical barmaid, he thought. Or at least not his idea of what a stereotypical barmaid was, the kind who had manned the pumps in the pubs he had drunk in on the estate during his youth. Not blonde and brassy, bosomy and blousy. The kind who would come on to you one minute, want to mother you the next, blank you the moment after that. Pearl was younger than him, the daughter of Dan and Elaine Ellacott who owned the pub. She had returned to the village, and the pub, after university. Only temporarily, she had said at first. Just till something comes up. A job I'm suited for in the city. Any city. Well away from here, thank God. She had been behind the bar for over five years.

He got on well with her, though. A good working relationship. The bar had become hers to run really, her parents concentrating on keeping the struggling hotel upstairs going. She did the hiring and firing, ordering, bookkeeping, everything. And Tom had no problem working for a woman. He might not be as young as her, but he wasn't a dinosaur. He did what he was told, dispensed drinks when asked, brought out food when required, listened to customers when they needed to talk. Although most still preferred to talk to Pearl. And he couldn't blame them for that.

'Go sit down,' Pearl said. 'Have something to eat before you start. Don't work if you don't have to. I'm not exactly snowed under here.'

'You're all right. I'll give you a hand.' His turn to smile now. 'Sure there's something that needs a man's touch rather than a young girl's.'

'Piss off, granddad.'

They both laughed. A good working relationship.

He started in the cellar, checking the barrels, stacking up the empties, carefully moving in the new ones. Doing all the lifting and carrying that, despite what she said, Pearl wasn't strong enough to do. In fact, he had been surprised at just how heavy the work was, even for someone as used to exercise as him. It was good, physical work. It passed the time and he didn't have to think too much about it. That suited him just fine. He came back up to the bar, wiping his hands on a towel.

'Anything happening today I should know about?' he asked Pearl.

'Round Table meeting tonight,' she said with a hint of a smile.

'Ah, the local civic toiletries all out in force. Have to be on our best behaviour. Do we need to salute?'

She laughed. 'Don't let them hear you say that. They'll find somewhere else to have their meetings. Then where would we be?'

'Yeah, like there's somewhere else round here for them to go.'

Pearl shrugged in agreement.

The Round Table meetings were one of the few things that brought in any kind of revenue to the pub. Locals got together in an upstairs room, trying to find ways to halt the decline of the village. Even Pearl's parents were involved. So far, thought Tom, they didn't seem to have come up with anything.

'Dad's all excited that the marina's on the agenda for tonight,' Pearl told him.

'Oh, that. Hope you can let him down gently.'

There had been rumours that Cornwall Council were looking to build a marina with the last of the EU regeneration money coming in. Areas had to bid and there were three in consideration. St Petroc thought they stood a chance. Tom knew it wasn't his place to tell them how delusional they were.

Pearl agreed again. 'Well, it gives them something to talk about. Makes them feel useful, bless them.'

Tom assumed position behind the bar, waited for customers. The same few regulars were still there, now using the storm as an excuse not to leave. Pirate John sat on his usual stool in the corner, rolling away at his skinny cigarette until it looked like a broken yellow twig. He was the friendliest of the locals so far, Tom had discovered. The least likely to treat him with suspicion. Although, as he had been keen to tell Tom on their first meeting, he hadn't lived in Cornwall all his life like the rest of them. No, not him. He'd actually spent some time in London. Tom didn't ask what had brought him back. He doubted he would get a truthful answer. And besides, he wasn't really interested.

He didn't know why he was called Pirate John. The only reason he could think of was that the front of his cottage had been decorated so enthusiastically and idiosyncratically, with a huge, thick horizontal flagpole sticking out of the wall, that it looked like the prow of a pirate galleon. He also didn't know what he did for a living. Pirate John drove round the village in a vintage blue-and-white two-tone Hillman, loading and unloading what could be junk, could be valuable vintage and retro items, or could be both. Plus a never-ending supply of anonymous, nod-and-a-wink cardboard boxes. Maybe he was called Pirate John, thought Tom, because he was some kind of twenty-first-century smuggler. He also – Tom had noticed, having been on the receiving end plenty of times – fancied himself as something of a barroom philosopher.

In the far corner were Mick and Stew. Both young men, all knotted muscle and sun-hardened skin, leathered beyond their years. Long hair in beanie hats, perma-stubbled chins, T-shirts and work clothes. Labourers or surfers, Tom hadn't pried. But their actions were always shadowed, hands constantly ducking beneath the table whenever the door opened. Tom guessed what that meant. But still refrained from becoming involved.

And representatives from the local hippy grungy surfer clan had put in an appearance. They all wore variations of the same uniform, hair long and tousled, beards unkempt. Tom had just begun to tell them apart but still hadn't learned any of their names. They kept themselves to themselves. Lived in tents and camper vans somewhere along the coast. A kind of commune. They weren't like the surfers he had seen earlier, the middle-class ones in their premium wetsuits on their expensive boards pitting their egos against the elements. This lot seemed to live off the earth, be part of it, even. Or liked to give that impression. But their very presence gave off an indefinable air of menace and danger. Like Hell's Angels with boards. The rest of the drinkers gave them a wide berth.

The other regulars, Isobel and Emlyn, retired history teachers, hadn't shown. The weather must have put them off. They would probably turn up later for the Round Table meeting.

Pirate John shook his empty glass in Tom's direction. Tom nodded in return. He could see that Pirate John's lips were moving in preparation for one of his usual philosophical rambles, the empty glass a ruse to find an audience. Tom crossed to him.

This was his life now. This was his world. Shrunk down to the inside of an old pub in a remote part of north Cornwall. Constantine nearby got the majority of the surfing trade, Port Isaac the TV tourist trade. St Petroc got neither. And, though he doubted others in the village agreed with him, he was happy with that. His only responsibilities to pour drinks correctly, listen and nod when talked to. A lot of people would find the repetition, the anonymity, the mundaneness of life behind the bar of a dying pub in a dying village stifling. Maddening, even. But not Tom Killgannon.

After what he had experienced, it was exactly what he wanted. The closest thing to nothingness he could find.

But that was all about to change.

3

Lila was scared. Really scared. She had run before but that had been away from something bad and hopefully towards something better. And nowhere near as bad as this. Now she was running for her life.

She was soaked. And cold. The garage she was sheltering in had a leaking roof and no matter where she tried to position herself, on the floor in the centre, in the corners, the rain found a way to soak her. She had tried covering up the gaps with things found around the place – old tarpaulin, plywood sheets – but nothing worked. The water still found her.

She pulled her clothes tight around her in an abortive attempt at warmth but that just added another layer of cold against her skin. She tried to think of somewhere to go. Somewhere she could be safe. Couldn't think of anything, anywhere. So she sat, huddled, shivering. Alone.

Again, she tried to work out how she had come to be in this situation, again she came up with no answer. She had done what was asked of her. Picked up the boy. Stood smoking with him so he got a good look at her, made sure he got in the van and Kai drove away. That was it. Her part, finished. When she asked what would happen to him she was told it was none of her business. Even Kai had ignored her. And she had left it at that. She knew not to ask too many questions. It wasn't healthy. Just accept, that's what Noah always said, what she was always told. So she did. Or tried to.

And then she saw him on TV. On the screen in the pub. A photo of the boy.

She turned to the other two she was sitting with. Kai and Noah.

'Hey, that's—'

A look from Noah silenced her. Kai looked away from her.

She kept watching. The sound was down low but she still managed to make things out. He had gone to Cornwall with his university friends for a small break before their exams. And hadn't come back. Police wanted to question a young woman who was seen with him on the night –

She stared at Noah once more.

'Do they mean me?'

'Keep your voice down,' he said, eyes half lidded, face blank. 'You're attracting attention.'

Lila did as she was told, but kept staring at the screen. Deliberately not looking at Noah, hoping he wouldn't watch her, gauge her reactions, knowing he'd be doing exactly that. Kai looked anywhere but at her.

A couple came on the screen, sitting at a table, flashlights going off all around them. The woman couldn't stop herself from crying and the man had his arm around her, was doing everything he could just to hold her upright. He looked like he wasn't far off joining her. Beyond the pain, they looked nice. That was the only word she could think of to describe them. Nice. Pleasant. A middle-aged, middle-class couple. The kind who were sure of their home and their life, their place in the world. And now their world had caved in, now they weren't sure of anything any more.

They were talking about their son, Kyle. How much they missed him, loved him. How they just wanted him to come home safe. The mother not keeping it together by this point, collapsed into a sack of grief. The father still going, pleading with the camera, looking directly at Lila.

'If anyone knows where our son is, please . . . any . . . anything at all. Please get in touch. We just want to know he's all right. We . . .'

And then he collapsed too. The screen changed, went back to a reporter frowning at the camera. He gave some contact information, emails, phone numbers, drew out an ending to the report in clichéd prose poetry, then it was back to the studio.

14

Lila didn't say any more for the rest of the night in the pub. But she was aware of Noah staring at her the whole time. And of Kai not staring at her.

That night she found herself lying awake, still thinking about the boy. But more importantly, about the boy's parents. To have someone care about you, love you, the way they did for their son. To be heartbroken when that person is gone from their lives. It was so alien to her, like she was watching a documentary on a different culture, a different world. One she had never been part of. A sudden revelation came to her: *That was the way it should be. That's what's supposed to happen in families.*

She lay awake the rest of the night.

The next day she started asking questions. Quietly, subtly. Or so she thought.

The first person she approached was Kai. But he was suddenly unavailable. Avoiding her, walking away when she came towards him, his friends surrounding him when she tried to get him alone. That hurt. He was the nearest thing to a boyfriend she had ever had. A saviour, even, considering how he had picked her up and brought her to the commune. And asked for nothing from her in return. Well, not much. Well, nothing she wasn't happy to give in order to feel safe and wanted in return. And she had become quite fond of him. More than she would admit. But now he just blanked her. So, trying not to let the hurt show, she tried again with others.

What had happened to the boy? Where was he now? And the answer was always the same. No one knew who he was, where he was, what she was talking about. Or if they did, they weren't telling her. And then she became aware of Noah. Watching her, watching those she questioned. Saying nothing, but warning them against talking to her all the same. Judging her.

A word kept cropping up. Slipped out when Noah wasn't looking. She didn't understand the meaning or significance but she knew it must be important.

Crow.

That night he approached her. 'Lot of questions,' he said.

She didn't know how to respond. He was right.

'Why?'

This one she knew she should answer. The way he'd said it told her there was a lot riding on the right answer. But she didn't know what to say. What could she say?

'Just . . . just thinking about that boy. That's all. Hoping he's all right.'

Noah's face was impassive, eyes hard. 'Best that you forget you ever saw him.'

She looked straight at him, questions tumbling through her mind, bubbling into form on her lips.

He stopped her. 'Just do it. For your own good. Right?'

And that was that.

But she couldn't let it go. Another sleepless night followed. And by morning she had reached a decision.

Before anyone else was up and without being seen, she left the commune and began walking. Down the steep, narrow lane towards the village of St Petroc. And its one working phone box. At least she hoped it was working. She had memorised the helpline number from the TV broadcast and she didn't care what Kai would say, what Noah would do. She thought of those two parents, grieving for their lost son in a way her own parents never had and never would over her. Heart hammering, hands shaking, she stepped up to the phone box, ready to pull open the door.

And Noah appeared from behind it.

'You going to phone one of those numbers, are you? Tell the crying mummy and daddy where their precious little boy is?'

She stared at him, dumbfounded. She didn't know what to say. Didn't need to say anything. It was written all over her face.

'Can't have that, can we?'

16

And he grabbed her by the hair, pulling her along behind him.

She screamed for help, but Kai was there with his camper van within seconds and she was thrown in the back, speedily driven off.

Back at the commune, Noah threw her into the yurt. Locked the door.

That was when the storm hit.

It raged all night. Smashing against the canvas walls, like it would tear it from its moorings. But despite its fierceness the yurt was in no danger of moving. It was why they'd put her in there. Well anchored to start with, the more rain that hit the canvas, the more rain it absorbed and the more its weight increased, pulling it further into the ground.

She ran through a whole range of emotions. Anger, denial, more anger. Stomping about, kicking the walls, trying to tear through the heavy canvas, leaving her nails, her fingertips, in stripped, bleeding stumps. Screaming all the time, before collapsing, exhausted. But no one came. Then eventually, giving in to fear, scared about what they would do to her next, how long they would keep her here. Too scared to move.

She knew it would be nothing good. She had heard stories of people who had challenged Noah, even just disagreed with him. They had disappeared. Suddenly. Left the camp, everyone said, their eyes darting round, seeing who was listening as they spoke. Didn't want to be here any more. But she knew – they all knew – there was more to it than that.

Because the bodies would show up eventually, washed ashore somewhere along the coast, bloated and chewed and smashed by the rocks. A surfing accident or a cliff walk gone horribly wrong. Unidentified at first, then someone would remember the commune. And come asking questions. And be met with shrugs, indifference. People come and go. Stay as long as they want, leave whenever they feel like it. Were they here? Probably. Do you know anything about this? No. Sad shake of the head from Noah and that would be that. Case closed. Accidental death, death by misadventure, whatever. But death all the same.

And that, she knew – feared – was what would happen to her. It was Noah's way of dealing with problems. And that's what she had become.

Knowing what she knew. There was only one way Noah would let her leave the camp.

Anger and fear spasmed through her. No . . . no . . . no . . . not her. Not this way. Not now. She stood up, looked round once more, her eyes long accustomed to the darkness.

There must be a way out, must be . . .

Nothing. They had cleared all the furniture from it except what she needed. A mattress on the ground. One of their home-made bio toilets in the corner with a bucket of sand next to it. And a strong lock on the wooden door. No light, not even a candle. She might use it to burn her way through the canvas.

So she sat in the dark, listened to the storm.

And that was when she felt it. Water. Dripping on her.

She looked up. Daring to hope, hating herself for that emotion.

She saw it. A chink of darkness against the lighter colour of the canvas. A possible way out.

Lila looked round, tried to find something she could stand on to reach the hole. Found only the bio toilet. An old wooden armchair with a hole cut out of the seat and a tin bucket placed underneath. Another bucket next to it filled with sand, a scoop to put the sand in the bucket with. That would have to do. She pulled the toilet chair until it was underneath the hole, stood on the seat, tried to reach it. There was a length of rope hanging down, a binding for the canvas that had come loose during the storm. Lila jumped for it, caught it. Tugged. The rope held. Good. She gave a grim smile and, heart hammering, pulled herself up the rope.

The hole was small and the more she pulled on the rope, the more she tightened it. But she managed to get her hands on the seams, her toes just about balancing on the back of the old armchair.

Her fingers were almost shredded from trying to find a way out through the walls. Earlier wounds were reopened, earlier pain revisited as she pulled, riving it apart until the hole was big enough for her to fit through. Her stomach muscles and arms were cramped from stretching, but every time she felt like stopping she reminded herself what lay in store for her if she didn't make it. That gave her the extra spurt of energy she needed.

Eventually the canvas started to give. The hole became big enough. She just had to pull herself through it . . .

That was the hardest part. Grasping the canvas with her bleeding fingers, pulling her cramping body up with her, the rain, wind and cold slicing against her exposed face.

But she had no choice. Eventually she managed it. Lay on the roof of the yurt, gasping for breath, gulping down oxygen, hoping it would rid her body of the pain of getting there. For a few seconds she didn't even feel the cold, the rain. The pain in her fingers.

But she couldn't lie there for ever. She sat up, looked around. Lights were burning inside the tents, camper vans and the old bus but no one was moving about, the storm having kept them all in.

She slid down the roof, clambered down the side of the yurt. Looked around. She couldn't go back to her tent for clothes or belongings. Too dangerous. So she would have to just go. Head into the town, see what she could find there. Set out on her own. Just get away from here.

And that was how she had ended up in the battered old garage.

She didn't know where she was, or how long she had been running. All she knew was that she had to keep moving, that she couldn't stay where she was for too long. She couldn't think about Noah or the commune, or about how much Kai had hurt her. That was all for later. No matter how cold she was, how wet, she would have to move on eventually.

So she opened the garage door, looked out. An old stone cottage was nearby. It looked empty. No lights on. Perhaps it was connected to the garage. Maybe a holiday let that no one would want out of season.

Looking around once more, knowing they could be anywhere, watching her, she left the garage and made her way quickly towards the back of the cottage.

It had to be warmer and drier than the garage.

4

The last of the Round Tablers – coming down to the bar for drinks after their meeting – eventually staggered off home and Tom and Pearl locked up the pub. Pearl called Tom stupid for venturing out along the cliffs when a storm was brewing and he had, reluctantly, agreed. She had insisted he couldn't do it again, especially not at night when the weather and darkness combined to make the path even more treacherous and had first offered him to stay the night in one of the many unused beds in the hotel upstairs. After he had politely turned the offer down she had insisted on driving him. Grateful, he thanked her and said yes.

She pulled up as near to the front of his cottage as she could. He was renting a place in Port Cain, just along the coast from St Petroc. When he first discovered it he had been surprised that somewhere so small actually had a name. A few stone cottages, mostly in bad repair, a shingle beach and cliffs on either side. Not even big enough to encourage tourists, developers or TV drama makers. But perfect for him.

Pearl looked at him. He knew he was expected to say something. 'Thank you.'

'You're welcome. I saved you from a soaking.'

She was right. The rain had, if anything, intensified during the journey.

'You going to be OK getting home?' He asked out of politeness because no matter how much he enjoyed her company he just wanted to get inside, wrap himself up in solitude, and not have to make conversation he wasn't being paid for.

She must have read his mind. 'I'd better be getting back.'

He thanked her again for the lift and got out. If there was a slight awkwardness between them, boss and employee together outside working hours, he didn't feel it. Or if he did, ignored it. As he approached the door he looked back at the car. She was still sitting there, watching him. He couldn't gauge her expression. Told himself the rain stopped him from doing so.

He waited until she had turned the car round and pulled away, then opened the door of his cottage. And stopped dead.

He heard a noise. Noise meant movement. Which in turn meant someone was inside.

He froze, the door key still in his hand. His first thought: *they've found me.*

Standing as still as he could, he listened. Tried to pinpoint the location of the noise over the blare of the wind. The back of the house. The kitchen.

As quietly as possible, without closing the front door in case he needed to get away quickly, and with the keys held firmly in his hand, the only weapon he could find close by, he stealthily made his way towards the kitchen.

As he crept along the hallway, he could see a figure through the open kitchen door, silhouetted against the window on the far wall. The window had been broken; rain blew in through the shattered panes.

He moved closer.

The figure hadn't heard him. He tried to force his eyes to become accustomed to the dark. Then didn't need to. A sudden light illuminated his invader. A girl, a teenager, he thought, bedraggled and shivering. Wearing too little clothing for the weather outside. And raiding his fridge.

Conflicting emotions ran through him. Relief at it not being whom he had expected. Confusion, amusement even, at who it actually was. And further puzzlement over how he was going to deal with the situation.

'Hey,' he said softly, knowing that if he said anything more she might just run. And he wasn't angry with her for breaking in. Curious, more than anything.

She froze, the full rabbit in the headlights. Or rather fridge light. He saw that she was about to bolt, held up his hands to show he meant her no harm.

'Hey,' he said again, 'It's OK. It's OK. I'm not going to hurt you.' He slowly stretched over, put his keys down on the kitchen table. 'It's OK. It's OK.'

Sensing no immediate threat, the girl relaxed slightly but still stood her ground, ready for fight or flight if she had to, a lump of cheese in her hand as a weapon.

'Help yourself,' he said, pulling out a chair and sitting by the table. 'Not much in there, though. Been meaning to stock up. Unless you like bacon. D'you like bacon? I could do you a bacon sandwich. And a cup of tea. Fancy that?'

The girl looked around, eyes darting to all corners of the room, sensing a trap.

'There's just me,' he told her. 'And I'm not going to hurt you. Put the light on instead of standing there in the dark.' He pointed to the wall where the switch was. She gingerly reached out and, eyes never leaving him, turned on the light. 'There. That's better.'

She stared at him and he realised for the first time just what a state she was in. Her clothing was thin, ripped and torn and covered in mud. It looked like she had been running through thorns. Very large thorns. Her hair was likewise matted and tangled. But it was her fingers he noticed the most. Bleeding and sore-looking, like she had tried to claw her way out of something.

'Sit down,' he said. 'Please. I'll put the kettle on.'

She did so. And sat round the opposite side of the table, as far away from him as possible.

He stood up carefully, not making any sudden movement, lifted the kettle and crossed to the sink, filled it. Switched it on. Turned back to her. 'Bacon sandwich? Or bacon and eggs?'

'I . . . either.'

'How about bacon and eggs with toast?' He looked at what she was still holding in her hand. 'With cheese if you want.'

She nodded. He set about making it.

She sat in silence while he prepared the meal, occasionally eating from the lump of cheese until it had disappeared. She volunteered nothing about herself and he didn't ask, not wanting to appear to be interrogating her, at least not until she had been fed. He glanced at her as he cooked, though. There was something familiar about her. He couldn't immediately place her, but he knew he had seen her before. Probably something to ask her when she felt more confident about talking.

So much for his solitude.

Although he found the house warm after the cold outside, she was shivering. He took off his jacket, handed it to her. 'Put that on for now. I'll build a fire in a while. Get you warmed through.'

He placed the bacon and eggs on the table, mug of tea next to it. 'Knock yourself out.'

She devoured it like she was starving.

After she had finished he slid his own plate over to her. 'Think you need this more than me.'

She devoured that too.

Once finished she sat back. Looked at him. And in that look, her defences began to come down. 'Thank you,' she said.

He shrugged. 'No problem. So,' he said, head cocked to one side, studying her, 'you're not a thief, I can see that. You wouldn't have broken in here if you weren't hungry.'

She nodded.

'And you look scared. So you must have been really hungry to let that overtake your fear.'

She didn't reply.

He leaned across the table towards her. She instinctively drew back. He stopped moving. 'Look, all I'm saying is, you needn't be scared. Not now. I'm not going to hurt you.'

She looked at him as though she wanted to believe, but still couldn't allow herself to.

'What's your name?' he asked. 'I'm Tom.'

Her mouth moved but nothing came out. He could tell she was deciding whether to tell the truth or make something up. 'Lila,' she said eventually.

'Lila. Nice name. Pleased to meet you, Lila. So what's got you so scared?'

Her lips clammed together. Eyes widened. Wrong question. Or rather right question, he thought, but too soon.

'Look, whoever, whatever it is, if you want to tell me, that's fine. If not . . .' He shrugged.

Why had he said that? Most people would immediately attempt to detain their intruder and call the police. He tried to analyse his actions. As far as he could tell, there was nothing malicious about Lila's break-in. She was hungry, wet and cold. There was also an element of relief for Tom that she wasn't who he had first imagined it might be. The remnants of his former life finally catching up with him. So why did he care who this girl was and what she was running away from? Was it for the same reason he found himself extra jobs to do in the bar? To stave off boredom, to not have to think too much? Or did he have another motive, one he couldn't yet admit even to himself?

'They . . . it's all about the boy,' she eventually said.

He was startled by her words. 'The boy?'

'The one who went missing, on the TV. His parents . . .' She sighed. 'It wasn't . . . wasn't me. I did . . . I saw . . . I didn't think they would . . . Not Noah, not even Noah . . . and Kai . . .' She sighed. 'The boy. The missing boy. He was . . . Crow . . . the Morrigan . . .'

Before she could speak further, they heard a voice.

'Hello? The door was open . . .'

5

Tom stood up, looked at Lila, put his fingers to his lips, calling out to the voice. 'Yeah, just a minute. Just stay there . . .'

He looked at Lila once more. She was standing, ready to make her way out of the broken window. He gestured at her to sit down, to stay where she was. Staring at him, not trusting him but wanting to, she did as he asked. He placed his fingers to his lip once more and stepped out of the kitchen, closing the door behind him, leaving her sitting huddled at the table in his oversized waterproof coat.

Once in the hallway he put the light on. The sudden illumination hurt his eyes. He squinted against it. Saw a figure standing there, backlit against the dark outside. Bulky, difficult to make out any features. 'Yeah?'

The figure stepped forward into the light and Tom realised who it was.

'Hello, constable.'

PC Rachel Bellfair pushed the hood of her police-issue waterproof back and shook her hair free. 'So formal.' She smiled. 'Your door was open. I was . . . passing.'

'Passing. Right.'

It was clear Rachel was expecting an invitation inside but Tom hadn't moved.

She gave him a sideways glance, frowned. 'Your front door's open. It's past midnight.' She stepped towards him. He could smell the sweetness of alcohol on her breath. She reached out a finger, ran it down his chest. 'Just thought there might be something wrong . . . that you might be in distress . . .'

Tom involuntarily stepped back. 'Everything's fine. Just forgot to shut it properly when I came in.'

She looked past him towards the closed kitchen door. Her expression changed. Wary. She looked back at him, found a smile. 'Any chance of a drink? Gasping.'

'You smell like you've had enough already.'

'I was at the Round Table meeting.'

'I know. I saw you.'

She moved forwards once more. 'And I saw you. Manfully pulling pints behind the bar.' Her finger extended once more. 'You know how big your arm muscle looks when you do that? Hmm? Really big . . .'

He looked round the cramped hall, realised he wasn't going to get rid of her straight away. 'Come in here.'

He led her into the living room. Like the rest of the cottage it was sparsely furnished. Functional furniture, a TV and DVD player, a small pile of DVDs, a bookshelf with a scattering of paperbacks. No pictures. No photos. He sat on the sofa, indicated an armchair but she ignored him, sat next to him.

'That's better,' she said, unzipping her jacket.

Tom glanced towards the door once more. Rachel caught the gesture and looked round, her fingers stopping on the zip.

'How'd you get back?' she said.

'Pearl drove me.'

Rachel's expression changed. A smile – if he had to describe it he would call it knowing – made its way across her lips. 'Did she now.'

'She did.'

'And that's why I can't go into the kitchen. That's why your door was open. You couldn't wait to get her inside, could you?' She leaned forward, aggression in her voice. 'Like a younger model, do you? Even younger than me?'

Tom felt his body respond to her closeness despite the situation. Not now, he thought. Not with Lila in the kitchen.

'The booze has made you brave,' he said, trying for levity. He regarded her. She was undoubtedly attractive, although the police uniform with its unflatteringly cut trousers, bulky belt, vest, accessories and high-vis jacket did its best to hide that. Well-built with long, dark, curly hair, a pleasant face that didn't need make-up to be good-looking, and an easy smile. She had caught his eye as soon as he had moved in. She was the first person he had spoken to. More than just spoken.

'So that's a yes, then?' More aggression, more bitterness in her voice.

He sighed, tiring of this. 'No. She's not here. Just me.'

Rachel smiled. 'All alone, then.' Another smile. This one less innocent. Her hands went to the front of her coat. 'Shall I slip into something more comfortable?'

Tom didn't move. 'I don't think so.'

She pulled the zip further down. 'That's not what you said last time . . .'

He sighed, shook his head. But his body once again responded. Even more so. He couldn't help it. He was a man. A lonely man.

Then he thought of the girl in the kitchen.

'I think you'd better go, Rachel. It's . . . not a good time.'

She pulled back, stared at him, a mixture of disappointment and anger in her eyes. 'Right. I see. That's the way it's going to be from now on, is it?'

'Rachel . . .'

'Got what you wanted, so that's that?' She stared at him. No warmth, no teasing in her eyes now.

'Please, Rachel . . .' He tried to put his hand on her, but she shook him off.

'Don't "Please, Rachel" me.'

'Look, you knew this would be difficult,' he said. 'You're my liaison. You'd be in trouble if your bosses found out. Not to mention your husband.'

'You didn't mind it last time. Or the time before.' She nodded in the direction of the kitchen. 'Maybe I should just make sure Pearl's not in there. Wouldn't want to be the laughing stock of the whole village, now, would I?'

'Pearl's not in there. There's nothing between me and Pearl. That's ridiculous. I just . . . I'm tired. This whole situation, sometimes I need to be alone. You should understand that. Know what it's like.'

She stared at him. Said nothing.

'Look, I think you'd better go now. I'll talk to you soon.'

She zipped up her coat. 'Whatever.' She swept out, slamming the door behind her.

Tom exhaled a breath he didn't know he had been holding.

When he'd first met Rachel he had been feeling particularly vulnerable. Forcibly moved to St Petroc, his emotions still raw from everything that had happened up North. He had needed someone. And there had been Rachel. And no matter how unprofessional it was, no matter how much he knew it could impact on their future working relationship, not to mention Rachel's husband and child, they had allowed it to happen. Wanted it to happen. And now, settled, steadier, he had realised it had been a mistake and he had to deal with the fallout from it.

He heard her car pull away, went to the window. Watched. Waited until the lights had disappeared up the hill and away. Then went back to the kitchen.

Lila was gone. And she had taken his coat.

And with it his whole identity.

6

Kyle couldn't tell if his eyes were open or not. It didn't matter. All he could see was darkness. Different shades, subtle shadowed hues, but darkness all the same.

Time had become elastic, as immeasurable as everything else about him. He had screamed and screamed, demanded answers, demanded anything, a response, even insults. Was rewarded with nothing. Eventually, exhausted, he had slept. And woken. And then a pattern of sleeping and waking became established but he didn't know how long each spell lasted.

He had replayed – again and again – what had led him to this situation. Tried to think what he might have done to cause it, what he could have done to avoid it. Came back to the same question every time: why him?

The girl in the camper van. He remembered her. Or sort of did. His memory of that night was more dark than light, portions coming back in flashes, snatched glances of dim scenes glimpsed through filthy windows. He tried to jigsaw them together. The weekend away in Bude with his uni friends. The pubs. That spliff. The girl. Always back to the girl.

The look on her face when he got out of the van, realised he wasn't at the campsite. Sadness. Actual pain. Like it hurt her to do what she was doing to him. Her melancholy eyes the last recognisable thing he saw as they put the bag over his head, held him tight from behind, bound his arms to his body, his legs together. She might have even mouthed she was sorry, but he didn't know if that was a real memory or one he had made up to comfort himself. Still, he allowed it to become part of his repeated narrative. Hoped it had been true.

Then he had been bundled into the back of another van, a proper one this time, stinking of diesel and sweat. Yelling all the while through the thick, loamy-smelling sacking, suddenly sober and alert, not knowing how far his voice was carrying, hearing it reverberate around his head. He tried to get his arms free but only succeeded in tightening his bindings. He smelled the muck from the floor he'd been roughly placed on.

He had no idea how long his journey was. In retrospect he chastised himself for not doing what he had seen done in films, listening for anything that stood out so he could make his way back to that point once he had escaped. But he was just paralysed with fear. Nausea rose within him and he had no capacity to do anything.

Eventually the van stopped, the doors opened. Kyle was dragged out between two bigger bodies. An overwhelming smell of alcohol and tobacco, sweat and weed.

The night air changed. The ground beneath his feet altered. He was now inside. Dragged along what felt like a stone floor. He came to a halt as his escorts stopped walking.

He found his voice, began to articulate. 'What d'you want? What's . . . what's going on?'

Nothing.

'Look, is this . . . is this a joke? Yeah? Rand? That you? Fucking joker, OK, Rand, very funny. You've made your point now . . . let me, let me go.'

A smack to the back of his head answered him. He shut up.

His bonds were cut off. He tried to rub his aching wrists, move his ankles, but again his escorts held him in too firm a grip. He tried to remove his hood but was given another smack for his trouble.

'Hey . . . Ow, that . . .'

And then he was pushed forward. Into nothing.

He put his hands out, screamed as he fell. With no idea how far, how long the drop would be, the scream turned into some kind of desperate animal bleat that he didn't recognise as coming from him. Then he hit the ground. Hard.

The screaming stopped as the air huffed out of him. His leg buckled, ankle twisted. He rolled onto his back, gasping, gripping his ankle, writhing in pain. Flinching all the while, waiting for the next horrific instalment.

Nothing happened. He just lay there. A scraping noise sounded above him, something being moved into place. Then reverberated off into silence.

Pulling breath back into his body, he put his hand on the wall, dragging himself upright, testing his ankle. He could move his foot with some painful effort and it felt swollen and tender so he didn't think it was broken, just badly sprained. He pulled the hood from his head. Saw nothing but blackness.

Kyle's eyes eventually grew accustomed and he explored his surroundings. Clammy stone walls, dirt floor, no door. The only entrance from above. An oubliette. A bucket with a rope attached to be hauled up and emptied. In one corner a rusted bed frame holding a thin wet mattress stinking of damp. And nothing else. No human contact, no noise. Nothing. Just darkness and confinement.

And that was where he had been all this time.

His mind, left alone, had drifted, played 'what if' games. 'If only's. If only he hadn't spoken to that girl. If only he hadn't come to Bude with Rand and Jack, his uni mates in Surf Soc. If only he hadn't joined Surf Soc. If only he hadn't gone to uni. If only . . .

Studying English Lit and wanting to stretch his artistic ambitions, he had wanted to join Drama Soc but found he was too shy to audition. Surf Soc was the next stall at Fresher's Week. The tall, blonde wannabe beach god behind the trestle table had told him it would impress the girls, give him 'awesome times with lots of chicks'.

That alone should have put him off but it was a late act of defiance against his parents, the doctors and his lonely childhood.

A weak heart, his parents had been told when he was tiny. Operations, in and out of hospital, so often that by the time he was six it had become a second home. His parents always anxious, treating him as if he would break. The doctors said it was healing, that he was becoming as strong as all the other kids his age, but his parents were wary, still wanting to protect him. He could understand that, objectively, but still felt the need to rebel, to prove himself. And becoming a surfer seemed like just the right way to do it. And of course, there were the awesome times with lots of chicks to look forward to.

Well, he had met one chick. But this definitely didn't count as an awesome time.

His heart was pumping so hard it felt like it would burst through his chest. He thought of his parents' warning. The doctors had never imagined him in this kind of situation. This might be the end of him. He tried to force his pulse down, his breathing to slow. Organise his thoughts.

His first time on a surfboard. He had barely managed to find his balance without being upended by some wave. And it was cold. Freezing cold. The others didn't seem to notice, but Kyle did. And when he took yet another battering, when the rain came down almost horizontally, pushed the waves, and himself, towards the rocks, when his head, his body went under once more into the stinging, salted ice water, he wished he had just auditioned. Just stood on stage, belting out Ibsen.

Then the bar with his mates, talking to a group of other surfers, hard-weathered faces, solid, farm-worked bodies beneath washed-out sweats and worn-out jeans. Eyes as jagged and flinty as the rocks in the cove they'd been surfing in. Bigging up their earlier exploits in almost legendary terms. Kyle standing separate, alone. The third wheel, the square peg.

Then the girl. Small, blonde, pretty. Asking him outside for a smoke.

He wasn't very experienced but didn't want to disappoint her, so in the cold night air at the back of the pub he drew the smoke deep into his lungs. A taste of bitter diesel herbs followed by prickly nausea, sudden empty-headedness. Like his mind was being sucked from his body, a tsunami pulling the sea back from the shore, the better to strike back with ferocity. But there was no strike, no force. Just a uselessness that left him hanging. A powerlessness.

Take another, she had said. And he had done so.

That was when the night began to dissolve.

She had talked. About herself and her friend Kai. About travelling. The future. And he tried to listen, answer, but the world was tilting on its axis, spinning away too fast for him to hold on to. And then he was lost to blackness.

And now, alone in his oubliette for who knew how long, he cried. So much, so loudly and so often that he had physically exhausted himself. Every emotion had been experienced, defiance, anger, all the way to fear, gradually moving to a weary acceptance. Every time he heard the covering over his cell being moved in preparation for food to be thrown down – a pre-packed sandwich and water usually – or a bucket change, he would call out, ask who was there, why they were doing this to him, plead for an answer. There was never a reply. Never a glimpse of another person.

Kyle still harboured a vain hope that he would be rescued, that someone would have seen his abduction, reported it, and would be out looking for him. A vain hope. But he clung hard to it, the only thing to stop him going insane.

His mother would be devastated. His dad too, although he had always considered him the tougher of the two. And even though it wasn't his fault, he felt a perverse guilt for putting them through that.

So there Kyle sat, alone in the dark with a smashed ankle, unable to escape even if he wasn't injured – the exit too high, the wall unscaleable. Playing 'what if' and 'if only' over and over again.

His only hope that someone – anyone – had missed him, would be out looking for him. And that they would find him.

Yes. They would find him.

They had to.

PART TWO

7

The storm broke, shifted off somewhere else, leaving behind soaked earth and a colour-cancelling grey gloom over St Petroc. The locals emerged from their homes once more, like moles blinking in the sun, and life struggled on as normal. But not for Tom.

He went back to work the next day. And the day after that. Doing his duties: lifting, fetching, serving, all the while giving no clue to the casual observer that anything was amiss. Bantering with Pearl. Chatting to customers when they initiated it. Pirate John seemed somewhat agitated, still giving his usual pseudo-philosophical rambles but pointing up certain words, like he was speaking in some special code Tom was expected to understand. Tom just zoned out, nodding occasionally to feign interest. He had more important things on his mind.

The first thing Tom had done after Rachel left a few nights ago was to go looking for the girl, Lila and, more importantly, his coat. And everything it contained. She couldn't have got far, not on foot and in the state she was in, so she must have hidden somewhere. Tom exhausted all the places he could think of, was as thorough as he could have been. No Lila. She was good, he admitted grudgingly to himself. He might have had the training, but she had the natural – or at least developed – skills of a survivor.

He had barely slept since then, out driving round the area on the lookout for her both before and after his shifts. Again, he found no sign of her. He hoped she hadn't attempted to use his cards. They would probably be flagged up on some database somewhere, making his whereabouts known, making him vulnerable. He couldn't have that. But he didn't know what to do. He felt he had run out of options.

All except one.

A big old Edwardian house just outside Truro, surrounded by trees and set away from any main roads. The downstairs rooms like a spread from *Country Living*, all original features, sumptuous decorations, tastefully complementing antiques and huge, filled bookcases. But it was upstairs that interested him. Tom was required to remove his shoes on every visit, make his way up to the attic. A Lloyd Loom armchair facing a Lloyd Loom sofa. Box of tissues and a carafe of water on a side table. One glass. Behind that set-up, the other half of the attic was an office, including desk and computer. Tom sat where he was expected to, on the sofa. He could see the sky through the slanted windows. It looked grey, distant.

A woman sat down opposite him. Late fifties or early sixties, well-dressed, trim and fit. Healthy looking. Intelligent eyes and refined, attractive features.

'Hello, Tom.'

'Hi, Janet.'

'Not your usual time for a session. So this is an emergency?'

'Yeah.'

She sat back, notepad on lap, waited.

'I've lost my identity,' said Tom.

And that was how he started the latest session with his therapist.

He told her what had happened. Lila. His coat. Rachel's unexpected arrival. His fruitless search.

'And I just can't ... it's ... I just don't know what to do next. I'm ...' He struggled to voice the word. 'I'm scared of what might happen.'

'Scared?' Janet frowned. 'Not a word you normally use.'

A ghost of a smile passed his lips. 'Maybe I'm getting more in touch with my feelings.'

She smiled also. 'Maybe. So what are you scared of? Somebody finding you?'

'Not so much that. I think I can take care of myself if I have to.'

A stern look. 'We've talked about that, Tom. That kind of thing's behind you now.'

Tom didn't reply. 'I'm scared of someone . . . yeah, finding out where I am. But letting people in the North know. Not so much for what they'd do to me, but what they'd do to . . . you know.'

Janet nodded. 'And that's worrying you, making you unable to see a way out of this?'

He nodded. 'Plus getting exposed where I am. I'll have to move again.'

'Well, that's a possibility. Obviously I'd prefer you to stay where you are, give these sessions some continuity, get you better again.'

Another nod.

'Any more dreams recently?'

Tom put his head down, shook it. 'Not yet. I can feel the shakes coming on again, though. Stress. Anxiety. You know.' The words seemed to be torn out of him.

'I know. So the best thing we can do is come up with some coping strategies to head off a full-blown attack. And I think the best way to do that is by looking at practicalities, wouldn't you agree?'

He nodded. Even if he didn't agree, and didn't feel able to do what she asked, he knew she was right.

'OK, then. First thing, can you tell anyone?'

Tom gave a bitter laugh. 'My point of contact is supposed to be Rachel. But you know what happened there.'

Janet, trying to keep her expression professional, allowed a frown of rebuke to settle on her forehead momentarily. 'I should have reported your affair. It could have compromised your safety.'

'I know.'

'But you assured me it was over.'

'It is. No long-term damage.'

'So you say. But now you can't talk to her.'

'Not ... yet. Not about this. If I tell her that there's a teenage runaway girl in my kitchen, stealing my stuff, while she's sitting in the living room coming on to me as I'm telling her there's no one else in the house ... I don't think so.'

'You don't think she would be professional about it? After all, you were just trying to help someone in trouble.'

'Yeah, I know, but ...' Tom sighed. 'I've already overstepped the mark with her. And yeah, I'm trying to back-pedal on that. But what if she doesn't act professionally? If she wants a bit of revenge? It's a small community. What if she starts telling them in the village, in the pub, that I entertain teenage girls in my house?'

'D'you think she'd do that? She would actually be angry enough to do that?'

Another sigh. 'I don't know. Maybe, maybe not. There's something ... dark about her. A bit dangerous. I think that was what attracted me to her in the first place. So, I don't know. But I don't want to take that risk.'

'So where does that leave us?'

Tom liked the way she said that. He had always expected therapists, counsellors and psychologists to sound patronising when they referred to 'him' as 'us'. But he didn't get that with Janet. It just made him feel that someone was on his side. That he didn't have to cope alone. Or not completely. He knew that held its own risks, mainly of dependency, but he would tackle that if and when it came to it.

'I ... I don't know,' he finally said.

'Is there no one else you could ask? Talk to? Have a quiet word with? Someone this girl knew who could help you?'

'Well, there's the travellers she came from. But I don't think so. She was running *from* them. I doubt they'd tell me much. If anything, I might make it worse.'

Janet nodded. Checked her notes. 'One thing I think I should ask. Why did you help this girl?'

'Because . . .' He knew what she was driving towards. He didn't want to answer this. Not yet. Because he'd asked himself the same question, repeatedly, and hadn't come up with an answer. Or not one he could admit to himself. 'Because she was wet through and cold and starving. I'd have done it with anyone. I'm sure you would have too.'

Janet didn't answer. 'Are you sure that's all? She didn't remind you of anyone? You didn't feel there was something about her situation, something familiar that you had to atone for?'

Tom sat back, closed his eyes. 'I think I've had enough for today.'

The TV in the bar played on. Property shows gave way to local news. The sound turned down, subtitles giving a rough – sometimes very rough – approximation of what was actually being said, out of sync with the images. They were reporting on the missing student. Tom knew that because the same photo had been used for days now. That smiling, happy image as familiar a face as the regulars in the pub. The parents were giving a new police press conference, faces blank and eyes darkened by sudden camera flashes, their grief rendered slightly comical by mismatched subtitles poorly reporting their words, their anxiety intensified. Desperate to be heard, begging to be understood, knowing as time went on that not only would the odds of finding him be lowered – at least alive – but that their newsworthiness was diminishing by the day. With no progress the press and the public would get bored and they would be off the air for good. Replaced by someone or something else for the public to become briefly angry, appalled or concerned about. They had already been relegated from headline to supporting feature, an anti-EU fishing industry protest taking the top spot. Soon Kyle would be just another open case, another unsolved mystery. Until somewhere down the line someone gave up a lead. Until a body turned up. Dead or alive.

Something about the missing boy hit a nerve within Tom. What was it Lila had said?

All about the boy . . . the one who went missing, on the TV . . .

He had overlooked her words in his desire for the return of his wallet. What else had she said?

His recall used to be near-perfect but it was a skill he had allowed to lapse. He concentrated once more, mind going back to a few nights previously.

It wasn't . . . wasn't me . . .

She had said a name. Something biblical. Moses? No.

Noah.

Noah. That was it. He remembered because of the downpour outside. But there was someone else. Another name. Not biblical. Hippyish . . .

Not Noah . . . and Kai . . .

Yes. Kai. And something else. Someone else? No. Something else.

Crow . . .

And the Morrigan.

'Miles away, you were.' The words accompanied by a small laugh, a giggle. High-pitched, girlish almost.

Tom blinked. In front of him stood Emlyn, the retired teacher, smiling, slowly waggling an empty beer glass.

'Sorry,' said Tom, recovering, 'What can I get you, Emlyn, same again?'

'Please.'

Tom took the glass, placed it to one side, produced a fresh one from the shelf, took it to the hand pump of an ale from a local brewery, began pouring.

Emlyn and his wife Isobel were regulars and proud Round Table members. Both retired history teachers, both small, always wrapped in shapeless fleeces and all-weather gear, always smiling, cheerful. They sat at the same corner table under a wall lamp, and slowly drank the same drinks, eking out the days and evenings reading books or newspapers, sometimes doing the crossword. Completely content with one another's company. Tom wondered how they had achieved that. How anyone could.

Tom placed the drink on the bar. Took the money, gave change.

'Must have been something serious, judging by your face,' Emlyn said, mouth crinkled into a smile.

Tom managed a smile of his own. 'Just the way my face looks when I get lost in thought. Been told I can look a bit fierce.'

Emlyn just wandered back to his seat, giggling.

Pirate John was sitting at the corner of the bar, glass nearly empty, trying to make eye contact with Tom again. Tom instead went into the kitchen on a flimsy pretext. Looked around, counted to thirty. Very, very slowly. When he emerged, there were two new customers at the bar. Two of the travellers, the surf communists, wearing variations of their counterculture uniform and sullen, withdrawn expressions. He gave them their pints and they took their seats, as far away from the few meagre customers as possible.

Tom studied them. Could they be Noah and Kai? Probably not. But they might know them. Should he just go over and ask them?

Pearl chose that moment to enter. She found him looking at the two surfers.

'You all right?'

'Yeah,' he said, her words breaking the spell. He turned to her. 'Just looking at those surfers. Travellers. Is that what you'd call them?'

'Whatever you like, I suppose. They've got a campsite over the rocks in the next bay. They're kind of . . . I don't know. A commune? You get a fair bit of that stuff down here. People who think they're getting back to nature. That kind of thing.'

'You sound like you don't agree with them.'

She shrugged. 'Don't care. As long as they pay their way and don't cause trouble they're welcome to drink in here. We need the money. We can't be fussy.'

Tom kept staring at them. 'They don't seem very peace and love.'

'Why are you so obsessed with them suddenly?'

'I'm not. It's just . . . curious, that's all. Thinking about what drew them to this "outlaw" lifestyle, as they'd say. I mean, they're not just hippies, they're more of a ragtag bunch, aren't they? Some just want to get wasted, some just do it at the weekends, go back to their day jobs on Monday . . .'

'Some of them are running towards things,' said Pearl. 'New lives, new futures.'

Tom turned, looked at her.

She smiled. 'I can be deep as well, you know.'

'Didn't doubt it.' He glanced back at the travellers, sitting there like they were in a world of their own. 'I reckon more of them are running away from something rather than running towards it, though.'

'Or from someone.'

'Yeah,' said Tom. 'Be the perfect little hideout, something like that, wouldn't it?'

She said nothing. Walked away.

Tom looked again at the two surfers. Thought. If Lila had been involved with that student's disappearance, if this Noah and Kai were involved, then if she used his cards he wouldn't just be flagged up on a database. He would be connected to that case. And that was something he couldn't allow to happen. That wouldn't just make him vulnerable, it would be putting him in danger. And not just him . . .

He made busy behind the bar, polishing the wooden surface once again, looking for any physical action to free up his mind. Planning the best way to approach them. He had to find Lila.

But first he needed to talk to Noah.

8

'Fancy a drink before heading off?' The pub had emptied – which hadn't taken that long – and Pearl was standing by his side, smiling.

'I do, but . . . I think I'd better be off,' he said, watching the two surfers through the window disappearing into the darkness.

Pearl frowned, concerned.

'Got a bit of a chill from the other night. Haven't been sleeping too well. Better get myself sorted before tomorrow's shift.'

'I'll run you home.'

'You don't need to do that. Put yourself out. I'll be fine.'

'You're not going to join the travellers, are you?'

He laughed, walked out. Feeling Pearl's eyes on him as he did so.

He knew where he was going. Or at least he had walked the route in daylight. And he had the two travellers in front to guide him.

Past the street lights of the village, onto single track lanes. Up the stone footpath carved out of the side of the hill, stumbling as the trees, foliage and darkness increased, the only illumination coming from the difference in dark grey and black between the land and the sky. He reached the top of the cliff, found the path along the edge, mindful about where he placed his feet. Below, the tide rhythmically crashed and receded, an indistinct background murmuring.

He should have waited. He knew that. Planned his actions, devised a risk assessment, made sure of an escape route if anything went wrong. He was only thinking like this because he'd sensed from Lila's words that this Noah was involved in the disappearance of the boy. And, given Tom's instinctive suspicions of these travellers, possibly other things too. If that was the case then it made him potentially dangerous. Possibly very dangerous. Tom shouldn't even have been contemplating confronting Noah. But his identity took precedence, missing student or not. Anything else, any kind of heroics, someone else would have to take care of.

In front of him, the two travellers had rounded a rock face and begun their downward descent. Tom followed and saw down below the travellers' camp. In a small, beachless inlet with towering rocks on two sides, was a field with a couple of old ambulances, tents both makeshift and genuine, a few yurts with permanent wooden front doors, camper vans in various states of disintegration. A wooden shack, presumably some kind of communal toilet block, had been inexpertly erected. Bare bulbs were strung around, their wires snaking down to a couple of old, black, smoke-belching generators. The last few campfires of the night were dying out.

As he got nearer, he realised the vehicles were pulled round the canvases, like Western wagons in a defensive formation. Keeping the Indians – or whoever – out. Him, perhaps. He revised his plan of action. Jogged on ahead to catch up with the two men from the pub.

'Hey, 'scuse me.'

They both turned, startled to see someone behind them. Silhouetted against the light from the camp, Tom noticed that at least one of them was afraid. The other one had tensed, his body language ready for a fight.

'Hi,' he said, keeping his voice as friendly as possible. 'I've been trying to catch you up. I work in the pub.'

The two of them relaxed slightly, recognising him.

'I need to speak to someone here. Noah? Is he about?'

'Why d'you want him?' The bigger of the two had a strong Northern accent and for a second Tom was thrown. Did they know each other? No, he told himself. That was ridiculous.

'Just need a chat. Can you take me to him?'

The second one looked between Tom and the bigger traveller. He seemed scared to speak, to intervene. Waiting for someone to give him instructions. Or at least see how things developed.

The bigger traveller turned, gave Tom his full attention. 'Why?' Less a question, more of a challenge.

Tom didn't back down. 'Because I want to see him.' Eyes holding the other man's unblinking, face impassive. 'You going to take me to him or shall I just go and find him myself?'

The smaller man was now looking between the two of them, head bobbing like a tennis spectator. Tom didn't blink, didn't back down. The other man eventually broke eye contact but turned abruptly into the darkness so Tom couldn't witness it. He had.

'Come on,' he said.

He started to walk towards one of the old ambulances, slipping through the gap between that and a Ford Fiesta. Tom followed, the other traveller behind him.

Tom was led to one of the yurts. Lights were still on inside. The man knocked on the door. 'Noah? Someone to see you.'

'Who?' A muffled reply.

'Barman from the local pub. Wants to talk to you.' He turned to Tom, eyes on his, smile playing at the corners of his mouth. 'Wouldn't say what for.' Noise from behind the door. It was opened. The traveller pointed at Tom. 'In you go.'

His eyes followed Tom as he entered. He came in behind him with the other man. Closed the door.

Tom looked round. The place looked as he had expected it to look. A bed area, a living area, a kitchen area. Like an untidy studio flat. A woman lay in the bed. She turned away from the men, seemingly bored by the intrusion. Tom noticed she looked a lot younger than the man in front of him.

Noah was smaller than he had expected. Dark hair, straggly and greasy, with an unconvincing attempt at a beard. He was wearing an old T-shirt and pyjama trousers, pulling a hoody on over the top. His eyes seemed wary, as if he was always expecting trouble or looking for an escape route.

'What d'you want?'

'To talk to you.' Tom gestured to the other two. 'Alone.'

Noah sniffed, looked at the other two men. 'Nah, they stay.'

Tom said nothing, just stared. Should he press the point or accept it? He decided, reluctantly, to accept it. Noah probably wanted the men to stay in case there was any trouble. He looked wiry and sneaky enough to handle himself, but numbers never hurt.

'Fair enough,' said Tom, aiming for nonchalance.

'And you are?'

'Tom Killgannon. I work at the pub that these two gentlemen have been frequenting this evening. I take it you're Noah?'

He nodded. Scrutinised Tom. 'You say you're a barman, you sure about that?'

'Sure.'

'You're not police?'

Tom frowned. 'No.'

'You look like police. Maybe you're undercover.'

Tom flinched at the words. He hoped that Noah didn't pick it up. 'I'm not police, I'm not undercover.'

'You sound like police.'

'I'm not.' His anger rising.

'If it looks like a pig and oinks like a pig –'

Tom struggled to keep his temper in check. 'I'm not fucking police, *OK*?'

Noah leaned back, smiled. Like he had just scored a point or had his argument proved. 'Whatever you say, mate.' He pointed to a pile of cushions. 'Sit down.'

Tom, knowing he would be at a disadvantage if he did so, didn't move. 'Fine where I am.'

Noah shrugged like he didn't care, but stayed standing also. 'What d'you want to see me for, then, barman?'

'I'm trying to find someone. I believe she lived here.'

'Yeah? We get a lot of people here. Don't know all of them. We're not a cult. We just live here 'cause we like it.'

Out of his peripheral vision, Tom saw one of the men, the smaller one, nod his head in agreement.

'Her name's Lila.'

The man stopped nodding. The room seemed to freeze.

'Lila.' Noah's voice sounded suddenly cracked. He nodded, slowly. Playing for time, thought Tom. Drawing his response out, deciding how to play it. '*Li-la.*'

The smaller man was looking between the other two, fear on his face. They ignored him.

'Yeah,' said Tom. 'Lila. She used to live here. She's gone. I want to know where I might find her.'

'What for?' Noah's voice too devoid of inflection, eyes too blank.

'She's got something that belongs to me. And I want it back.'

'What?'

'Between me and her.'

Silence once more. Eventually, Noah spoke. 'What's she said to you? When did you meet her?'

Tom's turn to keep his face impassive. 'The other night. During the storm.'

The same flat eyes. 'She's not here.'

'She mentioned your name. I thought you might know where she'd be. If there was anyone else she would have gone to.'

Noah shrugged. Aimed for casual. Missed. 'Not me. Lot of people come here. Lot of people just wander off. We don't ask them to come, we don't make them stay, we don't stop them leaving.' He stepped in closer, eyes locked with eyes. 'I don't know what she's said to you, but that's not the way we are here.'

Tom held his gaze. Felt emboldened by Noah's response, like he was on to something and should keep pressing. 'She said she'd done something wrong and you were after her. Sound about right?'

Tom was aware of the bigger man moving behind him. He tensed himself, fists ready. Noah gave the man a nod and he stayed where he was.

Attention back on Tom. 'She was lying. She does that. And steals stuff. She was trouble. I wasn't sorry to see her go.'

'What kind of trouble?'

Noah chose not to reply.

Tom tried again. 'She mentioned another name. A boyfriend. Kai?'

Tom was aware of the two men at his side once more. The smaller one stared at the bigger one, open-mouthed, on the verge of speaking. One look from the bigger one stopped him.

Noah gave another shrug. 'Can't help you there. Like I said—'

'Yeah, I get it.' Tom hated being lied to. And Noah was a terrible liar.

'Well, I'm sorry I can't help you, Mr . . .'

'Killgannon.'

'Mr Killgannon.' Noah frowned. 'Irish? You don't look it. Or sound it.'

Tom's gaze never faltered. 'Father's side. Second generation.'

Noah, unconvinced but not pressing the point, nodded towards the door. The bigger man opened it. Tom moved towards it, then stopped, turned.

'One last thing. What d'you know about the Morrigan?'

It wasn't the response Tom was expecting. Noah froze. Stared straight ahead, fear creeping into his eyes. He managed to regain his composure but it was too late. Instead he walked up to Tom, faced him, trying to replace the fear with a threat.

'I'm sorry you've had a wasted journey, Mr Killgannon. These two gentlemen will escort you to the perimeter of the camp. Do get home safely. I hear these cliffs can be treacherous at night.' Noah, feeling he was on familiar ground, smiled. It wasn't pleasant.

Tom returned the smile. Equally unpleasant. He glanced at the other two, then back to Noah. 'Don't worry. I can handle myself. It's others you should worry about.'

Noah didn't reply.

Tom was escorted to the old ambulance, then let go. He walked all the way back to the coastal path, feeling at least two sets of eyes on him.

It was a long walk home but he made it safely. His parting words obviously hadn't gone unheeded.

9

Pirate John let himself into his cottage and jumped in fright as the wind took the handle from him, slammed it shut. He stood there, hand clasped to his chest, waiting for his heart to slow down once more. He was scared of everything at the moment. Everything and everyone. And with good reason.

He locked the door, checking it twice, walked towards the kitchen, examining everything on the walls as he went, hoping familiarity would keep him calm. Bring him safety.

A framed brittle and yellowed copy of the *Daily Mirror* announcing Elvis Presley's death. An amateur watercolour of Port Isaac at sundown, made gauzy by extra layers of dust. A 1980 *Sandinista!* Clash album cover signed by Joe Strummer, record long since removed. A film poster for *Night and the City*, Richard Widmark's scared, shifty countenance seemingly following him as he went. Old model Second World War planes hung from the ceiling, Spitfires and Stukas frozen in a never-ending, unwinnable dogfight. On an old telephone table, at war between describing itself as antique or junk, were three made-up model kits of old Universal horror films monsters: Dracula, the Mummy, Frankenstein's monster. Well painted but like everything else, old and dust-laden. But cherished, after a fashion, like all the items on display.

He went into the kitchen, put the kettle on. Took milk from the fridge – the dress-up Liberace fridge magnet today wearing a long mink stole and a gold crown – a teabag from one cupboard and a mug from another. The mug had a reproduction film poster on the side, Hammer's *Hands of the Ripper*. He made his tea, moved to the living room, sighing as he sat in the armchair. It was never as comfortable as it looked. Old 1930s, overstuffed with horsehair. Part of a three-piece. All threadbare but still serviceable.

The room matched the furniture: the walls were tobacco-stained beige; an old, dark wood dresser held period gewgaws and knick-knacks. But here were examples that the world had moved on: a poster of Johnny Cash angrily giving the finger, a flat-screen TV in one corner with accompanying black plastic boxes underneath, shelves of DVDs. Broken Action Men and Barbie dolls arranged on the dresser like serious sculpture, fighting for space with old paperback books and filthy framed photos. A mini cityscape of cardboard boxes stacked to various heights all round the room. Most curiously of all was a hanging curtain of CDs in front of the window. Despite everything crammed in, the house didn't speak of a rich and full life, which was surely the intention, but rather of clutter and obfuscation, trying to disguise an emptiness at the heart of it. But to Pirate John it was home.

He found the TV remote, switched it on. *Newsnight*. Trump and Brexit, played on a seemingly endless loop. He flicked over. A late-night casino cash cow, exhorting the lonely, half-cut night owls to phone in and gamble away on rigged machines. Flick. Late-night local news. The student was still missing.

And off.

The student.

He sighed. There was no getting away from what he had heard, what he had seen. And he couldn't keep it to himself, couldn't keep quiet any more. It was wrong. And he had to tell someone about it.

What he had heard, what he had seen . . .

He was still shaking from it.

He got up, selected a Dave Brubeck album, put it on the turntable. Hoped the sounds would be enough to drown out the images in his head.

Pirate John ducked and dived, sailed close to the wind, or under it when he could. Out in his vintage – and barely roadworthy – two-tone Hillman; or in his house with the ship's mast out front turned into a makeshift birdfeeder, and reclaimed industrial pots and vessels turned into flower troughs; or just walking through the village wearing his Second World War sheepskin flying jacket over his MCC cricket jumper, his long grey hair flapping behind him; people thought him a harmless and possibly lovable eccentric. And maybe he was. But he was a lot more intelligent than he was given credit for and had a lot more compassion too. Empathy. And he wasn't going to go along with what he knew was happening.

The image came back to him: all that blood, the screaming, the howling, the smell . . .

He shuddered, turned the music up louder. Wished he had something stronger to hand than tea.

He had tried talking to Tom, the barman in the pub earlier. He thought that the outsider might be one of the few people he could trust round here. But it hadn't worked out the way he had expected it to. For whatever reason, Tom was either too busy or unresponsive to chat. Sometimes when he wasn't occupied he just stood at the side of the bar, staring away into nothingness. No matter how much Pirate John tried to catch his eye, Tom seemed not to see it. So Pirate John had left, alone, the burden he carried overwhelming him.

Before he could think further, there was a knock at the door. He had rigged up an industrial warning bell from an old factory as his front-door buzzer but it very rarely worked properly. So he knew the knock was for him.

He froze. A visitor at this time of night was never good. Never.

Another knock, harder this time, insistent.

His stomach flipped over. He knew who it would be.

There was no point not answering, the music was on. His caller knew he was in. So he turned down the volume, and, like a condemned man, went to answer the door.

A figure stood there, dark even against the night, huddled and hooded.

'Hello, John. Not going to leave me standing here all night, are you?'

He stepped aside, let the figure in. Straight to the living room, down on the settee. Pirate John followed, resumed his seat in the armchair.

'No tea, John?'

He hesitated. Should he get up and make tea for a visitor, no matter how unwelcome? A guest was a guest, as his mother used to say.

He stood up.

'I'm pulling your leg. I'm not thirsty. Sit down again.'

Pirate John did so. Waited.

The figure leaned forward. Smile in place, hands clasped together like a parish vicar. 'So how are you then?'

He swallowed. Hard. 'Fine.'

'You see, I'm not so sure. I've heard you've been having a few . . . shall we say, second thoughts? About our . . . endeavour?'

Pirate John said nothing.

'I heard you saw something up in one of Bill Watson's fields a couple of nights ago and that's made you less keen.'

The images blazed into his mind once more, unbidden: the ripped-open cow's carcass, the blood . . .

'You were talking to Bill Watson about it the other night. Asking questions.'

Again he said nothing.

'Looking like you were ready to back out.'

'No. Not me, Morrigan, not me.' Trying to keep the shake from his voice.

The figure's smile froze in place. Eyes penetrated. 'You sure?'

Pirate John didn't trust his mouth to speak. He nodded instead.

The figure stared at him, took in his features, scrutinising, an artisan looking for unwelcome and unexpected cracks in a job previously thought finished.

Pirate John tried to keep his gaze as steady as his interrogator's, hoped he was managing. Doubted it.

Morrigan sat back. Spoke almost conversationally. 'That can't happen, John. Second thoughts, cold feet, call it what you like. You agreed, remember?'

He didn't answer, unsure whether the question had been rhetorical or not. A stare from his guest told him an answer was expected. He nodded once more.

'We all agreed. But it's been noted that you're not as happy as the rest of us.'

'It's not that,' Pirate John said, unable to stop himself. 'It's just . . . it's . . .'

The figure stared, waiting for him to explain himself.

Pirate John sighed. 'Look, I know we have to, have to do this. It's just . . . I'm fine.' He nodded once more, hoping he displayed resolve, knowing he was just trying to convince himself. 'It'll be fine.'

'It will, John. It will. It has to be.' Morrigan sat forward once more. 'None of us want to do this, John. Really. And we wouldn't unless we had to. Unless there was absolutely no alternative. You agree?'

Another nod.

'Good.'

Silence fell. Pirate John waited.

'What were you trying to talk to that barman, Tom Killgannon, about?'

Pirate John almost jumped. It felt like Morrigan was reading his mind. 'Nothing. We . . . we often have chats. He's good company. An intelligent man.'

Morrigan stared, unblinking. Deciding whether he was telling the truth or not. Eventually a blink, but from the expression, the jury was still out. 'He's an outsider, John. And not to be trusted. Just bear that in mind.'

'I will.'

'Good.' Morrigan rose.

Pirate John breathed a sigh of relief that the ordeal was over and he hadn't given anything of himself away.

'Oh,' the figure said, turning before reaching the door. Delved a hand into a pocket. 'Just in case this conversation doesn't take hold.' Handed something to him.

He took it, staring at it in horror. A kind of rough doll with the skull of a crow, black feathers stuck on to give it a semblance of life, crossed and tied sticks for a body, more feathers to cover the raw wood. A black stone strung where a heart should be.

A crow warning.

He felt his legs give way, had to sit. He managed to rest on the back of the settee, heart pounding, stomach churning.

The figure smiled. 'Do I need to do this?'

'No . . . no . . .' Begging, pleading.

'Good.' Morrigan plucked the doll from his hand, made it disappear back into a pocket. 'I'll bid you goodnight then.'

Pirate John waited until the figure was gone before running upstairs and vomiting into the toilet.

He'd got the message.

10

Lila pulled the hood over her head, huddled down in the doorway. She was trying to simultaneously make herself anonymous, yet also be visible enough for someone to take pity on her and give her a few coins. Like every homeless person. She found that she didn't need to make herself invisible. The passers-by did it for her.

Newquay in the rain. She felt the wet and cold of the pavement through her thin shoes, the rain hitting her knees and calves, turning her jeans into a second skin. Thank God she had the warm, waterproof coat to huddle inside. A small mercy.

Newquay out of season. The days still cold, sky grey, the promised spring postponed once more. Midweek, out of season and lacking tourists. There was never a good time to be homeless but there were always worse times. And this was one of them. But she was still alive.

She repeated her mantra once more.

'Spare some change, please . . .' Said without effort, without hope.

Someone from the travellers' camp, who had been homeless a long time, once told her there was a reason people walked past and ignored you.

'They can see you perfectly well,' he had told her. 'But they don't want to acknowledge you. Because that would make you real. And then they might start to think of you as a human being. Someone who got into this situation, someone who was someone else before. Someone like them, even. And they start to think how easy it is, or could be, to go from where they are to where you are. So they ignore you. Go back to work. To a job they hate, suck up to their boss who they hate, be nice to their wife or husband that they're bored with, get on with things. Because the alternative's always sitting there, out of the corner of their eye.'

He had said plenty more on the subject, in fact too much; he was a regular philosopher, boringly so. But that was the thing that had stuck with Lila. And now she was experiencing it for herself.

She couldn't believe what her life had come to. She had never had a happy childhood, but she was beginning to think that her parents were right. That God hated her. God was punishing her. If so, he was a right vengeful fucker and it was really, really time he stopped now.

Head down, shoulders slumped, she felt tears once more welling at the corners of her eyes. No. She wouldn't give in. She would be strong, brave. She would go on. Things could be worse. She thought back to the yurt, to the fate that had awaited her. Yes, things could definitely be worse.

She looked up and down the street once more. A few shoppers about, heading for the Poundlands and Poundworlds, several early lunchers, builders and tradespeople. And that was it. No one gave her money. No one saw her.

She stood up, decided to take a walk.

After she'd left Tom's house with his coat she had returned to the leaking garage and spent the remainder of the night there, huddled under some old tarpaulin, disguised from her hunters. The coat proved warm, waterproof and over-large and she'd snuggled into it, managing to get some semblance of sleep.

She felt bad about stealing it. When she'd seen him standing there, framed in the light from the hallway, big and powerfully built, she had been scared. Terrified he would hurt her. She wouldn't have been able to put up much of a fight, if he had wanted to.

But he was nothing like that. Polite. Kind. He had even fed her. Listened to her story. And that was the trouble. She had said too much to him. Nice as he was, she didn't know if she could trust him. And when that policewoman had turned up at the door, she knew he definitely couldn't be trusted and that she had to go. She had grabbed what she could – the coat – and wished she could have taken some of his food but didn't have time or space. So it was back out the window.

As soon as dawn hit, she was out of the garage and away. Along the back roads, away from the travellers' campsite, the opposite direction of the village. Hands in pockets, hood pulled up. Shying from vehicles, hiding in bushes and hedgerows when something approached her that might have been familiar.

Eventually, following a road sign, she found herself in Newquay. She knew it from visiting with Kai and the others. They'd surfed, she'd watched. It was the first sizeable place on the map; far enough away from the travellers' campsite, near enough to walk. Just. Her feet were in pain, the thin, wet material rubbing and chafing, giving her massive, bursting, bleeding blisters. Dark was falling by the time she arrived and she couldn't walk any more. The rain had held off for the most part and the coat had kept out what had fallen. With no place to stay and no money, she had curled up in a doorway and pretended she wasn't there.

The first night had been awful. She had slept rough before, when she first left home, and she knew what to expect, but that didn't make it any easier. Cardboard from a metal cage behind Tesco, placed in a shop doorway, the coat huddling round her.

She barely slept. But she hadn't been disturbed and that was a relief. She had seen first-hand what could happen to homeless people. Getting attacked while they slept, pissed on, set on fire. No limit to what one human could do to another in order to feel superior. And just because it hadn't happened to her that night didn't mean it wouldn't. She had to sort herself out. Straight away.

She felt in her pockets. Brought out a handful of small change. A morning's work. She counted it as she walked. Three pounds seventy. Not bad. Maybe people were more generous than she had thought. She was starving, having not eaten anything since the food Tom had given her a few nights ago. She found a café. Nothing flash, as greasy a spoon as possible, all peeling formica tables and moulded plastic chairs, and ordered a cup of tea and a sausage sandwich. Sat down, waited for it.

The tea arrived. It tasted awful but it comforted her. And it was warm in the café. Very warm. She knew other customers were looking at her, thinking she must be one of those surfer beach bums, but most ignored her. She hadn't been sleeping rough for long enough to look totally homeless yet.

Very warm. She unzipped the coat, took it off.

And that's when she felt it.

A hidden pocket. She knew there had been a bulge, but thought it was just some part of the lining, an extra-thick section, padded pocket or something. But no. It was a well-disguised secret compartment. And something was in there.

Another look round. No one was paying any attention to her. Good. She opened the pocket. Took out a package tightly wrapped in plastic. Bound in elastic bands. She undid them. And suddenly she wasn't hungry any more.

Credit card. Debit card. Driving licence. Passport. NHS card.

Jackpot.

'There you go.'

She jumped as a bored-looking waitress slapped down a sausage sandwich in front of her. The plate spun a little, like a penny circling a drain, before coming to rest. The waitress was gone by that time.

She looked at her stash once more, her mind whirring with possibilities.

Her first thought: use the cards. Get as much out on them as she could, then run. As far away as possible. Think what she would do when she got to where she ended up at. But be careful with them; use contactless only, small amounts, or order online.

Her second thought: No. She would need an address for ordering online and the cards might already have been cancelled.

Or the police might be waiting for someone to use them. Like marked banknotes. Too risky. Reluctantly she put those thoughts aside, turned to the other contents of the package.

Passport. NHS card. She smiled. That was better. That was workable. She had someone she knew who could help her with that. Kai had introduced them. And he was in Newquay. Result. She smiled. Her sausage sandwich tasted like the best thing ever.

11

Time had stopped completely. Or was moving so rapidly he couldn't feel it. Sleeping. Waking. Both the same thing. Darkness. Cold. Loneliness. Pain. Kyle was barely aware if he was alive or dead.

He had stopped screaming. It did no good: no one heard, no one came, he just gave himself a sore throat and a hoarse voice.

He started talking to himself just to hear something. To tell himself that he was still alive, that this was actually happening. At first, once acceptance had set in and he realised he wasn't going anywhere soon, he started to talk aloud as a kind of diary.

'I've just woken up. My ankle still hurts like hell . . . I'm getting up, walking around . . .' Gasping in pain. 'Shit . . .' Sitting down again, hard. 'Fuck, that's . . . I think it might be broken . . . hurts . . .'

From that he progressed to reliving the events that had brought him there, paying particular attention to the girl who had enticed him, definite now that he had seen reticence in her eyes. And then on to who would be coming for him. How they could reach him.

'There'll be appeals on TV, national TV, got to be. And my mum and dad . . . my mum and dad will . . . someone'll see it, someone'll spot me. Rand and Jack'll be out looking for me. They'll find me, they'll find me . . .'

His voice always trailed off, echoed away to nothing when he reached that point.

Then on to his surroundings. 'Where am I? Think, Kyle, think. Stone. A hole in the ground. Hole in the ground . . . an old mine? Isn't that what this place is famous for? Cornwall? *Poldark* and all that?' Pacing while he thought this, his ankle starting to bear his weight. 'A mine. Tin mine, wasn't it?' No answer. He continued.

'I'm in a mine. Probably. Maybe. Underground.' A sigh. He sat back down. 'Underground . . .'

The enormity of his words sank in. Underground. If that was the case, they might never find him . . .

Tears at that thought. Self-pity, loss, fear rage, everything. All the stages of grieving for his situation in one. And finally, a prickly, heart-plummeting realisation. A dark and lonely acceptance. Alone. In the dark. And no one would find him.

He didn't know how long he continued to feel like that. Night and day had no meaning any more. He slept, but for how long he couldn't tell. Same for waking. So he turned his attention inwards.

Because some part of him was untouched by self-pity. Some tiny desperate kernel of rage was still there, glowing hot, building. Forcing him to think, to act. Or at least to try.

He got up, walked round his cell once more. There must be something, he thought. Some small chink, some crack he could work on, expose . . .

Fingers working on the wall, the floor. Methodical, probing one section at a time, not finishing with it until it had been fully explored. His fingernails tore. His fingers felt wet. He knew they were bleeding. He would stop, let them recover, then continue.

The walls were stone. Tightly placed atop other stones. The weight from whatever construction was above him pushing the bottom ones down even further. They wouldn't budge. No matter how hard he pushed and tried to pull, worked his fingers round the edges, tried to find cracks or crumbles of loose rock, he couldn't shift them.

It was exhausting work to begin with but in his weakened, damaged state even more so. The breaks in between trying became longer as the rational voice in his head built up and the hopeless, futile nature of his enterprise was exposed. Then the scales would tip, and the other part of him would be in the ascendancy. Up he would get and try again.

Standing on the bed, reaching as high as he could, feeling his way round the wall, he had an idea. Could he actually do something to get even higher? Could he even manage to reach the entrance above?

He jumped off the bed, looked at it. His eyes had accustomed well to the gloom now, enough to make out shapes and shadows, judge distances and perspectives. The bed was metal-framed. Springs stretched across the frame, an old, mildewed mattress on top. If he put the bed vertically against the wall, climbed up it, could he reach the top?

He looked up. Trying to gauge whether it was possible.

Worth a go . . .

Heart quickening, he pulled the bed away from the wall. Stripping the mattress, ignoring the pain in his ankle, he scraped the bed along the floor, tried to get it to a position where he would have enough space to stand it up. Another look at the place above that he was aiming for, and he slowly flipped the bed up onto its end. Panting from the sudden exertion, he waited until he had regained his breath, shaking from the sudden burst of adrenaline, and pushed the bed against the wall.

The floor was uneven and the bed rocked. He pulled it slightly away from the wall, then pushed the top end towards it creating a steep ramp to climb up. The top two legs of the bed hit the wall, stayed put. Smiling, Kyle began to climb.

Using the springs as ladder rungs, he made his way slowly upwards, his ankle crying out with every movement, every bit of pressure placed on it.

As he reached the top, gasping and stretching, the bed began to pull away from the wall and he felt himself beginning to move backwards into air.

'No . . .'

He pushed his body weight forward, moved the bed frame back to the wall once more. It landed with a thud. Kyle clung to it, getting his breath back, before continuing upward.

Eventually he reached the top of the bed. Balancing his feet in the spring rungs, wobbling before finding balance, ignoring the pain in his ankle, he stretched his arms up as high as he could.

His fingertips brushed the corrugated-metal covering. His heart skipped a beat, kept pounding on. He forced his body further, trying to elongate himself as much as possible. Get a grip, find an edge, push . . .

His fingers now touched the cold metal. He pushed harder. Moved his feet, tried to climb even higher.

And lost his balance.

Arms windmilling, Kyle tried to angle his body forward, grab the wall, keep himself and the bed upright.

No good. His damaged ankle had given way. The bed was detaching itself from the wall, swinging away, falling down. And Kyle went with it.

He landed on the mattress but didn't have time to consider his luck as the frame came crashing down after him. He rolled inwards, hoping to shield himself from the impact, tucking his head into his arms, curling foetally. The heavy metal frame avoided him for the most part but the taut coiled springs, with their sharp, pointed ends, hit him with full force.

He lay there unmoving.

It was a long time before he started to cry.

12

Crack Converters. That's what everyone Lila knew called it where she was from; she didn't think it would be any different here. No matter what name it was going by.

The shops had sprung up about twenty years ago. Modern pawnshops, second-hand shops, offering instant cash for electronics and electrical items. Always in poor areas, always busy. Always well stocked. The staff never asked where the stuff came from. It didn't matter, there was no law to compel them to. It was the nearest thing to legally fencing stolen goods around. Crack Converters because that's what the core clientele usually converted their sold items into.

Lila knew there was one in Newquay. She had been there with Kai when he was offloading some audio gear he had somehow acquired. He also knew that one of the guys who worked there dealt in more lucrative stuff under the counter. The kind of stuff she had found in the coat pocket.

It took her a while, but she remembered where the shop was. Away from the tourist front, back where the locals lived. Locals who didn't take part in the seafront bar culture. She entered the shop.

It was all strip lighting and outdated equipment, DVDs and games. The lights showed up the cheap plastic shells on the items, the years of wear, the obsolescence. Even on a rainy day like this one, the shop was busy. Mainly young men in tracksuits, trainers and hoodies that would never see the inside of a gym. Bad complexions and bad hair. Bargain-basement bargain hunters. The place smelled of sweat and damp, unwashed, smoke-infused, petrichoral clothing.

This is my kind of place now, thought Lila. These are the people I have to hang around with if I want to get by. The realisation made her feel like crying. Then another thought: No. Get this stuff fenced, get some money, get out of here. Where didn't matter. Anywhere was better than this.

She walked up to the counter. A black kid who looked younger than her waited for her to speak. 'Is Conroy in?'

'Yeah,' he said, then his eyes narrowed. He looked her up and down, appraising her. Seemed slightly put off by her shabby appearance, but from the leer on his lips was willing to put that aside. He leaned on the counter. 'You can talk to me, if you like.'

Lila wasn't in the mood for his shit. She gave him a stare that would have emasculated him if it could. 'Get him.'

The youth did as he was told.

Lila waited. For longer than she had expected. It seemed like Conroy was doing it deliberately. She scanned the kids in the shop as she stood, checking how much attention she had drawn to herself. Beyond casual glances, not much. She tried to see if there was anyone she recognised. There wasn't. Good sign.

Eventually Conroy appeared. He saw her, stopped walking and smiled. Not a good smile. The kind a mongoose gives before it hypnotises a snake and pounces.

But Conroy was bigger than a mongoose. Much bigger. He had so much fat on his body that his bones seemed to have shrivelled and shrunk beneath. Every part of him seemed spherical. His arms, unable to get closer to his body, stuck out at his sides like a doll, his legs also when he walked. He breathed through his mouth as he moved, panting from the effort and the strain he was putting on his lungs. His clothes – T-shirt, joggers – were enormous. By comparison his trainers looked small, or rather normal-sized. He had short, greasy black hair and somewhere in the back of his dough face, cunning little raisin eyes.

'I know you,' he said, wheezing as he approached her.

'I know you do.'

'You're usually here with that hippy. Where's he?'

She shrugged. 'I've got something for you, if you're interested.'

He smiled, revealing a wide array of teeth in various stages of distress. His breath matched them. 'Have you now? Let's see it.'

'Not here.'

He looked back the way he had come, down towards the rear of the shop. The prospect of walking there didn't fill him with enthusiasm. 'Better be worth it,' he said and set off.

Aware that the black kid was watching her as she went, Lila followed him.

The back office looked exactly like the kind of place Conroy would sit in. A wide armchair pummelled into submission sat behind an office-surplus desk that was so old it could have enjoyed an expensive second life in a Hoxton members' club. A large TV dominated the corner, a porn film frozen in mid-climax on the screen.

'Better be good,' Conroy said, manoeuvring his body into the armchair. 'I was busy.'

Lila didn't make any comment. Just stood in the centre of the room.

'What you got then?'

'You still dealing in cards?'

He shrugged. It took a while, sent ripples down his chest. 'Maybe.'

Lila waited. She wasn't as nervous as she had expected. Walking into the shop, asking for Conroy, staring down the kid behind the counter, it all just came to her. Naturally, she thought. Or what passed for naturally to her now. And here she was standing in front of the big man, expecting him to toy with her before giving her anything, probably undercutting her. Well, she wasn't prepared to do that. She had had enough.

'Well,' he said eventually, with an irritable sigh, 'what you got for me?'

She took the package out of her jacket – she was thinking of it as hers now – and extended her arm across the desk. He made to grab it. She pulled her hand back.

'First,' she said, 'I want to make sure you're going to pay me.'

'If what you've got's worth it, I'll pay you.'

'It's worth it. Just make sure you've got the money.' Her voice was steady, legs shaking only slightly from adrenaline. Where had this new-found confidence come from? A mental image of her parents flashed into her mind and what they had done to her, then Noah and Kai. Rage gave her new strength.

He raised an eyebrow. 'Sure of yourself, aren't you?'

'Yeah. I am.'

'Let's see it, then.'

She handed the package over. He opened the plastic bag, took the contents out one by one, laid them on the desk. Studied them. Looked up.

'Well, well, well,' he said.

'It's good stuff.'

He kept studying it. 'Hmm.' He picked up the passport, looked through it. Scrutinised something in the pages. Then the same with the NHS card, then the credit cards. He placed them all back down on the desk, looked at her. 'Very good,' he said. 'Too good.'

Lila frowned. 'What d'you mean? They're perfect. You should have no trouble shifting them.'

He held up a pudgy finger. 'One. You're right. Perfect.' Another finger. 'Two. I might get into a lot of trouble.'

'Why?'

He pushed them back across the desk towards her. 'Because I know hooky stuff when I see it.'

She was totally confused now.

He leaned forward. The effort seemed to cost him. 'Hooky. Snide. Whatever. Bent. This is . . .' He pointed to the passport. 'Too perfect. It's new.'

'So?'

'So are the cards, all of them. Brand new.' He shook his head. His neck moved several seconds afterwards. 'Means they're not real. Warning flag.'

Lila couldn't believe what she was hearing. 'But they are, look at them.'

'Yeah, they look real. And they might pass scrutiny. But I've seen stuff like this before.' He leaned back. 'I wouldn't touch them.'

Lila felt all the air, all the earlier confidence, leave her body. 'What . . . what d'you mean?'

'They're the kind of things you give to someone when they get a new identity, witness protection or something. Or when they're an undercover cop. Security services. Or they're on the run from something or someone. No, sorry. And since I don't know anything about them, or what I'm getting into, I'm not interested. More trouble than it's worth.'

Lila just stared, unable to speak. All her hopes had been pinned on that money. Her plans for escape, for . . .

Conroy leered at her. 'Pity,' he said, baring his rotten teeth once more. 'I was quite looking forward to . . . negotiating with you . . .'

She gave a shiver that was nothing to do with the temperature. 'So . . . what now?'

He held his hands up. 'Dunno. Pick your stuff up and off you go.'

'Will anyone else round here take it?'

'Me or no one.'

Numbly, she gathered the cards, passport back together, replaced them in the plastic bag, pocketed the bag. 'I was . . . counting on that.' As soon as she spoke she regretted it. Don't show weakness, no matter how desperate you feel. Especially in front of someone like him.

Conroy looked thoughtful. Lila didn't move because she sensed he was about to make some offer. She didn't know whether it would be something she wanted to hear, but she had to listen.

'You need money?'

She nodded.

'You want work?'

'Doing what?'

A laugh. As ugly as the rest of him. 'Don't think you're in a position to be choosy, darlin'. D'you want work? Money?'

Part of her wanted to tell him no, she didn't. She was worth better than anything he could offer her. But she found herself with that familiar feeling of a sinking heart, that dread, nodding.

'Thought you might. Go see Leon in the front shop.'

'Who's Leon?'

'You've already met him.'

The black kid. The leering one. She must have let her disgust show on her face.

Conroy laughed once more. 'He's not all that bad. Usually. Follow me. Oh.' He stopped. Held out his hand. 'I'll take those cards from you. Just in case.'

'You said you wouldn't touch them.'

He shrugged. It took a while. 'Give. If you want a job.'

Lila handed them over.

'Thank you. Come on.'

Her earlier confidence was now well and truly gone. Lila followed him, like the condemned on her way to the gallows.

13

If Crack Converters had been off the beaten tourist track, the house Leon took Lila to could have been in a different town entirely.

If it could actually be called a house. Lila had seen static caravans before. Had even accompanied her parents on several joyless holidays in one. But this was different. It was set out as a holiday park, regimented and grid-like, but with one crucial difference. The caravans were more than static – they had become permanent residences. Metal walls gave way to brick leading to the ground. Small fences indicated wooden-clad courtyard gardens with spaces made for cars. Some had been extended with aluminium second storeys added. Most had been kept in some semblance of good repair, but not the one Leon led her to.

'Where we going?' Lila asked.

'We're here.'

There hadn't been much conversation en route. Leon asked Lila questions: on her background, whether she had a boyfriend, where she was living, why she was here. Everything. But she had answered as monosyllabically as possible. Shrug, shrug, shrug, needed some money. Even that confession seemed to be too much for her and she hated herself for admitting it.

'Don't worry,' he had said. 'Where we're going, there's plenty money to be made.'

She couldn't place his accent. Definitely not Cornwall, more London. She could have asked him where he was from and why he was here, but that might make him think he could ask her things and expect answers. And that wasn't going to happen.

She looked at the house/caravan. The park was well away from the seafront, past the bars, restaurants, nightclubs, B & Bs and hotels, which made her think it wasn't for holiday homes. Retirement? Perhaps. But more likely a cheap alternative to buying a real house for economic strugglers. The one they stood in front of wasn't in good repair. The metal was dirty, as were the windows. Net curtains added to the darkness within. The space surrounding it was a weed-encrusted concrete patio with the rusted skeletal remains of garden furniture scattered about. Fag butts. Stretched black bin bags, torn and spewing their innards through rodent incursions. Chicken bones and fast-food wrappers rain-stuck to the ground. No brick around the bottom of this one, only mildewed, warping wood slats. The step that Leon stood on looked like it would collapse at any moment.

Leon knocked on the door, waited.

Eventually it was answered. 'Got someone to meet you,' he said, and stepped inside.

Lila, expected to follow, did so.

The inside was as she had imagined from the outside. Grease-stained cardboard pizza boxes littered the surfaces, given second lives as makeshift occasional tables for drug paraphernalia. Old cans and bottles were turned into ashtrays. The stink of weed was everywhere, along with sweat and dirt. A TV set in the corner had been turned into a games screen, wires and handsets snaking from it. A couple of off-brand laptops lay around. The furniture and carpet were covered with fractals of cigarette burns.

There were three people inside, all male. Two were the same age as Leon, dressed similarly in trainers and shiny sportswear. One black, one mixed race. The other one was older, fatter, dressed in stained jogging bottoms and an aged T-shirt, hair greasy, cut in no discernible style. Velcro-fastened old trainers on his feet. Lila knew the guys were looking at her, knew how they were looking at her and that made her feel uneasy. But it was this other one who drew her attention. He didn't belong there. He didn't look happy. In fact he looked scared. Very scared. His eyes darted from one youth to the other, watching their reactions to Lila's entrance before he dared give his own response. Looking at Lila, some kind of plea in the gaze.

'Who's this?' the black youth said.

'Name's Lila,' said Leon. 'Conroy sent her. Reckons she could be useful.'

At Leon's words, the third man became animated. 'Conroy? What did Conroy say? Me?'

If Lila hadn't worked it out already, his speech would have given him away. He had some kind of learning difficulty. Quite a severe one.

'No, he didn't mention you, Josey. This is work.'

Josey sat back down in his filthy armchair, head slumped, like he had just been switched off.

The darker kid got up from his game. Behind him a car crashed, bodies were torn apart, explosions boomed and screams came from the TV. Josey looked up, laughed at it.

'Fuck's sake, man,' said the lighter-skinned one, angry. 'We're playing here.'

The darker youth walked towards Lila, eyes all over her body. 'Playing. Yeah.' Despite the fact that she was bundled up in the big coat, he must have liked what he saw. Or what he imagined he saw.

Leon became territorial, stepped in front of her. 'She's here to work,' he said. 'Conroy said so.'

'Just being friendly, man.' He finally looked at her face. 'You're Lila, yeah?'

She nodded. 'And you?'

'Ashley. So you lookin' for work?' He smiled, showing lax dental work. 'I could give you a job.'

Again, Leon interceded. 'Conroy wants her out there. Reckons she's got connections. Can shift stuff easy.'

Lila frowned to herself. Conroy hadn't said any such thing. She said nothing, tried to pick up some more clues from the conversation.

Ashley turned away from Leon, looked towards her once more. 'That right? You got connections?'

'Yeah,' she said because it was expected of her.

'So have we. Yours better be good. Otherwise we won't need you.' Eyes hard, anger behind the words, unhappy at being challenged by Leon, taking it out on her.

'We could find something for her to do.'

The light-skinned guy had risen now and she could tell straight away that this one was the leader, the alpha male in their scrawny pack. Smaller than the other two, wiry, but with a glint of something in his eye. Or rather a lack of something. He moved towards her.

'We'll make use of you. Don't worry.'

And for the first time since she had arrived there, Lila felt scared.

'So what do I have to do?' She didn't want to ask the question but knew she had to.

Ashley smiled. 'Get out of that coat for a start . . .'

She pulled it further around her.

'Shut it, man,' said the smaller one. Ashley immediately became mute.

'I'm Aaron,' he said. Gestured: 'This is my crew. Lila, yeah?'

She said yeah, then fell silent, not knowing what else to say.

'And Conroy says you got contacts, yeah?'

She nodded. Hoped he wouldn't catch the tell in her eyes, the lie.

If he had done so, he didn't let on. 'Good. We're just waiting for a new batch. When we get it, you'll go out selling. You OK with that?'

'What am I selling?'

'Weed, mainly. Skunk. Some pills. Spice. E.'

'And the good stuff . . .'

Josey had stood up and was grinning at her. She looked once more at him. This time clearly noting the dried-up veins, the scabbed, ulcerated moonscape of his arms. Heroin.

'Shut the fuck up,' Aaron said without even looking at him. Josey shrank away, like a happy puppy that had been kicked. He turned back to Lila. 'So yeah, that's it.'

'So when's this new batch coming?'

'Any day now. Down from London.'

She nodded once more. 'So . . . what happens now?'

Aaron looked round. 'You find somewhere to sleep. If Conroy vouches for you, you're good. You're one of us.' He stepped in close. She smelled decay and sugary, fizzy drinks on his breath. 'But you fuck us over and you'll regret it. Right?'

She didn't doubt him.

'Make yourself at home, then. Have a drink, smoke, whatever.'

She looked round the cramped, squalid caravan once more. Wondered yet again why it was always other people who got to live happy lives.

14

Morrigan saw St Petroc as it really was. Not the crumbling, dilapidated, dying village everyone else saw, but the glorious, beautiful place that had once existed and could again, when all the premonitions, practices and rituals came to fruition.

Rain had swept the streets, cleansed them. A chance for a new beginning. Or an ancient one to return. Morrigan saw the drying buildings as they had once been, in childhood days. No mildew or mould, no disrepair. Shops flourishing, the streets full of happy, contented people. Homes well lived in. Obviously the church wouldn't survive. The state of neglect and disrepair it currently stood in, it would have to be completely abandoned. Or subsumed once more by the old gods. The old religion. For it was only through a return to them that the future would emerge.

When Morrigan was a child, the old religion had been everywhere.

'You're lucky to come from where you do,' Morrigan had been told at university. 'The wall between the two worlds is very thin here. And magic is strong. The spirits can cross over and back again. And when you ask them for help they will give it. If you ask correctly.'

Morrigan from that point on always asked correctly. And in returning to St Petroc after university, Morrigan's power grew.

Evidence of the old religion, the old ways, was everywhere. The church was there but Christianity never got much of a foothold in an area that still clung to the trade and practised its traditions. Pagan, in its purest definition, meant 'of the village'. That, Morrigan knew, was its true heart.

Morrigan always took pleasure from walking past an open window and smelling a working powder like witch or spirit or love being made up, or one of the working incenses. Morrigan would smile, content to know the craft was still being practised, and that no amount of fashionable surface cynicism could disguise that.

But those practitioners were dying out now, the evidence of them becoming sparser and sparser. The youngsters who could keep the traditions alive were moving away, turning their backs. It was up to Morrigan to keep them going, to bring the young ones back. To demonstrate that both they and these traditions were still central to the future of St Petroc. It didn't need much. Most people knew of the power of the old ways. Still believed in them.

Someone approached. Morrigan knew them, had known them all their life. A smile, a nod. They gave a brief incline of the head in return, hurried away. Morrigan's features remained set. Watching them go. Fear and respect. That was only right. That was the way of the old religion.

A quick watch check: Morrigan had to be somewhere. Saying a prayer for the future of the village, Morrigan got to the car, drove off.

Bill Watson's farm was just outside St Petroc. He still considered himself a local to the village though, proud member of the Round Table and contributor to the country show when it used to run. Stoic and capable-looking, he was the very epitome of the West Country farmer. He had only taken a weekend away from the farm when he got married, then it was back to business as usual, up at five, his new wife alongside him. He hadn't broken his routine when his daughters were born, nor when he became a grandfather. So the fearful expression that greeted Morrigan's arrival was totally out of place.

'Blessed be, Bill.'

He nodded. 'Did you speak to him?'

'I did. There'll be no more trouble from John. He saw sense.'

'Did you have to . . .?'

'No.' Morrigan's eyes darkened. 'But next time'll be a different matter. Not that there'll be a next time for him. It's all taken care of.'

Bill sighed, shoulders slumping, releasing a weight he wasn't aware of holding.

'Everything all right here?'

He nodded once more, eyes averted. 'Fine. Since the . . . you know. Everything's fine. Herd's back to normal. Defra said it was contaminated feed, that was all.'

Morrigan moved closer. 'And what d'you think, Bill?'

Again, he averted his gaze. His mouth worked but the words took a while to make their way out. 'It was a murrain.' His voice quiet, not even a shadow of the booming drinker's voice he used in the pub with his farmer mates.

'That's right, Bill. Murrain. The old religion is powerful and not to be sneered at or dismissed easily. If Defra explained why your cows were ill after you successfully completed the ritual then it means the ritual worked. The plague lifted. That's all.'

Bill nodded once more. Then looked up, a puzzled expression on his face. Fearfully, he asked a question. 'Why did you come here? You could have just called me to tell me about John.'

Morrigan stared at him, eyes dark beads, crow-like in their blackness. 'I could. But I wanted to remind you, Bill. Of what's at stake. John had second thoughts. But he won't any more. I'm just making sure that you don't either.'

'I don't . . . I don't, Morrigan.'

Morrigan nodded, smiling. 'I know you don't, Bill. I know you're with us . . . Till the end.'

He nodded once more, clearly wanting Morrigan to leave. Morrigan sensed that, stayed.

'Everyone else all right about the task ahead?'

'As far as I know, yes.'

Morrigan's features darkened. 'As far as you know?'

'I mean . . . yes. Everyone's still in.'

'Good. That's as it should be. We're family, remember. Family in the old ways.'

'I . . . yes, I know.'

'Good. I'll be off now. You've no doubt got your work to do. But remember. I'll always be watching.'

He said nothing.

'So mote it be.'

'So mote it be,' he mumbled in return.

Morrigan left him standing there, watching. Felt that delicious power well up within once more.

15

St Petroc was resting, Tom felt. In a grey lull between extreme weather conditions, like it was waiting for something. Life to return, perhaps. The morning sun hadn't broken through the clouds yet, if indeed it ever would. The day was dull. Tom ignored it. He had things to do.

The past few days had got him nowhere. He had searched all over but the girl wasn't to be found. And worse: his dream had returned.

Tom had discussed it with his therapist, his recurring dream. He knew what it represented, why he got it. Didn't need her to tell him that.

'It's always the same. She's lying there, dead. All broken. Twisted. Covered in blood. And I'm . . . I'm holding the gun. I've killed her.'

'But that's not how it happened, is it?'

'It may as well be.'

'But it's not how it happened. It's just how you've chosen to remember it. How your subconscious has chosen to reinterpret it. Does it happen often? Any particular times or triggers?'

'When I'm stressed. Or thinking about it, you know, dwelling on it. Or I'm depressed.' He gave a feeble laugh. 'So yeah, often.'

And it was back again now. He could see himself in the dream, leaning over, turning over the body and . . . then he wakes up. And sees her face everywhere in every waking hour.

He couldn't let it take hold of him again. He had to do something.

Kai was the best bet. Or the only bet. Tom had worked out that Kai was the smaller of the two travellers he had followed from the pub. He had given himself away on hearing his name. Now, Tom was looking out for him. He hadn't been back to the pub since Tom's nocturnal visit to the camp and Tom felt Noah must have warned him off. But that was OK. He had other methods of tracking him down.

During his first morning off, Tom had taken his binoculars and gone for a walk along the cliff edge, taking the route towards the camp but stopping short of it. Finding a patch of gorse on the top of the incline, crouching behind it, training the binoculars on the camp. They were powerful and he had no trouble seeing what was happening in relative close-up. The surf hippies going about their daily business. For a group that seemed to pride itself on its counterculture activities, thought Tom, their lives seemed to be as routine and dull as everyone else's. Washing, cooking, working. Keeping busy. Occasionally he would glimpse Noah and he studied the reactions of the others as he went about among them. Awe? Fear? Something like that. They seemed scared of him, drew away if he spoke to them. Measured their responses carefully, didn't initiate conversation. It didn't seem like a very happy camp. And Noah didn't seem like a benevolent ruler.

He watched Kai skulking around. He seemed to be Noah's delivery boy, frequently leaving the camp in his battered camper van, returning with boxes to be unloaded into what Tom assumed was some kind of supplies or mess tent.

He was so intent on watching and trying to formulate some kind of day-to-day timetable for Kai that he didn't realise he himself was being watched.

'Doing a spot of birdwatching?'

Tom looked up, startled. Emlyn and Isobel, the old couple from the pub, were standing beside him. Both bundled up in waterproofs and woollens, smiling down at him like garden gnomes come to life.

'Yeah,' he said, taking his binoculars away from his eyes, standing up. 'Ow. Didn't realise how long I've been sitting.'

'The knees are always the first to go,' said Isobel, laughing. 'Emlyn and I used to come out here regularly to watch the seabirds on the cliffs. Can't any more. Knees, you see.'

'See anything interesting?' asked Emlyn.

Shit, thought Tom. 'Erm . . . yeah. A few birds. Still looking for the right place, though. To see things.'

Emlyn pointed along the shoreline. 'You should head over that way. Next bay along. Used to be quite a collection of nesting boobies, didn't there, Isobel?'

'Oh, yes. It was a lovely sight.'

'Is that right.'

The three of them stared at each other, conversation having drained away.

'Well,' said Emlyn, 'must get on. Can't stand here chatting all day.'

'Right.'

'Will we be seeing you later?' asked Isobel. 'In the pub.'

'If you're in tonight you will.'

'We'll look forward to it.'

And off they both went.

Tom waited until they had disappeared over a ridge before resuming his spot.

That had been the first day. The second he had come back to the same place, notebook in hand, writing down the times that Kai disappeared and returned. Trying to judge from the time spent away just how far he had travelled and what for.

This continued for the next day as well, as Tom built up a picture of the lad's movements. The day after that he was ready for him.

He spotted the name of the local butcher on the side of a couple of the boxes he brought to the camp. That meant he was going into the village. So Tom didn't have far to travel to apprehend him.

And now he waited near to the butcher's shop, ready for Kai.

'Hello, stranger.'

Tom jumped, turned. Rachel stood behind him, smiling. He managed a hello, then looked round, hoping he hadn't missed Kai, or been spotted.

Rachel noticed his glances. 'What you doing round here at this time? Not like you.'

'Just . . . out for a stroll. A think, you know. Stopped off to . . . just look around, seeing as I live here now.'

Rachel kept scrutinising him. Though not looking convinced, she eventually nodded. 'Well, whatever, I'm glad I bumped into you. I wanted to say sorry for the other night.'

'Oh. Right.' Another glance. Still no sign of Kai.

Rachel frowned, looked closer at him. 'You listening to me?' Her voice changed. 'Or are you here to meet someone?'

Tom gave her his full attention. 'Sorry. Yes. I'm a bit . . . on edge at the moment. Just, you know. One of those things.'

'Right.' Clearly not convinced.

'But yes. Thank you. You don't have to apologise, though.'

'No, I do. I'd had a few at the meeting. I shouldn't have even been out driving, but you know.' She laughed. 'I mean, who's going to arrest me?'

Tom joined her in smiling, almost laughing. 'It's OK. I'm sorry if I seemed unfriendly.'

'I had no right to barge in like that. If you had someone there that's not my business. I'm in no position to get arsey with you. I know that.' Another smile. 'We still friends?'

He returned the smile this time. 'Sure. We've got to get on together, haven't we?'

'We do. Speaking of which . . . Mick's away for a few nights next week, if you're free?'

A shiver ran through Tom. He thought he was extricating himself from her but that didn't seem to be the case. She was persistent.

'Let me see.'

Rachel seemed to realise how that must have sounded, back-tracked. 'Sorry. Desperately bored local girl craves excitement. Sounds like an advert, doesn't it? But it's fine, we can just meet as, you know, friends.'

'Actually, I would like to talk to you about something.'

'Sounds important. What is it?'

Tom looked round once more. 'Not here. Later.'

Rachel's eyes widened in what looked like terror. 'You haven't given me an STD, have you?'

'What? No, nothing like that. Just give me a call. Come round when you can.'

'OK,' she said, looking slightly unnerved, 'I will. Right, I'd better get on. Got to go round the farms. Had a few vandalism calls. Never stops, does it?'

Tom said it didn't. Rachel leaned forward as if to kiss him good-bye, but then seemed to resist and left. He watched her go. She was undoubtedly attractive. And when she wasn't being so predatory around him she was good company. He still wished they hadn't become lovers but there was nothing he could do about what had happened in the past. His therapy was teaching him that. He put Rachel out of his mind, concentrated on the task in hand.

The village was quiet. But then it always was. It had a veneer of silence that he hadn't been able to break through in the short time he had been there. He saw regular faces but only recognised them because of their associations. The vicar always wore her dog collar. The butcher his bloodstained white apron. The woman in the local shop he recognised because it was the only local shop. They were polite towards him but not overly welcoming. He was a newcomer without an established place in the village hierarchy. He felt it was the kind of place someone could live for twenty-five years and still be thought of as the newcomer.

And away from the main street with its dwindling commerce, he had spotted another pattern, something else he wasn't part of, would never be part of no matter how long he lived there. Homes bearing things he didn't understand. Holed stones hanging above doors and windows. Small constructions, fetishes, of straw and bones, feather and fur placed on front doors. Too real to be tourist tat. Desperate, fearful pagan offerings for a safe life, a good night's sleep. For any kind of hope for the future. He could understand the thinking behind this, if not the acts themselves.

The village itself was built on a spiral, a collection of roads leading down towards the cove where the pub was, and it fell short of picture-postcard pretty. It was a casebook study of neglect. Local, national, cultural, economic. Since the Brexit vote the affluent South-East had left the more secluded rural areas alone, both for holidays and the mixed blessing of second homes, unwilling to be associated with those who had voted Leave, fearful of what kinds of people they might meet in those areas. Cornwall had been hit more than other areas in that respect. Places like St Petroc most of all. Tom knew they were desperate for the marina to be built nearby, but anyone looking dispassionately could see that no amount of pagan fetishes would make it happen.

Kai's camper van appeared at the end of the street. He parked up and got out.

Tom rotated his neck on his shoulders, heard a satisfying crack. This was the part he hadn't planned in detail.

This was the part he was looking forward to.

16

'Hello, Grant.'

Grant Jenner looked up suddenly, unable to hide the surprise, then fear, in his eyes. Morrigan smiled in return. Happy to have that effect on him. The fear curdled in his gaze, turned to something Morrigan was less pleased to see. Resentment. Anger.

'How did you get in? I didn't hear you.'

'You never do, Grant.'

'What d'you want?'

'I was just passing. Came to see you. That's all. A social visit. See how you're bearing up.'

Morrigan stood in the doorway to the kitchen. Grant was at the kitchen table, his wheelchair pushed underneath, piles of papers before him. The kitchen looked like it didn't belong to a traditional farmhouse, all gleaming, modern, hi-tech appliances, designer fixtures and fittings. Not a rustic wooden chair in sight.

He turned his chair to face Morrigan. Stared. Hard.

'Come to gloat, have you? See what your so-called magic powers did, is that it?'

The smile slipped from Morrigan's face. Replaced with something much colder. 'I did what you asked me to, Grant. I gave you the spell to get your cheating wife to come back to you. You've only got yourself to blame for the result.'

Grant pushed his wheelchair closer to Morrigan. 'Yeah. I did what you told me to. I got her back. No bloody use now, though, is it? Look at me.'

'You should have been more specific. *Caveat emptor.*'

The rage Grant was experiencing threatened to turn physical until he glanced down at his legs, realised he couldn't get up, do anything. He slumped back into his chair once more.

'Your wife was having an affair, Grant,' said Morrigan, tone more conciliatory. 'She was going to leave you because she didn't love you any more and because of your mismanagement of this farm. You came to me to bring her back. I gave you a spell to do so. At no time did I tell you to get so drunk you couldn't see and chase after her in your car.' Morrigan looked at his legs, back to his eyes. 'So you can't blame me for your actions.'

Grant said nothing.

'You got her back. Your farm's finances are much healthier.'

'Yeah,' he said, wheeling himself round the table, picking up the whisky bottle at the side of his paperwork and pouring himself a generous measure, clearly not the first one of the day. 'And she got her bloke. Paul fucking Priestly. Running this fucking place now. And her too.' He drank the whisky down in one painful gulp. 'She's just my fucking carer now . . .'

'Then be careful what you wish for, Grant. Be more specific next time.'

He stared at Morrigan once more. 'Why are you here?'

'Just to remind you,' Morrigan said, as easily and breezily as possible. 'To keep strong. Not to give in.' Morrigan began pacing round the kitchen, examining hanging pans, knives. Holding one up, catching the light. 'These are very sharp, Grant. Very. And sturdy. I can imagine them slicing clean through flesh to bone. I could make use of these, Grant.' Attention back on him now. 'Great use.'

Grant now looked scared. His outburst had had little to no effect; the whisky was doing its job, dulling his senses once more. The threat of a knife-wielding able-bodied Morrigan advancing on the useless, self-pitying farmer was much more terrifying.

'Have it if you want it,' he said, his voice small and parched, like he needed another drink.

'Thank you, Grant. I may just do that. It could come in very useful for our purposes, couldn't it? And of course, if we were to use it then it would only be a small matter to check which one of us had a missing blade from their kitchen, wouldn't it? If it came to that, of course. If things went horribly wrong because someone backed out and spoke when they shouldn't have. But it won't, will it? No, no, no.'

Grant sighed. He understood exactly the threat he was being given. 'No, Morrigan. It won't.'

Morrigan smiled. 'Good. Because I wouldn't want your anger at misusing my spell to become something bigger.'

Another sigh. He clearly just wanted Morrigan to leave now. 'It won't.'

'Good.' The knife disappeared somewhere on Morrigan's person. 'Then I'll leave you to it.'

Morrigan turned, walked towards the door, looked out. Stopped. Turned. Smiled once more. 'Oh, look, pulling up in front of the house, here comes your wife now. And Paul Priestly too. I wonder where they've been and what they've been up to?'

Grant seemed close to tears. He glanced up, his eyes pleading. 'Morrigan?' His voice sounded as pathetic as he looked.

'Yes?'

'Have you got another spell? Something for these?'

He curled his hands into fists, hammered them down hard on his useless legs. Clearly, he felt no pain.

'You mean to make you walk again?'

Grant nodded.

'Yes, that's possible.'

He looked up, hope appearing for the first time in his eyes. 'Really?'

'Oh, yes. But the most important ingredient in that spell is faith, Grant. Do you have faith that you could walk again?'

'Yes,' he said quickly.

'And more importantly, do you have faith that your wife would want you again if you could?'

He looked to the door where he could see his wife coming towards him, arm in arm with Paul Priestly, not even bothering to hide it now. His head dropped once more.

'I thought not, Grant. I'll bid you good day.'

Morrigan left, making small talk with the two incomers on the way out, while in the kitchen Grant reached for the whisky bottle once more, upended it into his glass.

17

Kai didn't see Tom as he exited the camper van. Didn't hear him tailing him down a side street leading towards the butcher's. Didn't feel him until Tom put his arm round Kai's throat and said: 'One word and I'll choke the fucking life out of you.'

Kai said nothing. Didn't move.

Tom waited until he was sure that he would receive no resistance, then spoke again. 'Good. Now if I take my arm away are you going to run? Are you going to shout out?'

Kai shook his head in response.

'Good.' He began to slacken his grip. Kai initially did the same, relaxing his body, but Tom felt him tense once more, getting ready to run or hit back. He grabbed him again, tighter this time. Kai gurgled as his air supply was restricted. 'What did I just say? And what did you just agree to? *Stay* where you fucking are.'

Kai stayed where he fucking was.

'Now,' said Tom, arm slackened slightly to allow his quarry to breathe, 'you and me are going to have a chat.'

Tom was surprised how quickly his training came back to him. More than that – the person he used to be who utilised that training. As he kept his muscles taut, Kai ceased struggling in his grasp, accepted his situation. Was he just pretending to be this new person, this Tom Killgannon? Was he really still the old him? Or had he just ceased being his old self without a new persona in place? Was that why the villagers didn't know where he fitted in, because he didn't know himself?

Too much thinking. Not enough action.

'Right,' he said. 'Answers.'

He grabbed Kai's shoulder, spun him round, slamming him against the stone wall, arm across his throat once more. Tom preferred to look in their eyes when he questioned them. Easier to spot lies that way.

'What . . . I don't know what . . .'

'I haven't asked the questions yet. First one, where's Lila?'

'I . . . I dunno . . .'

Tom pressed his arm harder against Kai's neck. 'I'll ask you again. 'Where's Lila?'

Kai's face began to redden, hands clutching at Tom's unyielding arm. 'I . . .'

Tom kept his voice steady. Every time he had done something like this it was almost an out-of-body experience. Like someone else was doing the driving and he was just in the passenger seat. 'Where's Lila?'

'I dunno . . . honest . . .'

'Explain.' Tom removed the pressure slightly, allowed him to breathe, to talk.

'She . . . she was . . . she'd been . . . she'd done something wrong. Noah told you that. He put her in the punishment tent. Waitin' to decide what we were goin' to do with her. An' she . . . escaped . . .'

'What had she done wrong?'

No reply. Tom pushed harder once more.

'What had she done wrong?'

'I can't . . . can't . . .'

'You can.'

'They'll . . . they'll . . .'

'What, kill you? Hurt you? What d'you think I'll do to you? Now, again. What had she done wrong?'

'She . . .' He shook his head, screwed his eyes shut. 'No . . . no, if Noah . . . I can't . . .'

'If Noah hears that you've told me something he'll be mad at you? Is that it?'

Kai nodded.

'I'll be mad at you if you don't.'

Kai said nothing. Couldn't speak.

'This is getting tedious. What had she done wrong and where is she now?'

'I don't know where she is now. If . . . if we knew that we'd have got her . . .'

Tom began to understand. 'Right. So you're looking for her as well? For this thing she did wrong?'

Kai nodded, relief on his features. It seemed like he had said the right thing, been believed and would soon be released.

Tom disabused him of that notion. 'So what had she done wrong? You're not walking away from this until you've told me.'

'No . . . no . . .'

Despite his threats, Tom didn't seem to be getting anywhere. Whatever hold Noah had on Kai was a strong one. He took a chance. 'Was it something to do with that student? That missing student?'

The words hit hard. Kai's mouth dropped open, he stopped moving.

Tom felt a frisson of excitement. Bullseye. 'It was, wasn't it? What had she to do with the missing student? Kyle, isn't that his name?'

'She . . .' He shook his head, thought better of himself. 'I can't. Can't tell you.'

Tom squeezed his neck harder. 'You can. You will.'

Kai gasped for air. 'No . . .'

Pushing harder. 'What about crows? What have they got to do with it?'

Kai's eyes looked about to pop. Like he couldn't believe what Tom was coming out with. It terrified him, rooted him to the spot.

'Morrigan . . .'

'Everything all right?'

Tom and Kai both turned at the same time. At the end of the alleyway stood a middle-aged woman dressed in waterproofs and carrying a walking stick. She was staring at them both.

Tom relaxed his grip slightly. 'Just a friendly disagreement.'

'Doesn't look that friendly to me.' Steel in her voice. Completely unafraid of the two of them. She scrutinised them once more. Looked at Kai. 'You're one of the chaps from the campsite, aren't you?' Then at Tom. 'I've never seen you before.'

'He owes me money,' said Tom. 'Just making sure I get it back.'

She kept staring at them both.

No one moved.

She looked at Kai. 'Is that correct?'

Tom tried to stare at Kai, make him answer the way he wanted him to.

'No, it's not . . .'

'Then I shall call the police.' She put her hand inside her pocket, brought out an ancient mobile phone.

That was the last thing Tom wanted, and Kai presumably. 'It's all right,' said Tom, attempting a smile. 'We'll go somewhere else. Settle our differences more amicably.'

He put his arm round Kai's shoulder, tried to move the other man away.

'You'll stay where you are until the police arrive,' she told him.

Tom turned to Kai. Smiled. 'We'll do that, shall we? I'm sure they'd like to hear what you were about to tell me.'

Tom didn't see the blow coming but he felt it. Kai's knee came up swiftly between his legs. The pain, unexpected and sharp, hit him and he bent double, removing his grip from the other man. Kai didn't follow it up, didn't wait for anything. He ran.

'Fuck . . .'

'And there's no need for that kind of language, either.' The woman tutted, turned and walked away, muttering to herself all the while.

Tom bit his lip. Said nothing. Heard Kai's camper van revving up and driving off.

18

Lila stared at the ceiling. She heard noise from the rest of the caravan: loud voices, music, games. She lay still, tried to pretend she was somewhere else entirely. Somewhere warm, safe. Happy.

She closed her eyes, tried to block out everything in her present. She knew that other people in a situation like hers – if there was anyone else in a situation like hers – would try to cast their minds back to a time when life was better. Lila had to go way, way back for that to happen. Almost to birth.

She could barely remember a time when she had been happy or felt safe and wanted. Her infanthood was the nearest thing to that. A time recalled only as a kind of rosy glow, nothing specific, no memories that stood out. But her big sister was there. That's the thing she clung on to. The only good thing.

Sophie.

Lila had idolised her. She was everything Lila wasn't, everything Lila wanted to be. Tall, confident, popular, good-looking, fun to be with. Most siblings – or sisters at any rate – didn't get on when they were children. Lila and Sophie did. Her elder sister looked out for her, took her to the park, made time for her. Didn't put her down, laugh at her, try to lose her and go off with her friends when her mother told them to be together. And Lila loved her for that. And for everything else.

And her mother. She was fun to be around then too. And her father, when she saw him. When he wasn't at work. She remembered weekends when they were all together. Holidays where they found somewhere new to explore. That was when she felt happy. That was the time in her life she remembered laughing like someone with nothing to fear.

Then that rosy glow faded.

Sophie disappeared. That's what Lila was told. Sophie had gone to live with other people and wouldn't be coming back. Lila was devastated. Why would her sister do that? Why would her sister leave her that way? And who had she gone to live with? Who wanted her more than Lila did? Apart from breaking her heart, none of it made any sense.

Her parents wouldn't explain further. They stuck to their story. Lila noticed a change in them straight away. Especially her mother. The fun drained from her, replaced by a kind of over-cautious anger. She didn't want to let Lila out of her sight yet punished her for whatever she did. Lila suddenly developed faults in her mother's eyes. Lila believed she was behaving as she always had, but her mother insisted that those faults were there and they were sudden and huge. Angrily insisted. Sometimes with threats of violence, sometimes with actual violence.

The rosy glow had completely disappeared now, just darkness all around. Cast adrift by her sister's disappearance, left with an increasingly unstable mother. Her father began to spend longer and longer at work, sometimes not coming home for days on end. When he did eventually turn up he would be distant, sad-looking. As if he wanted to say something to Lila, something important, but couldn't find the words or the time or the energy to do so. And her mother would ensure that the two of them were never alone long enough for him to do it, always seeking some excuse to break them up, to be there with them, even though she made it abundantly clear she didn't want to spend time with either of them. Her father began to take on the defeated, haunted look that prisoners had in films.

He seemed to just fade in and out of her life from that point, more like a ghost than a real person. But her mother was there. All the time. Much more corporeal than Lila would have wanted.

Years went by.

Lila's schoolwork began to suffer. Her friendships. She wasn't like Sophie had been, popular and confident. She felt herself becoming awkward, shy. Unable to express herself emotionally but with a well of rage building within her. The other kids at school laughed at her, bullied her. She became more and more withdrawn. Unable to tell her mother, unable to tell her teachers. She felt so alone, like she didn't even want to be alive.

Then her mother started to change. Began to visit church regularly. Not just any old C of E church either. But an extreme evangelical one, the kind that would have handled snakes had health-and-safety regulations let them. Her mother's behaviour became even more erratic and extreme. She still took everything out on Lila but now she had a reason. God told her to do it.

Lila didn't know what to make of that. Her parents had never been religious. Her father in particular had always mocked religion, laughed at bishops and priests when they came on TV. Lila had always laughed along with him. But now he said nothing. Just let her mother continue.

Then something miraculous happened. Sophie had contacted her mother.

Lila was overjoyed. When? How? And more importantly, when was she coming home? Her mother spoke with a kind of cold triumph in her voice. Sophie wasn't coming home. Not here, not now. Not to this place. Lila was devastated. She didn't understand. Sophie was in a better place now. A much better place. Sophie was in heaven.

Sophie wasn't coming back. This place wasn't good enough for her. You – her mother pointed at Lila – aren't good enough for her. She's with God now. And we'll all go and meet her one glorious day. We'll all be with her then. But first we have to suffer down here. Like she did. We can't be at one with God until we've suffered like she did.

Lila looked to her father. He said nothing. He was beyond broken, a dead man walking. Going along with whatever his wife said.

Lila couldn't believe what she was hearing. At first she was too stunned to speak, to question. But she eventually found her voice. And the questions didn't stop.

How was Sophie in heaven?

How was she with God?

Where had she actually gone?

Had her mother and father been lying to her all this time?

What had been happening?

It was her father who eventually told her. In a voice as small as he now looked. His words were few and simple but like an iceberg held masses beneath them.

'Sophie's dead,' he said. 'She was killed by a car. We don't know who was driving. He didn't stop. He was never found. He got away with murder.'

Lila couldn't believe what she was hearing. On one level it all made sense, the way things had been the last few years, but it still didn't begin to answer her questions. The main one being the next thing she shouted out:

'Why didn't you tell me?'

No reply.

'You lied to me . . . You both lied to me . . .'

'We were trying to protect you . . .' Her father's words as weak as his voice. 'We didn't know what to do for the best . . . We thought . . . When you were older . . .'

'That's enough.' Her mother strong, imperious. 'We did what we thought was best. And that's that.'

'You lied to me, you—'

The slap was as sudden as it was unexpected. Lila put her hand to her face, the shock even stronger than the pain. And the pain was intense.

'You will not talk to me like that. You. Of all people. You will not talk to your mother like that.' Standing over her, ready with the next blow.

Lila looked to her father, hoping for some guidance, some resistance. He just sighed, shook his head. Said nothing.

'You will not disrespect your mother. You will not disrespect your sister. And most importantly, you will not disrespect God.'

Lila stared.

'You're a monster. Nothing but a monster. He took the wrong one.'

After that there was no way back.

The rage inside her welled up, spilled over. If Lila was a monster, she would behave like one. If she couldn't be good, she would be bad. If the only response she could get out of her mother was negative, then she would really give her something to be angry about. And as for her father . . . He wasn't worth considering. She had no respect for him. He might as well not be there.

And that was the majority of her teenage years. Living in a house where she was actively hated or at best ignored, constantly having to measure up against a deified dead sister, constantly being found wanting.

It all came to a head one day when she came in from school. Or at least what her parents assumed was school. Lila had actually been in the park all day, hanging around with a like-minded group that spent all of their money on cheap booze and even cheaper drugs. She didn't like them much but felt she had no choice. These people were her friends now.

There was a man waiting in the living room, sitting on the sofa. Well dressed – too well dressed, Lila thought – smiling insincerely.

'This is Father Gerald. From our church. He's here to help you, Lila.'

Lila looked at him, saw the cruel hunger in his eyes, the kind that was usually disguised behind good manners and good clothes. She saw through him straight away. Saw him for what he was. Hiding behind his position in the Church to excuse any sadism he wanted.

'What's he want?'

Father Gerald stood up. The smile still in place. 'Your mother tells me you're troubled, Lila.' Softly spoken, soothing, like a lullaby.

Lila said nothing, just clenched her fists, steadied her legs, ready for whatever he was going to do.

Her mother came and stood at Father Gerald's side, both moving slowly towards her.

'Your mother tells me you're beset by demons, Lila. That they need casting out?' His ridiculous words rendered reasonable by his calm and even tone.

'What the fuck?' Lila said.

Her mother looked at the priest in triumph. 'You see? You see what I have to put up with, Father Gerald? The way she talks to me?'

Father Gerald smiled. 'Don't worry. She won't be like that for much longer.'

The signal must have been prearranged. Lila had no time to move, didn't see them pounce. Father Gerald pinning her down, her mother pulling her arms behind her, tying something round her wrists.

Lila screamed, shouted, kicked against them all the harder. To no avail. They seemed to receive strength from her struggles, her fear. Soon she was trussed up, cable ties at her wrists and ankles, writhing on the floor trying to get up, get out of the room, the house. Screaming obscenities, shouting for help.

'The devil is strong in this one,' said Father Gerald, voice like someone explaining a PowerPoint presentation. He gagged her, pulled the cloth tight in her mouth.

Lila felt it cut into the sides of her lips. The more she screamed, the more she worked against it, the more it bit into her.

'Now we can begin the exorcism,' he said.

And Lila screamed even more.

Later, when it was all over, when Lila had stopped crying, stopped shaking, her mother came back into the living room. Sat down opposite her, stared at her. Face blank, voice flat.

'It was for your own good. We had to find some way to get the demons out of you. To turn you into a good girl. It was for the best.' Her mother smiled. It didn't come naturally. 'Don't you feel better? Don't you feel like you've been renewed in the body of Christ?'

'I fucking hate you.'

Her mother sighed. 'I thought we'd got rid of all this.'

'I fucking hate you.'

'Lila . . .'

'I hope you get cancer and die alone. Really painfully. I hope you fucking suffer.'

'Lila, that isn't . . .'

'I hope you get to heaven and Sophie isn't there.'

Her mother looked wounded. Lila felt empowered. She continued. 'I hope she's in hell. Burning in hell. Rotting in hell.'

Her mother's mouth fell open.

'I hope you go there too. I hope you fucking burn.'

Tears sprang to the corners of Lila's mother's eyes. Lila felt triumph at the sight of that and smiled. The smile turned into a laugh. And the laugh didn't stop.

She heard her mother crying, telling her to get out of the house, that she was no longer a daughter of hers. She heard her screaming that Lila had let God down, let her sister down, let her own mother down, after all the things she had done to help her. She heard all that. And she never stopped laughing.

And that night, she left.

And now she was here. In a caravan in Cornwall with drug dealers who didn't know her or trust her but would like to fuck her, and a giant man with the mind of a baby.

She kept staring at the ceiling, desperately trying to think of those times when she was happy. Desperately hoping that a time would come when she could be happy once more.

Knowing that there was no point in even thinking that.

She stayed screwed up in the sleeping bag, a foetal ball for as long as possible. But she knew she would have to leave the room at some point, face the living hell her life had become.

She thought of her mother, wondered what she was doing now. Hoped that whatever it was, she was suffering more than Lila was.

Sometimes that feeling was the only thing keeping her going.

19

'What's the matter with you?' Noah stared at Kai. Unflinching, unblinking. Hard, cold eyes.

Kai both flinched and blinked. 'It's . . . can we talk somewhere private?'

He had driven straight back to the camp after his encounter with Tom Killgannon. Didn't even stop to pick up what he had gone for. This was more important.

Noah walked away from Kai, expecting him to follow and he did. Noah led him to the yurt that had held Lila. It seemed to Kai that months had passed since then. He tried to work out how he felt about entering the place Lila had escaped from. He thought about Lila, tried to work out his feelings towards her. They had been lovers once, of a sort. He'd always got the impression that he was more into her than she was into him, that she was only with him for the sake of convenience. In the camper van he had somewhere they could stay, a method of transport and, with the bits of dealing he was doing, an income. And she said she liked surfing although she never actually did it. She seemed happy to be with him, though, and he liked that. But he also thought that if someone else had come along when he did she would have been just as happy to go off with them.

And now she was gone completely. Again, he still didn't know how he felt about that. Especially under the circumstances.

Noah turned to him, stopping any further introspection.

'Talk to me.'

Kai stared at the ground, unsure where to start.

'What's happened?'

'It's . . . it was that barman. The one who was here the other night.'

Noah's fists clenched, back straightened. 'What about him?'

'He . . . he was waiting for me in the village. Pulled me into a back alley. Started asking questions. Threatening me. His hands . . .'

Noah stared straight at him. 'About what? Questions about what?'

'About . . . Lila.'

'So the same thing as the other night.'

Kai nodded, avoided Noah's gaze. Unsure of how much to tell him.

'What?' More a command than a question.

'He asked more than that. Knew more than that.'

Noah stiffened. His voice, when he spoke, dropped to a near-whisper. 'What did he tell you? What does he know?'

'He . . . he asked about the student. The missing one. He . . . said Lila had something to do with that.'

Noah thought for a few seconds. It seemed to Kai like hours.

'He said Lila had something to do with that?'

Kai nodded.

'He knew Lila had something to do with that?'

Another nod.

'That's what he told you.'

Another nod, avoiding eye contact all the time.

Noah stepped forward. Invading Kai's personal space. Kai didn't dare move.

'Are you sure that's what he said? Those exact words? That he knew she was involved?'

Kai said nothing.

'Because he could have just as easily said something about it and hoped your answer would confirm it for him. Couldn't he?'

Again, Kai said nothing.

Noah moved in closer.

'Couldn't he?'

Kai, realising he had no choice, nodded.

'You gave yourself away.'

Kai looked up. 'No, I . . .' Wilted under Noah's stare. He tried again. 'He knew about the crows.'

This seemed to genuinely interest Noah. He frowned. 'Really? He knew about the crows?'

Kai nodded, desperate to be believed. 'That's what he said. And something else. He mentioned . . . Morrigan.' He flinched as he said the name.

Noah's expression hardened, the iron gate descending. But before it did, Kai thought he glimpsed a second of fear in Noah's eyes.

'Morrigan? You're sure?'

Kai nodded.

'Tell me everything that happened.' Noah paced over to the other side of the yurt as Kai talked, made a play of thinking. Kai stayed where he was. Noah looked at the ceiling, pointed.

'Look,' he said, finger raised. 'That's where she got out, see?'

Kai looked. The cords had been loosened. There was dried blood on the canvas. He wondered how much it had hurt her to do that. Felt a pang of sympathy but tried not to let that show in front of Noah.

'It's been repaired, of course. Can't happen again. This place is perfectly escape-proof now.'

Silence. Kai felt he was expected to fill the void.

'Good.'

'Yes,' Noah said, turning to face him. 'It is good. Because this is where you're going to be staying for the foreseeable future.'

Kai couldn't quite take in what was being said to him. 'What . . . why?'

'Yes, Kai, I'm afraid so. I've been thinking this for a long time now but what you've just told me has confirmed it. You have your uses, in small, menial ways. But you've become a liability to me, Kai. Just like Lila was. And that means I have to leave you here while I decide what to do with you.'

'But . . . I . . . I told you about this straight away. I, I attacked him, hurt him. I . . .'

'You told me an old woman from the village showed up and recognised you. She was your rescuer.'

'Well, yeah, but—'

'Well, nothing, Kai. If she hadn't appeared who knows what you would have told him? What secrets you would have divulged? No, you'll be staying here. Till I decide what to do with you.'

Kai knew what that meant. Anyone who entered the yurt under these circumstances – and there had been quite a few – was never seen again. No one asked what happened to them but there were rumours. Sometimes more than that. No. He wouldn't let that happen.

Kai looked round. Noah was at the opposite end of the yurt, watching him. The door was behind Kai. He could easily reach it. He did so, turning quickly, making a run for it. Pulling it open, dashing outside.

To be met with a baseball bat to the stomach, end on, taking his breath away. He dropped to the ground, hands grasping his injured stomach, curled into a foetal ball, gasping, pain flooding his torso.

Jason, one of Noah's closest 'advisors', stepped inside.

'Thank you,' said Noah, stepping over Kai's body and making his way outside. He locked the door behind him.

Kai lay there, too damaged to move.

20

Pirate John had committed one of the bravest acts of his life: he had left the house.

After Morrigan's visit he had pulled the curtains closed and, panic flooding his system, lived like the only survivor of some terrible apocalypse: eating from cans and dried food saved up from his emergency pantry supplies, drinking only bottled water, no phone, internet or even TV. Alone with himself. He found it wearyingly frightening.

He couldn't trust anyone or anything around him. Had they poisoned his water supply? Substituted his regular canned beer for something else? His fresh food, had that been deliberately contaminated in some way? It was easy to do. The Russians did that kind of thing all the time. He kept away from the windows, used only strategically placed diffuse lighting in case his silhouette appeared through the curtains, making too clear a target for any putative marksman.

And all the while thinking, planning. Trying to find a way to get through what was happening around him not only with a clear conscience, but more importantly, alive. To stop himself from going insane he had started writing down everything that was happening, keeping a journal containing as many factual accounts of the madness as he could find. He had a stack of A5 ring-bound notebooks that he hadn't been able to shift so he'd torn into them and got started.

Bill Watson. Pirate John knew what he had seen that night. The usually taciturn farmer naked, covered in the blood of a cow he had just slaughtered in his barn, standing in the middle of one of his fields, flinging buckets of cow's blood around him, all the while howling at the night sky. Morrigan was behind that, Pirate John had no doubt. Bill Watson had been in trouble, seen his herd struck down by some mystery illness. Everything was apparently fine now, though. Defra had cleared it up, pointed to contaminated feed. But Morrigan had developed such a hold on the area with talk of the old ways, the old religion, that Bill Watson had been convinced it was his ritual alone that was responsible for his cows' recovery.

Bill had led him to ask around, find out what else had been happening that some people might not have been aware of. The plight of Grant Jenner, another farmer who he was familiar with, had come up in conversation. A car crash had left him in a wheelchair, but Pirate John knew that Morrigan's hand – to some degree – was behind it. He didn't yet know how or why, but he would find out.

Jack Tillis was another one of the village's close-knit group of farmers, a man Pirate John personally disliked and whose political views he had little time for. But something had happened to him, too. Something involving migrant workers and unharvested crops.

Tony Williamson was a down-from-London newbie farmer, spending an awful lot of money on organic principles. Pirate John wasn't sure where he fit in yet, but he was certain to play a part in Morrigan's design.

Everywhere he looked he could see Morrigan's work.

And all of them had something to do with the bid for the new marina. Not to mention the missing student. Pirate John was sure he was vital to that.

Looking at his notes made him feel brave once more. Or at least able to come to a decision. He would have to leave the house, do something about it. What was the worst that could happen? Well he knew the answer to that, but still he had to do something, even after being warned. He didn't think they would go so far as to kill him, although with all the madness that was happening at the moment with the resurgence of the old religion, he wouldn't put anything past anyone. It was a chance he would have to take. Because if he didn't, things would get an awful lot worse.

He would have to be clever, sneaky. That was fine, he was used to ducking and diving. Let them all believe he was doing one thing – towing the line – when in reality he was doing another – gathering evidence against them. His bravery increased the more he considered what he was doing. This wasn't just being brave and standing up to bullies, this was actual heroism. Pirate John could save the day.

But he couldn't do it on his own. He needed an ally. And there was only one person he would consider. An outsider. Someone who definitely didn't know what was going on.

He left the house, set out to find him.

'Tom in today?'

Pirate John tried to ask the question as casually as possible but there was no doubting the urgency behind it.

'Sorry,' said Pearl, 'day off.' Then smiled at him. 'You'll have to make do with me, I'm afraid.'

Ordinarily he wouldn't have minded that. Pearl was a real looker, even if she was Dan and Elaine's daughter and probably young enough to be his too. But not tonight.

'That's no hardship,' Pirate John said, not wanting to give any indication that there was something on his mind. He didn't know how much Pearl knew, how deeply she was involved. He hadn't seen her at the gatherings but that didn't mean anything. 'Always a pleasure.'

She leaned on the bar, looked at him. Smiled. Hardly rushed off her feet. 'What's on your mind, John?'

'Oh, nothing much. This an' that. You know.'

Her smile didn't fade. 'Good to hear it.' She walked away, busied herself along the bar.

Pirate John watched her. Was she involved? It didn't seem like it. Surely he would have known by now. She would have said something. Even a nod and a wink, something like that. Just to let him know. Others in the village had when he'd walked to the pub. Had looked at him in such a way that he was left in no doubt that they knew what he had been doing, thinking, knew all about Morrigan's call. And what it entailed. Eyes on him like never before. But not Pearl. He didn't get anything like that from her. So either she was very good at hiding it or she genuinely wasn't involved. He tried again.

'Know what Tom's up to today? Is he at home?'

'No idea,' she said, coming back to his end of the bar. 'Could be out somewhere, could be . . .' She sighed, shrugged. 'No idea.'

Pirate John detected a kind of sadness when she spoke of Tom. A wistfulness. He didn't have time to dwell on it. He came to a decision.

'What time d'you get off work?'

She laughed. 'You asking me out for a date, John?'

He felt himself redden. 'No, nothing like that. I was just . . .' He looked round, checking that no one was listening to them. He had no idea if anyone was or wasn't. 'D'you get a break? I want to have a word. About something important. Just not here. In private.'

Pearl frowned but still didn't seem to be taking him seriously. 'Sounds ominous.'

Pirate John kept a straight face. 'Can we talk when you're finished? Please?'

She shrugged. 'Fair enough. But you're not getting me into one of your schemes, are you? I've told you, we have suppliers for everything we need here.'

'No, no, nothing like that. Just . . . a chat.'

'OK then. I'll be off in a couple of hours. We can have a coffee.'

He thanked her, waited. Time couldn't move fast enough.

21

Lila pulled her coat around her. It was warm but not comforting. And it didn't stop the coldness gathering around her heart.

An amusement arcade on the seafront at Newquay. It looked like the end of the world. Run down, rain-lashed, even the electronic bleeps sounded mournful. She had spent most of the day in and around there, only spending money on a takeaway cup of tea from the café next door that both looked and tasted like the water hitting the shore. She hadn't eaten anything. She was saving what little money she had for later, hoping to make some more in the meantime.

It wasn't looking promising.

'You've got contacts,' Leon had said earlier, in the caravan. Getting ready for work, doing up the buttons on his Crack Converters red polo shirt. 'Conroy said so.'

She didn't reply for fear of being caught out in a lie but cocked her head to one side slightly to show him she was listening and not contradicting.

'So he wants you to use them. Says some guy – your boyfriend?'

She shrugged. 'I know who he means.'

'Yeah.' Leon scrutinised her, her non-committal answer making him wonder whether this boy was still around. 'Well, Conroy says he doesn't need him. You can do instead. You get the gear from here, go and sell to them.' Leon gave her his entrepreneur smile. 'Another revenue stream coming online.'

Again she didn't contradict, didn't agree or disagree. 'So what do I do, then?' she asked. 'What's the prices, do I haggle?'

'Yeah. You're a self-employed small businesswoman now. You're the backbone of the economy. You've got targets and profit margins and all that shit. Course you haggle. You get the best price possible. You've got something they want. And soon, there's only gonna be us supplying it. Bargainin' from a position of strength, innit?'

She could have laughed at his appropriation of business-speak. 'OK then,' was all she said instead.

But she couldn't go back to the camp. And couldn't tell them that. She'd be out and homeless all over again. So she had to do something. She had to be smart.

And that was why she had found herself in the amusement arcade. This, she had decided, was to be her new territory.

Except it didn't seem to be working.

She had wandered around, trying to catch kids' eyes, even giving a sotto voce indication of what she was there for. 'Weed, Charlie, ecstasy . . .' And if that didn't work: 'Spice, meow meow, whatever you want I've got . . .' But the kids all seemed to be sorted. None of them approached her. A few older men did, cruising the aisles looking for young, fresh meat, not too fussy about which sex they'd settle for. She told them where to go. And they did. No bother, no drama, usually. It was a numbers game to them: keep trying till they found one that would say yes. And they did. Or they wouldn't have kept going there.

The kids staring at the games, immersed in dancing figures on the screens, the cars, the guns, the monsters, the women, the gore. Deaf to everything but the tinny beeping and bleeping of the theme tunes, the screams of the dying, the screech of tyres, the incessant emission of ammunition. The rush they got from what they were doing as potent as any drug. Lila saw that.

She made another round of the place as the clientele refreshed itself. Began her whispered litany once more.

No interest. No sale.

Well, some interest, but unwelcome.

The guy behind the counter of the change booth was staring at her. She had noticed him looking over earlier and panicked, thinking she was about to be detained and arrested but he hadn't done anything. Hadn't approached her, confronted her, stopped her. Just looked and allowed her to go on. So she let it go, thought it was just the kind of place where dealing – and everything else – was tolerated.

But now he was really giving her attention. Making his earlier glances seem casual. And that wasn't a good thing.

He got out of his booth, began to walk towards her. Young. Tall, but not carrying it well, like he was used to sitting down all day, his back curled and hunched. Thin and gangly, turn sideways and he'd be flat. Hair long and greasy, skin pallid from lack of daylight, spotty and pitted from fast food. But his eyes, the look on his face. Like the bullied kid at school who never got a chance to get even until he grew older and achieved a small kind of power. Victim turned persecutor. But cruelly so. And his latest victim, he had obviously decided, was Lila.

He stopped in front of her. 'I've been watching you.'

His breath stank. Whatever unpleasantness curled behind his eyes curdled in his body too.

'And?' she said, refusing to be scared.

Not the response he had expected, she could tell. He tried to regain his upper hand. 'I know what you're doing.'

'That right? How nice for you.'

Anger flamed in his eyes. This wasn't going to plan. He moved nearer to her. She didn't flinch. 'You're a drug dealer, aren't you?'

Lila crossed her arms. 'You tell me, you've been watching me.'

'You are.'

'Really? You seen me sell anything?'

'Yeah.' Quickly, not thinking.

She raised an eyebrow. 'You sure about that?' She could have laughed at how suddenly absurd the situation had become. Caught dealing, except she hadn't been.

Anger boiling over, he reached out for her. 'You're coming with me.' Grabbed her by the hair, pulled.

Lila twisted, tried to get away. Couldn't. For all the apparent weakness in his frame he was strong. Anger did that. And she had made him angry. He pulled at her hair. The pain was excruciating. She tried to claw his hands, but he ignored her. She screamed, trying to attract attention, but everyone became suddenly blind and deaf. He dragged her off the main floor to the back of the arcade, pausing to enter a pin code into a lock, waiting for the door to open. He pushed her inside, threw her down on the floor of a tiny, filthy office. Exactly the kind of office she would have expected the arcade to have.

He pulled up an old office chair, sat down right in front of her, legs apart, so she had no choice but to look up at him. Instead she looked at the floor.

He kicked her arms away. Vicious, quick, hard. She fell to the floor, her face thudding off the cracked vinyl.

'I'll have some fucking respect from you . . .'

Lila, reluctantly, looked at him. But she took her time about it. She stared him straight in the eyes. Didn't blink. Her own anger overriding any fear she might have had.

'That's better,' he said, although the shake in his voice, the doubt in his eyes, made her think that it possibly wasn't.

'What d'you want?' she asked.

'To talk to you.'

'So talk.' She gave a false yawn. 'Haven't got all day.'

Again his anger rose. He stood up, stood over her. 'Listen, you druggie bitch, I am that close –' he gestured an infinitesimal gap between his thumb and forefinger – 'to calling the police on you. Tell them what you've been doing here.'

She attempted a shrug. It hurt her shoulders. 'Call them, then. I'll talk to them.'

'No, you won't. Because you're not going to get out of here. Not unless you do what I say.'

'That a fact?' She kept the anger in her voice but she was starting to get scared now.

'Oh, yeah.' He reached over to the desk, picked up a long, old-fashioned wooden ruler, the kind that schools stopped using in the 1960s. 'Because that's what happens to skanks like you. Skanks that I find in the arcade doing what you were doing. Or worse. Selling their snatches. Oh, yeah, I've sorted them all out.'

She could have giggled at his choice of words if she hadn't seen the ruler. She spoke, again trying to sound brave, hoping she managed it. 'You're not going to do that with me. You're really not.'

'You think so?'

She could see the erection in his jeans. It turned her stomach. She started to pull herself up off the floor.

'Stay where you are!'

She didn't, kept moving. And didn't see the blow coming until it was too late.

It hit her shoulder, knocking her back to the floor again. Christ, that thing hurt. Shockwaves all down her arm.

'My dad was a school teacher,' he said. 'He brought this home one day. Said they weren't allowed to use it on the kids any more. But that didn't stop him from using it on me. I hated him. I stole it from him. And now I use it on people like you. And I put it to very good use . . .'

She just rubbed her arm, stared at him.

He giggled. 'That's better. Get to know your place . . .' He began to undo his jeans. 'You know what's coming next, don't you?'

She did. And she had had enough. Of being used, of being abused, of being ignored, and of being patronised. She was worth more than this. She had to be. And she wasn't going to take it any more. Especially not from creeps like him.

He was taking his short, stubby penis out of his hideous old boxers. She noticed that he had loosened his grip on the ruler, keeping it slack in his left hand. She knelt upwards as if she had given in, was being submissive towards him.

He giggled. 'Yeah, you bitch, that's right . . .' Made to grab her hair once more with his right hand.

Her eyes never left the ruler in his other hand. Before she reached his groin she had grabbed it from him. He was so surprised he let go. She pulled her arm back, brought the hard, flat wood down in a straight line. She aimed for his stomach, missed. Hit him on the penis instead.

He howled.

She got to her feet. He was lying curled up, pain etched on his features, tears falling. She stared down at him. Felt all that hate, that anger well up within her. She felt the ruler in her hand, the hard, smooth wood. Thought of the damage it could inflict. Imagined how much she would enjoy it.

She brought it up, made ready to strike as hard as she could.

'No, please . . .' Lying on the floor, whimpering, crying.

'You're fucking pathetic.' She brought it down as hard as she could.

And now, later, she was on the seafront, looking out at the water. Grey. All grey. The coloured fronts of the bars behind her washed out in the overcast weather. She could see something on the horizon, a boat or a ship, she couldn't tell. But whatever it was she wished she were on it. Or at least on something that would take her far away from here.

She thought of her actions in the arcade. Felt herself raising the ruler again, bringing it down once more. Hard. She tried to work out how she felt about what she had done. He hadn't got up when she left. She wondered whether he was able to. And now that the anger had subsided she felt guilty. She shouldn't have given in to that feeling, but she'd wanted to hurt him, wanted to make him pay for what he had tried to do to her. The more she thought about him, the more she understood him. The bullied, abused kid taking his revenge out on anyone he could. Pathetic, really. In every sense. But were her actions any better?

'Heard you ran into a bit of trouble.'

She jumped. Turned. Ashley stood behind her.

'You gave me a fright.'

He smiled as if that was his intention. 'Heard you were in the arcade. Got into a scene with Arcade Phil.'

A shudder of dread ran through her. What had happened to him? Had he reported her to the police? Was he dead?

Ashley laughed. 'You left the man in a real fucked-up state. Fucking funny.'

'He . . . what did he say?'

'Said you attacked him. Tried to rob him.'

'But I didn't, I—'

'Don' worry. I know exactly what happened. Not the first time he's tried that. Not the first time he's ended up hurt, neither. He'll get better again.'

'Good.' She breathed out a sigh of relief she didn't realise she had been holding.

The smile dropped from Ashley's face. His eyes became instantly hard. 'You don't go back there. That's my territory. Got it sweet there, you don't fuck it up for me. Get me?'

She nodded.

'You got your own territory. Stick to it.'

He turned, walked away.

'Come on, back home now.'

She followed him. Gave a quick final glance at the sea. The boat or ship was long gone.

22

Kai had known terror before. But that involved waves, a lack of self-belief, getting out of his depth and fearing his lungs would fill with water and choke him.

That was not like this.

He was face down in the back of a van, hands tied behind his back, ankles similarly so. An old sack on his head. They had come for him during the night. Or he assumed it was during the night – the yurt had blackout curtains all around it.

When Noah left him he had shouted, tried to take out the door, the walls. Find a way of escape. But there was none. His prison had been reinforced since Lila was there. Noah wasn't in the habit of making the same mistakes twice.

Eventually, realising he was getting nowhere, he had sunk back against the bed, suddenly exhausted. The adrenaline that had given him such a rush, from his confrontation with the barman onwards, had abated, leaving him washed out, ready for sleep. So with nothing else to do, the only method of escape he had was to curl up on the bed and do so. Roughly and sporadically. And when he woke he reassessed his situation.

Fear had now given way to anger. Directed at Noah. Kai had done nothing wrong. He had been attacked and had given a good account of himself. That was that. What was he supposed to do? Not tell Noah? That would make things even worse. No. He had done the right thing. And look where it had got him.

His next target was himself. He had allowed this to happen, allowed himself to get into this situation. He should never have gone along with it, never have even agreed to it. And never let Lila be part of it either. Yes, looking at it dispassionately he hadn't been given a choice and probably would have been forced to do it anyway, but still. He should have said no. He kept thinking. And thinking. What could he have done instead, how could he have changed things? Every avenue led to the same conclusion, the same direction: here.

So he sighed, tried to tamp down his rising terror, accept his situation. Control it. He thought of Lila, wondered where she was, hoped she had managed to escape. Hoped she was happy.

He missed her. Yeah, that was it. He missed her. He knew she probably wouldn't be missing him, not after everything that had happened, but he had felt things for her he had never felt for anyone else. Was it love? Could be.

He was still thinking about Lila when they rushed him.

He knew who it was, could identify every one of them. He had shared exploits, drinks, drugs, meals, a life with them. They were his friends. Or had been. Because above all they were loyal to Noah and if he told them to kill Kai, they would do so. Not because of any great love for Noah but because they knew how the camp was structured. They knew that it could just as easily be one of them in Kai's place. And they would do whatever it took to ensure that didn't happen.

So they forced him to the ground, beat him, kicked him, pulled his arms behind his back, tied them, then his ankles, and hooded him. Then they dragged him out.

He felt himself being thrown in the back of a vehicle. Could have been any one of the vans, could even have been his. And then he was driven off.

That was when the terror really kicked in.

When he realised where they were taking him.

23

They all looked at Lila differently now.

They'd heard what she had done to Arcade Phil and were wary of her. Kept their distance. Treated her with something like respect. The previous nights she hadn't been so lucky. They thought she was there for the taking. Something for the pack to squabble over, the alpha being the one who managed to fuck her. And she had fought them off. Not physically, not yet, but with body language, stares, words or the lack of them. She wasn't just unresponsive to them, she had tried to appear downright hostile. And it had worked. But it was only a temporary measure. There would be a reckoning. Of that she was certain.

Now that had been put on hold. Indefinitely. They were in no further hurry to try anything with her. For now she scared them. All she had to do was sell some drugs, make some money. But when they realised she couldn't do that . . .

She didn't want to think about it. She needed a get-out plan.

It was becoming a typical evening in the caravan. Ashley and Aaron were playing games on the PS4, Josey watching. Leon was still out. She sat on the sofa, said nothing.

'Get me a can of Coke,' said Ashley, never taking his eyes off the screen.

Lila looked around to see who he was talking to.

Silently, Josey got up, made his way to the kitchen area. Picked up a can of Coke from the countertop, brought it over, held it outstretched.

'Open it.'

Josey did so. Ashley took it, downed a mouthful, grimaced.

'It's warm, you fat stupid fuck. Get me a cold one.'

'Yeah, yeah, sorry, sorry . . .'

Josey, half cringing, half running, made his way back to the kitchen area, took one out of the fridge. Brought it over, opened it. Handed it to Ashley who, without turning round, threw the warm Coke can back at Josey. Not expecting it, Josey fumbled it and ended up wearing most of the contents before it eventually landed on the floor.

'Look what you done now, you stupid cunt,' said Aaron, again not looking at him. 'Clean it up. Filthy fucking pig.'

'Yeah,' chimed in Ashley, 'filthy fucking pig.' Then laughed.

Josey looked like he was about to burst into tears. He stared at the can on the floor, brown liquid fizzing onto the carpet. He slowly bent down, picked it up. Looked around as if confused what to do next.

'Let me help you,' said Lila, going towards him.

'Sit down,' Aaron told her. 'He's got to learn and it's his place, his responsibility.'

Josey, head bowed, carried the can over to the kitchen, located the bin, put it in. He then found a cloth and got to work mopping up the spilled drink.

Lila watched. Josey's place. He owned the caravan? What had he to do with the rest of them, beyond using? Why were they here? With him in particular? Plenty of questions, no answers as yet. Not wanting another fight, she said nothing. Remained still.

The next flashpoint wasn't long in coming.

'Hey, fat fuck, get me some food.' Ashley again.

Josey immediately jumped up as if he was about to be hit. He looked round, confused.

'Food. Now.' A real threat in Ashley's voice.

Josey ran to the back of the caravan, picked up a mobile phone. Pressed a button. When it was answered, he spoke as if repeating a well-worn litany. 'Extra-large All the Meats, stuffed crust; extra-large The Works.'

Ashley looked at Lila. 'What d'you want?'

Lila looked between the others. She hadn't realised how hungry she was. 'Erm . . .'

'Hurry up.'

'Tuna. Something with tuna.'

Ashley nodded at Josey who was waiting for his cue to speak. 'And tuna. Yeah.' He listened to the voice on the phone. 'Yeah. Yeah.' Then gave a plaintive look towards Ashley and Aaron. 'Money?'

'The usual,' said Aaron without looking up.

Josey felt in his pockets. 'I haven't . . .'

'Yes, you fucking have. Don't try that one again. Remember last time.' His voice flat, disinterested, but the threat implicit.

Josey, defeated, mumbled something into the phone, ended the call.

'You know you've got money,' said Aaron. 'And you know what you have to use it on.'

Josey nodded. Resumed his seat in silence.

'Hey.'

An empty Coke can hit Josey in the head. He flinched, rubbed the spot where it had struck. Looked like he was about to cry.

'Don't sit down, you fat fuck, you've got work to do. Get me another one of these.'

Josey immediately stood up, crossed to the fridge, opened it, looked in. He straightened up, fear and confusion on his face. 'There's . . . there's none left . . .'

Aaron stood up. Even at the far end of the caravan Josey shrank back, scared.

'Whose fucking fault is that, then?'

Josey began to shake his head as Aaron advanced towards him, mumbling something incoherent.

'Eh? Whose fault?'

Aaron drew level with Josey, stared at him. Josey just curled up on the floor. 'Don't . . . don't . . .' Hands covering his head, wailing, like an abused puppy who knew what was coming next and was dreading it.

Aaron stood there, unmoving, staring.

Eventually he smiled. It wasn't pleasant.

'Don't let it happen again.'

Walked back to the front of the caravan, laughing. Ashley joined in. Lila just stared at them. Aaron saw her reaction, turned to face her.

'What?'

'Nothing.'

He nodded. 'Good.'

The boys resumed their game.

Later, when the pizza had been consumed – Lila having little appetite by then but eating just to keep her strength up – Josey started to fidget.

'What's wrong with you? Got crabs, or something?'

Ashley smirked at Aaron's joke.

'I want . . .' said Josey. 'Want some medicine . . .' He pronounced it *medsin*.

'Do you now?' said Aaron.

Josey nodded. 'Please . . .'

The boys looked at each other, smiled as a private joke or sense of anticipation passed between them. They sat back on the sofa, looked at Josey.

'What you goin' to do for it?' asked Aaron.

'Yeah,' said Ashley, 'what?'

'I . . .' Josey looked between the two of them. Lila saw the fear and humiliation in his eyes.

Slowly he began to throw his body around, as if to some music only he could hear. The two boys started to laugh, made encouraging whoops.

'Sing!'

'Yeah, sing!'

In a voice that sounded more suited to crying, he began to sing. Or gave an approximation of singing: it was some time before Lila realised he was performing Kylie Minogue's 'I Should Be So Lucky'.

By this time the two boys were in hysterics. Laughing not only at the spectacle before them but at the power they had to command him to do it. Lila wanted to be sick.

She saw tears roll down Josey's face, saw the pain in his eyes. She stood up.

'Fucking hell, just give him what he wants.'

The other three all stopped and stared at her. She suddenly became self-conscious, embarrassed, but had to continue.

'Just . . . let him have what he wants.'

'Talk about killin' the party,' said Aaron, eyes glittering darkly. He stared at her. His eyes said she should be taught a lesson. But she knew that her treatment of Arcade Phil stopped him from doing so. Also, her anger made her match his gaze. Eventually his eyes dropped. He hit Ashley in the arm. 'Get him his stuff.'

Ashley got up off the sofa, walked towards the door leading to the bedrooms. Josey flinched as he passed him.

Lila watched him walk down the hall, not closing the doors behind him. She clearly saw him kneel down before a bedside cabinet in the master bedroom, take out a small bag of heroin. Also in that cupboard were piles and piles of money. She couldn't make out the denominations, but she knew there was plenty there. Enough to start a new life with. And enough gear to sell, just to keep things ticking along while she got established.

Ashley came back, threw the little plastic bag at Josey who scrambled for it, thanking them profusely, and going to the kitchen to start cooking it.

Lila sat back. Plenty to think about now. The money. The drugs. Her way out. She looked at Josey in the kitchen. And when she went, she knew whom she would take with her.

Her thoughts didn't last long. The door opened. Leon entered. 'Look who I've found . . .'

He stepped inside, letting someone come in behind him. Another black youth, smaller than the others, dressed for the street in London or Manchester but not Newquay. And, Lila soon discovered, full of himself.

'Danny!' Ashley and Aaron stood up.

Danny basked in their adoration. Then held up a sports bag. 'Been to the shops, boys. Brought back supplies. Got something for me?'

Lila watched the others become even more excited, talking over themselves, telling him they did and how good it was to see him again. Then he saw Lila. Smiled. She felt his eyes travel all over her body. He was either underage or stunted, but his gaze went well beyond his years. And not in a healthy way.

'Who's this?'

'Lila,' said Leon. 'One I was tellin' you about.'

Danny walked over to her. His breath smelled of alcohol and Haribo. Looked right in her eyes. 'Lila.' The way he said her name made her feel unclean. 'Lila . . .'

She held his gaze. Tried to imagine he was Arcade Phil. No threat. Easily beatable. Found it hard.

'Conroy sent her,' Aaron told him. 'New recruit. Openin' up new avenues of trade an' that.'

'Good to hear it,' said Danny. Then his attention was back on Lila. 'Think you and me're gonna become friends, ain't we?'

Lila said nothing. Just tried to look through him.

'Ooh, a challenge. I like that.' He turned to the rest of the room. 'Right. Get your gear on. We're off out. Wanna combine business with pleasure?'

They did. Lila didn't move.

'Let's go, then.'

24

Kyle was broken. Mentally, spiritually, physically.

He had pulled the bed back into place after his abortive escape attempt. It hadn't been easy: his body was wrecked from the fall, the impact of the rusted but still sharp springs having gouged bloody tracks along his torso, arms and face, the weight of the frame bruising his muscles and bones. Added to the already existing pain in his ankle and he could barely move.

After moving the bed back he had just lain on it, too damaged and exhausted to get up again. Certainly in no condition to make another escape attempt.

Eventually – he didn't know how long, it could have been minutes, hours or days – he heard the metal sheeting at the top of the oubliette being pulled across. Despite everything a small glimmer of something welled within him. He wasn't sure what: hope? Fear? It surprised him; he had thought he was beyond feeling anything any more.

He waited. Told himself it was only for another sandwich and bottle of water to be dropped, or the bucket to be hauled up.

But it wasn't.

He heard voices. Or at least one.

'Don't, I . . . look, I'm sorry, I . . . please . . .'

Kyle was suddenly interested. He attempted to sit up.

No reply. Instead, just more pleading followed. 'Please, look, we can, we can stop this. I'll . . . I'll not say anything. You can trust me.' Then a final, plaintive, 'Please . . .'

Kyle heard movement. Scuffling, shuffling, grunting, like a fight was going on above him.

'No . . . no . . .'

Then a body fell into the oubliette. It landed with a dull thud, hitting the packed earth hard, as he had once done, the breath huffing out to be replaced by wheezing, as the body struggled to reinflate its lungs.

Kyle stared at the figure. His eyes had grown accustomed enough to the gloom to make out that it was a male, with long hair, dressed like a hippy. As he looked, something dropped from above, hit the figure. Kyle knew what it was immediately. A torch.

The metal sheeting was replaced over the hole, there was the sound of retreating boots, then silence.

Kyle waited for the figure to speak. Eventually he rolled over onto his side. Coughed.

'You OK?' said Kyle.

The figure jumped. He hadn't realised there was someone else there.

'Who's . . . who's that?' Struggling to speak, still gasping.

'Who are you?' asked Kyle. He had been used to being alone for so long that to have company was somehow surreal. Part of him doubted that this person was actually physically here. It could just be a hallucination. The figure moved, attempted to rise. Soon gave up on that and remained where he was. He sighed, finally regaining his breath.

Kyle stared. 'Why are you here?'

The man rose slowly until he was resting on his elbows. He turned towards where Kyle's voice was coming from. 'I . . .' Another sigh. 'Said the wrong thing, did the wrong thing. Somethin' like that.'

Kyle couldn't make out his features but there was something in the man's voice that sounded familiar. He couldn't place it, decided to encourage him to keep talking until it came to him.

'Said the wrong thing to who?'

Another sigh. This time of resignation, acceptance. 'I know who you are. Your name's Kyle, isn't it?'

Kyle was taken aback. He hadn't expected the man to know him. 'How d'you know that?'

The man laughed. Harsh and bitter; Kyle heard in it failed dreams and missed opportunities. And self-loathing.

'Yeah,' was the only answer the man gave.

Kyle was interested now. He sat up, ignoring the pain the effort involved. 'How d'you know my name? Who are you?'

'You really don't know?' The man was moving around, checking his limbs still worked, trying to get up. His hand fell on the torch. 'You really don't know?'

'No. I don't. Who are you?'

It took some effort but the man stood up. He clicked on the torch. The light was sudden, intense and blinding to Kyle after the long enforced darkness.

The man laughed once more. This time like a private joke. Kyle was getting impatient and a little angry. He couldn't see anything funny in the situation.

'I said who are you?'

The man swung the beam round the cell. Eventually brought it to rest on himself.

'Don't you recognise me? I'm the guy who put you in here.'

25

'Hello again.'

'Hi.'

Rachel smiled. 'Invited this time. Things are looking up.'

Tom stood to one side. 'Come in.'

Rachel walked straight to the living room. He closed the front door, followed her. When he reached the room she had taken off her jacket, sat down on the sofa. Rubbed her arms.

'You got the heating on? Place's cold.'

'Takes a while to warm up. It's on, though.'

Tom placed himself on the armchair opposite. He noticed a smile on Rachel's face, disappearing as quickly as it had appeared. He didn't know what to make of it.

'So,' she said. 'Do I get a cup of tea this time?'

Tom went into the kitchen, put the kettle on. It was about the same time at night that she had made her last call. Her visits were always late. Or most of them were.

Asking her round had been an impulsive gesture, done to get rid of her while he waited for Kai. Afterwards, he had agonised as to whether it was a good idea or not, but he was committed now. He had to act and hoped he had made the right choice.

He busied himself with getting mugs, milk and teabags, didn't notice that she had crept in behind him.

'Broken window?' she said, walking over to it, flexing the piece of MDF Tom had wedged in place as a makeshift deterrent. 'You had burglars? Should report that to the police, you know.'

Again, Tom wasn't sure how to answer. He turned to her. 'Look, I've got some stuff to tell you. I don't know quite how to say it – I'm not good at this kind of thing – so you'll have to bear with me. Let's get our tea, sit down. And talk.'

She pulled out an old wooden chair, sat at the table. 'It's warmer in here. I can sit near the Aga.'

They sat facing each other, table used for holding mugs, Aga keeping them warm. Both knowing it was difficult to get their relationship back on a professional footing after being on a personal one for so long.

'I've ...' He looked at his mug. Watched the steam swirl. 'The other night. I wasn't being a hundred per cent honest with you.'

'No shit, Sherlock. I'm police. We're trained to spot liars.'

He nodded. 'But it's not what you think. It's not—'

She placed a hand on his forearm. Looked him in the eye. 'It doesn't matter. I was out of order. You don't owe me anything. I know the rules and I have to stick with them. Even if ... well, it doesn't matter.'

'Is something wrong?'

'Nothing I can't cope with. And I shouldn't take it out on you.'

Tom didn't want to ask the next question. – didn't want to become more involved – but he felt he had no choice. 'Is something wrong at home?'

Rachel gave a sad smile. 'It doesn't matter. Tell me what you were going to say.'

Tom looked at her, unsure how to continue.

'What?' she said. 'Why you looking at me like that?'

'I just want to know what's wrong, that's all.'

Rachel sighed. 'You're a good-looking bloke, Tom. Christ knows we don't get many of them round here. And when we do ...' She tailed off. 'Well, I wanted you. You know that. And I ... I like you a lot. And that complicates things. That's all.'

Tom was amazed at what he was hearing. Amazed and wary. 'So what are you trying to say, Rachel?'

'What about Pearl?'

It wasn't the answer he had expected. 'What about Pearl?'

'Are you seeing her?' She gave a short laugh that Tom couldn't guess the intention behind. 'Is she my rival?'

138

'Rival? Pearl?'

'Oh, come on, I've seen the way she looks at you.' Trying to be playful but an undercurrent of anger behind the words.

'She's younger than me.'

'So what? So am I.'

'Not as young as her.'

'She must be, what? Ten years younger than you?'

'Little bit more. Not much.'

'That means nothing.' Rachel sighed again. Thought long and hard before she spoke again. Auditioned several words in her mouth, didn't speak any of them. 'Look,' she said eventually, 'just forget I said anything.'

Tom tried to speak but didn't know what to say.

'Let's get down to business. What did you want to talk to me about?'

Grateful for an escape from the way the way the conversation was heading, he told her everything.

When he had finished he sat back, looked into his mug. Empty. He got up, filled and boiled the kettle once more. Sat back down, waited for her to process what he'd said and speak.

'Wow,' she said eventually. 'I can honestly say that wasn't what I was expecting.'

'No,' said Tom. 'But that's it. Now I have no identity, and maybe she's got something to do with the disappearance of that student. Noah and his crowd too.'

Rachel looked like she didn't know what to say, how to react.

'So will you help me?'

'To do what?'

'Monitor my cards. See if they've been used anywhere. Or if anything's popped up for sale. If someone's been brought in with a bent passport, something like that. And, I don't know, put out a description of her. Last seen wearing.'

'Last seen wearing your coat.'

'Exactly.'

'I'll do what I can. Obviously.'

'Thank you. I do appreciate it.' He paused. Looked at his new mug of tea as if seeking strength there. 'Do you have to report this?'

'What, you losing all your plastic? Course I do.'

'Keep it discreet, though.'

She smiled. 'No, I'll put an advert in the paper. Course I'll keep it discreet.' She laughed. Her eyes kind of slid sideways. 'Thought you'd know that about me by now.'

Tom looked away, not wanting to meet her gaze. Or part of him didn't. 'What about the surfers? Will you look into them?'

'Someone will. I'll pass it up the line. Not me, though, not in my local bobby remit.'

'Too big for the rural police. Have to bring in the city boys.'

Rachel looked at him, eyebrows raised. 'Oh, you think we're all useless here in the country? Good for herding cows, crap at catching criminals?'

'That's not what I meant. I know you're still police.'

'Obviously. The uniform tends to be a giveaway.'

'Yeah, but . . . city policing's different. You know that.'

'Different, yeah. But not easier.'

'City police see people at their worst,' said Tom. 'Either as victims or perps. On one end of hurting or the other. You never realise the ways humans have got to hurt other humans. You think you've seen it all. But you haven't.'

'And you think it's different here?'

'Isn't it?'

She laughed. 'Rural policing's like a fence. There to keep things straight. Keep things put, or keep things out. You try and fence off people's emotions, stop them from turning into actions.'

'City policing's like that too.'

'No doubt. But there's fewer people living here so it becomes a different thing. You try and do things with a gentle word here and there, but . . .'

'But what?'

Rachel thought hard before answering. 'You're in the countryside now. Nature. Red in tooth and claw and all that. And the people living here can be just as bad. And sometimes, even worse.'

She fell silent. Lost in what was behind her words, Tom said nothing.

They both held their mugs, looked into them.

Eventually Rachel looked up.

'So are we having a fuck or what?'

26

Kyle couldn't find words. The newcomer kept moving the torch over the walls, the floor of the cell. Part of Kyle's brain was registering that it was the first time he had seen his surroundings properly. Most of his brain was flailing as to what to do next.

He didn't know whether to attack the man, channel whatever anger he might be feeling, or ask him where they were, if there was a way out. Or maybe get a view from the outside world, find out what was being done to find him, rescue him. Or just be grateful for some company. He did none of these things. He just stared, mouth open.

The man finished swinging his torch round, brought it to rest pointing downwards. 'I'm Kai,' he said, 'and before you ask, I'm just as much a prisoner as you are.' The words bitter, edged with despair, self-pity.

Kyle found his voice. 'Why ... what have they put you down here for?'

'They think I betrayed them.' A bitter laugh, spat out like coal dust and phlegm. 'Yeah. Fuckers.'

Questions bubbled up in Kyle's mind, all trying to surface at once. He moved his lips but nothing coherent came out.

'I'm sure there's plenty you wanna know. But for now, we've got to find a way out of here. We can't stay here.'

'Why not?'

'We just can't. Believe me.' Kai's eyes caught the light. Kyle noticed that the man was as scared as he was. Perhaps more so. It made sense. He knew who had put them here. He knew why. It couldn't be good. Kai's fear transmitted itself to Kyle. He felt panic rising once more.

'There's no way out. I've tried. I ... got hurt trying. Badly.' He pointed to his injuries. 'There's no way out ...'

Kai turned away, seeming to survey the room once more, but Kyle noticed his words had ramped up the other man's fear, which Kai didn't want to let him witness.

'Why are you here, then? I mean really? What have you done to them?'

Kai sighed. Kept looking, kept turned away from Kyle. 'You don't want to know.'

That was when Kyle felt the anger rising within him. All the way to the surface, ready to blow. He grabbed Kai by the shoulders, swung him round to face him. 'I do want to know. And you need to fucking tell me . . .' He shook him, hard. 'Tell me . . .'

Kai tried to wriggle away from Kyle's grasp, but he just held on all the harder. Which in turn made Kai pull all the harder. Soon the two of them were grappling, Kai trying to escape, Kyle venting his anger, no longer trying to restrain the other man, just hitting him as much as possible. Letting out God knew how many days' and nights' worth of pain and fear, channelling it all onto the body of the man who had put him there.

Eventually Kai stopped trying to fight back, just accepted the blows. He slumped to the ground, curling into himself as he did so. Kyle, exhausted, slumped down next to him. They remained in silence, the only sound that of their harsh breathing echoing off the stone and hard-packed earth walls.

'I probably . . .' said Kai eventually. 'Probably deserved that . . .'

Kyle said nothing. Didn't know if he was relieved, exulted or ashamed by his sudden burst of violence.

'I just mean,' Kai continued, 'I don't blame you for doin' it. That's all.'

Nothing.

'If I was in your place, if you'd . . . you know what I mean.'

Kyle, eventually, nodded.

The two of them sat in silence once more.

It was Kyle who broke it this time. His voice quieter, reasoned.

'So why am I here?'

Kai sat up, back against the wall. Neither looked at the other man, both stared ahead into the gloom.

'Dunno.'

'You don't know?'

Kai shook his head. 'Dunno. Just did what I was asked to. Me and Lila.'

'She was the girl. The blonde one.'

'Yeah, that's her.'

'You were told to . . . what? Pick me up?'

Kai nodded. Kyle felt that anger rise within him once more. He turned, stared at Kai's shadowed profile.

'Why me?'

Kai shrugged. 'You were there.' He turned to face him. 'Sorry, mate. All there is to it.'

Kyle stared at him, unable to speak. Kai began to feel uncomfortable under the gaze, gave an apologetic shrug.

'Sorry.'

'So . . . it could have been anyone, is that what you're saying? Just anyone?'

'Yeah.' Kai's voice was small.

Kyle didn't know whether this made him feel better or not. Didn't know what to think.

'So you must have known why they wanted me. Or, sorry, someone like me.' He couldn't hide the sarcasm in his voice.

'I told you, no. They never said.'

'Who never said?'

Kai sighed. 'Does it matter? You're here now. And I'm here as well. And we've got to get out.'

Again, Kyle saw the panic beginning in the other man's eyes as he spoke. He remembered the symptoms. He was behaving just as Kyle had when he was first imprisoned.

'Where's the girl?' asked Kyle. 'Lila?'

Kai shrugged again. 'Dunno. Gone. She didn't like what she'd done either. Wasn't happy about it. So she did a runner.'

'And you're here because you're unhappy about what you did to me?'

Kai didn't answer straight away. 'Yeah,' he said eventually.

Kyle said nothing. He knew a lie when he heard one.

'So what do they want me for, then?'

Again, Kai didn't answer straight away. 'I dunno,' he said eventually, his face averted.

Kyle didn't know if that was a lie or not.

Again, silence descended.

So what are we going to do then?' he asked finally.

'Find a way out,' said Kai. 'We can do that, can't we? I mean, there must be a way out.'

Kyle said nothing. It was his turn not to speak. Not to lie.

27

Coasters Club, Newquay. Fresh and Friendly Night. Lila stood at the edge of the dance floor, watching. Dance music pounding, she felt it in her ribcage. Lights spinning, flashing, combining with the music to send coded enticing messages around the room. Undecipherable to most, but the ones who got them really got them. Sweet sour stink of alcohol and energy drinks. Lynx Africa and Tommy Girl. Perspiration and desperation, all sweating for one reason or another: booze, drugs, dance, sex. Everyone wanting to get but not give out. And all around, shadowed nooks, crannies and corners made blind eyes easier to turn.

Danny had told them to get ready to go out. Newquay had tried to reinvent itself in recent years as a family resort with bars and restaurants instead of clubs but Coasters was a hangover from the town's glory days as the party drugs capital of the south-west. A mixed clientele: new kids who wanted it to be like it was, old timers who refused to believe it wasn't. Aaron, Ashley and Leon all took turns working there, put in shifts to ensure they had a presence. Clubbers knew who to talk to if they wanted anything. And they always supplied. For a small – or rather not so small – percentage the management blindly faked innocence. Sympathetic coppers on the payroll always ensured someone called ahead to inform them of any drugs raid. Everyone was happy. Everyone got what they wanted.

The boys were treated like local celebrities: free drinks, genuflection. They loved it, played up to it. Lila wondered where the local dealers were. She hadn't seen anyone else selling since she'd come to Newquay. The boys sometimes talked of London, or rather Hackney, but not why they had made the trip, why there was no opposition to them. If she had been more interested she would have asked. But she just wanted to get as far away from them as possible with as much as she could carry. And, watching them drinking, partaking of their own stuff and letting their guard down, she thought tonight might be the time to do it. She had stayed sober, clean. Building herself up to it.

She was wearing a dress. The first change of clothes since arriving at the caravan. It was short, tight, a good job the place was warm otherwise she would be freezing. New but cheap looking. The kind of thing a teenage boy would imagine a girl wanting to wear. Which was just what had happened. When Leon had brought Danny in with him he had stopped off at New Look and picked up something for her to wear to the club.

'You can't go out with those hippy-shit rags on, girl, you got to style it a bit, smarten up,' he had said, the other boys nodding along with him, experts suddenly.

From the expression on his face when he handed the carrier bag over he expected to be congratulated for it. Or even, his eyes said, repaid in some way. But once Lila put it on, felt the tight, clingy fabric mould itself to her thin body and ride up over her thighs whenever she moved, then saw the undisguised way the boys all stared at her, she knew she had nothing to thank him for. She had insisted on wearing Tom's coat over the top of it on the walk to the club, keeping her body as covered up as possible. And she wouldn't part with her old Converses.

'Dance,' said Danny, standing directly in front of her, can of Red Bull in hand. He turned, walked towards the dance floor where some heavy, slow-grinding, gangsta rap was blasting out. Didn't even turn to see if she was following him, just expected it. Lila didn't move.

Once he reached the edge of the floor he turned, realised she wasn't there. Walked back towards her, features angry.

'I said dance,' he repeated, a chemical fire burning behind his eyes.

Her first instinct was to ignore him, stay where she was. But something in her, the thing that had hurt Arcade Phil, had made her stand up to Conroy, had kept the boys in the caravan at a distance, jumped up inside her.

'All right then,' she said, not waiting for him to walk to the floor this time, just crossing there herself, letting him catch up.

The other boys stopped what they were doing and turned to watch. This was serious. This was real. Danny had managed to do what they had not.

On the floor she closed her eyes, tried to let the music carry her. She danced for herself, threw out arms and legs, gyrated and moved in ways that made her feel good, and her alone. Hands in her hair, running over her body. She felt Danny's hands attempt to touch her but moved away from them, shook them off. Kept dancing. Found a rhythm in herself that matched the music. Moved to it. Enjoyed herself for her own sake.

The song finished. She opened her eyes. Danny and the other three boys were all staring at her. She smiled, enjoying the new-found power that she had over them. Now that the sullen, dowdy-looking girl from the caravan had chrysalised into a sexy young woman, they wanted her more than ever.

'You got some moves, babe,' said Danny. He kept talking but she ignored him.

A thought came to her: I don't have to leave. I could be in charge of this outfit. They're boys. They're weak. They'll do anything I say. Danny's the one who pulls the strings. If he says I'm in charge, I'm in charge.

She turned back to Danny, gave him a dazzling smile.

'Let's find somewhere to sit down,' she said. 'We've got things to talk about.'

More Red Bull. More vodka. More speed. Lila found Danny easier and easier to talk to the more he had. Or at least to get her own way with. Get him to agree to whatever she wanted.

She leaned forward as she spoke. Her breasts were small but she knew his eyes would be drawn to them. Knew he'd be staring at them all the time she was talking. *These boys always want what they can't have.*

'So you run this outfit then, Danny, yeah?'

He shrugged, looked around. An emperor surveying his empire. 'Yeah. These are my boys. They do what I say.'

'You're a long way from home.'

He sniffed. He'd taken more than speed. 'Way it goes now, innit? Way we do business. We movin' out of town into the little places. Takin' over.'

'How d'you do it?' All breathless admiration.

If he'd had peacock feathers they would have been fully displayed. 'Move into a small town, somewhere like this. Cuckoo someone's house. That way we stay off the books.'

'Cuckoo?'

'Take over. Move in.'

She thought of Josey, how they were treating him. Tried not to let the revulsion show on her features.

'Go on.'

'Then bring in my homies. Set up shop. That's it.'

'Any opposition?'

He smiled. 'Not here. Smooth as a shaven pussy.' He laughed, locked his eyes on hers. Waiting to hear her response, thinking she would bask in his wit.

She didn't disappoint. 'Very smooth, then.'

Danny laughed. Lila laughed. She couldn't believe it was this easy.

Her smile faded. Back to business. 'You think they're up to it? Running your empire for you down here?'

She pointed at the three boys. They were all disappointed that Danny was talking to Lila but trying not to express it. Instead they were talking to other girls, trying to pull off deals. They looked like three little boys playing gangsters.

Danny must have seen what she had seen in them. He looked back at her. 'What you proposin'?'

She took a sip of her Coke, sucking down on the straw, eyes locked with his. Perfect dead-eyed blowjob pose. 'Think you need some new blood in your organisation. In fact, I think you need some new blood running it.'

She sat back, waited for his response.

A smile split his face. 'Who might that be?'

She placed her hand on his. 'I think you know.'

As easy as that, she thought.

28

A night like any other at the encampment: fires burning, mongrels barking. Old buses, ambulances, vans and campers turned into homes, with oil, candles, generator-powered electricity keeping them lit. Music playing. People sitting in groups, people sitting alone. Noah holding court.

He was inside his home – an old single-decker bus – away from the rest, surrounded by his inner circle. His praetorian guard.

An emergency meeting.

He looked at the three of them gathered before him. Sitting wherever they could, the bus's regimented seats having long since been torn out. His most trusted lieutenants. All hair, muscle, tattoos, leather and denim. Peace and love just alien words to them. Loyalty, order and violent enforcement more their style. They sat waiting for him to speak, impassive.

Kai should be here, thought Noah. Then immediately chastised himself for feeling sentimental. Kai would have been here, he told himself, if he hadn't been so weak. He put Kai out of his mind, turned to the three before him.

'We've got a problem. As you're aware, Kai was becoming a liability. If not, he'd have been here. But he leaves us with a problem to sort out. You know what happened. You know who hurt him, who made him talk. He calls himself Tom Killgannon. He's a barman at the Sail Makers. And he's trouble. He's been asking too many questions. He's been putting things together. It's time he was taken care of.'

The three before him perked up at his words. Here was something they could understand. A way to employ their talents. They waited while he told them what he had planned.

Noah looked at them. He loved this feeling. Power. Making people do what he wanted them to. Restructuring a little part of the world to his liking. Got a thrill every time he gave an order.

But Noah didn't get that far. His phone rang.

He took it out of his pocket, ready to angrily dismiss whoever was calling him.

Then he saw the name.

Morrigan.

His heart skipped a beat. And in that moment he was reminded that the world wasn't always his to rearrange. And that loss of power, of control, was something he hated. And feared.

'I've got to take this . . .'

He stood up, accepted the call, and made his way off the bus.

'We need to talk,' said the voice on the other end.

'Yeah,' he said. His earlier composure had deserted him. He was no longer the boss, the one who inspired terror. He was now the one who terror was inspired in. 'I was just going to—'

'I don't care what you were going to do. I hear you've had a problem.'

'Yeah,' he said, trying to shrug it off as no big deal. 'But I'm dealing with it. I was doing that when you phoned, actually.'

Silence.

'So, you know, no harm done. It's all in hand.'

'No, it's not.'

His heart skipped another beat.

'Meet me. Now.'

'But I'm . . .'

'Now.'

The connection was broken.

He looked back at the other three. Tried to get his breathing under control, tried not to show his fear before them.

Deep breath. Another. Returned to the bus.

'Change of plan . . .'

*

154

The St Petroc stone circle sat in the shelter of several trees, atop a grassy plateau looking out to sea. Like other places of interest local to St Petroc it was known about but not often visited. Nine white lichen-covered stones made up the circle. Quartz in the rock sparkled when the sun's reflection hit it. But there was no sun now. No moon, either. Just dark grey clouded night. With a chill wind coming in off the water.

Noah never admitted to being scared. Ever. Fear belonged to the scrawny kid he used to be. Now he was Noah. A leader. A figure of strength, respect. But not tonight. As he approached the stone circle, footstep after reluctant footstep, he knew he was none of those things. He was that scared, scrawny kid again.

One of the stones had fallen down over the years, lying on its side, grass and moss growing around it. Its position gave rise to fanciful rumours that it was meant to be there, some kind of mono-lithic sacrificial altar. Local folklore, desperate to spark interest, had never made much of an effort to correct that impression.

The altar stone was occupied. Noah swallowed hard. The figure was swathed in darkness, without shape. Folds of cloth settled all around it like the resting wings of a giant black bird. Noah's heart beat against the cage of his ribs like a wild animal trying to escape.

'You're late.'

'I came as quickly as I could.' He tried to stop himself making excuses. Willed his mouth to shut, his voice to stop. Failed. 'It's . . . difficult to find this place at night. Hard not to be seen.'

The figure just stared at him. Cold, hard, birdlike eyes.

'Sorry, Morrigan . . .'

Morrigan ignored him, looked around. Looked towards the sky, spoke. 'Every land has its magical places, its ancient and continuing concentrations of power . . .' Then looked directly at him. 'But you wouldn't know about that, would you?'

Not knowing the right thing to say he silently shook his head.

'Or even what I was quoting?'

Another silent shake.

Morrigan took this for an answer. 'You've had trouble.'

'It's . . . being taken care of.'

'I know what happened. I just wanted to hear it from you.'

Again, he didn't reply.

Morrigan continued. 'You've had trouble with both of those who you chose to deliver the boy. The girl's disappeared. And the other one?'

'He's . . . been taken care of.'

'I very much doubt that. Where is he?'

'I . . . had him placed with the boy.'

Morrigan stared at him. Noah wanted to step backwards but didn't dare.

'Placed with the boy.'

Not trusting his voice once more, he nodded.

'Actually with the boy? Alongside him?'

'Yeah. Thought it was better. Keep him out of harm's way while this is all going on. Get rid of him later so as not to create a fuss if anyone comes looking for him. Which is highly unlikely.'

'Alongside the boy.'

Noah swallowed. He couldn't see a problem with his plan. Waited. Hoped Morrigan didn't see the fear in his eyes. Knew that Morrigan missed nothing.

'The girl's in the wind.'

'I'm looking for—'

'The girl's in the wind.' Noah fell silent. 'Who knows what she's said, who she's spoken to. And this other . . . person . . .' Morrigan spoke the word like it was poison, '. . . is currently telling our boy just what we have planned for him. You think that's a good idea?'

Noah shook his head, almost too quickly to take in Morrigan's words.

Morrigan stood up. Like a giant bird about to strike. Noah inhaled a sharp breath. The cold hurt his lungs. He stepped back. His legs were shaking.

'Get him out of there. Get him dealt with. And pray you're not too late.'

'Yes, Morrigan.'

'What are you doing about the girl?'

'We're . . . looking for her. We're watching the last person to have seen her. See if he . . . if he knows where she is. If he goes to her. Then we've got her.'

'This person. Is it that barman?'

Noah just stared. 'Yeah. How did—'

'He's been making quite a nuisance of himself. He feels wrong. Gives off a false scent. Not what he appears to be. Watch him by all means. But don't be afraid to take care of him.'

'No. Right.' Noah now nodding stupidly.

'Just remember what will happen if you mess this up.'

'I . . . I won't.'

Morrigan stepped towards him, smelling of fire, burning branches. 'Don't make me regret letting you do this. Just remember what you're getting out of it.'

Morrigan stared at him. And he knew his audience was over.

He turned, walked away as quickly as he could without running.

Then just ran.

29

Tom couldn't sleep. Wasn't sure he wanted to.

Rachel had left a couple of hours ago. The usual goodbyes, breathless kisses, hands over bodies, then off to her car, phone out, number called and speaking to her husband before she was behind the wheel. Reassuring him she was on her way, that work had taken longer than expected. A small wave to Tom with one hand, the phone still pressed to her ear with the other as she drove off.

The night outside was cold, still. As though Rachel's departure hadn't made a ripple. Like she had never been there. Inside, Tom could still smell her perfume, their sex. The house reverberated with her absence.

He had tried to settle. But sitting in an armchair with a novel he had failed to get involved with, spine cracked and pages splayed out on the table next to him, he was anxious, on edge. The glass of whisky didn't help, nor the music. He usually listened to something on a soothingly low level before sleep; Nick Cave's *Skeleton Tree* or *The Civil Wars* were the usual ones. Dark, deep, from the playlist he and his therapist had come up with. Tonight it was the turn of Erik Satie's *Gymnopédies and Gnossiennes*. Lamps threw pools of glowing warm light round the living room. But he only saw the shadowed pools between them. None of his trusted late-night sleep inducers were working and he knew why. The dream. He was frightened to sleep in case it came back again. He needed to try something else.

Tom was a big man, kept himself in good shape. He had both the physique and the features of a rugby player. Bones that had been reset. Scars that hadn't fully healed. He came across as someone who could handle himself. And he could, if he had to. But his eyes, when looked into directly, betrayed a sensitivity, an intelligence – a hurt, even – at odds with his build. He closed those eyes now. Sat still, letting the music wash over him. Listened to the silences between those sparse, beautiful, melancholic notes, trying to find space within to crawl inside, to go deep. Or as deep as he dared.

Think. Feel. Tune everything else out, meditate the way his therapist had shown him.

He hadn't believed meditation would work. Not after everything he had been through, what those experiences had made him. But surprisingly it had. It brought him face to face with himself, the world. It calmed him, centred him. And he wasn't too big or too close-minded to admit it.

So now he let his mind drift, waited to see what would come to him.

Rachel. The first thought in his head, the first picture in his mind. And his conscious thought when he had invited her back:

I won't have sex with her.

I won't have sex with her.

I've only called her here because of my cards, the identity theft. That's all. Honestly.

Lies. Self-deluding lies.

She fulfils my needs. We have sex, my needs are fulfilled and she leaves. Don't want involvement, don't need involvement. Can't risk involvement. And when she's gone I don't miss her. Perfect.

Were these lies too that he told himself?

He saw Rachel's face. In his bed. Under him. On top of him. Rachel in ecstasy. Eyes locked on his, smiling. And now, sitting in his lounge, he smiled at the image. In his kitchen drinking coffee, talking. Her eyes, again. Still that warmth, that returned smile. She fulfilled his needs all right. He just hadn't been honest with himself about what his needs were.

And then walking away from him. The smile faltered now, faded. Talking on her phone, readying herself to go back to her life. Her more important life. The smile gone completely now. And an emptiness inside him taking its place.

He tried to blink it out of his mind, kept thinking.

Lila. He had to find her. Not just because of what she had taken of his. More than that. She might be in trouble. She could be dead, for all he knew. No. Don't think that. She had to be alive. She had to be. If she died after leaving him he would . . .

No. It wasn't his fault, whatever happened to her. He couldn't be responsible for everyone. He couldn't get involved. Kept telling himself: don't get involved. But still. He couldn't have another death on his conscience. Even if he wasn't the direct cause of it, he would feel it, shoulder at least part of the responsibility. So let her be alive. Let that be that. And don't get involved.

Because when he got involved . . .

Another face. Another name. About Lila's age, looking up at him with happy eyes. Trusting eyes. Loving eyes. Then later, her sprawled and bloodied body, a Picasso version of her earlier self.

And a gun in his hand.

The dream.

He opened his eyes, stood up, moved quickly to the CD player, snapped it off. Poured another whisky, drained it in one, not savouring, feeling it burn, hoping it burned. Then another. Then –

Stop.

His heart was hammering. He felt out of breath. That emptiness inside him was curdling, turning in on itself. Poisoning him. He had to get out.

Pounding along the cliff edge, Tom ran as hard as he could, chest burning, legs and arms jelly-shaking, but never fast enough, never far enough to outrun what was inside him.

Wherever he went, his sister used to say to him when they were little, there he was.

His sister.

161

He ran even harder.

Half an hour later he reached St Petroc. Slowed as he came down from the cliff, approached the main street. It was dead. The odd street light cast a sparse sodium glow over the buildings and roads. Too late for traffic, for pubs, for people. Most of the windows were dark, curtains drawn.

Tom walked the streets aimlessly, blind to his surroundings, trying to get his breath back, his limbs to work properly. He felt alone in the world, as though there had been some catastrophe and he was the last man left alive. No one to talk to, no one for company. No one to judge him, to look for him. He didn't know whether it made him feel better or worse.

He walked, wondered what he was going to do now that he was actually here. Run back home? Walk back home? Too cold to walk. He would have to run, if he could summon up the energy.

Off the main road and down past a row of old cottages, he noticed a light on in one of them. He knew straight away which one. The flagpole sticking out pretending to be the prow of an old sailing ship gave it away. Pirate John's place.

Tom saw movement at the window. Quick, furtive. A curtain fell back into place.

'Tom?' A whisper rather than a call.

Tom turned. Pirate John had opened his front door, poked his head round it, then withdrawn it fast, like a tortoise on speed.

'Hi, John.'

The last thing he needed right now. Some conspiracy-theory bullshit. Sleep gives you cancer or something. That must be why he was still awake.

'Just out for a run. I—'

'Come in. Now.' An urgency in Pirate John's voice, the words whispered once more.

'I—'

'Now. Please.'

Might be just the thing I need, Tom told himself. Take my mind off things.

Pirate John quickly shut the door behind them.

Pirate John's house was the idiosyncratic yet dowdy museum of the last sixty years of pop culture that Tom had expected. And like its owner, its passions were displayed with often important points missed.

They stood in the living room. Piled boxes and empty food tins made it look like it was under siege. Pirate John smiled apologetically.

'Sorry about the mess, I . . .' He stumbled. 'I haven't been out much, lately.'

'No,' said Tom, wondering whether he should sit down or just leave. 'Haven't seen you in the pub for a while.'

'Yes, yes . . . that's . . .' A sigh. 'Sit down, sit down, Tom. I've . . . sit down, please.'

Tom cleared the remains of a meal – tinned corned beef and baked beans, eaten cold from the tin – and sat on the settee. His host took the armchair, perched forward. Like a bird about to fly off. Or attack.

'Sorry about the mess.'

'You've already apologised.'

'Yes, yes, I have. Yes.' Another sigh. 'Haven't been out of the house much recently. Sorry for the mess.'

Tom looked at him. Pirate John never seemed like the healthiest of people but tonight he looked decidedly ill. Although if cold corned beef and beans was his diet Tom wasn't surprised. But there was something more than that. He looked scared – haunted.

'I've . . . this must be, I don't know, providence? Is that right?'

'Is it?' asked Tom.

'Yes, I've . . .' Another sigh. 'Sorry. I've been wanting to talk to you. Needing to see you.'

163

Tom remembered him saying something like that in the pub one day. He hadn't thought too much about it and then Pirate John had disappeared for a while. Probably saved him from a boring evening, he had thought. Dodged a bullet. 'Right, well, I'm here now.'

Pirate John looked down, as if he had suddenly lost the power of speech. 'Oh, God,' he said eventually. 'It's . . . I don't know how to start. Where to begin.'

'At the beginning?'

Pirate John looked at him and laughed. It sounded simultaneously preposterous and like a smoker's death rattle. 'Not that easy.'

Another sigh. Tom waited.

'It's . . . I wanted to talk to you because you're . . . not from here.'

Tom nodded, waited.

'An outsider.'

'Is that good?'

'In this case, yes. Very good. I mean, I've talked to Pearl about this, took a chance that she might not . . . anyway. You're the one I wanted to speak to. Needed to. Because they can't have gotten to you yet, can they?'

Tom frowned. 'What are you talking about, John?'

'They . . .' He looked round nervously, as if he was being watched or listened to. Then back at Tom. 'You're looking for that girl, aren't you?'

Tom blinked. Not what he had been expecting. 'What?'

'That girl. The blonde one from the travellers' camp.'

'How . . . how did you know that?'

'Never mind how I know. I just . . . I just do. You're looking for her.'

'D'you know where she is?'

Another glance to each side. 'I wish. It would make it a lot easier. Then I could tell you. Then you could find her. And all this . . .' he searched for the right word, couldn't find it, '. . . *this* will be over.'

'All what, John?'

'You . . .' A violent shake of his head. 'I shouldn't . . .' Another sigh. 'Sorry. I know I'm not making much sense. I know you think I'm just some mental old . . . I dunno.' His eyes on Tom's. Desperate to be heard, to be believed. 'But I'm not. I'm deadly serious. You've got to find her.'

'And how do I do that?'

'Find Kai.'

'I did. It didn't end well.'

Pirate John gave Tom a fearful look. He didn't want to ask what had happened.

'Let's just say he won't be telling me anything in the near future.'

He looked downwards, the pictures in his mind probably worse than what really happened, thought Tom.

'Right. Right.' Pirate John nodded to himself, thinking. He looked up. 'Newquay.'

'Newquay? What about it?'

'Kai used to make drug runs there. Nothing bad, though. Just a bit of puff an' that. Try Newquay.'

'You think she's there?'

'Might be worth a try. If you can find Kai's drug source. They might be able to help you.'

'D'you know who it is?'

Pirate John shook his head. 'All changed there now. Used to be a bloke called Conroy. He might know. I've dealt with him before. But don't trust him.'

'I wasn't planning on it. Where can I find him?'

Pirate John told him.

'Thanks.'

Once more Pirate John looked around, checking for eavesdroppers. Tom became uncomfortable.

'Well, it's getting late, I think I'd better . . .'

'Yes, yes, yes . . .'

Tom stood up. 'Thanks for the chat.'

Pirate John stood also. 'I hope there'll be lots more like it, when we have the time. When it's all ...' He tailed off again, watching whatever movie was playing behind his eyes.

Tom saw himself out.

And ran all the way back home.

30

The metal bed frame was back up against the side of the cell. Kai and Kyle sat looking at it, exhausted by the effort. They had turned off the torch to preserve the batteries.

Kyle had been horrified when he had looked down at himself in the torchlight. His arms, legs and body scratched and bloodied, blackened with dirt, his clothes filthy and torn. As though he had regressed to some kind of cave-dwelling Neanderthal.

They sat there, listening to each other's breathing. Kyle could make out only the dim outlines of their surroundings. They had both calmed down considerably. Decided that, even if they didn't like each other, even if one blamed the other for his predicament, the best thing to do was work together to escape. Whatever animosity remaining between them could be resolved afterwards.

'So this is what you did?' asked Kai. 'Put it there, climbed up it.'

Kyle nodded. Then spoke, unsure whether Kai could see him. 'Yes.'

'And what did you hope to do when you got up there?'

'Dunno. Escape. Run.'

Silence fell as Kai thought over Kyle's words. 'You probably wouldn't have got very far.'

'Why not?'

'Have you worked out where you are yet?'

'Dunno. An old castle? A cave? Something like that? Oubliette?'

'Try tin mine,' said Kai. 'Or at least an ex-tin mine.'

'Aren't they all closed now? Tourist museums, or something?'

'A couple. Most of them were just left to rot. The caves filled in, mostly, and that was that.'

'And we're in some of the caves.'

Kai's turn to nod, then speak. 'Yeah. Well, underground.'

Panic rose within Kyle. 'How far underground?'

'No idea. These caves could go on for miles. Some even go out under the sea.'

Panic notched in Kyle's voice. 'Could we be there? Under the water?'

'Doubt it, think those ones have been closed. But, you never know . . .' He shrugged. Kyle didn't see it.

They sat in silence once again. Eventually Kyle spoke.

'How d'you know so much about this? Tin mines and that? Did they tell you all this?'

'They?'

'The ones who put me here.'

'Already knew. Studied it at university. History. Geology. All that. What I wanted to be, a geologist.'

'So why didn't you?'

A sigh. 'Long story. Really boring, really clichéd. Got into drugs. Had a bit of a . . . dunno what you'd call it. Got in with a bunch of . . . don't know what you'd call them, either. Druggies, travellers, surfers. Whatever. Friends, that's what I called them.' He fell silent once more. His mind slipped into the past, thinking of how difficult he had found his course, of seeing all his uni friends doing well, of trying to run away from his problems using dope and booze and, what he always told himself, some minor shenanigans. Wasn't that what being a student was all about? In reality he was lying to himself and he knew it. And his course friends moved on, further away from him, and his life went in a different direction. Or rather he coasted, having no direction. Soon, his new friends were all he had and he was too scared, too ashamed to try uni again. So he just stayed with them. Told himself he had made the right decision. Yeah. The right decision.

'Friends, yeah. That's what I called them. I dropped out of uni, that was that.'

'And was it your friends who put you in here?'

168

Kai laughed. The darkness accentuated the bitterness of it. 'Can we stop calling them that? They're not my friends. Not any more.' He choked off an angry sob at the end of his sentence. It echoed away to nothing.

Kyle didn't know whether to feel any pity for Kai. His emotions were so confused he couldn't identify which one he was experiencing. But he was pretty sure that pity, after all that Kai had done to him, wasn't it.

Silence fell once more. Kyle broke it. 'So how we going to get out of here, then?'

Kai said nothing.

'I said how we going—'

'I heard you. *Jesus*.'

It sounded to Kyle as though Kai had been crying. Quietly. In the dark. Doesn't need my pity, he thought, anger coursing through him, he's got enough of his own. He wasn't going to let him wallow.

'Come on,' Kyle said, 'we need to make a move. They could be back at any time.'

He got slowly to his feet. His body felt wrecked, pain from his fall enveloped his torso, his ankle screaming at the slightest pressure he placed on it. But he wasn't going to let it slow him down. He wasn't going to let it keep him prisoner here.

'Come on,' he said again, more urgency in his voice this time. 'Let's go.'

He heard a sigh from beside him in the dark, followed by the sound of reluctant movement.

'What d'we do?' Kai sounded defeated.

Kyle found it ironic. For so long he had been sitting here, alone, not knowing what his ultimate fate would be but guessing it wasn't going to be good. Feeling that, as time passed, no help would actually be coming for him. And now he felt a tiny sliver of hope enter his heart. He couldn't do this on his own, but together they could accomplish something. Together they had a chance.

'Put the torch on and I'll show you.'

Kai did so, the illumination of their surroundings sudden, painful and stark.

'There,' said Kyle, pointing. 'The bed frame's propped against the wall. It should hold in that position. Now point the torch up there.'

Kai did so. The ceiling showed a sheet of corrugated, rusted metal pulled across the entrance to their oubliette.

'There's . . . that's a big gap between the frame and the top.'

'Yeah,' said Kyle, 'I know. I tried to reach it and fell. But there's two of us now. If you climb up first, I'll hold the frame still. That way we can put it flush against the wall and we should be able to reach the top. Or rather you can. Your ankle's not fucked like mine is. Then you get out and I climb up. There's rope up there, they use it to lower the bucket. Throw that over for me and I'll attach it round my waist. Then I'll climb to the top and you pull me out.' Kyle allowed himself a smile. 'That sound like a plan?'

Kai nodded, his eyes hooded, rendered dark and unreadable by the angle of the torch.

Kyle felt like laughing. They were going to do it. They were going to escape. When he spoke he couldn't keep the excitement and joy from his voice.

'Let's go, then.'

31

Lila opened her eyes. The morning had arrived hard.

The caravan's curtains and nets didn't stop the light getting through. The room was bathed in washed-out grey. But she believed that was the caravan's natural colour. The boys didn't seem to mind, but then they were just kids, really, playing at being gangsters. They didn't know any different. Lila felt apart from them, not just through experience but also outlook. Temperament.

She turned over. And froze.

Danny was lying next to her. Asleep.

Her heart stopped, then began again, hammering so fast and loud she could hear it in her ears. Danny. Questions pinballed through her head. How? Why? What? She tried to think back to the club the night before. She had been sitting with Danny. Made a play to take over the gang. Danny was up for that. Told her she could do it. Gave her his blessing, his encouragement. He would tell the gang tomorrow, he had said. In the meantime, we celebrate. And she had stayed on Coke. Not wanting to lose control.

And that was the last thing she could remember. Until waking up now.

She checked her body. She was naked. Looked round the room. Her clothes were on the floor by the bottom of the bed. That dress Leon had bought her. She never wanted to see it again. Made her feel nauseous just looking at it.

She sat up. And Danny stirred. Opened sleep-fogged eyes, heavy with the previous night's excesses, looked at her. Smiled.

'Hey,' he said.

Lila didn't know how to respond. Should she start asking him questions straight away? Should she just be polite and smile back at him? She sketched the ghost of smile around the corners of her lips and moved to get up. She took the top sheet, gathered it round her body.

'You don't need to do that, hon.'

She turned. He was propped up on one elbow, watching her. Smile even broader now. She could see from the outline of the sheet that he had an erection.

'Come back to bed. Got somethin' for you . . .'

She stayed where she was. Stared at him. 'What happened last night?'

That smile reached his eyes. Like a wolf or a shark, she thought. Getting off on her question.

'You had the time of your life, girl.' His smile changed. 'Don' you remember?'

She didn't. That was the thing. She said nothing.

'Come back to bed . . .' He began to move the cover down his body.

'I've got work to do,' she said, turning away from him once more.

'Nothin' that won't keep.'

She stopped once more. 'You said I was in charge now. That still right?'

'Business later. Pleasure first.'

'Business now,' she said, trying to keep her voice steady, hoping he didn't catch the rising note of hysteria. 'What happened last night?' She hadn't meant to ask the question for a second time, the words just came out on their own.

He laughed. 'You had a great time. That's it.'

She dropped the sheet, stared at him. 'How come I don't remember it, then?'

He ran his eyes over her naked body. So intensely she felt like he was penetrating her. It made her feel violated. Grabbed the sheet, covered herself up again.

He pulled a mock hurt face. 'Hey, that's an insult. I was pretty fuckin' good. You don' remember, you don' remember. Dunno why.' Dismissively, like the conversation was over. 'Got some stuff in the fridge. You know what I mean. Go get me it.'

Anger swelled within her, mixing with the uncertainty, the hysteria she was already feeling. 'I'm not your fucking slave. Get it yourself.'

She didn't see him move, didn't think he could have moved so quickly, not after the night he had had. But he did. Suddenly right beside her, grabbing her wrist, twisting it. Eyes right on hers. Morning breath with a sour chemical undertone.

'I ask you to get somethin' you fuckin' get it. Right?'

Another twist. She gasped. Nodded. Got it.

'Good. Get my stuff from the fridge.'

Pulling the sheet tightly round her, she left the room.

She walked into the main body of the caravan. Josey was staring at the TV. He didn't seem to have moved for hours. He barely glanced up as she entered. Leon was gone, already at work. Ashley and Aaron were just waking up.

She opened the fridge door. Saw a bottle of champagne. Where had that come from? Something else to join the list of things she couldn't remember. She took it out, shut the door. Was ready to return to the bedroom when she felt the other two staring at her.

She looked at them. They looked away. Faces filled with shame, embarrassment. She just stared at them.

'What the fuck happened last night?' She hadn't intended her voice to be so loud, shrill.

Neither of them answered. Both looked away from her.

'I said what happened last night?'

Aaron looked up. 'Ask Danny.'

Ashley nodded beside him. His usual swagger gone. 'Yeah. Danny.'

An idea was forming in her mind. A dark, ugly idea. She hoped it wasn't what she was thinking. She really, really hoped it wasn't.

She took the champagne back into the bedroom. Danny had resumed his position in the bed, lying there like nothing had happened. He patted the side of the bed next to him.

'Anything come back to you yet?' he asked, a smirk splitting his features.

She stared at him. Nothing but contempt in her eyes. She knew what he had done to her. That smirk said it all. She could barely keep her hands steady as she held the champagne bottle.

'Yeah,' she said, once again struggling to keep her voice steady. 'You put something in my drink, didn't you?'

He held his hands up, gave an exaggerated shrug. 'Did I?'

'What was it, roofies?'

Another shrug.

'And then you –' Her voice, breath, deserted her. She tried to keep calm, controlled. 'You . . . fucked me.'

'Yeah.' Another shrug. 'But I don't remember you arguing.'

'I don't remember anything about it . . .' The words screamed at him.

He blinked, surprised by her ferocity. She kept going.

'You . . . you drugged me, knocked me out. Then . . . then . . .' She couldn't bring herself to say the word. The one word she had to say to get what had happened to her in perspective. That would make it real. And that could change her life for ever, define her as someone else. A person she didn't want to be. 'You know what you fucking did . . .' Screamed once more.

He moved slowly out of bed, came towards her, arms out in a consoling manner. Smiling all the while. 'What was I supposed to do, babe? You weren't coming across for me. And man, you looked hot. In that dress. Like, proper hot. Had to have you, gorgeous. Had to be done.' He laughed. 'An' I know you enjoyed it too. Don't pretend you didn't.'

She closed her eyes. Splinters of memory glistened in the darkness of her mind.

Fragments: the club swirling round her, arms holding her upright. Being able to collapse but not fall. Someone keeping her up.

Then blackness.

Another fragment: cold night air. Walking, her feet not touching the ground, legs not working properly.

Blackness.

Then: someone breathing on her heavily, face in her face, body jumping up and down. Wanting it to be over so she could slip back in blackness once more.

She opened her eyes. Danny was right beside her now. Arms snaking round her body, pulling the sheet off.

'Come on, baby, don' be mad at me. Come on. We had fun. It was—'

The bottle hit him in the side of the head before she even realised she had swung it.

He staggered away, hand to his head. Reeling like a drunk or a concussed boxer. When he took his hand away, his fingers, palm, were red with blood.

'Wha . . . what you do that for?'

She didn't answer him. Couldn't answer him. Just swung the bottle once more, connecting with the same spot.

He hit the floor. Groaning, trying to touch his head, his hands moving in slow motion, like his battery was winding down.

Lila stood and watched. Expressionless.

The bottle slid from her hand to the floor.

Danny stopped moving.

Lila just stared.

32

Tom had never been to Newquay before. He often found that out-of-season seaside towns possessed a kind of melancholic beauty, a sort of run-down gothic charm. Not this one. The fuzzy grey TV static of the falling rain left it looking washed out and near-abandoned, the heavy clouds made the purgatorial time between the fag end of winter and the glimmer of spring seem oppressive and never-ending. Or maybe it was just the mood he was in. Whatever, he hoped his business here went as quickly as possible.

He sat in his car, watching the pawnshop on the opposite side of the road. He knew what those kinds of shops were usually referred to as, and he saw a steady stream of people going in and coming out. It wasn't hard to pick out the ones who were dealing in stolen goods. Dressed as though they lived on the streets – which they may have done – carrying equipment there was no way they could afford. But coming out happy.

There was something else going on too. Some of the customers exiting seemed to have been directed to a light-skinned black youth, hanging about on the street corner, trying not to draw attention to himself and therefore drawing even more attention to himself. Tom knew immediately what he was. Dealer. And not a very adept one at that. He was trying to practise various surreptitious moves to place product into the punters' hands but he just ended up looking like a terrible magician, showing how it was done the whole time.

Tom wasn't bothered about the business ethics of the place or the kid on the corner. They could do what they liked. He just wanted to find Lila and get his stuff back.

He wondered which approach would work best. The kid, or the shop? Since Pirate John had given him a name and address, he would try the shop. He locked the car, pulled a new coat around him, made his way across.

Inside was exactly as he had expected. All electrical gear and dyna-bright strip lighting. Another black youth stood behind the counter. His demeanour changed when Tom walked in. He wasn't the usual clientele. He knew the kid thought he was trouble.

Good.

He walked up to the counter. 'I'm looking for Conroy.'

The youth looked surprised, and a little scared. He tried not to let it show.

'What's it about?'

'Between me and him.'

'D'you know him?'

'Nope.'

'Conroy doesn't see people he doesn't know.'

Tom smiled. He hoped it wasn't pleasant. 'Tell him there's no such thing as a stranger, just a friend you haven't managed to piss off yet.'

The guy made up his mind. 'Wait here.' Disappeared into the back of the shop.

Tom waited. But not for long. He soon re-emerged.

'Conroy says to come this way.'

Tom walked around the counter, followed the youth down a corridor. The decor became drab, functional. Conroy's office was exactly as he had imagined it would be. And there sat the man himself in a broken-down armchair. Like a fat spider welcoming his prey into his web.

'Thank you, Leon,' he said, dismissively.

Leon left. Conroy gave Tom his full attention.

'One of the boys in blue I don't know about?'

'What makes you say that?'

'You look like a copper. Smell like one, if you know what I mean.' He gave a loud sniff, as if he was just about to exhale phlegm on the filthy floor. 'No offence.'

'None taken. But I'm not police.'

If Tom thought his words would have relaxed Conroy, he was mistaken. The man remained on guard. 'Who are you, then?'

'My name's Killgannon. Tom Killgannon.'

Something sparked behind Conroy's eyes. He tried to hide it, but Tom had seen it.

'Ring a bell?' Tom asked.

Conroy attempted a shrug. His body made oily ripples as he did so. 'Not really.'

'Not really? So it might have done?'

'I meant no. I don't know you. I don't know your name.' He sighed, tried to seem impatient. Tom wasn't fooled for a second. He had confronted better liars than this one. 'Now if you want something, tell me. I'm busy.'

Tom glanced at the TV screen. A porn film played silently. 'So I see.'

He moved slowly towards Conroy. The seated man didn't like that. Squirmed, looked uncomfortable.

'Just stay where you are. Where I can see you.'

Tom ignored him. Stood right over him.

'I'll come to the point. I recently lost something. Something very personal. It was stolen from me. I have reason to believe it ended up here.'

Conroy tried a smile. 'Reason to believe? You even talk like a copper. What thing? What reason? And who told you?'

'Credit cards mainly. Few other things. Passport. As to who told me to come here, that's none of your business.'

'I think it is.' Conroy had picked up a stick from the side of the chair. Dark, heavy wood, heavy metal globe on the top. Tom would have wagered money on him using it more as a weapon than a walking aid. 'If someone's giving out my name for . . . well, something that sounds like criminal practice to me, I should know about it.'

'Look, Conroy, cut the bullshit. I know a fence when I see one.'
Conroy began to protest. Tom ignored him, kept talking. 'And I
haven't got all day. Just tell me where my stuff is, give me it and I'll
be away. You'll never see me again.'

Conroy just stared at him. His little raisin eyes looked almost
black as he tried to scheme his way out of the situation. Tom could
see him weighing up the odds, deciding what the best approach
would be. How much money he could make for himself.

Eventually he spoke. 'Yes, I recognised you. Yes, I've seen your
passport. And your cards. A girl brought them in here. Tried to sell
them to me.'

Tom felt a thrill run through him. Tamped it down. Kept focused.
'So where are they?'

Conroy attempted another shrug. His body, not given sufficient
warning, protested and it didn't last long. 'Who knows? Maybe she
tried somewhere else.'

'Newquay is a small place. I doubt there's many other people
who would deal in the stuff you deal with. So where are they?'

Another silence, another calculation from Conroy. He smiled.
'I could get them for you.'

'When?'

'Later today.'

'If you know where they are, if they haven't been used, why don't
you just get them for me now?'

'Oh, it's not as easy as that, Mr . . . Killgannon? Is that what you
said your name was? Is that your real name? Just out of interest.'

Tom felt a shiver of unease. Conroy knew. Or at least suspected.

'Just give me them back. That's all. And I'll say no more about it.'

Conroy laughed. It was the sound a bullied kid makes when he
inadvertently manages to gain power over his abuser. A victim's
victory.

'So what is it, then? New identity? On the run? Is that it? Or are
you some kind of spy?'

Conroy's words were getting too near the mark. Tom snatched the walking stick from Conroy's hands, held it at the fat man's neck. Conroy gurgled, choked. Tom pushed harder.

'Just give me the fucking cards back . . .'

Conroy's face, red to begin with, was turning purple. Spit and dribble appeared at the corners of his mouth, his eyes bulged. Tom kept pressing. Stared at him.

'You going to give me my stuff back?'

Conroy nodded.

'Sure?'

Another nod.

Tom took the cane away. Conroy's hands went to his throat, massaged his wounded chins.

'I'll have to get them for you.' His voice sounded like it was bubbling up through oil and water. 'Come back later.'

'When?'

'Later. When the shop shuts.'

Tom didn't want to leave the shop, didn't want to let Conroy out of his sight. But he knew he had no option. 'You'd better not be fucking me about. You'll be sorry if you are.'

'When my shop shuts. Come back then.' He gave a smile. It looked like the kind of grimace a condemned man on Death Row would make. 'I give you my word.'

'You'd better. Because I wouldn't like to be you if you disappoint me.'

'Wouldn't dream of it, Mr . . . Killgannon.'

Tom left the office.

He got back into his car, sat there thinking. He didn't trust Conroy at all. Didn't have any faith that the cards would be there when he said they would. Didn't even believe Conroy would be there. He knew he was going to be crossed in some way. He decided to just sit there, watch the shop. All day if necessary.

But something stopped him.

The youth from behind the counter, Leon, came hurrying out. A quick look up and down the street, seeing if anyone was watching him. Tom instinctively knew who Leon was looking for. Him.

Leon walked to the corner, exchanged a few words with the dealing youth. Then turned and hurried off in the opposite direction.

Tom wondered what to do next: stay and wait or follow the boy. As Leon almost disappeared from sight along the pavement, Tom made up his mind. He got out of his car, locked it, and followed.

33

Danny still hadn't moved.

The boys had gone, calling after Danny, after Lila, before they did. She had mumbled something that she couldn't remember in response. It seemed to have placated them as they had left without looking in the bedroom.

And still Danny hadn't moved.

Lila thought it was time to get up. She didn't know how long she had been sitting there, slumped against the door, staring at the body, not wanting to touch it, go near it – already thinking of Danny as it, not him – but she knew she couldn't stay there for ever. She didn't want to. She didn't want to move, either, though. She just wanted to be somewhere else, someone else, entirely. But she knew she couldn't do that so she had to move.

She stood slowly, looked for her clothes. The scrappy dress from the night before was thrown in a heap on the floor. Anger rose once more as she thought of what Danny had done to her, followed by disgust, then nausea. She swallowed hard, tried not to dwell on it. There would be enough time for that later. For now she had to make a plan. She had to disappear.

Her other clothes – jeans, top – were folded in the wardrobe, where she had left them before changing. She quickly pulled them on. Looked around once more, trying not to stare at *it*.

Think. *Think.* Put the jumble of thoughts and emotions into some semblance of order. Make a plan.

She had it. Her getaway plan. The money. The drugs.

Before she left there was something she had to do. She knelt down, forced herself to put her face close to the body. She closed her eyes, held her breath. Concentrated. Felt it. On her cheek. Slow, weak, but definitely there. Danny's breath. He was still alive. Relief flooded her body. Whatever else she was, she wasn't a murderer. But he wasn't moving. Did that mean he was just unconscious? Or had she put him in a coma? Either way, she wasn't going to hang around to find out.

Heart quickening, she nudged open the door, looked down the caravan's corridor. No one there. She stepped out, turned left, went into the main bedroom. Knelt down at the bedside cabinet where she had seen them store drugs and money. Opened it.

Smiled.

There it all was. An old carrier bag full of money, crumpled notes and a few coins, and on the shelf above, plastic-wrapped packages. Her escape fund.

She went back to the other room, still ignoring the body, grabbed her coat, and began stuffing the deep pockets with notes. The coins she slid into her jeans pocket. Then she turned her attention to the packages. The white bricks were cocaine, the brown ones heroin. God knew what the pills were but the cannabis was all in separate bags. She started with the bricks.

When she had as much as she could carry she stood up. Turned.

And there stood Josey, blocking her exit, blocking out nearly all the light in the room. He was frowning.

'What you doin'?'

'Just . . . getting a few things. I . . . the boys need a few things. They, they called me. Told me to take them to them.' For some reason she felt panicked by his presence. She had regarded him as harmless until this point but now she was struck by just how large he was. And how unhinged his mind was too.

He looked into the bedside cabinet, frown deepening, then back to her. 'Where's my medsin?'

'It's . . . I've got it here, Josey.' She patted her pocket. 'Just here. I'm taking it to the boys. They . . . they need to . . . have some. They need me to take it to them. So I'll just . . .'

He didn't move.

'You're takin' my medsin . . .'

'Just for a little while. The boys need it. They'll bring it back. Promise.'

He stood immobile, thinking.

'No,' he said, eventually. 'The boys are my friends. They told me that must never be taken away by anyone but them. They told me.'

'Well, they've asked me to—'

He took a step towards her. Another, steadied himself before her. No way she was going to get past him.

'No.' He said it with such finality. He had clearly made up his mind and was not going to change it. 'No. The medsin stays here.'

Lila had to think quickly or she would never get out of the caravan. 'Fine. Fine, I'll put it back.' But before she did so, she had an idea. It was risky, but it felt like the right thing to do. She couldn't leave him in the caravan at the mercy of the others. She had to do something.

'Look, Josey,' she said. 'I'm . . . I'm not coming back. I'm leaving.'

Another frown. This one tinged with panic as his eyes went to her pockets. 'You're takin' my medsin an' you're not comin' back?'

'No, Josey, I'll leave you your medsin. I'll just . . . Look. Why don't you come with me? Both of us? We can get away from the others, you can be happy again. Free.'

She paused, looked at him. Seeing if her words were penetrating. His features softened. She thought she might be getting through. Emboldened, she continued.

'I bet you were happy before the boys came, weren't you? Well, you can be happy again. No one to boss you round, no one to hurt you.'

A smile almost appeared on his face.

185

'Just think. You could be like that again. That would be good, wouldn't it?'

He nodded. Slowly.

'And you won't need your medicine anymore. You could—'

'*No* . . .'

The strength of the word shocked her. She fell silent.

'No . . . they said . . . they said you might . . . might try to do this . . .' His hands at his temples rubbing, as if the action would make his thoughts come quicker.

'But Josey, you can be happy again. You can—'

She didn't see the blow but she felt it. Or rather the aftermath, as she tripped, stumbled and slid down the opposite wall, the caravan shaking from her impact. Dazed, she looked up at him. His face looked like it was splitting apart, as if whatever emotions and ideas were in his head were being violently birthed.

He screamed.

'They're my friends! My friends! An' you want to take them away from me! An' my medsin . . . No . . . you're a bad lady, a bad lady . . . no . . .'

He grabbed her coat, began going through the pockets, pulling out the wrapped bundles, the money, she had stuffed in there. In doing so he pulled her to her feet, flung her around like something boneless and weightless.

'Bad lady . . . bad lady . . .'

She tried to pull away from him but there was no way he would let go. Drugs and money showered the bedroom as he screamed.

Lila managed to extricate an arm from the coat. Vitalised, she tried the other. And found that she could slip free. One part of her mind – a large part – was reluctant to leave the coat behind, or rather what it contained, but she knew it had gone beyond that. Now it was just a question of survival.

186

Josey's tearful fury was all-encompassing but she had ceased to be at the centre of it. She managed to move past him and through the bedroom door.

And stopped dead.

Leon was standing there, looking in the other bedroom, staring wide-eyed, open-mouthed at the still body of Danny. Then he saw Lila.

'What the fuck's gone on here?'

34

Kyle felt better than he had for a long time, despite his injuries. Holding the bed frame against the wall, keeping it secure while Kai climbed up it first, as well as making sure the light was positioned correctly so Kai could see where his feet went, he felt the anguish and emotional turmoil of the time spent in his prison slip off him like shed skin. He could stand on his ankle, hold his arms aloft, feel strength in them and his body. On some level he knew that it was just adrenaline keeping him going but he didn't mind at all. Weren't people capable of miraculous things because of adrenaline? Mothers lifting up cars to rescue their trapped children, that kind of thing? If they could do that, he could do this.

He watched Kai as he climbed. Quicker than he had been, but then Kai hadn't spent nearly as long locked up as he had. He was almost to the top. He watched as Kai reached for the sheet of corrugated metal. Nearly there. Another step more. Another reach. Got it.

A thrill ran through Kyle. He was smiling. It felt like such an alien expression for his face to be pulling. Like his muscles had forgotten how to do it and had to be taught again.

Kai managed to get a grip on the metal, pushed it away so that a gap developed.

'You there?'

'Yeah . . .' The exertion told in Kai's voice.

Kai gripped the edge of the opening, tested it to see if it would take his weight, make sure the stone was strong enough. It was. He transferred his weight to his arms, pulled, his legs coming off the frame. Kyle felt his heart in his mouth. This was further than he had managed. The mattress was on the ground just in case, but he had a feeling Kai wouldn't need it. He knew they were going to escape. And that feeling – hope – was the most delicious emotion he had ever experienced.

Kai managed to pull himself clear of the hole. He was out of their prison.

Kyle punched the air, shouted. 'Yes . . . What's there?'

No reply.

Kyle waited. There was no sign of him. That tentative feeling of hope began to be replaced by something altogether more distressing.

'Kai?'

Nothing.

'Kai . . .' Panic in his voice now.

Kai's head appeared over the lip of the hole. 'Sorry. Just having a look round. Need that torch. Can't see a thing.'

'I'll bring it up with me. Ready?'

'Yeah.' He leaned over, grabbed the top of the frame, steadied it against the wall.

Kyle started his climb.

It didn't take him nearly as long this time. Last time, if he was honest, he was climbing without any real hope of escaping. This time it was definite. No turning back. And he wouldn't need the mattress either.

He worked his way up, the torch in the waistband of his jeans. The light was slightly diffuse as a result, but he could still make out where he had to go.

As he reached the top Kai's grip disappeared. The bedframe shook, began to move away from the wall.

'Kai . . .'

Kyle made a desperate grab at the rim of the hole. His fingers caught. He managed to push the frame back against the wall but found himself unable to move. He looked up into the gaping blackness above him.

'Kai? You there?'

No reply.

'Kai.' Anger in his tone now, more insistent. 'Come on, mate, I'm stuck here.'

'Yeah, I'm here.' Kai's head appeared over the rim of the hole. 'Pass the torch up so I can see you.'

Kyle released one hand and, fingers still gripping on to the edge above him, fumbled for the torch in his waistband. It was difficult to balance with only one hand. He swayed backwards a couple of times, felt that near-giddy thrill that he might fall run through him, but recovered, managed to hang on. Eventually he passed the torch across.

'There you go.'

Kai took the torch, placed it on the rim. It shone directly into his eyes.

'OK, now get my arm . . .' Kyle stretched outwards and upwards. This was what they had planned. Kai up first, pull Kyle up after him. Then both of them away. But Kai didn't reach for him.

'Kai, what you playing at? Get my arm . . .'

He could see, behind the blinding halo of the torchlight, Kai's head move slowly from side to side.

'Sorry, mate. Only room for one of us on this trip.'

Kyle thought he had been mistaken, that he had misheard Kai's words. He tried again.

'Stop fucking about. Grab my arm . . .'

'I've been having a think. And you know what? I don't see much of a future for myself on the run. Especially not running from these people. I don't think I'd get very far, to be honest. But I do have a plan. You see, if I can talk to them, tell them a few things, then everything might be OK again. The only trouble is, you can't be there.'

'Kai, please . . .'

That by now familiar feeling of depression, hopelessness, anger and overriding fear flooded back into Kyle. He couldn't believe what he was hearing.

'Kai, come on, don't leave me here, please. *Please* . . .'

Kyle felt tears, hot and desperate, forming in his eyes.

'I can't leave you here,' said Kai, voice curiously flat.

Kyle felt a glimmer of hope once more. 'Then get me out . . . please . . .'

'Don't think you understand. You see, my plan can't involve you. At all. So when I say I can't leave you here, I mean I can't leave you here alive . . .'

Before Kyle could respond or even process what Kai had said, the other man's arms had found his hands and were pushing him away from the wall.

Kyle scrambled, frantic not to fall, desperate to keep his balance on the bed frame.

'Sorry, mate,' Kai said, and pushed. Hard.

Kyle felt his limbs freewheeling, pedalling in mid-air, as he lost his grip and balance simultaneously. The bed frame moved away from the wall, began to fall over once more. Kyle was in freefall, trying to grab on to it, hoping the mattress would break his fall again.

It didn't.

The momentum took him away from it and he landed on the stone floor with such a thick, jarring thud that he didn't feel the pain of the impact for a few seconds. When it did hit, it hit hard.

Then the frame landed on him. And he felt what was left of his body shatter.

He tried to breathe. Couldn't. Thought at first he had winded himself, that air would soon return, but the more he tried to breathe, the harder it became. Like he was drowning inside.

He tried to move. Couldn't. His hands went to his chest. Felt a spongy, wet substance where his ribcage should have been. Tried again to breathe. Spluttered liquid from his mouth. He tasted old pennies.

He knew what had happened. His lung was punctured by his ribs, filling with blood. He was drowning.

Panic gripped him once more as he struggled to breathe.

But it was no use. The blackness of the cell was being replaced by another kind of darkness. A more permanent one.

He wanted to scream, to shout, to cry. This was unfair, this wasn't supposed to happen. *Not to me, not to me . . . Not yet, not now . . .*

But no sound came out. No sound could come out.

That other darkness clouded over him.

35

'She was goin' to leave, take the medsin . . .'

Josey seemed to have finally found his voice, Lila thought.

Leon looked from one to the other, back to Danny's body again. Head shaking, mouth slack. Like it was all too much to take in, like there was nothing he could think of to say.

Lila moved, made for the door. That was Leon's cue to snap out of his trance. He grabbed for her as she went past. She tried to duck under his grip, but he used both hands, held on tight.

'Whoa, whoa . . .'

They tussled. His grip became more determined. Lila realised he wasn't going to let her go. She relented, allowed him to hold her. Bided her time until he relaxed, until she could bolt.

'What . . . what . . .'

'Danny raped me,' she said. 'He tried it again, just before. I . . .' She gestured towards the body, saw the champagne bottle lying on the floor. Looked back at Leon. 'He raped me, Leon.' The words spat in his face.

'She's takin' the medsin . . .' Josey, behind her now. 'She's runnin' away . . .'

'No, she's not.' Leon shoved Lila back into Josey's body. 'Hold her, Josey. Don't let her go.'

The big man did as he was told. Lila's chances of escaping were diminishing by the second.

Leon looked at the body once more. Put his hands to his head, closed his eyes. 'Fuck . . . fuck . . .'

'Just let me go,' Lila told him. 'You can keep the stuff, keep the money. I won't take any of it. Just let me go, yeah? And that's that. You'll never see me again.'

Leon looked between her and the body once more, panic etched on his features. He knelt down beside Danny, examined him. Bent in close. Straightened up quickly.

'He's still breathing . . .' The words almost not coming out due to shock.

'I know. So you can let me go now, yeah? You've got no reason to keep me here. I'll just . . . go.'

Leon seemed to be making his mind up.

'Can't do that.'

'Why not? Who's going to know? Just say he fell over. Or he was attacked. When he comes round, or whatever, he might not even remember what happened.' She tried to shrug off Josey's grip, move towards Leon, smiling. It didn't work. 'Come on. Just let me go . . .'

'I can't. There's people who'll want to know what happened.'

'Which people?'

'Just people. And they won't be happy. So no. You can't go. You have to stay here. Otherwise they might think it was one of us that did it. And I'm not taking the blame for that.'

Lila noticed how his eyes widened as he talked, saw fear enter them.

'No. You're staying here.' Firmer now.

And in that moment Lila knew that she was broken. She had no more to give, no more drive, no more ideas. She couldn't escape, didn't have the energy to keep running. She would just take what was coming to her.

'Fine, then,' she said.

Silence fell once more.

Then they heard the door open.

36

Tom was close to giving up and going back to the shop. His pursuit of the youth seemed to be getting him nowhere. He felt like he was just following him home. But he persisted, some intuition he couldn't place driving him on.

Always at a discreet distance, never risking being recognised. He thought he had been made on a couple of occasions and had pretended to go into a shop or look as though he was going to cross the road, before continuing his pursuit. He knew from experience that the trick was not to panic, not to make sudden, rash movements. That was the way to draw attention to himself. But, it seemed, his quarry hadn't suspected a thing and Tom was being over-cautious. Better that, he thought, than the alternative.

He hadn't been impressed with Newquay from its seafront facade and as he walked away from that he became even less enamoured. The front was run-down, ancient amusement arcades with their incessant beeping and sickly light thrown out onto the pavement, threatening-looking fish-and-chip shops that offered more of a dare than an encouragement to enter, and boarded-up businesses that had failed to entice the populace and whatever tourists happened upon the place. A few chain-store surf-gear shops were dotted about and the kind of shops that only exist in old seaside towns selling everything no one needs but for some reason will buy. One, Tom noticed, had a plastic dispenser outside that he took on first glance to be offering bubblegum and gob stoppers but on closer inspection was revealed to be selling his-and-her thongs for a pound. Judging from the yellowed, laminated, photo-display advertising, it had been there some time and it looked like very few had taken them up on their offer.

The back streets were equally depressing. Rows of old houses, pebbledashed with aluminium windows, lined the narrow streets. Some had been painted bright pastel colours, the desperation of which had the reverse effect of making them seem even more drab.

Tom was careful during this section as he was more exposed. The boy had only to turn to see him. But he didn't. At first Tom put that down to luck but then noticed the telltale sign of white wires stretching from each ear. He was lost in whatever he was listening to.

Eventually the houses gave way and a static caravan park appeared before him. If the houses had looked bad, this was even worse. It felt like some metaphorical end of the road. The houses had become increasingly grim as he walked, telling a cautionary tale of what could happen if a life went astray. The caravans were the end result. The dead-end result. The youth headed towards the door of one of them. A particularly run-down specimen even by the standards of those surrounding it. His hand was at the door, ready to enter. But he stopped.

Tom did too.

The guy removed his headphones, cocked his head to one side, listening. Then, when he had heard enough, he twisted the door handle, ran inside.

An alarm went off inside Tom at that point. It felt like his decision to follow had been vindicated. Something was happening here and he had a feeling – intuition again – that it was connected to his business with Conroy. Abandoning all pretence of subterfuge, he ran towards the caravan, opened the door.

It took him several seconds to process the scene. Several more to realise who the young blonde was. He recognised the youth from the shop but had no idea who the other one was. He was the most intriguing of the three. Obese yet malnourished-looking, with sunken dark-rimmed eyes in his sunlight-starved face, his clothes stained and filthy, his hair dark with grease and dirt. He didn't look as though he belonged with the other two; but taking in the appearance of the caravan, more like he belonged there than they did. Tom noticed something else about the obese man. Tracks on his arm. Right. Thought of the young dealer on the street outside Conroy's place.

'Who the fuck are you?' The youth spoke first.

'Don't you remember me? I've just been talking to Conroy.'

Recognition sparked in the kid's eyes. 'What you doin' here?'

'Followed you. Wondered where you were going.' He dismissed him, turned his attention to Lila. 'Hello again.'

Lila just stared at him, unsure whether his appearance here was a good development or a bad one.

'Believe you've got something belonging to me. That right?'

She looked between the other two, then back to Tom. It was clear he was the last person she expected to see and she couldn't hide her surprise.

Tom felt like he had the upper hand. He pressed on. 'Well?'

'Conroy's . . . Conroy's got your stuff.'

'He told me someone else had it. And I have to go back later and pick it up.'

'He's lying,' she said.

'How d'you know that?'

'Because it's what he does.' She looked at the other two. 'It's what they all do here.' No disguising the hostility in her voice. Her eyes travelled over to the other bedroom. Tom followed her gaze.

'Oh, dear. What did he do?'

'Raped me,' she said, her earlier anger returning, the words spat out.

Tom nodded. 'And these two? They your friends?'

'No. Definitely not. This is Josey. He lives here. This is Leon. He ponces off him. With his two mates.'

Leon was about to argue but a look from Tom silenced him.

'Are they keeping you here against your will?'

She nodded, not holding his gaze. Shame on her face.

'I'm walking out of here. You want to come with me?'

She looked up once more, wary. Then glanced at the other two. Weighed up her options. Nodded once more.

'OK then,' he said. 'Off we go.'

Leon found his voice once more. 'Whoa, whoa, you can't just walk away with her. No way, man.'

'You're right,' said Tom. He pointed to his coat lying on the floor. 'I'll take that too.'

'No . . .' Josey roared.

Tom looked between the three of them. 'What's up with him?'

Lila picked up the coat. The movement agitated Josey further. She held the coat up, emptied what remained of the drugs from the pocket, let the parcels drop on the floor.

'Here,' she said. 'Have it. Have the lot.'

She passed the coat to Tom. He didn't take it.

'Cold outside,' he told her. 'You might want to put it on.'

She did, almost smiling at him.

Tom turned to Leon. 'We're leaving now. Whatever happened to him in there – ' pointing to Danny – 'is nothing to do with me. And she's coming with me.'

'But she's almost killed him . . .'

Tom knew he was inviting trouble. He knew he should have just walked out of there on his own, gone back to see Conroy, got his stuff and gone home. End of. But there was something about the girl and the lost, frightened way she had looked at him when he entered the caravan. He couldn't just leave her to be torn apart by whatever fate awaited her. He had to do something.

And he knew why, even if he wouldn't admit it to himself.

'You can sort things out here. She's coming with me.'

They walked out together.

No one followed.

Outside, she pulled the coat around herself, seemed unsure what to say or how to act. Tom felt the same.

'Thank you,' she said eventually.' Her voice sounded small, fragile.

'Don't thank me just yet. We're going back to see Conroy.'

37

Kai didn't know where he was going. He had thought it would be easy. Get out of the pit, use the torch to retrace the route he had taken in getting Kyle there. Stroll to the exit. Or if he had to, do that thing he'd seen in films, check for air currents or cracks of light and follow them. But there was nothing like that. No clues. Just tunnels. None of them looked familiar. And there were no directions as to which one he should take.

It wasn't like the cave tunnels he had been on school trips with. Where they could walk around with no real sense of danger, always keeping an exit in mind.

These caves were by turns cavernous and tiny. Occasionally wooden supports held up huge shelves of rock. Sheets of corrugated metal provided makeshift ceilings where the rock and earth had crumbled above, rusted away in sections to allow mini roof-falls. He could walk upright in some sections, could have played football in them even, but in others had to go bent double and in some might have found himself screaming in claustrophobic terror at their narrowness. Axe and drill marks covered the walls and ceilings like post-industrialist cave markings. Sometimes he felt that his route took him upwards, sometimes downwards. He reached different levels, all with tunnels branching off in differing directions. Hoped he chose the right one, the one that went to the surface. All the way through the floors were uneven, strewn with all sizes of stones and gravel he kept stumbling on and tripping over; sometimes he would sink more than ankle deep, like being pulled down by a kind of dry, sucking quicksand. Bone dry, he thought with a shiver. He moved carefully, watching where he stepped, hoping his torch battery would hold out. If that went, he feared he would be completely lost.

The caves seemed to go on for ever. Kai didn't realise that there was so much space under the ground. It was like a mini town carved out of solid rock.

He kept moving. Then saw something up ahead. It looked familiar. He moved quickly towards it, heart increasing, thinking it might be some kind of exit. It wasn't. It was the entrance to the pit he had been held captive in with Kyle. He pointed the torch downwards. There was Kyle's lifeless body lying at the bottom, the bed frame over him like a cage. Kai turned away. Sat on the ground.

He was going to be stuck underground for ever. That was that.

He tried to keep himself together, not give in to tears or screaming. Not to look down at the body lying in the pit, reminding him of what he had done. Taunting him. Kai wasn't a killer. No, he was the opposite of that, one of the good guys, always had been. He couldn't think of himself any other way. If he did he would just collapse completely and it wouldn't matter whether he made it out or not. He had only done what was necessary to survive. That's what he told himself. Kept telling himself.

But other thoughts slithered into his mind in the darkness. Kyle. Not just his death, but his capture. And Kai's part in that. He had gone along with it readily enough. Yeah, he'd tried to rationalise it to himself by saying that if he hadn't done it Noah would have found someone else. And then where would Kai have been? Knowing too much but not wanting to take part. Yeah. He knew what would have happened then. So he had been pragmatic. That was it. Pragmatic.

Then there was Lila. Something much deeper might have developed between them given time. But no. She had to do what she did. And there was nothing Kai – or anyone – could have done to stop her. What had happened to her was definitely her own fault. Definitely.

So he sat there, telling himself what he tried desperately to believe was the truth.

And all the while, his torch battery was running down. Soon it would be gone completely. And that would be that.

Desperation driving him once more, he stood up, set off in the opposite direction from the one he had taken last time. Or at least he hoped so. Soon he was in another maze of tunnels just like the previous ones. It was hopeless. He was totally lost.

He tripped, fell into a wall. Dropped the torch. The light went out. He slumped to the ground.

'Fuck . . .'

His head hurt. He put his hand to it, felt something wet. Tried not to panic at what he knew it could be. Hoped it wouldn't be too serious. He couldn't pass out as well as get lost. That really would be the end of him.

Willing himself to move once more, he managed to get up onto all fours. Felt around on the ground for the torch. Felt something else.

Metal. Rusted old metal. But streamlined.

He felt further. Wooden sleepers underneath going crossways.

His heart beat more rapidly. This must have been the track they used for taking the ore in and out of the mine. That meant it must lead somewhere. That meant . . .

He searched around once again for the torch. Managed to find it after skinning his fingers red raw in the darkness. Turned it on. It wouldn't light. Exasperated, he threw it to the ground. No, he thought. The rusted metal rail would have to do. That would be his way out. He didn't need the torch.

Crawling on his hands and knees, he followed the rail.

For how long, he had no idea. All he knew was that the initial burst of euphoria he had experienced on finding it subsided the further he crawled. He began to feel tired as the adrenaline high of the discovery deserted him and doubts crept in once more. Was he heading in the right direction? What would he do if the rail ran out and he still hadn't found an escape route? Or came to a dead end, blocked in by rock? He tried to stop these thoughts, to concentrate on just moving forward. Hoping the worst wouldn't happen.

But the worst did happen. The rail ran out.

He tried not to panic. Keep going. Just because the track's not there any more doesn't mean that this isn't the way out. Keep going.

Soon the ground became coarse once more. The sleepers had disappeared beneath him too. He felt around for signs of where it could have continued, found nothing. He patted the ground, trying to work out if it was smoother in one place than another, give himself a clue as to which way to head. All he found were different tunnels. He had no choice. He kept going in the same direction.

Finding no reason to continue on his hands and knees he risked standing up, hoped the ceiling wasn't too low. It wasn't. Slowly he moved forward, hands on the walls. He put one foot in front of him, pressed down, expecting the ground beneath him. It wasn't there. The blackness acted as a sensory deprivation chamber and, trying to pull back, he lost his balance and fell.

He landed hard, the air momentarily leaving his lungs, a searing pain in his chest. Breathing was hard. So was moving. Pain coursed like electricity all round his body. Exhausted, he just lay where he was.

This is it, he thought. This is the end.

Kyle came into his head. Lila.

This is what I deserve, he thought. I'm a fucking coward. I even lie to myself. This is what I deserve.

He closed his eyes. Blackness against blackness.

The light was blinding. He squinted, closed his eyes, opened them again. The light was still there. Heaven, he thought. This must be heaven. Like the religious ones always said. They must be right after all. Walk towards the bright light. That's all he had to do and he'd be in eternity. Except he couldn't move his body. And he was still in pain.

'Jesus Christ, what's he doin' here?' said a voice that Kai found familiar.

'The other one's not moving. Looks like he's dead.'

'So does this one. Shit . . .'

'What do we do?'

These weren't angels. Kai realised that now. And he wasn't dead, although parts of him felt like it.

'Can't leave him here. Let's stick him in the pit with the other one.'

They picked him up. Roughly. He cried out in pain. They dropped him quickly. He cried out in more pain.

'Jesus, he's still alive . . .'

'What d'we do?'

A pause while they thought.

'Get him out of here. See what Noah wants doin' with 'im.'

They grabbed Kai once more. He didn't know whether it hurt or not. He had blacked out again.

38

Conroy's shop was in darkness when Tom and Lila arrived. They had barely spoken to each other as they walked away from the caravan, leaving unsaid whatever questions either of them had. There would be time enough for that later. Tom had more immediate things to concentrate on.

They stopped before the closed door. Tom looked at Lila.

'This natural for him? Closing up when he's waiting for someone?'

'No idea,' said Lila. 'I don't know him well. At all, really.'

'You just handed my stuff over to him.'

Even in the darkness Tom saw Lila's face redden. 'He's a fence, right? That's all I knew. He deals in stuff like that. I just wanted some money so I could get off.'

'But it didn't turn out like that.'

She sighed. Shook her head.

Tom saw the pain on her face, in her eyes. She was being honest with him and he couldn't stay angry at her.

'Let's get this sorted,' he said, 'then we'll see what happens next.'

He placed his hand on the door. It opened.

'He's expecting you,' said Lila. 'That's good.'

'You think so? Walking into a dark, closed shop? Anything could happen. Anyone could be waiting for us.' He looked at her again. She was scared to go in, he could tell. 'Look, why don't you wait here? I won't be long.'

Her eyes lit up at being given a way out and from the speed with which her mouth moved her first response was to do as he had offered. But something changed in her expression. An uncertainty. A weight.

'No. I got you into this. Only fair I come with you.'

'You don't have to.'

'I know.'

He was starting to like this girl. Everything she had been through and she still had spirit.

'Come on then.'

He pushed the door open. They stepped inside.

He closed the door behind them. Stopped. Listened. Nothing. No sign or sound of anyone there. He listened closer. Heard something. Breathing. Heavy breathing.

Conroy. Had to be.

'I know you're there, Conroy. I can hear you.'

The breathing was followed by grunting and groaning. A darker shadow moved against the back wall. Conroy getting to his feet. 'So you came back, Tom Killgannon.'

'Didn't you expect me to?'

'Who's that with you?'

'A friend.'

'Come closer.'

'Put the light on and I will.'

A sound that could have been a laugh. 'I like it the way it is.'

Tom was trying to get his eyes accustomed to the gloom. He was sure there was more than Conroy waiting for him. He just had to know where they were, be able to deal with them if he had to. If he could. He hoped it wouldn't come to that.

'Where's my stuff, Conroy? I want it now.'

Another gravelly sound. 'Oh, you do, do you? Just like that.'

'Yeah, just like that.' Tom felt anger rising within him at Conroy's words, tried to channel it. He knew he would be no good angry. 'Just like we agreed.'

'Well, that's the thing, Tom Killgannon. Our agreement's changed.'

'Why?'

'Because I ... well, I'm not saying I won't give you what you want. But I think you should pay for it. Or pay something now and I'll give you part of what you want. Then another payment next week, say, and on like that. What d'you think?'

The anger within Tom threatened to explode. 'Blackmail, then. That's what you're talking about.'

'I know a fake identity when I see one, Tom Killgannon. And I know that you must need it for a reason. And that reason must be important. Important enough to pay to keep it secret, perhaps? I think so.'

Tom walked all the way across the floor of the shop to where Conroy's voice was coming from. As he approached him, two huge shadows detached themselves from the wall at either side of him. Tom stopped walking.

'You didn't think I'd invite you here unprepared, did you?'

Tom's fists clenched and unclenched. Clenched once more, stayed that way.

'Give me my stuff. Now.'

'Ball's in my court, wouldn't you say? Seller's market.'

'I could just walk out of here. Call the police. Tell them what you're doing.'

'You could. But then I'd sing like fuckin' Sinatra, Tom Killgannon.' He relished saying Tom's name. 'And I don't think you'd want that, would you?'

'I didn't mean about my stuff. I meant the other things.'

'What other things?'

'Your brother? What you've done to him?'

Conroy's voice flattened. 'What about my brother? What d'you know about him?'

'County line drugs gangs,' said Tom. 'Clue's in the name. They come down from somewhere else, London usually, and move in with someone. Someone a bit fragile, easily manipulated. Who won't complain. And to make sure they don't complain, they get them hooked. On heroin, say. Like your brother. Like Josey.'

Conroy said nothing. Tom continued.

'Cuckooing, I believe it's called. That person has all the responsibility of having their name on the books for the place, the cuckoos use it as a base for operations. Knock out the local competition

– usually with the help of someone local, isn't that right, Conroy? Then take over the market for themselves.'

'How d'you know all this?'

'Your boy Leon. Careless talk costs lives, and all that.'

Tom was aware of Lila standing behind him. He was thankful of the dark because he knew that the look of incredulity on her face would betray the story Tom was telling. He just hoped she wouldn't interrupt.

'Leon . . .'

'Followed him home. Not a happy place, that. Especially the way Danny is at the moment.'

'What d'you mean? Danny? I don't know—'

'Oh, please. Don't even. You know who Danny is. Or rather was.'

'What d'you mean, was?'

'Well, he's either playing the longest game of statues known to man or he's dead, I'm afraid.' Again, he was grateful not to be able to see Lila's expression.

'Dead?'

'Yeah. Leon again, I think. Could be. Or maybe he's just covering up for Josey. That was the impression I got.'

Silence. Tom could hear Conroy's breathing, harder and more ragged than before.

'Quid pro quo, Clarice,' said Tom eventually.

'What the fuck you on about?'

'It means give me my stuff and I'm out of here. I don't say a word. And you can clean up your own mess and make up whatever story you want to. You just don't bring me into it. What d'you say? We got a deal?'

'How do I . . . how do I know you're telling the truth?'

'How come I know everything if I'm lying? How come I know names and places? Think about it, Conroy. Makes sense.'

Silence. Then a huge sigh, like foul air leaving a tied black bin bag. One of the shadows came forward, stretched out a hand. Tom took the plastic package, opened it, checked everything was there. Pocketed it.

'Pleasure doing business with you.'

'Fuck off out of my sight.'

'Gladly.'

Tom, with Lila in tow, turned and left.

Out in the street they looked at each other. Lila couldn't believe what she had just heard him say. Tom wasn't sure he believed it either.

'What was all that about?' she said, shock and admiration mingling in her voice.

Tom shrugged. 'I've always been good at talking my way out of things. And into them too, if I'm honest.'

He looked up and down the street. It was near-deserted, a cold wind whipping in from the sea. He turned back to Lila. She looked small, lost.

'You got anywhere to go now?'

She shook her head, her hair obscuring her face.

'Come on then.'

'Where?'

'My car's here. We'll go back to mine. Sort things out from there.'

She smiled. She couldn't speak, didn't know what to say.

They drove off.

Later, they pulled up at his house and both went inside. Neither of them was aware of the car that had been parked just off the road by Tom's house with an unimpeded view of his front door. Nor did they see the two men sitting inside put down their binoculars on their arrival. And they certainly didn't see the car slowly move off, as it didn't have its lights on.

But they would know about it soon enough.

PART THREE

PART THREE

39

'So how's your week been?'

Tom looked at his therapist, sitting opposite him in her Lloyd Loom chair, half-smile on her lips, notes on her lap, waiting for him to respond. He pursed his lips, exhaled. Sat back, tried to get comfortable on the small sofa. Sat forward again, clasped his hands together.

'Busy,' he said.

'Good.' She looked straight at him. Eyes watching for things he wasn't aware he was doing. 'Is that good?'

'I found the girl.'

'Oh.' Janet's eyes widened. She quickly composed herself. 'And?'

Tom paused for a moment. Looked out of the window in the slanted ceiling of the converted attic room, saw the tops of trees attempting to throw off winter and burst into bud, saw blue sky, sun. Things were struggling to come to life again. Then back in the room, watching Janet waiting for him to speak.

He told her everything. Knowing that the session was like a confessional, that it wouldn't go any further. Or at least he hoped it wouldn't. He knew Janet had a duty to report anything illegal to the police and although he wanted to be honest, he didn't want to admit anything that would attract attention to himself. She would have to balance her professionalism against his confession. He would have to hope she came down on his side.

Finishing, he sat back. Almost as exhausted by the telling of his actions as he had been in the execution of them.

Her eyes widened, eyebrows raised. 'Well. Quite a week. Especially when you're trying to keep a low profile.'

'I felt I had no choice. Needed to get my stuff back. I had to do something.'

'So where is this girl now? I presume you didn't just let her walk off.'

'No. She's at my house.'

She looked at him, waited for him to expand further.

'Didn't know where else I could take her. She couldn't stay where she was. Anyway, it's only till she gets herself sorted out, then she'll be off.'

She kept looking at him. 'You sure about that?'

'Yeah,' said Tom, pouring himself a glass of water from the carafe on the side table, throat suddenly dry. 'I've done my bit. Got her out of there, got my stuff back. That's that.'

'Where will she go?'

He shrugged, body language, words, closed now. 'Wherever.'

She nodded. Looked down at her notes, back up again. 'I don't need to tell you what you're doing, do I?'

'Probably not.'

'Or what you think you're doing. Making up for earlier mistakes, as you see them. Creating a surrogate.'

'I know.'

'I'd be remiss in my duty if I didn't point out the dangers. They're two very different people. Remember that.'

'I'm well aware.' He leaned forward, knotting and unknotting his knuckles. 'It's . . . you know that poem by T. S. Eliot? The one where he talks about measuring out your days with coffee spoons?'

Janet's eyes widened. Surprised. Whatever else she thought of him as, it clearly wasn't a reader of poetry. He liked to surprise people that way. 'I know it, yes.'

'Well, for me it's not coffee spoons. It's blister packs of antidepressants. Each one with the day of the week on. That's my diary. That's how I measure my life. I'm trying to keep my head down, get sorted, but sometimes I just have to . . . do something. And hope it's the right thing. For whatever reasons.'

218

Janet thought before answering. 'But this is more than just wanting to play the hero, though, isn't it? It's an apology for what happened, a chance to right wrongs at one remove. As you see it, of course.'

He felt the impact of her words almost physically. But he had to accept the challenge she had laid down for him and respond. Otherwise there was no point in him being here. 'Maybe.'

'Is it redemption?'

'You think I need redeeming?'

'I'm just using your own words back at you. You told me that before in our first session. That you want to think of yourself as a good person again. Be proud of who you are. Do you see helping this girl as a way to do that?'

'I don't know. Really, I don't. I don't know if she's got parents, a family who could come and get her, I don't know anything about her. Just that she got in with some bad people and needed help to get away from them.'

'Is she a bad kid? She stole from you. You sure you're not just projecting an image of how you want her to be so you can help her rather than look at how she really is?'

Tom thought before answering. 'I don't think so. I think she was scared and desperate. Not thinking straight. She just needs a bit of help, that's all.'

'So you see yourself as her protector?'

'I'm just trying to put her on the right path.'

She said nothing, looked at him for a while, thinking, hoping that the silence would give him a chance for reflection also.

'Look,' said Tom eventually. 'It won't bring Hayley back. I know that. It won't change the past, or anything that happened there. She's gone and I have to accept that. I've tried to come to terms with it. But this is different. She's different. This girl. Lila.'

'No, you're right, it won't change the past. But you helping this girl, Lila, are you hoping it'll change the future?'

'Whose future?'

'Hers. Yours. Both.'

'I don't know.' He leaned forward once more. Clasped and unclasped his hands. Watched the muscles moving under his skin. 'I just . . . I saw her there, in that caravan, with those people . . . and . . . I couldn't leave her there. I couldn't walk away and, you know, just take my stuff and leave her. I couldn't.'

'But you didn't bring any of the others with you. Why not? Did they not need saving? Rescuing? Were they in a horrible situation too?'

He looked away. From her, from his own introspective gaze. 'I don't know. I didn't see them, I just saw her.'

She nodded. Understanding what he meant. Hoping Tom would too.

'And what about now? How does it feel to have someone with you who you're taking responsibility for?'

'I'm not responsible for her.'

'You feel you have a duty of care for her, though, don't you?'

'I suppose so. And I don't know why, because I haven't. She's nothing to do with me.' He looked up once more. 'You think I'm just doing this for myself? That she's just a stop on my . . . road to redemption?' He tried to be mock grand when he said the words but the intention fell flat.

She looked at him. A level, honest gaze. 'Can you look after her? Can you keep her safe?'

'I don't know. Like I said, it's only temporary.'

'Nevertheless, are you going to try and keep her safe? Even if it's only temporary? She's clearly in some kind of trouble.'

He thought. Looked up once more. 'Yeah. I'm going to try.'

'Then I think you've just answered your own question.'

40

Pirate John opened his eyes, just lay there, smiling. Enjoying the moment, breathing deeply, no constriction in his chest at all. Like a weight had been lifted from him giving him the best night's sleep for ages.

He knew why. Talking to Tom Killgannon and previously Pearl Ellacott. Simple as that. Sharing his burden, finding allies. He now had something he hadn't had for ages. Hope. Hope that he wouldn't have to go through with what he was supposed to. Hope that this madness would stop, that he – and they – would step back from the brink.

He swung his legs to the floor, got up. He had found living there depressing due to barricading himself in for days and watching the clutter rising. But he saw it differently this morning. The boxes and piles of junk were a towering cityscape that giant Pirate John could loom over and make his way through. A benevolent Godzilla negotiating his beloved Tokyo. He made his way to the stairs, playing his recent conversations with Tom and Pearl over and over once again.

The words were enshrined in his mind. So much so that he was beginning to wonder whether it had actually happened, or, more to the point, whether he had remembered it correctly. Was he saying things in his mental retelling that were never discussed in the actual conversation? He wasn't sure. Perhaps memory was just remembering things as you wanted them to be, not as they actually had been. Did it matter? Not really. Because he had allies. And even if he hadn't said the words his mind told him he had, he knew both of them knew what he had been thinking.

Into the kitchen, kettle on. Tea before anything else, the first one in days. He crossed to the fridge, took out the milk, smelled it. On the turn. But he could get one last mugful out of it before it went completely. Then he could go and buy some more. Because he felt like leaving the house today. Bit of fresh air, mingled with the hope he was feeling, do him the power of good. Let people see him in the village, show he wasn't afraid of them. Yeah. Good plan.

Tea drunk, he showered, dressed. Jeans, trainers, cricket jumper, vintage paisley scarf and – why not? – panama straw hat. Sorted.

He checked himself in the mirror. Looking good. But more than just the clothes; his features looked better than they had been. Less haggard, fewer dark patches under his eyes. He smiled at himself, planning his day.

Pop to the bakery café for breakfast. Treat himself. Then call on a few business contacts, see if he had anything they needed, or there was anything he could get them. Then a few pints in the Sail Makers, maybe. Tom might be there, Pearl too. They could get their heads together, sort out what to do next.

He stepped outside, closed the door behind him.

And stopped dead.

There it was, on the door. Nailed. For everyone to see.

A crow warning.

And Pirate John's world collapsed again.

41

Kai was lucky to be alive. Or so he thought.

He lay on his back, staring upwards, unable to position himself otherwise, his body wracked with agony, tightly bound to the bed. The ropes round his chest added to the pain in his broken ribs making shallow breathing hurt, deep breathing excruciating and movement impossible. The two who had carried him out of the mine hadn't been especially gentle, adding to his injuries. By the time he was in the van, driven to the site and decanted into the yurt he had passed out several times.

The yurt was becoming a familiar sight. Almost welcoming, compared to where he had just been. He hadn't seen Noah yet, though, so that might all change. In fact he hadn't seen anyone or anything, unable to turn his head or move his body. A bottle of water with a straw in the neck had been placed by the side of his head and he occasionally drank from that, but he had received nothing more. When he was first left there he had been scared that his back was broken, that he would never be able to walk again. But he could wiggle his feet, move his toes and even attempt to lift his legs so that was some relief. He hadn't coughed up any blood either so he took that as a sign his lungs weren't punctured. Now all he had to deal with was Noah. And that would make everything else he had endured seem easy.

Noah didn't keep him waiting long. He heard the man's voice as he entered. 'Well, well, well. Thought I'd seen the last of you.'

'Hello, Noah. You'll forgive me if I don't get up,' he said, the words coming in painful gasps.

Noah laughed. An actual, holding-his-back laugh. It was such a strange sound it unnerved Kai.

'That was funny. Really funny. I never had you down as that. Many things, yeah, most of them disappointing, but funny wasn't one of them. Keep it up. I might change my opinion of you.'

'What's your opinion of me now, then?'

Noah stopped moving. Even without seeing him Kai knew he was being studied. 'Brave as well, talking to me like that. Very brave, considering everything you've done recently.' Noah's voice hard now, no longer any trace of the laughter.

Kai said nothing. His earlier wit and defiance had left him. He was aware of Noah crouching down beside him, could feel his breath on his ear and neck. Deep, even. Like a fighter psyching himself up, focusing on a target.

'I'm extremely unhappy with you, Kai. Extremely unhappy. And that's putting it mildly. You've fucked everything up, son. For everyone.'

Again, Kai said nothing. He didn't feel this was the right time to mount a defence. Waiting to hear what Noah had to say was the best thing to do.

'What you did . . .' Noah sighed. 'Tell me why I shouldn't just put you back in there now, eh? Back in that pit. And fucking leave you there. Tell me why I shouldn't.'

Kai didn't know if the question was rhetorical or not.

'Well?'

It wasn't rhetorical. 'I . . . I don't know, Noah. I . . .' He sighed. 'I did nothing wrong. Nothing.' Desperation crept into his voice. Pleading. It sounded ugly, desperate. But, the realisation hit him, he *was* desperate. He might not get out of this room alive. Or Noah might have been serious about his threat. Kai knew from experience he didn't joke about such things.

'You did nothing wrong? Do we really have to go over this again? You talked, Kai. Talked.'

'I didn't . . .'

'To that barman. Killgannon.'

'Honestly, I didn't . . .'

'But that's kind of beside the point now, isn't it? Because you've done much worse than that, haven't you? You know what I mean.'

'It was an accident . . . I didn't mean for him to . . .' Kai trailed off. Even he didn't believe his own words.

And Noah certainly didn't. 'I know exactly what you thought you were doing. Escaping. Getting as far away as possible. And the student would just slow you down. Or even worse, he would go to the police when he got away, incriminate you in his kidnaping. Wouldn't he?'

Again, Kai said nothing.

'In fact it was quite clever of you, Kai. Ruthless. Wouldn't have thought you had it in you. This has been a day of surprises where you're concerned.'

Kai could feel Noah's breath, faster now, hotter, against his neck.

'So how do we go forward? You've fucked everything up so badly that we're back to square one. I'm tempted to just put you in the student's place. You might say it was meant to be. Kyle, Kai. Almost the same.' He paused. Kai knew he was smiling. 'I know someone who would believe that. You know who I mean.'

Kai knew. And his terror and fear increased. 'I'm sorry . . .'

'Well, that makes it all right, then.'

'I am sorry . . .'

Noah's voice was right beside his ear now. 'Not good enough. You tried to run, save your shitty little skin. Get rid of the student while you're at it too. Didn't think about us at all. The community. Did you?'

Those were the words that broke Kai. But he didn't crumble the way he had expected to. He found strength in them. The strength of someone who knows his fate is terminal and therefore has nothing to lose.

'No, I didn't think about the community,' he spat angrily, turning his head to face Noah, ignoring the pain that caused. 'And why

225

should I? The community couldn't give a toss about me. The community didn't trust me, the community put me in the pit. Or you did. Same thing, though, isn't it? So why should I give a fuck about anyone except myself?'

He turned his head back towards the roof. Couldn't bear the sight of Noah's face for a second longer.

'Go on then,' Kai continued. 'Do what you're going to do. I'm in agony right now, so just do it. I'm not going to hurt more than I already do. So just save all the bullshit speeches and get it over with.' He sighed, exhausted beyond words.

Silence fell. It could have stayed like that for all eternity, thought Kai.

Then something unexpected happened. Noah laughed again.

He stood up, moved round the room, laughing all the while. 'Wow,' he said eventually, between gasps. 'A day of firsts, it really is. I thought there was nothing you could do or say that would surprise me. I admit it, I got you all wrong. You've grown a backbone, even if it doesn't look like it when you're lying there – you've got a mouth on you, you stand up for yourself and you've developed a sense of humour. Wonders will never cease.'

'Whatever,' said Kai, totally fed up now. 'Just get on with it.'

'Get on with what? I'm not going to do anything. Not yet, at any rate. No, get yourself well again. Then we'll see what you can do for us.' He leaned in close once more. 'For the community.'

He was laughing while he said it. Kai didn't know what to make of that.

Next, he felt Noah's hands on his bindings, cutting the ropes.

'Sit up if you like. Want something to eat?'

Kai nodded, still wary.

'I'll get it sorted.'

Kai rose slowly, body screaming with every millimetre, turned and looked at Noah.

'A few minutes ago I'd done something unforgivable, so bad that I was going to have to die for it. And now I'm your best mate. Think I'm going to trust you?'

Noah shrugged. 'Up to you. Yes, you did the worst thing imaginable. But you know I can't replace the student with you. You know that really.'

'Has to be an outsider.'

'Has to be an outsider, exactly. But don't think that you're not useful to me. Because you are.'

'How?'

Again, Noah smiled. It wasn't pleasant. 'I've got an outsider in mind. A last-minute replacement. And you're just the one to get them.'

42

Tom stacked the glasses, wiped down the back bar. Filled the optics, stocked the bottles in the fridges. Prepped the kegs in the cellar. Even checked that the crisps and snacks were topped up. Anything to keep busy.

After leaving his therapist he had phoned Rachel. It was too early to go to work and he didn't want to crowd Lila at home. He thought giving her space and time might help her to come to terms with what she had been through. And if she needed to talk then he would be there for her. So, sitting in a chain coffee shop in Truro, nursing his Americano and trying to be interested in a chocolate brownie, he picked up his phone, dialled a number that seemed to be becoming familiar to him.

She answered, her voice official. Not alone, he thought. She would have seen his number, knew it was him.

'Can I help?'

'You busy? Not a good time?'

'Just a minute.' A rustling sound from the other end, movement of some kind. Then a door closing. 'That's better. In the office. Just popped outside. So. What can I do for you?'

A note of flirtation had entered her voice with that last sentence. Tom wasn't sure whether to respond to it or not.

'Oh, just . . .'

'Thinking of me?'

'Yeah.' That wasn't convincing, he thought, not even to himself. He moved on before she either noticed or kept on flirting. 'Listen. I just wanted to say . . . about my cards and things. If you put an alert out, or whatever, you can cancel it now. Everything's OK.'

'You found them? Where were they?'

He had intended to tell her but something – he couldn't explain to himself what – stopped him. 'I got them back. That's the main thing.'

'Did that girl bring them back? Sounds unlikely.'

'No, someone told me where she was. So I went there and got them back from her. Simple as that.'

Silence.

'You all right, Tom? You sound a bit off.'

'No, I'm fine. So, yeah. She just gave me them back. That's that.' And because he didn't feel like he was being believed he threw in a semi-truthful embellishment. The most believable kind. 'She was trying to fence them but not having any luck. Good job I found her when I did.'

'Where was she?'

Again, he didn't want to answer. He knew it was Rachel he was talking to and she was on his side, but she was also police and if he told her anything incriminating she would have to report it. And he thought, for Lila's sake, she should remain under the radar for now. Even if it meant lying to his lover. If that's what she was.

'She's . . .' He wanted to say safe, thinking of his conversation with his therapist, but again he didn't think it was the right thing to say to Rachel. 'I don't know. But I'm not pressing charges. So just leave it as it is.'

He wondered if she'd noticed his attempt at deflection.

'You don't know where she is?' The tone of her voice told him it hadn't worked.

Tom had checked the local news that morning. TV, internet, papers. Nothing about Conroy or the gang or Danny. So either it hadn't registered yet or it had all been covered up. Either way he didn't see what good it would do Lila to be involved in it. Or himself for that matter. He'd almost had his identity compromised. He might not be so lucky next time.

'No,' he said. 'She was running away when I met her the other night. She hadn't got far but she wasn't coming back here. That's as much as I know.'

Muscle memory had helped in his confrontations with Kai and Conroy. A different kind of muscle memory was resurfacing now. The ability to lie convincingly. He had forgotten how good at it he used to be.

More silence on the line.

'You're sheltering her, aren't you?'

Maybe he wasn't that good a liar after all, he thought.

He sighed. 'She's somewhere safe. She's been through a bit of an ordeal and she doesn't seem a bad kid really. Like I said, I'm not pressing charges so everything's fine. That's all I phoned to tell you. Everything's fine now.'

'Is it?'

'What d'you mean?'

'I don't know, Tom. It sounds like you're hiding something from me. I don't know what and I don't know why. But that's what it sounds like.'

'I'm not, I—'

'Please. You'd say that whatever. But if you're keeping something from me . . . If it's about you and me and it concerns us, then we need to talk about it. If it's police business, then I really don't know what to say.'

Tom wished he hadn't phoned her now. 'I'm going to go. We'll talk soon.'

He cut the call before she could answer back, turned the ringer off, pocketed the phone.

His coffee was cold, his brownie unappetising. He stood up, left the café.

*

231

'You having a bet with someone?'

'Sorry?'

Tom looked round. He had been miles away, lost in his own world of memories and conjecture. Pearl was standing beside him, hands on hips, smile on face.

'Just that you're working so hard. It's like you're in a race or you've bet someone you can get everything done in, I don't know, fifteen minutes by the looks of things.'

He found a smile. 'Sorry. Was just keeping busy, that's all.'

Pearl looked round the near-empty bar. 'Hardly worth knocking yourself out for, is it?'

'Suppose not.'

'Something we used to say at uni: why should a student not look out of the window in the morning?'

'Don't know. Why not?'

'Because they'll have nothing to do in the afternoon.' Another look round the bar. 'Save something for the afternoon. Metaphorically speaking.'

He smiled, almost laughed. 'Good joke. And point taken.'

'You won't get any more money for working harder.'

'Fine. I'll sit and read, then.'

'Or we could talk. Chat, you know, like two people who are friends.'

Tom smiled. He liked the idea of being Pearl's friend. 'What shall we talk about? Brexit? Trump? The European Championships?'

Pearl paused, the smile dying on her face. He sensed there was something she actually wanted to talk about. He waited.

'John had a word with me the other night.'

Tom aimed for flippancy. 'Lucky you.'

'He said he'd been talking to you recently. About things that've been going on round here. Bad things. That right?'

Tom didn't know what to say, how much to give away. Like a game of Jenga, if he said something, took out one fact, Pearl would want to hear another. And eventually the whole edifice of carefully constructed secrets and lies surrounding Lila and his new identity would come tumbling down.

Pearl continued, without waiting for a reply. 'About Tony Williamson?'

Tom frowned. Not what he had been expecting. 'Who?'

'Farmer. Came down from London. Ex-City boy with loads of plans for going organic, full of it. Like no one had ever heard of it before. Anyway, threw himself off a cliff. Not long before you arrived.'

'Business that bad? I would reckon he's not the only farmer thought of doing that round here.'

'True. But John says he didn't commit suicide. And it wasn't an accident.'

'Murder, you mean?'

'So John says. His latest conspiracy theory. And he wanted to share it with me.'

'So what was it for? Secrets of raising dairy herds?'

'Something to do with the bid for the marina, apparently. And that missing student. Chuck in Shergar and you've got a full house.' She turned to him. 'Is this what he's been talking to you about? Not Shergar, obviously.'

'No, nothing like that.'

'What was it, then?'

Tom didn't want to tell Pearl about Lila. 'Just another of his theories. Nothing like that.'

Pearl looked disappointed. 'Oh. He said you would know all about it. That I should talk to you and we could both investigate. Like Mulder and Scully.'

Tom smiled. 'Bit before your time.'

Pearl smiled in return. Punched him on the arm. 'I'm not that young, granddad.'

Tom looked at her, holding his smile seconds longer than he should have. Pearl, he noticed, did the same. They broke looks. Silence fell.

'So what d'you think? Should we turn detective? I mean, there's nothing else to do round here.'

'That's not the first time you've said how dull this place is. Why'd you come back, then?'

'Truthfully?' Pearl thought. 'I don't know. Maybe I just didn't know where to go next or what to do. And my parents were struggling with this place. I wanted to help, I suppose.' She smiled. 'Or maybe I was waiting for a knight in shining armour to sweep me off my feet.'

'Round here?' said Tom. 'He'd be driving a tractor.'

She just smiled.

The conversation was becoming uncomfortable for Tom. He steered it back to firmer ground. 'Anyway, let's talk to John about this. He'll be in later no doubt.'

She agreed. Then went and found something else to do.

Early evening was the emptiest Tom had seen it since starting there. No one from the travellers' site, no Emlyn and Isobel, just a couple of farmhands and they didn't look like they would be staying for long.

'If it wasn't for the Round Table and their monthly meetings upstairs,' Pearl had said on occasion, 'we'd have gone under ages ago.'

The farmhands looked away, not wanting to return his gaze. He didn't know what to make of that. He knew he was an outsider but he thought he was on the road to being accepted, even begrudgingly. Perhaps not.

He had noticed it more and more recently, people looking at him like he didn't belong there. Or maybe they had always regarded him that way and he had been oblivious to it. Perhaps recent events had just sharpened his focus, made him more attuned to the way others were towards him. He tried to put it out of his mind. Hoped Lila was all right.

He picked up his cloth, looked at the countertops once more. Put it down again.

There was nothing he could do for the present.

Just wait for Pirate John.

But Pirate John didn't turn up.

43

The bed was more comfortable than Lila had been in for a long time. Easily better than sleeping in a garage or a hedgerow or a caravan with dealers. Or even Kai's tiny bed in his van, pushed up against his unwashed, sweaty body night after night. But this had been a great night's sleep. At least until she woke up and remembered what she had been through. Those memories fell on her like a huge heavy blanket, too dark and dense to throw off immediately, leaving her no choice but to lie curled beneath, pressed down by the weight of them.

Danny. What he had done to her. What she had done to him. She felt no remorse over her actions. No guilt, no upset. Just a kind of numbness. Uncaring whether she had taken his life or not. His actions had made her feel like that. His fault, not hers.

She replayed those memories over and over again. It was like watching a movie in a smoke-filled cinema, the other viewers constantly coming and going, obscuring her vision, the film itself stopping and restarting from different places, preventing her from following the narrative. She saw only glimpses, tried to relate to them, contextualise them.

His face leering over her, sweating, his teeth yellow, eyes narrowed. Sickly triumph on his face. Laughing.

Then:

The pillow shifting, revealing the edge of the bed. Her face up against it, pushing against the frame, a rhythmic pounding behind her. Mouth against wood, unable to breathe properly, to call out, to make him stop.

Then:

Nothing. Blackness. An oblivious kind of peace.

Then:

Rage. An anxious, desperate anger, staring at Danny's grinning face, seething.

Then:

Danny's unmoving body.

Then:

Nothing. Here. Now.

She didn't want to say the words again. Admit to herself what had happened. What he had done to her. It was something she would have to come to terms with. Get help for, even. But not now. Not today. Today she had to make sense of where she was, what was happening. And where she was going to go.

She pushed back the duvet. It was heavy, warm, moved slowly. Still weighed down by her recent ordeal, she stood up.

Tom had been good to her. Left a towel in the bathroom, an old dressing gown that was so big she could have gone camping in it, slipper socks and the oversized T-shirt she had slept in. It had an old, worn design on it for Richmond Fontaine. She had no idea what that was, presumed it was a brand of beer.

More than that, he had left her alone to sleep for a whole day and night. She knew he had gone to work and heard him return, but she just kept her distance from him for now. And he did the same, giving her the space she needed to re-orientate herself. To relax and heal. Not that any of that was possible yet. But he was trying.

She visited the bathroom, walked downstairs. It was strange being back in that kitchen again. By choice this time, not necessity. And not planning on running straight away, either. She looked at the window she had broken. Still temporarily boarded up. She kept studying it. Reached out, touched it. It didn't seem real, somehow, everything she had been through recently. Like a particularly bad dream or bad trip she would soon wake from. She looked at her hands. Her ruined fingers were healing. She stroked her hand over the wood of the window again. It was only through touching physical items, experiencing a memory connected to them, that she was able to divine reality. To realise that everything she had been through had actually happened. That it was real and she would have to confront it, cope with it and – hopefully, eventually – move on from it. If she ever could.

She poured herself a glass of orange juice from the fridge, sat at the table. Tried to make sense once more of the jumble in her mind.

Tom Killgannon. She couldn't make him out. He seemed decent enough, and in fact had proved himself to be decent enough, but she still couldn't work out his motives. He appeared to be driven by complex engines that perhaps even he didn't understand. He had been good to her bringing her here, not demanding anything and even forgiving her for stealing his stuff, but she just wondered if he had another motive for doing all this. When she looked at him, really looked at him, she saw something surprising. He was physically big and strong but his eyes betrayed him. They were softer, kinder than you'd expect. She hesitated to say soulful because that kind of word just made her want to heave. But there was something there that she recognised. Some kind of damage, something broken in him, like he wasn't complete. A missing piece he was looking for. She could relate to that.

She was grateful for what he had done for her. But should she be suspicious of him? She hoped not. She was tired of running, escaping one bad scenario just to jump into an even worse one. She just wanted some peace. But she couldn't rest fully here. Not being so close to Noah and everyone else. If she stayed here they would find her.

So she would have to leave. Preferably sooner rather than later. Hopefully Tom would help her. But in the meantime she had to decide whether she was going to trust him or not. She didn't think he would tell anyone or bring anyone round who would be a threat to her. At least she hoped not.

She took her glass of juice with her into the living room. It was neat, especially for a man living alone. There were CDs on shelves, some DVDs but mainly books. She studied the titles, looking for something to read to pass the time. She didn't know any of them. Cormac McCarthy. Don DeLillo. Hubert Selby Jr. And plenty more like that. Nelson Algren. John Steinbeck. And some heavy, thick books by Charles Bukowski. She took one down, found it was full of poems. This would do, she thought. Take her mind off things, pass the time. She sat down, started to read.

Waiting for Tom to return.

Waiting for the next phase of her life to start.

44

The windows were closed and curtained, the doors locked and bolted. Pirate John had checked and rechecked. And still he was terrified.

Back in siege mode again, he had moved anything he thought he needed into the centre of the living room, pushing everything else back to the walls, creating a mini island for himself. His phone, the TV remote, a huge plastic bottle of water and cans of food. He would have to go to the toilet at some point but he would put it off as long as possible and even then force himself to vary when and the length of time he needed to go. Just in case anyone was watching and thought there was a discernible pattern to his behaviour. Make it as hard for them as possible.

He had the crow warning in the room with him. He tried not to stare at it but couldn't help himself. He didn't know what to do with it. He couldn't leave it on the door for everyone to see. And he couldn't just destroy it. He hadn't thought of himself as superstitious but he supposed he must be if he wasn't able to bring himself to do that. Why couldn't he destroy it? He had asked himself that enough times, even gone so far as to put it in the rubbish, then feel unwell and take it out again. Or stand over the sink holding a lighter to its feathers, unable to bring the flame towards it. So it sat there in the living room, tossed into a far corner, supposedly out of sight. But he knew exactly where it was. Could feel those dead black beady eyes staring at him if he moved. Like it had some kind of evil power over him.

The rational part of him knew it was all garbage, that there was no such thing as a malign influence. But he felt it now. Penetrating to his core. Like a chill he couldn't get warm from, no matter how many hot baths he took or layers of clothing he swaddled himself in – or even if he turned the heating up as high as he could. No. It chilled him bone-deep and there was no way he could change it.

He didn't know what to do. He knew that sometime soon, or when he least expected it, something bad would happen to him. Perhaps something fatal. And he had agreed to that. They had all agreed to that. But he had never actually thought that it would happen to him. He didn't think he would be the one to have a change of heart, to want out. Or as he now understood it, to see sense and try and stop this ridiculous mass hysteria. And he certainly didn't think they would actually try and punish him for it. Not seriously. What had they all been thinking?

He couldn't get away without being spotted. His car was too noticeable. And he couldn't seek forgiveness either. Not once he'd received the crow warning. They weren't messing about. Look what happened to Tony Williamson, the posh City-boy farmer. Suicide? Everyone knew it wasn't. He had hoped Pearl Ellacott and Tom Killgannon would look into it for him. See for themselves what had taken place. He doubted that would happen now. It was too late for him. He couldn't even phone Morrigan – he shuddered at just thinking the name – and say he was sorry. There was nothing he could do. They had won. And he knew it.

He picked up the remote, flicked on the TV. Local news. He watched in case there was any mention of St Petroc, of the marina development. Nothing. Then he saw the photo of the missing student.

The parents were making yet another plea but they looked as though they had accepted that he would never turn up again. At least not alive. Pirate John could feel their pain and hurt coming through the screen. It touched him, what they must be going through. That feeling that these things always happen to someone else. The soul-searching, desperately wondering what they had done to deserve this, what had gone wrong. Why were they being punished? He wished he could help them in some way. He felt dreadful, knowing what he had done and not being able to speak about it.

The report ended and a number flashed up on the screen. For help in finding Kyle. Pirate John stared at it. And realised there was something he could do to help them. Not much, but it was something.

He committed the number to memory, picked up his phone. Punched in the digits, waited. While he was listening to hold music, a voice came on and told him that the information he was giving would be treated in confidence although calls were recorded. He didn't care. He waited, feeling his heart hammering, the fingers which held the phone shaking. Eventually it was answered.

'Crimestoppers, how can we help you?' A professionally cheerful voice.

His turn now. 'I . . .' A deep breath. Another. 'I . . . it's about that missing student. Kyle Tanner.'

'Do you have information?' The voice was interested now, but wary. Trying to coax him along but clearly tired of all the sick practical jokers these kinds of appeals attract, he thought.

'I . . . yes. He's . . .' The crow warning caught his eye, sitting in the corner, dominating the room, its dead eyes locked on him. Judging him. Warning him.

'Hello?'

'Yes, I . . . he's . . .'

The crow's gaze unwavering.

'Take your time, sir. We're here to help.'

'Yes, I know. He's . . .'

Turning away so the crow couldn't see him any more.

'He's . . .'

But still it judged him. Watched him. Like it was reporting back. Like they would know what he was trying to do.

'Sir? Hello?'

He ended the call. Threw the phone on the floor.

He was shaking, trembling all over and sweating as if he had just completed a five-mile run. He felt sick to his stomach.

And still the crow stared at him.

He stood up, crossed to it. Was about to pick it up but stopped himself. Didn't even want to touch it. He just stared at it.

'You bastard . . . you fucking bastard . . . I fucking hate you . . .'

Again his hands went towards it, outstretched, fingers turned to grasping talons, ready to rip it apart, throw it away.

But he couldn't reach for it. Unable to let his fingers touch those black, oily feathers, begin to rend it into pieces. Unable or unwilling. He didn't know which. All he could feel was its malevolent power washing towards him. Its eyes glinting darkly, beak sharp, ready to fight back if he tried anything.

He turned away, slumped onto the sofa. And burst into tears.

He was too weak to stop them from doing anything, to fight back. Even too weak to put a pair of grieving parents' minds at rest. How pathetic was that? How pathetic was he?

He needed to talk to someone. He needed help.

He had to talk to Tom Killgannon again.

Somehow.

In the meantime he would just sit in his room and wait.

For the end of his world to arrive.

45

'Feeling better?'

Kai opened his eyes. He wasn't used to Noah being this charming and happily disposed towards him. Usually it was hostility or, at best, indifference. But now the man seemed genuinely pleased to see him all the time. It made Kai nervous.

'Yeah,' he said, sitting upright. 'I've been walking around for a bit, getting used to being on my feet ag—'

'Good,' said Noah, cutting him off. He handed him a mug of something.

'What's this?'

'Tea. Get you strong again.'

This was definitely out of the ordinary. Kai went from being nervous to openly suspicious.

Noah read his features, smiled. 'You're an important member of the team, Kai. We need you back on your feet as soon as possible.'

'Why?' He took a sip of the tea. Too hot. Burned his mouth. He grimaced.

'Got something for you to do. Something only your particular talents will be handy for. Listen to me,' he said, laughing. 'I sound like that Neeson bloke in that action film. "I have a particular skill set . . ."' He laughed again.

Kai put the tea down by the side of the bed, wary. 'What kind of thing?'

'Like I said, something you'll be good at. In fact, it's probably something that only you could do. We just need a few more things to fall into place and then you're on.'

'What d'you mean, fall into place? You said there was an outsider that you needed me to get. I either do it or I don't. They're either there or they're not. What has to fall into place first?'

A flash of something appeared on Noah's face. Just for a second or two, then it was gone. But Kai saw it. He recognised it. That old intolerance bordering on anger that talking back, asking questions, always brought. And in that moment he knew – definitely knew – that Noah's new approach was just a sham. And he should be wary about what was being lined up for him.

'This and that,' he said. 'Don't worry about it. Just get yourself well again.'

Kai nodded. Attempted the tea once more. It was still too hot to drink.

'I'll hear soon. Then we'll be full speed ahead. And it'll all be over.'

There was something else in Noah's voice, behind his words, that gave Kai pause. Like he wasn't actually talking to him, just repeating things to himself. The man looked, and was trying to disguise sounding, weary. There was almost sadness there. Or fear, thought Kai. No. That was unthinkable. Not for Noah. He was the one who instilled fear in people, not the other way round. Wasn't he?

'So who is it, then?' asked Kai.

Noah just smiled. 'A surprise.'

'A surprise.'

'Yeah. But you'll like it. Poetic justice, let's call it.'

Kai didn't like the way he had said that. There was some kind of sickness in the words.

'And what if I don't like it?'

'You don't want to think like that, Kai. Believe me.' Noah let himself out. The implied threat hung heavy in the air.

Kai tried to move, felt pain lance through his body, bringing back memories of the pit. He shuddered, reached for his tea, brought it to his lips.

It had gone cold.

46

They sat in the living room, Tom and Lila, both on separate seats, both giving each other plenty of space, drinking mugs of tea. Keeping their own silence like two people who had met at a party with plenty in common but no idea how to start a conversation about it. Music was playing.

'What's this we're listening to?' asked Lila eventually. She was sitting in an armchair, curled up, legs underneath her, Tom's T-shirt, pyjama bottoms and slipper socks dwarfing her body.

'*Skeleton Tree* by Nick Cave. And the Bad Seeds, of course.'

'Right.'

'You like it?'

Lila made the kind of face someone makes when they're grateful to their host but don't want to hurt their feelings.

Tom smiled. 'I'll put something else on.'

'No, no, it's OK . . .'

'It's fine. Probably a bit too depressing, really. Those lyrics, the sentiment behind it . . .' He stood up, crossed to the CD player. 'Any requests?'

'Whatever you like. What d'you mean by the sentiment behind it?'

Tom changed CDs. 'He wrote it just before his son died accidentally. Recorded it afterwards. Not the most cheerful of listens, but cathartic. Very cathartic.' He drifted slightly, came back. 'Try this instead. See what you think.' Al Green's 'Tired of Being Alone' came on.

'I know this one.'

'But d'you like it?'

'Yeah. It's good.'

'Right. We'll leave it there, then.'

'Why is your music so depressing? That last one about the dead son, this one about how lonely he is. You not got anything cheerful?'

'What you got in mind – Little Mix?'

'Fuck off.'

He laughed. After she realised she hadn't offended him or upset him, she joined in. It eased the mood between them a little.

'Thought you'd be into rave music and stuff like that.'

'Why?'

'Traveller culture, surfer, that sort of thing.'

'Nah, not me. That was Kai's kind of thing, though. I used to just tag along and pretend to like it.' She fell silent for a few seconds. 'Did that a lot, then. No, I like my Zayde Wølf, Joseph. Stuff like that. Passion Pit.'

'Right,' said Tom, none the wiser.

It was late. He had worked a full shift but left straight afterwards, not staying to join Pearl for a drink and a chat the way he often did. It hadn't been a particularly arduous shift, just a few regulars there. The retired teachers were in, a few farmers and farm workers but that was it. No Pirate John or anyone from Noah's site. Their talk with Pirate John would have to wait.

Often, he would take some food home – whatever was left in the kitchen – and as usual, Pearl had offered. He had to stop himself from asking for double portions so as not to give away the fact that Lila was staying with him. He just took one portion home, gave it to Lila, and made himself cheese on toast. She was very grateful.

'I didn't know if you'd eaten or not.' He had come in to find her asleep in the armchair. An open book of Charles Bukowski poetry beside her.

She jumped up, a look of terror on her face, ready to run, then calmed down when she realised it was him.

'Sorry,' she said, I must have dozed off.'

'Don't worry about it. I reckon you needed it.' He went into the kitchen to prepare her food.

They ate in the living room, music on. Stayed there after they had finished.

'So,' said Tom, putting aside his empty mug, arching his back and stretching, 'how did you end up down here?'

'You know how I ended up here.' Her eyes looked wary, on guard, not wanting to give anything away.

'Not here in my house. I mean here in St Petroc. With Kai.'

'What d'you want to know for?'

Tom shrugged. 'Just interested, that's all.' He smiled in what he hoped was a reassuring way. 'Like to know who my housemates are. Whether I need to hide the peanut butter. You know.'

'Love peanut butter. You got any?'

'You still hungry?'

'Just checking. For later.'

'Yes, I've got peanut butter. You needn't panic.'

She looked at him over the rim of her mug. 'So what about you? Where are you from? You're not from round these parts.' She assumed a terrible Cornish accent when she said it. Made both of them laugh.

'No. I'm Northern.'

'Right. Which bit?'

Tom wondered which answer he should give her. 'Middlesbrough.'

'Where's that? Scotland?'

'No, Teesside. You probably haven't heard of it. Don't worry, you haven't missed anything.' He stood up, crossed to the cabinet in the corner, took a half-empty bottle of Lagavulin off the shelf, poured himself a generous amount. Sat back down again, Lila watching him all the time. 'What about you? Where you from?'

'You keeping that to yourself?' she said, deflecting the question, nodding towards the whisky.

'You really want some of this? OK.' He found another glass, poured her some. She smelled it, wrinkled her face. Tried it. And couldn't stop coughing and gagging.

Tom smiled. 'Hey, that's expensive stuff.'

In between coughs she handed the glass back to him. 'Have it . . .'

He took it. 'So,' he said again when she had calmed down, 'what's your story? How did you get here?'

She wiped her mouth with her sleeve, swallowed some tea. Gave the question, and the answer, some thought. 'I . . . didn't get on with my parents. I couldn't live there any more.'

'What happened?'

She looked at him, frowning. 'Why d'you want to know all this?'

'I'm interested. Getting to know each other. Just thought you might want to talk. But if you'd rather not, fair enough. Your story's your story.'

'No, it's OK.' She felt slightly ashamed at her defensiveness. 'I'll tell you.' She paused, readied herself. 'I don't look back on what happened much.' She paused again, thinking. 'Actually, that's not true. I think about it a lot. Especially my sister.'

'What happened to her?'

'She died.' Lila saw Sophie's face again in her mind's eye. Smiling, vibrant. Beautiful. 'Suddenly. Accident. And I don't suppose my parents ever got over it. This is the bit I think about a lot. About what happened to them afterwards. At the time I just hated them.' She stopped talking.

'And now?' said Tom, sipping his whisky.

'Oh, I still hate them, but I try to understand them more. I mean, I'll never forgive them for what they did to me. My mother especially.'

'Which was?' Tom readied himself for something horrific.

'She brought in an exorcist.'

He nearly spat out his whisky. 'Jesus Christ. Do they still have them?'

'Yeah. But the Church keeps quiet about them. She brought one in for me. Said I was running wild, that I had a demon in me.'

'A demon?'

Lila nodded. 'When Sophie died they told me she'd gone away on a holiday. Then when she didn't come back they told me she'd left them and gone to live somewhere else, somewhere better. And we weren't supposed to talk about her. I didn't know what was happening. My sister loved me. And I loved her. She wouldn't just get up and leave. I knew it. But when I tried to ask them about it they got angry and told me to shut up. Then one day my mother said she'd heard from her. I thought this was brilliant. You know, Sophie's coming back, hooray.' Lila smiled sadly at the memory. 'What she meant was, she'd been to a spiritualist and they'd told her Sophie was in heaven.'

'Shit . . .'

'Yeah. So then they had to tell me that Sophie was dead. And that was when shit got real.'

Tom poured himself another glass. 'What happened?'

'I was furious with them. You know, why haven't you told me this? Why did you pretend she'd gone away? All of that. They said that they were going to tell me when I was older but they just hadn't got round to it. I mean, I know now it was just their way of coping with it – that's the part of me trying to understand it – but you know, I still can't forgive them for it. For lying to me.'

'No, you wouldn't. So where does the exorcist come in? Seems like quite an escalation.'

'Yeah, it was. After that my mother got worse. Church all the time, everything I did was wrong.' Lila stopped talking, horrific memories being dredged up.

'It's OK. You can stop if you want.'

She shook her head. 'No, I want to finish. It's helpful, you know? Takes my mind off what's just happened. Gets things in perspective.'

'It's up to you.'

'So yeah. Church. She just got worse and worse. And my dad didn't want to know, didn't even try to stop her. And I tried to make it work, I tried to be nice to them, but she wouldn't let me. So I just stayed away as much as possible. Went to see my friends in the park. Sat with them. Drinking, smoking. At least they made me feel wanted. Then when we were having an argument, my mother said that God had taken the wrong one. It should have been me, not Sophie.'

'Really?'

'Yeah. Well, you can imagine how I reacted. And then she brought in this exorcist. A vicious evil fucker called Father Gerald. I can still see him now. His eyes, his . . .'

She broke off, shuddering. Tom was concerned for her. Talking had stirred up more than unpleasant memories but he knew she was putting it into context with what had happened between her and Danny. 'You don't have to—'

'No.' Said louder than she had expected. She stared at him, tears appearing, eyes displaying hurt. 'I do.'

'OK.'

'Father. Gerald. Father fucking Gerald . . . he held me down. He . . .' She shook her head. 'He called it getting rid of demons. I've got another word for what he did. And you know what? You know what the worst thing about it was? My mother didn't just stand there while he did it. She helped him. Helped him tie me down, helped him do whatever he said. And all the time she smiled at me.' Lila sighed. 'Can I try some of that whisky again?'

Tom handed her his glass. She took a large sip. Grimaced as it went down, but held it. Like the pain of it helped her cope with an even greater pain.

'And that's that. I left home. Ended up meeting Kai. I knew he fancied me more than I fancied him but he had somewhere to sleep and he was all right, you know? All right to hang about with. So

252

I did. And we ended up here.' Another sigh. 'And that's when . . . well, you know.'

Tom knew some of it and wanted to ask her about the rest, about the missing student, but Lila kept talking.

'What about you then?' she said, wiping the tears away from her cheeks. 'I've shown you mine, you show me yours.' She tried to laugh. 'Heart, I mean.'

He smiled at her words. 'Well . . .' Should he tell her? He wasn't supposed to tell anyone but he felt she was owed something after what she had just admitted to him. The truth. Or something like it. As much truth as he could own up to. 'OK, then. The first thing is, I'm not from Middlesbrough.'

'Wow,' she said, severely unimpressed. 'That's a shocker.'

He smiled. 'I'll tell you more. Then you'll see why it's important.'

'OK, then.'

'I'm from Manchester. Grew up there. Didn't really have much family, just a sister who I loved more than anyone else. She was older than me, always there for me. Got me out of trouble. All of that. I wasn't a bad kid, but I was easily led. Or at least that's how I like to think of it. Maybe I was a bad kid. Or I just enjoyed doing iffy things.'

Lila looked wary. 'Like what?'

'Oh, nothing too bad,' he said, trying to reassure her. 'Breaking in to places, fights, that kind of thing. Nicking cars. Tabloid teenage tearaway, that was me.' He smiled as he spoke. 'I was just full of, I don't know, anger. Rage. My dad had died when I was little and my mother left me with my older sister. She brought me up. And I think I took that anger out on, well, just about anyone who looked at me the wrong way. But it couldn't last. I knew it couldn't. Or at least I had enough sense not to keep doing it. I was going to end up in serious trouble.'

'So what did you do?'

'Joined the Royal Marines. What kids like me did then. Kids who hadn't had a good education, but who wanted to get out from where they were. Wanted to do something with themselves.'

'Like killing people.'

'Yeah, I heard that a lot. But that's not what I signed up for. Honestly. I don't even like guns. I just wanted to learn a trade, you know. University was, like, a million miles away. No way I could ever do that. So it was the Marines for me. Plus Julie, my sister, had a kid by then, Hayley, and she was living with this bloke she'd met. I got the feeling I was, I don't know, surplus to requirements. It was time to move on.'

'So where did you go?'

'Not far from here, actually.' Tom was aware of his Northern accent coming back. He hadn't spoken in this much detail to anyone for a long time, apart from his therapist. He didn't find it as bad or as awkward as he had expected. 'Lympstone Commando Training Centre in Devon. Toughest place in the country. If they couldn't sort me out, no one could.'

'And they did.'

'Yeah. Got nine GCSEs, graduated top of the class. Told you I wasn't thick. Then off to Afghanistan.' He swirled the whisky in his glass, emptied it. Refilled it. 'Did twelve years as a commando. Saw some ...' He kept staring into the whisky. 'Some things. Horrific things. Friends dying in front of me, all of that. But I didn't just witness it. I helped create it.'

Lila stared at him, nervous again about sharing a house with this man she knew very little about. He noticed her concern.

'Don't worry. It was a long time ago. I was a different person then.'

'What did you do?'

He shrugged, downed more whisky. It was lubricating his voice, freeing up his words. Helping him to get things out. 'You don't want to know. Really. You don't. I'm still in therapy for it. And what came after. PTSD, depression, the lot. So anyway.' He refilled his glass. Knew he needed to slow down. 'Twelve years up, I left. Joined the Met as a copper.'

254

'You were police?' Again Lila looked wary.

'Yeah. I was a DC in CID. Didn't like it much. So I joined the Specialist Crime and Operations unit working undercover. That was more like it.' He became thoughtful. 'I suppose I'd become a bit of an adrenaline junkie. I needed something to . . . give me that kind of thrill. But something that still had structure to it. An outcome to work towards. Catch the bad guys. You know?'

He took another mouthful. Stopped talking. This was the bit, he thought. The part I shouldn't admit to. He looked at Lila. Young, damaged but trying to work through it. He recognised something of himself in her. And because of that he felt able to share what he was about to say next.

'Then I got sent up to Manchester. Back to Moss Side, where I'd grown up. I was supposed to infiltrate the drug gangs there.' He stopped, looked at her. 'Can I trust you?'

She looked suddenly shocked at the question. 'What?'

'Can I trust you? Really trust you.'

'Yes . . .' She looked at him strangely, trying to gauge why he had said that.

'Only, I'm about to tell you something that's going to compromise me.'

She looked very confused now. 'Compromise? You're talking like you're still a copper.'

'No, honestly. It's just if I'm going to tell you the next bit, I need to know you won't tell anyone else.'

'Why would I tell anyone else?'

Tom smiled, had an idea. 'OK, how about this. I'll make a deal with you. I'll tell you the next bit if you tell me what happened to that missing student. Or what you know about him. Yeah?'

Lila's eyes widened. She looked like she was going to get up, make a run for it. Tom realised he had said the wrong thing.

'Sorry,' he said quickly. 'Don't get upset. We're just talking here.'

'You got me here to ask me questions. You're a copper . . .'

255

'Seriously, I'm not. I'm an ex-copper. Ex-Marine. I'm ex-lots of things. I'm just here. Me. A barman. This is it.' He gestured round the room. 'This is all I am. Here and now.'

'So why d'you want to know about the student?'

'Because I'm curious. There's something going on round here and he's connected to it. And I think you're connected to it too, which is why people are looking for you. And I think the people looking for you are bad guys. And I'm trying to help you. I don't want the bad guys to find you. But to do that, I need to know what you know. Simple as that.'

And it was, she thought, when he explained it that way. She scrutinised him once more. He seemed like a good man. She could usually spot the ones who were a bit off, who were lying to her. She'd had enough practice. But she didn't get that vibe from Tom. He seemed genuine. And also, she recognised something in him that mirrored something in her. Some kind of damage, of looking for healing. A way back. Or a way forward.

'OK then,' she said. 'But this had better be good.'

'Oh, it's good.'

Then the doorbell rang.

47

Tom and Lila looked at each other, shocked at first. Then Tom smiled.

'If I go and answer that, will you still be here when I come back?'

'Yeah.'

'You sure? You won't head out the window?'

'Ha. Ha.' She smiled when she said it.

'OK. Won't be a minute.'

He went to the front door, thinking he knew who it would be. The only person who called at this time of night. He opened it.

'Hi, Rachel.'

He was right.

'Hi, yourself.' She smiled. 'Saw your light on. Can I come in?'

He knew what that smile meant. 'If you like, but . . .'

She stiffened. The smile faded. 'You've got company.'

'Haven't we done this already?'

She relaxed. 'Yeah, we have.' She paused. They looked at each other.

There was something about her that made him want her. Like she had put some kind of spell on him. She knew how to make the base, reptilian part of his brain respond, even if he had previously been in deep conversation with Lila.

If Lila hadn't been in the front room he wouldn't have thought twice about asking her in and taking her upstairs. It was what they both wanted. An honest relationship in that sense, neither under any illusion. Or at least Tom hoped not. Part of him thought he should just send Rachel away now. But another part thought it might be possible for her to stay. Lila wasn't his daughter, she didn't have a say in who he slept with. Or when. He did have to take her into consideration, though. Especially bearing in mind what she had been about to tell him. And there was something else. On the phone, he had been wary of telling Rachel where Lila was. Looking at her now – and admittedly he probably wasn't using his brain as his primary thinking organ – he didn't see what the problem was.

'You can come in if you like,' he said. 'But yeah. I do have company.'

She arched an eyebrow. 'If you're after a threesome you can forget it.'

'It's not like that.' He sighed, decision made. 'Come in.'

He walked into the living room. She followed. And stopped at the door.

'This is Lila. I suppose it's about time you two met. Lila, this is Rachel.'

Lila stood up quickly, ready to run again. Tom crossed to her, hands out. She flinched away. He didn't touch her, dropped his hands to his sides. 'It's OK. She's a friend of mine. That's why she's here. That's why she came here last time. She often calls in at this time of night.' He smiled in what he hoped was a reassuring way. 'Nothing more than that, promise.'

Lila relaxed slightly. But if she had been holding a knife, thought Tom, she would still have kept a tight grip on it.

Rachel entered the room. Smiled at Lila. 'Hiya. Don't worry. I'm off duty.' She helped herself to a whisky, sat down on the sofa.

'I'm not pressing charges,' said Tom. 'That's all over with. Lila and I've sorted it out.'

Rachel shrugged. 'Off duty, like I said. Not my problem. You two do what you want to do.' She looked at the whisky, smelled it, put it down untouched. She stood up once more. 'I'll put the kettle on instead. Tea?'

'Lovely,' said Tom.

Rachel left the room.

Tom looked at Lila. 'Sorry,' he said. 'She pops in from time to time, like I said. When she's finished work.'

Lila still looked wary. 'And she's a friend?'

'Well –' Tom felt himself reddening – 'bit more than that, actually.'

Lila understood. Relaxed a little more.

'That's all. I couldn't not let her in. Not again.'

Lila sat back down, but remained perched on the edge of the chair. 'She's married, isn't she? She's got a wedding ring on.'

'Yeah, she's married. And I don't pry into that. It's up to her what she does and how she copes with it. Her marriage might be in a dreadful state for all I know. Her husband might be doing the same thing.' He shrugged. 'I never said I was perfect, or a saint or anything like that. I'm probably the opposite.'

'Well, it's up to you what you do.' She looked at the door that Rachel had gone through once more. 'I'm going to bed.'

'No, don't do that. Stay. Talk. We were having a good old chinwag.'

She rolled her eyes at his choice of words. He smiled. Both movements felt slightly strained. As though they were trying to pretend they were still having a good time.

'Yeah, well, she's put a stop to that. Goodnight.'

'Wait.' Tom laid his hand on Lila's arm.

She looked at it. Some kind of boundary had been crossed but neither of them knew what. Tom had always kept a physical distance from her, making sure she was comfortable in his presence. This broke that rule completely. He withdrew it.

'Sorry,' he said. 'Don't go, though. Stay.'

She glanced at the door again. Tom thought she looked nervous, agitated.

'Is something wrong? Is it Rachel? Have you had a run-in with her already? You needn't worry. I told you, you're safe here.'

Lila looked as though she wanted to believe him. Tom didn't think she was convinced.

'I'm still going to bed.'

'You're not going to run off again, are you?'

'Why d'you care?'

Tom's eyes widened. He was genuinely shocked by her words. 'What?'

Lila dropped her head. 'Sorry. 'Night.'

She left the room before Tom could say or do anything else.

He stood there alone. Heard her going upstairs, her bedroom door slam shut.

It was his turn to feel on edge now. He just hoped she wouldn't run. Not again. He had taken a liking to her in a short space of time. And he genuinely wanted to help her. If he could.

'Right, three cups of . . .' Rachel stopped in the doorway. 'Where's she gone?'

'Bed.'

'Oh. Well.' She placed the mugs down on a side table. 'Just us, then.' She sat on the sofa. Looked up at him. 'Come and join me.'

Tom's earlier arousal at the sight of her had vanished completely. He now regretted letting Rachel into the house. He wished he had listened to his earlier instincts. He wanted to go back in time, do it all again. Lila was spooked by Rachel and he didn't know why. He hoped she would tell him in the morning. He hoped he hadn't lost her trust completely.

'Right,' she said again, patting the seat. 'Sit down. I've had a hard day and I need to release some tension.' She began taking her jacket off. 'Come on, haven't got all night.'

Seemingly bewitched by her, Tom sat. Hating himself for what he had just done.

48

'Here we are again.'

Noah nodded at the words. Said nothing more. The St Petroc stone circle, bleached bone in moonlight against the surrounding darkness. And in the centre like a shadow detached from that darkness sat Morrigan.

'Sit by me.'

Morrigan was sitting on the flattened stone, the supposed sacrificial altar. Noah moved slowly forward, took his seat. Kept as much distance as he could between them. Said nothing. Waited.

'I'm not happy, Noah. Really not happy. Nor is anyone else. And neither should you be.'

'No, Morrigan.'

Morrigan turned, stared at him. '*No, Morrigan*? Is that all you have to say? Where's your explanation, your plan to make things work? To save something of the disaster you've created? I'm waiting.'

'I'm sorry,' he said, knowing it was the only person he ever said it to or would ever say it to.

'Well, I suppose that's a start. And how are you going to make things better, hmm? Put things back on track? There's a lot riding on this. A lot of people's futures are hanging on it. On what you're going to do next, what the next words out of your mouth will be. So?'

How did Morrigan always do this to him? It was as though Morrigan had some kind of power, some method to look right inside him, find the part of him that was full of fears and self-pity, self-disgust and self-loathing, that cordoned-off area he didn't show to anyone, not even himself if he could help it, and rip it out for all to see? And he didn't know how it was done. If it was a mind trick then it was a damned good one. If was some kind of witchcraft, then that really terrified him.

'I've got a plan,' he said.

'I'm waiting.'

'We need an outsider. It must be an outsider, yeah?'

'That's what was agreed.'

'Well, I've got one.'

'Look how you messed the last one up. A simple grab and what happened? People who you promised me wouldn't talk, talked. And then one of them goes and kills the outsider. Then we're back to square one. And everyone's waiting on you to make it right. Why should I listen to anything you have to say?'

'I've got someone in mind. And I've got someone in mind to get them. There won't be any fuss and nothing'll go wrong. I promise you.'

'Your promises are worth nothing.'

'But . . .' Despite the cold he was sweating. 'I can do this. Please. I know I messed up.' He took a deep breath after those words. They didn't come easy to him. 'Let me sort it. Give me a chance to make things right.'

Morrigan stared. Those unblinking, black eyes, a crow's eyes, seemed to bore right into him. 'I've got no choice but to trust you. We're all waiting for you.'

'I won't let you down.'

'You'd better not. Otherwise your past life might catch up with you.'

Morrigan knew. The only person here, or anywhere. Morrigan knew who he had been, what he had done. Morrigan had made the past go away. But Morrigan could bring it back again. He didn't doubt that.

'It's a girl,' he said quickly. 'The girl who ran. We've tracked her down. We know where she is. And we're going to get her.'

'We agreed an outsider.'

'She is an outsider. After what she did, what she tried to do, she's not one of us any more. And she won't be missed.'

'She'd better not be.'

'She won't. I promise you.'

'We've already had that conversation.' Dismissive, smiling maliciously.

Noah said nothing.

Morrigan stared at him once more, then looked straight ahead. Silence. Noah could hear the waves crashing against the cliffs, the wind susurrating through the trees behind, as though they were talking about him behind his back.

'I wanted to hear the screams,' said Morrigan, almost wistfully.

Again, Noah said nothing. Waited.

'That's the best part. The screams. When you prepare the victim for what awaits them. Soften them up. When they see their own blood, feel their own pain, their insides on the outside, parts that should be attached, unattached, even forced to eat parts of themselves for sustenance . . . when they can't believe what's happening to them, they've never experienced anything to compare with it before. When they look death in the face and feel so suddenly, amazingly alive. That's beautiful . . .'

Noah just stared straight ahead, silently hoping – begging – to be dismissed.

Morrigan continued. 'That's what we all feed on, what gives us strength. Nourishment. Sustenance. The screams, the fear, the blood. Their death gives us life. The more they scream, the more they suffer, the more we take from it, the more powerful we become.' Morrigan turned to face him. 'And because of you, that's what we shall miss.'

Noah was too scared to reply.

'The anticipation is everything. The final act is for the community to share. It is the beginning of the next phase. But the anticipation . . . is all mine to savour. And you are going to deprive me of that. Of sustenance. Of power.'

Noah felt he should say something. 'But you . . . you can still do all that.'

'No, Noah. I can't. The date has to be kept, does it not?'

Noah nodded.

'Then don't tell me what I can still do.' Morrigan's voice rose. 'You have deprived me of it. My pleasure. The ritual can still go ahead as it must do. But I will never forget what you have done to me. *Never*.'

Noah couldn't move, couldn't speak.

'Why are you still here? Haven't you got things to do?'

'Yuh – yes . . .'

Noah rose slowly to his feet, a puppet whose strings had been pulled.

'Go on then. And don't fail this time. Because it won't be just me you have to answer to. You know that.'

49

Noah watched the dawn rise. Sitting on the edge of the cliff, staring at the sea, lost in the distance. Crows swooped and cawed, reminding him he wasn't alone. Mocking him, laughing at him. Ahead were the gulls, sharp-eyed, sharp-beaked, opportunistic scavengers, razoring the cliff sides for prey. He knew all about gulls. Remembered them from the trawlers. Wheeling and diving. Flat eyes and knife-beaks, coming towards him. Fish guts or hands, they didn't care as long as they got fed.

The trawlers. He barely thought about them now. But Morrigan had brought all of that back. The past he had tried to keep hidden. The past Morrigan could unearth on a whim if he caused displeasure. The accompanying fear had kept him up all night. He couldn't go back to the camp, couldn't let them see that fear in him. His respect would be gone.

So he had sat on the cliff, remembering. When he used to be someone else. Someone ordinary. Dean Bosley. Failed fisherman turned local drug dealer, somewhere further down the coast. Happy with his good car and his rural ghetto-flash clothes, his easy money and his very local notoriety. Fishing was dying. Brexit had seen to that. When the opportunity to peddle drugs came along, he took it. And found most of his customers in his old sailing mates, all needing something to help keep them awake on the forty-eight-hour trips. And that had been him. Until the deaths.

The first involved both crew-members of a trawler. Steering their boat back to harbour they misjudged their distance and capsized. Drowned. Both high on amphetamines.

The second was out at sea. A miscalculation with the net-gathering equipment and one of the fishermen went overboard. Tangled up in netting, he couldn't be saved. Amphetamines again.

The third was Ron, Dean's old skipper. Heart attack. Whisky and amphetamines.

It didn't take the rest of the small town long to work out that Dean was the common denominator in all the deaths. He was the supplier. The locals came for him like angry, pitchfork-wielding villagers in an old horror movie. So he ran. And ended up lying low in a traveller commune in north Cornwall. Surfing, scrounging, dealing, whatever. He did all right.

And he changed his name. Noah. A nod to his fisherman past.

Some of the travellers he found tedious. Middle-class university dropouts railing against all manner of injustices done to them by the Man, the Pigs, the System or whoever. But always popping back to Mum and Dad's every other weekend with a pile of washing. Noah had no time for them. And their blow wasn't as good as the stuff he could get.

But there was a hardcore band of those who thought like him, acted like him. He became the gang's dealer, getting stuff from his old contact Conroy, who had relocated to Newquay, and selling it to the travellers. They liked him, or tolerated him at least because he kept them supplied. And slowly he slithered up the hierarchy. Not that there was one to start with; he created it. And a few months later he was top of the heap. The boss. Dean was long gone.

And he found an added bonus. Lots of rich people had second homes in the area, empty most of the time. His gang would do the places over, Conroy would fence the stuff. And everyone was happy. Until a new face arrived.

'Detective Sergeant Hickox,' said the newcomer, holding his warrant card in front of Noah's face, impossible to miss. Medium height, medium build, wearing an anorak over a shirt and tie. Every inch a nondescript person. But his eyes told a different story. They held the gaze of whoever they looked at, scrutinised, judged. Knew things about you that you would never tell another person.

'Noah,' he said. 'What can I do for you?'

Hickox smiled. 'I don't think so, Dean.'

Noah blinked. Tried not to let the surprise show. Didn't know how successful he was at it. Regained his composure quickly, kept talking. 'No one by that name here, mate. Noah. That's me.'

'Stop the bullshit, Dean. Let's have a chat, you and me.'

Noah wanted to run. He looked around to see if anyone else had heard. No one in earshot. He turned back to Hickox. 'Think you got the wrong bloke, mate.'

'You're Dean, who used to work on the boats until you got a better offer. Supplied amphetamines that killed at least five people. Then did a runner and hoped people would forget you.' He stepped in closer. Noah smelled breath mints. 'But I didn't, Dean. It's taken a few years, but here we are.' He looked around. 'Nice place. Not your camp, obviously. The area, I meant. Or at least I bet it was before your lot turned up.'

'You've got the wrong bloke.'

'No, I haven't. Want to know how I found you? Big spike in burglaries in this area. Had a sniff around. What do I find? You lot. Did a bit of surveillance. And who do I see? Our old friend Dean. Killed those fishermen, then ran away. Now he's all ready to come home.'

Noah stepped in close. 'Listen. I'm not Dean Bosley.'

'Never said he was called Bosley.'

Noah reddened. Fear became anger. 'Get out. I'll get a lawyer and fuckin' have you.'

'Be my guest.'

He took another step closer, held what he hoped was a menacing stare. 'This is private property. Come back when you've got a warrant.'

Hickox stared at him like he wanted to kill him. Then his features cracked into a smile.

'Fair enough, squire. See you soon, Dean.'

He turned and left.

Noah was straight on the phone to Conroy. The big man managed to convince him it was just a fishing trip, that Hickox had nothing on him. Noah wasn't convinced. Wanted Hickox dealt with properly.

Conroy thought. 'There is something you could do. Or rather, someone you could talk to.'

'Who?'

'Someone I know who does things for people. I can set up a meeting if you like. But I've got to warn you. It's not what you're expecting. Keep an open mind.'

'What d'you mean?'

'Just keep an open mind, that's all.'

Conroy was right. It wasn't what he had been expecting.

Morrigan's house was so ordinary he almost missed it. He knocked at the door, was ushered inside. He looked around, not quite sure what he was doing there, what he was about to say.

'Don't be shy. Just tell me what you want.'

Noah weighed up his choices. He wasn't good at talking to strangers, sharing intimate facts of his life with them. He didn't want them to have something over him, some kind of leverage they could use. That was his job.

Morrigan glanced at a watch. 'Haven't got all night. You going to talk or not?'

Noah made a decision. It was to be the most momentous one he ever made or would ever make. 'Someone from my past's come back. And I want rid of him. Is there a way to do that?'

'There's always a way.' Morrigan smiled, the flames from the fire reflecting in those crow-like eyes. 'What d'you want to have happen to him?'

'I just want him to . . . to go away. Forget about me. Never come back.'

Morrigan became thoughtful, nodded. 'That can be done. I have a ritual for that.'

'A what? Fuck you on about?'

Morrigan became angry. 'What did you think this was? Why did you come to me? A ritual. To get rid of this policeman once and for all. D'you want to do it or d'you want to leave?'

Noah thought. This must be what Conroy meant about keeping an open mind. But a ritual. That meant witchcraft. Demons. Satan. Shit . . . Horror films had always scared him. He never let on, didn't want to appear weak before his friends, but he couldn't watch anything like that. Because it was all real. The occult terrified him.

Morrigan kept staring, waiting for an answer.

Noah felt like he had no choice. 'Yeah,' he said, voice weak, 'give me the ritual.'

Morrigan did. Gave him instructions to carry out, told him what items he would need for it to be successful, when to do it. He made notes. Looked round the room once more. This wasn't like in films or on TV. Demons always meet in scary places, not someone's front room. He would have laughed, if he hadn't been so terrified.

'Now remember,' said Morrigan, 'I shall also be casting spells and performing rituals while you do yours. These are for the completion of your task. I'll be aiding you. Never forget, I am with you. *Always* with you.' Those crow eyes glinted.

He left the house, went back to the site. Not quite believing what he had just done.

It wasn't until later that night when, unable to sleep, he thought of something: how did Morrigan know it was a policeman he wanted rid of? He hadn't mentioned that.

Never forget, I am with you. Always with you . . .

He lay staring and scared, until the morning light appeared.

The ritual was all he concentrated on. Getting it right. Ensuring Hickox was gone for ever. First, he had to make a doll.

Clay, the instructions said. Noah tried with earth, wetting it, mixing it, before realising that wasn't the kind of clay it meant.

So he found an art supplies shop in Truro, bought some mod-elling clay. He had never been good with his hands, unless it was rolling spliffs, chopping out lines or putting someone in their place, and he found the creation of the doll difficult. The instructions said to keep the person in mind the whole time and he did, hoping that the mental image of Hickox would be translated into the doll's likeness. Looking at the lumpen, mis-shapen thing he ended up with, he wasn't sure. But it was the best he could make. He left it to harden, followed the rest of the instructions.

The ritual had to take place at midnight. He had to be alone. He was expected to starve himself for twenty-four hours previously and take nothing but water and, if needed, a couple of spliffs. He needed them, he decided. He also had to have some needles, the bigger the better, and had to repeat an incantation as he plunged the needles into the body of the doll.

He learned the incantation off by heart:

'Three times I wound thee,

Three times you burn,

Three times I curse you,

To hell, never to return . . .'

And he learned the actions that accompanied it.

He invested so much time and effort into it that he began to believe the spell would work. And then the night before it was to go ahead, he received an unexpected visitor. Morrigan.

His heart beat faster. Fear overtook him.

'While you perform your ritual I will be performing mine. To help you.'

'Doing what?' Curious despite himself.

'Preparing hag-stones for him, blasting him working in the Circle of Arte . . . many ways.'

Noah didn't have a clue what Morrigan was talking about. 'Why?'

Morrigan smiled. 'Because you will become a useful ally to me. And you need to see my power demonstrated.'

As soon as this is done, he thought, I'm off. Get that copper off my back and you won't see me for dust.

The night arrived. Cloudy but dry. Cold. He drew the chalk circle round the fire he had made, sat in it. Waited until midnight. To make sure no one from the site was around, he had taken himself off to a quiet spot where he wouldn't be disturbed. Then he propped the doll in front of him, took the needles from his pocket. Began the ritual.

'Three times I wound thee . . .'

He stuck the needle in as far as it would go, left it there.

'Three times I wound thee . . .'

Another needle, another stab.

'Three times I wound thee . . .'

And again.

'Three times you burn . . .'

He took the doll, stuck it into the flames three times. Each time holding it until his fingers threatened to burn as well, then withdrawing it. It sat in his hand glistening, starting to melt.

'Three times I curse you . . .'

That part was easy. He hurled as much invective as he could at the doll. Found it difficult to stop at three.

'To hell, never to return . . .'

He threw the doll in the flames, watched it burn.

Now what?

'Thought I might find you here.'

Noah looked up, startled. There stood Detective Sergeant Hickox, arms folded, cigarette in mouth, smile on his face.

'Got a tip-off you were thinking of doing a runner. Got down here real quick.' He looked at the fire. 'Been watching you for a while. Didn't want to interrupt.' He laughed. 'Like playing with dolls, do you?'

Noah didn't stop to think, just became action and reaction. He jumped to his feet and lunged at Hickox, who, taken by surprise, fell under Noah's first blow.

'You're supposed to be dead . . .' Noah screamed. '*Dead* . . .'

Hickox retaliated quickly, landing a punch on the side of Noah's head, trying to scramble to his feet. Noah was knocked off balance. Hickox got up.

'Right, you little fucker, I've got something to haul you in for now . . .'

Noah realised he had done just what the copper wanted him to do. But he wouldn't go with him. No way. Desperation kicked in. He picked up the dry end of a burning log from the fire, swung it at Hickox. It connected with the man's face. He screamed, hands moving up instinctively. Emboldened, Noah shoved the burning log directly at his face.

Hickox tried to duck and dodge out of the way, soon lost his footing. Fell to the ground beside the flames.

Noah didn't stop to think. He picked up a second burning log, flung it into Hickox's face. Then another. Hickox screamed. Noah smelled burning flesh, heard sizzling, knelt down next to him.

'I'm not going back, I'm not going back . . .'

He took the log, raised it and brought it down on Hickox's head. Again and again until he lay still.

Now he looks like the clay doll, thought Noah, and started to laugh.

His laugh became so hysterical he didn't think it would ever stop.

Noah sat next to Hickox's dead body all night. The adrenaline come-down left him shaking and sobbing. He had killed a man. Actually killed a man. And not just any man, but a copper. He knew how they looked after their own. Knew what they did to a cop killer.

He had to get away. Hide the body. Had to . . .

Calm down. Think. Plan.

Hiding the body was easy. Just bundled it up in an old tarp, stuck it in the back of a van at the site. Said no one was to go in there. Nobody argued.

Deciding what to do with it was the hard part. And then deciding what to do with himself. The more he planned, the more he thought of Morrigan. He couldn't shake the feeling that he had been set up. Fear or not, he had to go and see Morrigan.

'How did it go, Noah?'

'How d'you think?'

'Please keep your voice down. I have neighbours.'

Noah began pacing the floor. 'It was a fuckin' disaster. You know it was.'

Morrigan arched an eyebrow. Smiled. It wasn't pleasant. 'That's what you wanted, isn't it?'

'Yeah, but not like this. I killed him.'

Another smile from Morrigan. Like a chill that had entered the room.

'Well, aren't you going to say anything?'

'What would you like me to say, Noah? Or should I call you Dean?'

Noah stopped, mouth open. Whatever he had been about to say left him immediately. What had he just heard?

'I know who you are. I know what you've done, and who was after you.'

It was too much for Noah. His head swam, pulse pounded. 'Why?' It was all he could manage, his voice feeble and broken.

'Because I needed you. You're going to be useful to me.'

'Why didn't you just ask?'

'Oh, that wouldn't have worked. You needed a demonstration of what I'm capable of. Otherwise . . .' Morrigan shrugged. 'Where's the loyalty?'

'So this was all just . . . this ritual, it was just bullshit?'

273

'Rituals are never bullshit, Dean. This one worked perfectly. I wanted you in a position where you would be able to assist me, let us say, and you needed to get rid of an irritant from your past.'

'But I killed him . . .'

'Yes, you did. And when you get rid of the body, I'll be the only other person who knows. The only living person, of course. And that's how I want it to be.'

Noah looked round the room again. So boring, so mundane. He couldn't believe that anything special happened here. But it did. He was witnessing a very special kind of evil. 'So you're going to blackmail me, that it?'

'Remember I said I was performing rituals of my own last night? Those, along with your actions, will aid me. Your ritual was for my benefit. Not yours.'

'You told him I was there, you knew I'd . . . I'd do something to him.'

'Hoped. Not knew. But I did think something like this would happen. It's not difficult to plan if you know what you're doing. It's all about power, Dean. And that's what I have now. Over you.'

He just stared ahead, like an animal trapped in a cage realising there's no escape.

'Power, Dean. The most potent magic of all. Power gives one the ability to transform things, to remake them in one's own image. To create willing acolytes. Power. That's real magic.'

He said nothing.

'You can keep on calling yourself Noah. In fact, I prefer it. You will get rid of the body to my specifications. As I said, I'm the only other person who knows what has happened and where the late, unlamented Detective Sergeant Hickox's final resting place will be. And in the meantime, I will need your services.'

'For what?' Noah almost didn't dare to ask. He certainly didn't want to hear the answer.

274

'There is a time coming when I will need you. And you will be there for me. Because you know what happens if you aren't.'

It was a warm sunny day when he left Morrigan's house but none of that touched him. It felt like a giant open jail that he was walking around in only through the grace of Morrigan, but in reality he was trapped in it.

Noah stood up. The day, in all its bleakness, was in full swing now. His reverie had got him nowhere, just reminded him of how much he hated and feared Morrigan.

He turned his back on the sea, walked slowly back to the camp. Waiting to see what fresh hell awaited him.

50

Tom had barely spoken to Lila during the day. Or rather, she had barely spoken to him.

She had clammed up, whatever was on her mind staying there. All the good work of getting her to trust him, to open up the previous evening, had been undone by Rachel's arrival. Or by his response to Rachel's arrival. And he felt as bad as he could about that.

It was always the same with Rachel. Sex followed by remorse. Never again, he always told himself. I'll be stronger next time. But he knew he wouldn't be. She would turn up, weave her sex magic on him and the cycle would begin again.

Rachel had only stayed for a couple of hours. The sex hadn't been great; he had been distracted throughout, disappointed in himself. Like pushing rope, Rachel had said at one point which made him feel even worse.

As he went to bed he was sure he could hear noises from behind Lila's bedroom door. She was still awake. That made him feel even more guilty. If she couldn't sleep and was having night terrors then he should have been there to help her. He felt like he had let her down.

She communicated only through shrugs and monosyllables. Picked up the Bukowski collection she had been reading the previous day, continued with that. Ignored him. Or tried to. She sneaked glances at him from the corner of her eye when she thought he wasn't looking. He tried to read her features. She didn't seem scared; maybe she was just as disappointed in him as he was. If so, she had every right to be.

'I'm just going to work. Will you be OK here?'

They had eaten and she had picked up the book again. 'Yeah,' she said, eyes never leaving the page.

'I'll try not to be late. If you're still up maybe we could spend some time together? If you like.'

'Yeah.' A shrug. Non-committal.

'OK then. See you later.'

She didn't reply. He looked at her, pretending to read.

'Listen, I . . . I'm sorry.'

She almost looked up. 'For what?'

'For last night. For inviting Rachel in. I shouldn't have done it.'

Another shrug. 'Your house. If you want your girlfriend here, that's up to you. Nothing to do with me.'

He knew she was suppressing what she really wanted to say.

'It was the wrong thing to do. I won't do it again.'

Another shrug. 'Do what you like.' The words said so casually, the emotion behind them anything but.

Tom stared at her some more but she was affecting not to look at him. He left the house.

All the way to work he thought of her, how he could make things right again. But he was surprised out of his reverie when he reached the Sail Makers. It was busy.

'What's going on?' he asked Pearl, taken aback by the number of people, the noise.

'Round Table again,' she replied. 'Upstairs. Special meeting about the marina. Sometimes they stop off down here, get fortified before tackling work of national importance.' She smiled while she spoke.

'Hey,' said Tom, 'maybe they'll ask me to become a member.'

Pearl laughed. 'Yeah, if you're still here in thirty years' time. You might not be considered the newcomer by then.'

'Don't worry,' said Tom, smiling. 'I bet I will.'

'I'm sure. They won't even let me join. Mum and Dad say it's not for me, I wouldn't be interested.'

'Dodged a bullet there.'

She laughed. He joined in.

'It used to be organising local fetes and stuff like that. But the marina's all they talk about now.'

'Spent the money before they've got it?'

'No, more like a real determination to make it happen here.'

'What, like finding which local councillors to bribe and having a whip-round?'

Pearl's smile faded. 'Don't know what they're doing or what they're planning but they take it very seriously. Never seen them like this before. Fixated. Only thing they talk about.' Someone came to the bar, a middle-aged farmer. 'Evening, Bill. What'll it be?'

Bill Watson asked for a pint of bitter. Pearl poured it. Tom looked at the clientele once more.

There was a guy in a wheelchair who two other people were helping up the stairs. A woman walked up behind him, presumably his wife, although from her body language she seemed more attached to the strapping, handsome man who was holding on to the wheelchair's base. A few farmers he didn't know came in and went upstairs, all waiting patiently for the wheelchair to be moved. Pearl was right, Tom decided. All of them seemed to have the same kind of expression. Driven. Determined. Desperate, even. And something about the eyes too. Wide, even flickering with fear or apprehension. On all of them.

Then Rachel entered. Tom looked surprised. He smiled at her. She was out of uniform and he couldn't help but stare. Despite what he had thought earlier he could feel his body responding just at the sight of her.

'Evening,' he said.

'Hello, Tom,' she replied, as if she barely knew him, eyes anywhere but on him.

Her attitude took him aback. He knew they couldn't be seen to be overly friendly in public, but she seemed decidedly frosty towards him.

279

'You OK?' he asked.

'Fine. I'll have a gin and tonic while I'm waiting, please.'

'Right.' He didn't know what else to say and she offered nothing in the way of conversation. He handed the drink to her, took her money.

'Thanks.' She turned, made her way upstairs.

He watched her go. Wondering what had just happened.

The retired teachers, Emlyn and Isobel, came in next, all smiles as usual. They also took their drinks upstairs. Tom was thinking again about Rachel but didn't get far. The next person through the door was Pirate John.

Tom stared. Pirate John looked terrible. He seemed to have aged about ten years. His face was grey, his features sunken and sallow.

'You OK?' he asked as John came towards the bar.

Pirate John looked at him, opened his mouth, but whatever was going to come out was stopped. A farmer came up, put his arm round Pirate John's shoulder.

'Good to have you with us,' he said, his voice hearty, his red face smiling. 'Coming up?'

Pirate John nodded and allowed himself to be led upstairs. He gave a backward glance towards Tom, his eyes begging, imploring. Tom stared back, concerned. He crossed over to Pearl.

'You seen the state of John?'

'Yeah. Awful.'

'And he looked scared. You don't think it's got anything to do with what he wanted to talk to us about?"

Pearl looked at him, frowned, eyes widened. 'You think?'

'Let's nab him afterwards. Maybe he actually does have something important to tell us.'

'For once,' said Pearl, aiming for levity. Missing.

51

Pirate John sat at the back of the room. It seemed like the whole village was crammed in there. People he had grown up amongst, been to school with, shared his life with. His friends. Now they couldn't bring themselves to look at him. He reckoned he knew why. When they looked at him, noted his defiance, they were looking at the part of themselves they couldn't bear to see.

He had been thinking a lot recently. About his situation in the village, about his life in general. About fear. And he had come to understand something. People were capable of anything if they were given permission to do it. The Stanford Prison experiments where half the student volunteers were made jailers and half prisoners. No matter what they were like before they took part, they all soon lived up to their roles. Especially the jailers. The civil war in the former Yugoslavia in the nineties. Rwanda. Neighbour turning on neighbour. As viciously as possible. Coming home from work and slaughtering the family next door. Because they were told they could. Given permission by a higher authority to let their basest urges run free.

As he kept looking round the room, searching for a face that would look towards him, smile even, his mind slipped back to when it all started. It was a kind of end of innocence, in a way. He had thought he knew people, knew what was going on in the village. But he was blissfully unaware of what was really happening. That first Round Table meeting. When everything changed. When Tony Williamson disappeared and Morrigan took over.

It had started as normal. All milling about in the bar, enjoying a few pre-meeting drinks, bit of chat. They were all there. The farmers drinking their ale, herding together looking slightly lost in a social situation. The retired teachers, Emlyn and Isobel, the local policewoman Rachel Bellfair, Dan and Elaine, of course. The usual production of getting Grant Jenner, head of the Round Table, and his wheelchair up the stairs.

Shame about Grant, thought Pirate John. Crashed his car one night and was now paralysed. He liked a drink and, it was agreed by common consent, he was lucky to be alive.

Tempers were going to be high that night. It was to be expected. They were there to discuss the proposed marina.

Grant was wheeled to the front. 'Thank you all for coming. As you know, this is a special meeting. Or at least a meeting with one agenda. The marina. I'm sure you've all heard about it by now. There's a shortlist, and St Petroc's on it. I don't need to tell you just how important this is for our village, for the whole area. After the government threw us over the cliff with the whole Brexit thing – and no, I don't want an argument, thanks – we need this. Desperately. We need this investment, the jobs. We need it or, quite simply, we die.'

He waited, let that sink in.

'We've got the economic figures for St Petroc and the surrounding area. The demographics of who's living here. The young people have all but gone. The businesses in the town are closing at a rate much higher than the national average. Wages are falling. Unemployment is rising rapidly, again much faster than it is nationally. The Brexit crowd, Gove and Johnson and their ilk, lied to us. Things aren't going to be the same for farmers, they're not going to get better. They're going to be worse. Much worse. Without an EU deal, the subsidies, the Common Agricultural Policy, sheep farmers are going to go to the wall. We're not getting seasonal labour from Europe. I don't need to tell you all how much we've already lost in letting crops rot because we can't get pickers.'

Murmurs of assent in the room.

'Smaller farmers are already selling up, letting big agri-business concerns take over their land and do what they like. We supply sixty per cent of our own food in this country. We're only ever nine meals away from empty supermarket shelves. And it's going to get worse. We're in a dying land. And we have to do something about it.'

Again he paused, hoping his message had sunk in to the whole room. It had: they all looked concerned, angry, despairing.

Grant spoke once more. 'These are desperate times. And desperate times call for desperate measures. Now, I want you to listen carefully to what I have to say. And listen with an open mind. Several of us have been taking part in, shall we say, unorthodox practices recently, in order to keep our land, our livelihoods, our –' He paused, looked at his wife who was sitting next to Paul Priestly. He looked away again. 'As I say, unorthodox practices. But they've worked. So I want to say to all of you, what worked for us might work for the whole village.'

He scanned the room once more, making sure his message was hitting home. It looked like it was. Pirate John just frowned. Wondered how – and what – he had missed out on.

'You all know what I'm talking about. Most of you have been part of it. We've tried everything to make our voices heard, to get our position understood, and we've got nowhere. So we've been delving back into the old ways. Making them work for us. And the results have been nothing less than astonishing. So I'm asking you now to take the next step in our crusade to get that marina built here and save St Petroc. Are we all agreed?'

A loud murmur of assent went round the room. Pirate John had no idea what was happening.

And then it clicked. He remembered Bill Watson, alone in his field, covered in cow's blood, howling at the moon. Bill Watson with his problems that mysteriously got sorted out after that night. Pirate John understood. The old religion. That's what they were talking about.

'Good. Then let me welcome to the floor someone you're all familiar with.'

Morrigan stood up, walked slowly to the front of the room, turned and looked at the crowd. Smiled.

'You all know me. I've been active in the Round Table for years. Born and bred here. And, as you know, I'm something of an expert on the old ways. Looking round this room I see plenty of faces that I've helped over the years. I've turned sceptics to believers. I've shown you that the old ways may have fallen out of fashion but they still retain their power. And you believe that. All of you. Or you wouldn't be here tonight, listening to me.'

A few nods, no dissent. Morrigan continued.

'I can ensure that the marina comes here. I can ensure wealth, jobs and stability for all our futures. There are plenty of people in this room who will vouch for me and what I can do. What I have done. The question is, do you want me to do it this time? And are you with me if I do?'

They all looked at each other. A few shrugs, a few nods. Grunts of assent.

'Anyone against?'

No one. Pirate John wondered what he had got himself into but still didn't dare raise his hand.

'Carried unanimously,' Morrigan said, those dark crow eyes smiling.

A few laughs. Morrigan became serious.

'Now. Before we proceed there are a few things you all need to be aware of. What we will be doing may not be strictly within the law. But I assure you, if my instructions are carried out to the letter, no harm will come to anyone in this room. OK? Now. Anyone who doesn't want to take part should leave now.'

Pirate John wanted to get up, to speak out. What was happening? He certainly hadn't got the memo. But no one else moved. So he stayed where he was too. Morrigan smiled once more.

'Good.' Morrigan looked towards the back of the room. Kept smiling as the door opened and some newcomers arrived. 'Noah. Good of you to turn up. Oh. You've brought friends.'

Noah entered. Some of his travellers, tall, well-built ones with flattened noses, prison tattoos and scarred arms, entered with him. They stood at the back, arms folded. People turned round to look, faces all concerned, worried.

'Please don't be alarmed. I invited Noah and his friends to attend. They're part of our community as well and after all, we're going to be allies from now on. Working together for all of our futures. So again, if anyone has a problem with this, leave now. If you stay, then we must all assume each other's complicity in what we are about to achieve.'

No one spoke. No one moved. Pirate John felt like he had slipped outside his body and was watching it from above. Numb, unable to move, to speak.

'Now. I'm going to ask you all to open your minds. As Grant said. To embrace practices and beliefs that you may never have had any dealings with before. Powerful beliefs that can change not just the way you think and feel, but the way you live. For all of us. You must be prepared to think the unthinkable, do the undoable. Whatever we decide, we go forward together. As one. You have all agreed, you are now committed. You are part of this. And no one will be permitted to drop out. So for the last time, are we all together on this?'

A few murmurings, anxious glances around to look at Noah and his boys. Someone stood up and, head down, walked out. Another followed. Then silence. Pirate John wanted to move but felt he was rooted to his chair.

'We are an army now, waging a war we cannot lose. The Morrigan is flying above you all. The crow who sees everything. The Morrigan can foretell the death of our enemies, the victory of our forces. The Morrigan will reward the righteous, punish the blasphemers, the weak. The Morrigan is the goddess of fate and battle. The Celtic great queen, the crow, the raven. You will all now henceforth address me as Morrigan.'

Morrigan talked. Outlined the plan, the parts everyone was to play.

'Follow my instructions to the letter and we will not fail. I have never failed yet. This will not be the first time.'

'If this is to proceed and we are to get the right and just outcome, we need one thing above all. A sacrifice.'

No one interrupted.

'This sacrifice should be an outsider. Not one of our own. No one we know. No one we love. No one we can be in any way attached to. Their suffering, their screams, will fortify us. Give us power. Make us unstoppable. Their ultimate death according to ritual will provide us with what we need to fertilise our earth, to make the future grow from it. The ritual must be carried out on a specific date and at a specific time. The sacrifice will be chosen by—'

'What the hell is going on here?'

All eyes turned to the source of the new voice. They moved slowly, like sleepers wakened from a dream or enchantment, mesmerised by Morrigan's presence and words.

Tony Williamson had stood up.

'Just listen to yourselves. Listen to what you're actually proposing. It's madness.'

'It's the will of the people,' Morrigan replied. 'And you have to serve the will of the people.'

'Is it bollocks the will of the people,' said Tony. 'It's mass hysteria, is what it is. It's desperation. It's lies.'

'Lies? Desperation? Aren't there enough examples of what I've achieved from the people in this room tonight? Haven't they witnessed my power first-hand?'

'No, they haven't. Just auto-suggestion and mass hysteria. That's all. It's pathetic. Don't you agree?' He looked at some of his friends.

Or those he had thought were his friends. None of them would make eye contact now. 'Really? You're going to say nothing, let this charade continue? Bill, what about it? It's all bollocks, you said so yourself. Tell them that.'

Bill Watson turned away. Mumbled at the floor. 'Reckon there might be something in it.'

Tony shook his head. 'Grant? Please. Please, Grant . . .'

Grant looked away from him also. 'Please, Tony. You don't know what you're talking about.'

'But Grant—'

'You don't know the full facts. You've got to see the bigger picture.' He looked across at his wife, smiled. She returned it.

'Jack, what about you?'

Jack, resplendent in his new tweeds, just shrugged. 'Sorry, Tony.'

Morrigan smiled. 'Shall we take a vote?'

Tony stood up. 'Do what you fucking like. I'm not going to be part of this.'

'Where are you going?'

'Away. From here. From all of you mentalists. Jesus Christ . . .'

'You are forbidden to speak of what has been discussed in this room tonight.'

'Am I bollocks. First opportunity I get, I'll be shouting it.'

Everyone seemed to move uncomfortably as one.

Morrigan's eyes glittered darkly. 'I would advise you not to, Tony.'

'Really? Or what? You're going to kill me or something? Put a spell on me?' He gave a bitter laugh. 'Get real.'

'I don't need to kill you, Tony Williamson.' Morrigan leaned forward. 'Consider yourself crow-warned. You know what that means.'

'Yeah. And I'm terrified.' He didn't hide the sarcasm in his voice.

'Remember one thing, Tony Williamson.' Morrigan again.

He turned, waited.

'Beware the calling of the dead.'

He laughed. 'Oh, for fuck's sake.'

'Mock all you like. But if you walk along the cliffs around here, where there have been shipwrecks off the coast, you can hear the dead calling out their names. And sometimes they call out the names of those about to join them. Take care you don't hear your name among them.'

'Well, that's wonderful to hear but I've got to go,' he said. 'The twenty-first century called. They want me back. Fucking superstitious inbreds, the lot of you. I hope you're all disgusted with yourselves. You should be.'

And he left, slamming the door behind him.

Morrigan waited until the hubbub had died down, then nodded towards Noah. He nodded in return, gestured to two of his boys who also slipped out of the door. Morrigan looked at the rest of the room and smiled.

'I trust no one else wants to follow his example?'

Everyone stayed where they were. Pirate John didn't dare move. He was part of it now, whether he liked it or not.

Morrigan smiled. 'Good. Now that we're all on the same page, is there any other business?'

That was the last time anyone saw Tony Williamson alive. His body washed up several months later, further down the shore. It was barely recognisable; partially eaten by animals and fish, buffeted and torn by rocks. Only identifiable by the remaining contents of his wallet. There was a coroner's inquest. No one called told of the argument, of his leaving the Round Table meeting early. Nor of Noah's men leaving at the same time. The verdict: death by misadventure. Walking too close to the cliff edge at night. No one from the village contradicted it. No one dared.

Pirate John came awake, reverie over, back to the present meeting. A lot had happened since that first one. He hadn't listened to the details tonight, didn't want to know too much, even though he was already implicated by his presence. Morrigan was concluding.

'Go. To your homes, your places of work. Wait. Not long now: the time is almost upon us. There is one last piece to be moved into place tonight. The most important piece. That is already under way. Then you will all receive the call. You know where to gather, what to do. And once our task has been accomplished, we can all look forward to a bright and prosperous future for each and every one of us.' Morrigan smiled, lifted wing-like arms. 'Go.'

52

Lila couldn't concentrate on her book, on the TV, on anything. She was scared. Every creak, every groan in the house made her jump. The branches outside hitting the windows, the distant sea washing up on the shore. Everything conspired to make her feel unsafe.

She had felt safe with Tom. For the first time in a long time – years, even – and that, she thought bitterly, had been her biggest mistake. To think, she had been about to share secrets with him, tell him things that might have made him hate her, might have led him to turning her in. She was beginning to think he wouldn't. But the policewoman's arrival changed all that.

So she and Tom were lovers. And she'd said she was off duty, not interested in Lila. It shouldn't have mattered, but it did. If she told Tom everything, he might tell the policewoman. And she wouldn't be off duty then. Lila couldn't take that chance. She would have to go. She didn't know where, but she couldn't stay here any more.

He had tried to talk to her before he left but she hadn't given him anything in return. Afraid of what would come out, she had said nothing. Just waited for him to leave, then sat, afraid all night.

There was a knock at the door.

Lila froze. It wasn't Tom. He wouldn't be knocking at his own house. And it couldn't be the policewoman, she knew Tom was out. Lila shuddered. Or could it be? Perhaps she'd come back to talk to her on her own, make her confess, take her in.

Another knock.

She listened, unmoving. No voices. She hadn't heard a car or anything approach. And she had been listening intently.

Another knock. And with it, a voice:

'Lila . . . Lila . . . you in there?'

A fist slammed into her stomach, her heart. She knew that voice.

'Lila . . .'

Kai.

She could hear her blood pumping all round her body. She had thought the policewoman was the last person she wanted to see. She was wrong.

'Lila, please . . . I know you're in there. Please . . . talk to me, it's . . . you've got to let me in . . .'

His voice was so pathetic. Pleading. Desperate. Scared. But she wouldn't open the door. No way.

'They're . . . I've got to get away. They're coming after me now, I . . . please, just . . . talk to me, please . . .'

And then he started sobbing.

'*Please*, Lila . . . help me, please . . .'

She moved to the front door, put her back against it, said nothing. Listened.

'They . . . I'm sorry. For what I did. I'm sorry. So, so sorry . . .'

More crying.

'It was . . . I had no choice . . . they, they made me do it . . . I'm sorry. So sorry . . .'

Lila listened. Because after all, it was Kai. The man who had loved her – *said* he'd loved her. And he was breaking his heart now. Her own heart softened slightly.

'Kai . . .'

'Lila? You're there? You're there? Please, let me in, please . . .' Frantic scrabbling at the door. 'I need to talk, I need to say sorry . . . please . . .'

'Why? Why should I believe you? Why should I let you in?'

'Please, you have to believe me, please . . . they're after me, they . . . I escaped. They . . . Noah and them, they . . . Kyle. That student. He's . . . oh, God, he's . . . they killed, him Lila. He's dead . . .'

'What?'

'And now they want me to take his place. They want me to ... please, Lila, *plea-sse* ... I've got ... I don't know who else to turn to ...'

She said nothing. Listened.

'I'm ... I'm running. Getting away. They're after me and ... I'm running.'

'How did you escape?'

'They weren't as clever as they thought. Same way you did. And I'm sorry. Sorry for what I put you though. For what I did to you. I know that now and I hate myself for it. But I'm getting away from here. And it's not safe for you, either. They're still looking for you ... Come with me, Lila. Come on. Come with me. We can escape together. Start a new life somewhere where they can't find us ...'

Lila's hand went to the lock, paused.

'Are you lying to me?'

'No ...' Almost hysterical in his reply. 'Please, please ... why would I come here? Why would I warn you, help you, try to get away? Why?'

She could hear her own breathing, deafening in her ears.

'Please, Lila ... hurry ... they know you're here ... come with me ... we haven't got much time ...'

Lila's hand went to the door handle once more, faltered. Tom was a good man. Or had seemed to be, until the policewoman showed up. Now, she didn't know if she could trust him any more.

Kai ... she didn't know how she felt about him. She had never loved him, not really, or at least she didn't think so. And she hated him for how he had betrayed her. But maybe ...

Maybe he was what she deserved. Who she deserved.

The thought hit her hard.

Maybe her mother was right. She was worthless, the wrong one to die. She had a demon inside her and didn't need saving, didn't need a new life. Maybe Kai was her destiny. The life she had to live.

So, with a heavy heart, she opened the door.

He looked dreadful. She had never seen him looking so bad. Bruises on his face were fading to sickly yellow but still held hearts of dark purple. His clothing was torn, tattered, his eyes wide and staring. Haunted. He smiled when he saw her. The kind of smile to break a heart.

'Lila . . .'

He grabbed her to him, held her close.

'Kai, come on, we'd better . . .'

She tried to pull away. He kept her tight to him.

She felt other arms on her, gripping her from behind. Strong, immovable.

'Kai, what—'

The arms pulled her away from him. He looked behind her, gestured. She heard a motor, saw headlights starting up, rounding the corner coming towards her. The men pulled her towards the vehicle.

She stared at him.

Kai shrugged.

'Sorry, Lila. You or me. What could I do?'

Lila tried to scream. It was cut off by a gag in her mouth. She was bundled into the van, Kai jumped in after her, slid the door shut, and they disappeared into the night.

53

Tom was restocking the back shelves with pint glasses when the meeting broke up and the Round Tablers collectively made their way downstairs.

'Here we go,' Pearl said to him, smiling. 'Brace yourself for the rush.'

There were only ever a few who stayed after the meeting to drink; Tom understood her sarcasm.

Emlyn was the first to the bar, beating the others who were manhandling the wheelchair down the stairs.

'Usual?' asked Tom.

'Please,' said Emlyn with his nervous giggle.

Tom began to pour a pint and a half of the local ale he and Isobel liked.

'Good meeting? Get a lot done?'

'Oh, yes.' Another nervous giggle. 'Lots. Really making head-way.' He gave a curious look straight at Tom. 'Won't be long now.'

'What won't?'

'You'll see.' He paid for the beer and walked away.

Tom frowned, shook his head, went back to his duties, serving what customers there were, until he noticed Pirate John come down.

Pirate John had waited until everyone else had gone before him, was hovering around the base of the stairs, putting a clear distance between himself and the rest of the Round Tablers. He had looked bad when he entered, but whatever had gone on up there seemed to have made him even worse. He kept looking at Tom, then nervously glancing round at the rest of the pub, hoping he wasn't attracting attention to himself.

He gestured for Tom to come over.

'You OK?'

Pirate John was shaking. 'No. I'm not. I . . . I need to . . .'

'Get you a drink, John?'

One of the farmers came over, a semi-regular that Tom could never remember the name of. Jack? Bill? They were all called something like that round here.

Pirate John allowed himself to be led away. He glanced back over his shoulder, seemingly pleading with Tom. Tom nodded, understanding. He went back behind the bar.

Pearl came up to Tom, stood alongside him. 'What was all that about?'

'Don't know,' said Tom. 'John tried to talk to me. That farmer took him off. He's terrified though, look at him.'

Pearl looked over to where Pirate John stood, surrounded by farmers like he was their prisoner. She looked back at Tom. 'Let's wait until we close, then go over to his. Both of us.'

Tom thought of Lila at home. 'I should get back.'

'Look at him. This is serious. What if he's got cancer, or something?'

'What would Tony Williamson's death have to do with that?'

'I don't know. Maybe it's, oh, he was in trouble for using banned or dangerous fertiliser or something. Or he topped himself because of money problems and John wants to blow the whistle but the others won't let him, because they're in for a share of his farm. I don't know.'

'Could be. He did say other people are in on it.'

Pearl laughed. 'What, even me?'

Tom looked at her, studied her reactions. He was trained to spot a liar. Pearl wasn't lying.

'No, not you.'

Trust didn't come easily to Tom. But he'd felt, since the first day he'd met Pearl, that he could trust her. He hoped his instincts were still right.

'Well,' she said, 'if there's something happening round here then I should be aware of it, yeah?'

'OK, let's do it.'

They went back to work. Rachel didn't stay. Just gave Tom the briefest, smallest of smiles and left.

Tom occasionally looked up to check that Pirate John was all right. He was sitting in amongst the farmers like their hostage. Drinking beer like a condemned man.

54

Lila wasn't hooded or blindfolded. Her captors made no attempt to hide their faces from her. If she could have managed to get up from the floor of the van she could have looked out of the back window and seen where she was. That told her one thing: her fate had already been decided. And it was terminal.

The van hit a rocky stretch of road. Lila's bound body bounced around, hitting the floor, the sides of the van. Kai laughed.

'Like being at Alton Towers,' he said.

Lila, gag in mouth, didn't reply.

Eventually the van stopped. Lila rolled, hit the side for the last time, stayed still. She felt bruises blossoming on her body.

'Last stop,' said Kai. 'For you, anyway.'

She stared at him with hatred. If she had been free she would have clawed his face off, ripped his eyes out.

Kai just smiled. 'Yeah, I know what you're thinking. And you know what? Rather you than me, darlin'.'

She yelled from behind the gag. Kai laughed.

'Get her out.'

The two who had manhandled her into the van dragged her out into darkness. She could hear the sea pounding against the cliffs, see dark silhouettes against the night sky. She knew where she was. The disused tin mine along the coast.

Most of them were now reclaimed as picturesque heritage sites, educational museums or backdrops for period TV drama. But some were beyond salvage and had been left to fall into disrepair and ruin. The outbuildings left with only the main chimney, pointing at the sky like the barrel of an ancient revolver, and underneath the ground their tunnels too dangerous and unsafe to block off. They could stretch for miles both inland and out to sea, into the rock of the cliffs and way down.

They dragged her towards the entrance.

The opening was small, enclosed by loose rocks and the collapsed side of an old outbuilding. Her two captors propelled her forwards, pushing her through the gap. They both followed, Kai bringing up the rear.

It had been dark outside but inside the cave it was a kind of pitch-black darkness, more intense than she had ever experienced. They turned on torches, pulled her along. She crouched, bent double initially, until the cave opened out and she could walk, or rather stumble, upright.

They were in a massive cavern with sections of old, rusted tracks beneath her feet. Roughly hollowed out, the ceiling was propped up by ancient timbers. Piles of rock and rubble were scattered all around, evidence of old cave-ins, just left there, the topography changed as a result. The floor abruptly stopped. She peered down. There was a sheet of corrugated iron nearby, a pit ahead of her. Inside was an old metal bed frame and underneath it a body, broken, bloodied. With a lurch of her stomach, she recognised it. Kyle the student.

Oh, God . . . Oh, God . . .

It hit Lila then: that was what she had been helping with. And it didn't matter whether she was directly involved, or that she hadn't known what was going to happen, she was at least partly responsible for the boy's death. She thought of her mother once more. Everything that had happened to her, everything she had done.

'Don't worry,' said Kai from behind her, 'you won't be here long.' He looked down at the boy's body. 'Long enough to get reacquainted, though.'

He drew a knife from his jacket, slit her bindings. She rubbed her sore wrists, turned round to hit him. She didn't get the chance. One of her two captors pushed her and she fell into the pit.

She landed awkwardly, the breath huffing out of her, but not in too much pain. More surprise and shock than anything else. She reached out, trying to find something to lean on, to pull herself up with. She found a hand.

She screamed, recoiled. Tried to put as much distance between herself and the dead student as she possibly could.

'If it's any consolation,' shouted Kai from above, 'I am genuinely sorry about all this.'

'Then get me out of here.'

Her initial anger had dissipated, replaced by a kind of desperate, depressive acceptance of the facts.

'Sorry. Already told you. You or me. Even so, I wish things could have gone differently for us. Genuinely.'

She sighed. 'You know why you're doing this, Kai? Behaving like this to me? Because you're weak. I've been with you long enough to know that. To know what you're like. When you came to the door, I only opened it out of pity for you.'

Kai laughed. 'Nah. You loved me. It breaks your heart, this. I know it.'

'Kai, I was only ever with you for what I could get from you. You're one of the saddest fuckers I've ever met. And you're a typical bully. The sad little loser who gets a bit of power.' She felt the anger rising within her once more. 'Fuck you. Fuck you . . .'

Kai tried to laugh her words off.

'You're a coward, a fucking coward . . .'

She heard them walk away, the light bobbing away along with them.

'I fucking hate you . . . I hope you die screaming, you sad fuck . . .'

Her voice rang out until the light faded. Then she was left all alone.

Not quite alone. Kyle's lifeless body was nearby. She couldn't see it but she could sense it.

She stayed where she was. Too hurt, too scared to move.

55

Tom knocked on Pirate John's front door, stepped back, waited. Nothing. There was a light on inside so Tom assumed he was in there. He looked at Pearl who shrugged, tried again.

Nothing.

He crouched down, flipped the letter box. 'John? It's Tom and Pearl. From the pub. Open up, mate.'

From somewhere within the house, a small defeated response: 'Go away. Leave me alone. Please . . .'

Pearl glanced at Tom, her face expressing deep concern.

Tom tried again. 'Come on, John, open up.' He stood up, turned to Pearl. 'If he doesn't come now, then—'

The door opened.

'Get in, quick.'

Pirate John bundled the pair of them inside, locked the door behind him.

'John, what's—'

He shushed them both, ushered them into the living room. Closed that door behind him. The room was in semi-darkness; the only illumination came from candles dotted about.

'Stay away from the windows,' he told them. 'Don't let them see you.'

Pearl was about to speak. Tom saw from the look on her face that she was going to say something, probably questioning Pirate John's sanity. He gently shook his head.

Pirate John kept talking. 'It's like a mass hysteria, that's what it is. The whole village. Gripped by this . . . desperation.'

'About what?' asked Pearl.

'The marina,' he said, as if it was obvious. 'If they don't get that ... well, they will get it. They've seen to that. They've gone to ... they'll go to any lengths to do it. That's the endgame. That's what it's all about.'

'What have they done?' asked Pearl. 'And who are they?'

'All of them ... They're all in on it.'

'But—'

'Wrong question. Not important.'

'What lengths have they gone to?' asked Tom.

'Right question,' said Pirate John, nodding as if unable to stop.

'And?' asked Pearl.

'The old ways. The old religion. Like Nietzsche said, when people stop believing in God, they don't believe in nothing ...'

'So, they'll believe in anything,' Tom completed.

Pirate John jumped forward, snapping his fingers. 'Exactly right. Exactly right ...'

'OK,' said Pearl, 'that's the abstract, what about the specific? What are they planning to do?'

'Sacrifice,' said Pirate John, his eyes fearfully lit by the candlelight.

Tom frowned. 'Sacrifice?'

'The student. The boy who went missing. That was the plan. An outsider, they said. Not one of our own, they said. Someone who wouldn't be missed. Not by us. But someone who could contribute to the greater good. Because you have to do that, they said. Do bad things for the greater good. It's the way of the world.'

'So where is he now?' asked Tom.

'Well, he's dead, isn't he?' Like Pirate John was explaining something everyone knew. 'It all went wrong. He died.'

'How?' asked Pearl.

'Wrong question again.'

Pearl looked put out at the reply. 'OK then, if he's dead ... what do they do instead?'

Pirate John gave a queasy smile, nodded. 'What d'you think they do?'

'Get a replacement?' said Tom.

Another nod.

'Who?'

Pirate John tried looking at Tom, couldn't hold his gaze. 'I think you know.'

He did. 'Lila.'

Pirate John nodded, his head down, like someone awaiting the noose.

'Who's Lila?' asked Pearl.

Tom dashed towards the door. 'I've got to get home. Now.'

'Why?'

'Because she's there.' He reached the front door, began opening it. 'I've been sheltering her. She's—'

And stopped dead.

Rachel stood with a gun in her hand. Behind her, two of the farmers from the pub, both holding shotguns.

'Rachel? What—'

'Back inside please, Tom,' she said, moving over the threshold.

Tom did as he was told. Staring at her all the time. 'I've got to go. Lila—'

'Is long gone by now,' she finished. Then her face became compassionate. Sad, even. 'I'm sorry, Tom. We could have really made a go of things. If circumstances had been different.'

Pearl looked between the two of them, understanding dawning. Tom, despite everything that was happening, felt a rush of shame.

Not knowing how to react, he allowed himself to be moved backwards, Pearl also.

Rachel herded them back into the living room.

'This is all bullshit, Rachel,' said Tom. 'All of it. Sacrifice? Is this for real?'

Rachel shrugged.

'It's bullshit. Superstitious bullshit. I can't believe you fell for it. Any of you. Pure bullshit.'

'Maybe it is,' she said, 'but it works. These two gentlemen here can attest to that. Can't you?'

She glanced at them both. Neither spoke.

Tom stepped towards her. Three guns focused on him. He stayed where he was.

'You're planning to kill someone. Murder them.' He shook his head. 'This is insane . . .'

'Yes, it's unfortunate, but what can you do? When you're born here, brought up here, you know the way things really work. You're brought up believing that the wall between this world and the other is very thin in St Petroc.'

'Yeah, I heard all that too but it's utter crap,' said Pearl.

Rachel stared at her. 'We heard the evidence, we took a vote. We're all in it together. We had to be.'

'And what if someone decides they don't want to go through with it?'

She nodded towards Pirate John. 'Ask him.'

'They get this.' Pirate John held up the crow-warning doll. 'It's a warning. You know what'll happen if you ignore it, if you try to deny it. They make sure. If you don't get back in line . . .'

'You get dealt with,' said Rachel. 'Rules are rules.'

'This is . . . ridiculous . . .' Tom shook his head. He could barely believe what he was hearing. Like his mind had jumped track and he was on a parallel Earth with the same people he knew but who were behaving in completely different ways. Stuck there, unable to get back.

'We have to have rules,' Rachel told them. 'This has to work. We all have to make it work. If one drops out and doesn't get punished what's to stop someone else doing it? And then someone else? It's harsh. But it has to be. For the greater good.'

'It's barbaric,' said Pearl.

Rachel said nothing.

'You're not going to get me,' shouted Pirate John. 'You're not going to deal with me . . .'

He flung the crow warning directly at Rachel who ducked to avoid it, while he dodged past her and the two farmers, reached the front door and was away. One of the farmers turned, made to go after him but Rachel placed a restraining hand on his arm.

'Leave him. He won't get far.'

'So when and where is this all taking place?' asked Tom.

Rachel smiled. 'So you can try and disrupt it? No, thank you. You've played the big hero and rescued her once before. You're not going to get another chance.'

'Listen to yourself. Just listen. What are you doing? This isn't you. Not the Rachel I got to know.'

Rachel gave a small, sad sigh. 'It isn't any of us. Not really. Or not most of us, at any rate. But what can we do? We all agreed to it. We all signed up for it when it seemed like the only chance we had for any kind of future. We're too far into it now. We have to see it through. And any fallout from that, we'll just have to cope with as best we can.'

'Presumably the marina'll make it all worthwhile.'

'Yes, it will. Peace and prosperity for all. And all of that. The ends will have justified the means. This area's steeped in the old ways. If you've lived here all your life, you'll have seen the old religion in action. You turn back to what you know works best when you're threatened, when you're desperate.' She sighed, shook her head. 'You're not from round here. I don't expect you to understand.'

Tom squared up to her. 'Listen, Rachel. Putting aside all your mumbo-jumbo bullshit, I've seen people who believed that the ends justified any kind of monstrous things. And who acted on that, for whatever justification they gave. And sometimes they got what they wanted. But there was always a price to pay. And they never stopped paying it. Usually for the rest of their lives. Sometimes they hated what they'd done so much that their lives afterwards were pretty short. And ended by their own hand. And the others? The ones who didn't care? They became some of the biggest monsters I've ever seen. So which one are you, Rachel?' He looked at the two farmers. 'And you two? What'll it be?'

She thought before answering. He had hit a nerve, he could see that from the expression on her face. Then she shook her head. 'I'll deal with that when it happens.'

'Look at yourself. What you're doing. It's already happened, Rachel.'

She closed her eyes, shook her head. Tom saw it as his chance. Kept talking.

'It's not too late, Rachel. Come on. Put the gun down. Walk away. Stop this . . . this madness. You can do it. Come on . . .'

He held out his hand towards her. She looked up at him, torn. Slowly, she reached out a wavering hand towards his.

The first farmer, Bill Watson, stepped forward, smashed his shotgun barrel down on Tom's outstretched arm. He collapsed to the floor, grasping his arm in pain. 'Get back. We've heard enough from you . . .'

Rachel's head snapped upwards like she had just wakened from a trance. She re-aimed her gun at Tom. Her voice when she spoke was rich with a desperate kind of self-belief. 'Like I said, it's a chance I'll take. That we'll all take. If it goes wrong what have we lost? Nothing. Just some outsider who we didn't know is dead, that's all. Happens all the time round here. Cliff edges are dangerous places. We can't get sentimental about every tourist who has an accident.'

Tom got to his feet, nursing his injured arm. 'But this isn't an accident. *This* is murder.'

Rachel gave a cruel smile. 'You telling me you haven't done anything similar? In Afghanistan? Or when you were undercover? I've seen your file, remember.'

'That was different.'

'Was it? There were ends, there were means. You justified one to reach the other.'

'No,' he said, but memories were montaging inside his mind. One in particular. He sighed. 'Yes. I was speaking from experience. I know what happens to you when you commit monstrous acts. You spend the rest of your life trying to atone for it. And you know what? I don't think you ever can.'

Rachel thought for a moment. It seemed as though Tom's words had this time reached her. Then the farmers moved closer once more, reminding her with upraised shotguns which side she was on, and the spell was broken.

'It doesn't matter,' she said. 'It's been agreed on and that's it.'

Pearl, Tom noticed, was having an even harder time trying to cope with what was happening. She looked like she didn't know whether to cry or scream. Instead she spoke, trying to make sense of it.

'And none of you'll speak up about it, because you'll all implicate each other.'

Rachel turned her attention to her. 'Absolutely right, Pearl. Like you say, all of us.' She stepped in closer. 'Know what I mean by that?'

Pearl frowned. 'No.'

'Where do the Round Table meet?'

Eyes wide, Pearl understood. 'My mum and dad.'

'Yes. Your mum and dad. Dan and Elaine. Hosting the Round Table's meetings all this time. You didn't think they just left when the meetings were on, did you?'

Pearl sank down on the sofa, head in hands. Finally defeated. 'No . . . no . . .'

'Ignore her,' said Tom. 'She's just messing with you. Don't listen to her.'

'Messing? You think? I'm telling the truth to the girl, Tom. Dan and Elaine didn't want her involved. I disagreed. I think it's about time she heard it. She's one of us, after all.'

'So what are you going to do now?' asked Tom.

'Up to you both.' Rachel looked down at Pearl. 'You've got the choice. You know what's happening. You know what we've done. This is your home. We're your people. You should be with us, not with this, this –' she gestured towards Tom – 'outsider.' She leaned in closer. 'So what'll it be, girl? You with us or against us?'

Pearl rubbed her fists into her eyes, pushing away the tears. She looked between Tom and Rachel, stood up. Went to Tom. Held his hand. 'I'm sorry, I don't . . . I'm sorry . . .'

She let it go. Walked over to join Rachel and the two farmers.

'Pearl? What—'

He said no more. Bill Watson swung the butt of his shotgun, connecting it with the side of Tom's head. He was unconscious before he hit the floor.

56

Light and pain. That was what woke Tom up.

He tried to sit upright, failed at the first attempt. The room swam in and out of focus, like a fairground ride he was trying to either jump on or off. He couldn't decide which, but it led him to the point of nausea. He lay back, eyes closed, tried again. Took it slowly, one muscle at a time. This time it worked. He opened his eyes. Still in Pirate John's living room.

Tom sighed, let his head drop forward, cradled it in his hands.

'Ah,' said a voice. 'You're back with us.'

Tom looked up sharply, immediately regretted it. Tried again, slowly this time. Pirate John sat on the edge of the armchair opposite him. Anxious, wired, as though he hadn't slept. Probably hadn't.

'What are you doing here?' he said. 'Thought you'd legged it.'

'I did,' said Pirate John, shame in his voice, 'but I had nowhere to go. So I just . . . hung around in my car, kept my head down till I knew they'd gone. Then, when nothing else happened and no one else turned up, I just crept back inside. And there you were. I tried to wake you but you were spark out. So I arranged you on the sofa, let you sleep. And here we are.'

'Where's . . . what happened to everyone else?'

'They left. Obviously didn't think we were important enough to deal with.'

Tom nodded. Wished he hadn't. 'You got any paracetamol? Ibuprofen? Anything like that?'

'Just a minute.' Pirate John stood up, disappeared into the kitchen. Came back with an ancient packet of pills and a glass of water. 'They'll be fine. Bit out of date, but that just makes them stronger, right?'

Tom didn't bother to argue, just took two. Swallowed them down.

'So what happens next?' he asked.

Pirate John sat down again. 'Well, tomorrow's M Day.'

'M Day?'

'Marina decision day. The day all this has been leading up to.'

'So, what? They're all going to be at the council offices doing some last-minute lobbying?'

Pirate John gave a bitter laugh. 'You really haven't been following this, have you?'

'Tell me.'

'Tonight's the night. The big ritual. Blood sacrifice, all of that. Then tomorrow the marina's ours. And then the world . . .' Another bitter laugh.

'You're remarkably cheerful.'

'I'm still alive, aren't I? A few hours ago I didn't think that would be a possibility.'

'Why did they leave you then?'

'Like I said. We're obviously not important enough to them. They think we're no threat.'

'And what if we are?'

'I'm sure they've plans in place to deal with that today.'

'Aren't they worried we'll go to the police or something? Tell everything?'

'They've got this sown up, Tom. Or think they have.'

'They might not.'

Pirate John shook his head. 'They're not all as direct as that lot last night. You know the Scientologists?'

'Yeah . . .'

'Bunch of evil brainwashing arseholes. I watched this documentary on them once. A reporter sat in his car watching their church, or whatever they call it. Then this young girl, really smiley and pretty, came out and took his photo. Ten minutes later they were all out sticking leaflets under everyone's windscreen wipers

312

and through everyone's front doors with his photo on and words saying he was a paedophile and was in the area.' He sniffed, nodded. 'Like I said, subtle.'

'So you're saying there's nothing we can do.'

'Dunno.'

Tom leaned forward. 'But John, you've been trying to talk to me for ages, get me to join you in doing something. Now that I'm here, are you bottling it?'

Pirate John became uncomfortable. 'No . . . no, I'm not . . . it's just . . .'

'What?'

'Well, it's all out in the open now. And there's nothing you or me or anyone can do about it.'

'So you're not going to try.'

He shrugged, sighed. 'What's the point?'

'The point is, John, someone I had a duty of care for is going to die a very horrible and unnecessary death. And I don't want that to happen. And I'm going to do something about it. Even if you're not.'

Pirate John stared at the floor.

Tom stood up. 'Where's this ceremony, ritual thing being held?'

'The stone circle. Midnight. They won't do anything before then.'

'Then that gives us the rest of today and most of the evening to put something together. You with me?'

'I don't know . . .'

'John, a few hours ago you were in fear for your life.'

'Yeah, well . . . now that I'm still here I might want to hang around for a bit.' He dropped his head, couldn't meet Tom's eyes. 'Sorry.'

'Right.'

'I'm sorry . . .'

'Whatever.'

Tom walked towards the door.

'Where you going?'

'Lila must be being kept somewhere. So I'm going to find some-one who knows where. Make them talk.'

'Who's that, then?'

Tom smiled. 'I've got someone in mind.'

57

Lila still hadn't moved from where she was sitting. All she could hear was the sound of her own breathing, the wind through the caves. She could see nothing. But she could sense Kyle's lifeless body right next to her.

She had run herself through every stage of despair several times, like a rollercoaster on a loop, round and round, each time as nauseous as the first. She had screamed herself hoarse after Kai had left until all she heard was her own voice echoing off stone. Then a ringing, deafening silence once she stopped. Then sobbing, self-pity overwhelming her. Then pleading, with herself, her captors, her mother even. She made wagers with everyone, sent prayers up into the darkness. To a God she had never believed in, a mother she still hated but promised she wouldn't if she got out alive. Now she just sat there, numb.

She felt there was no longer anything – if there ever had been – to live for. She had nothing left. And it was, as her mother had told her repeatedly, no more nor less than she deserved.

She didn't know how long she sat there. Then above her she saw the weak light of a torch as it bobbed slowly along the tunnel towards her, getting stronger, brighter, the nearer it came to the edge of the pit.

At first, her heart leapt at the improbability of it. She was being rescued. Saved. They hadn't forgotten about her, Tom had found her. But, as the light approached and she stood up to see the cloaked figure behind the beam, her heart dipped again. Whoever this was, they weren't bringing good news.

A figure stopped at the rim of the pit, shone the torch down. Lila squinted, pulled away from the light as it hurt her eyes.

'I've come to see how you are, dear. How you're shaping up.'

Lila knew immediately who it was. Morrigan. The one behind all this.

She said nothing.

'So how are you holding up?' A smile in the voice. An unpleasant, curdling smile.

Lila still didn't reply.

'Not talking? What a pity.'

'Why should I?' answered Lila. 'You're going to kill me, so why should you be bothered about how I am? And why should I tell you?'

A laugh. As unpleasant as the accompanying smile. 'Because, my petal, you should be pleased. Your death will bring new life to this village. To the whole area. To all these people who live here and for generations to come. Isn't that something to be excited about?'

Lila looked straight up. At the person behind the light. She saw through the clothes, the carefully constructed persona. She was fed up with having to take everything life threw at her. Now, she had nothing to lose.

'Listen,' said Lila. 'Drop the act. It doesn't impress me.'

A tightening in the voice. A warning. 'This is not an act. This is real. You of all people should appreciate that fact.'

'Yeah, whatevs. I've met frauds before. Pretending they were something they weren't, that they had some grand old calling, twisted old shits who hid their hatred and their perversions behind whatever it was they tried to get others to believe in. Usually religion. Just like you're doing.'

'I'm not like that.' Ice in the voice now. 'You have never met anyone like me.'

'Yeah, I have. Different religion, same shit. I've dealt with the best, mate, been fucked over by the lot of them. And you don't impress me at all.'

316

Morrigan laughed.

Lila was warming to her theme. 'I can see through you a mile off. Could from the start.'

'Then why did you do my bidding?'

'I don't know. I've thought about that over and over since it happened. And hated myself for what I did. For how weak and stupid I was to be led along. I didn't do it because I was scared of you. I did it because I didn't know what would happen to me if I didn't. I wouldn't have anywhere to live, nothing to eat. I didn't know how I'd survive.' Anger rose inside her. 'You think I wanted to be where I was? Living with that shit Kai? I'd have done any-thing to get away. And I did.'

'But you didn't get far, did you?'

'I tried . . .' Lila began to run out of words, feel tired. She kept going. Determined not to give in before Morrigan. 'So yeah. That's why I did it. Not for you. You're pathetic.'

Morrigan laughed. 'And yet, here I am up here, and you're down there.'

'Yeah?' Lila stood up. 'Well, come down here, you shit-headed pervert and we'll see who's the strongest, shall we?'

Morrigan didn't reply. Just kept the light shining down.

Lila continued. 'Did you come here to see me cry? Hear me beg? You get off on that shit? Bet you do. Well, tough. You're out of luck.'

The light moved. Morrigan had stood up. 'You're a foul-mouthed little girl. You'll never be a lady.'

Lila laughed. 'Considering you're going to kill me I'd say you were right.'

Morrigan turned, began to leave.

'Listen. I know what you're planning to do to me. But I'm going to fight you. Every step of the fucking way, for every fucking second. I'll fight you. I'm not going to make it easy for you. And you know what? If I'm going, then I'll make damn sure you're coming with me. You hear that? Where I'm going, you're going too.'

317

But Morrigan, and the light, had gone.

Lila, no longer content to lie down and die, had discovered a new-found strength she hadn't been aware she possessed.

She screamed defiance at Morrigan, at the world, until she had no more words left.

58

Late afternoon, and Tom could feel the chill in the air.

He approached Noah's travellers' camp the same way he had last time, hiding in the gorse bushes on the edge of the cliff, looking down to get the lay of the land. Standard commando procedure. He expected to be able to get into the site again, get close to Noah, make him talk.

He was wrong.

They were waiting for him on both sides. All of them big enough, and in plentiful supply, to make a fight redundant. He stood up, allowed himself to be walked into the camp.

He was led into the yurt he had been taken to on his previous incursion. This time, in the light, he noticed how much better it was than all the other dwellings he had seen on the way in. Almost like a house. Clearly Noah wasn't some communist egalitarian.

Noah was waiting for him.

'How predictable is this?' he said, laughing. 'You think the same thing'll work twice in a row? Well, obviously you do or you wouldn't have tried it.'

Tom shrugged. 'Got me what I wanted, didn't it? Only wanted to talk to you. That's all.'

Noah looked slightly put out at Tom's words.

'Were you expecting a fight?' said Tom, smiling.

Noah ignored him. 'What did you want to say? Get it over with.'

Tom gestured to a rug-covered bench. 'Can I sit down, please? Easier to have a chat.'

Noah looked uncertain how to answer him. This wasn't going the way he had expected. Tom had wrong-footed him and he clearly didn't like that. 'Do what you like.'

Tom sat down. 'Thank you.' He gestured to another seat nearby. 'Help yourself. Much more civilised.'

Again, Noah didn't know what to do. He had been about to sit down when Tom spoke. Now it looked as if Tom had the upper hand. Instead of sitting straight away, he turned, dismissed his followers. Then, when it was just the two of them, sat down.

'What d'you want?'

Tom leaned forward. 'What you doing, Noah? Eh? What you doing?'

Noah tried to sigh. 'What are you talking about?'

'Morrigan.' He watched Noah carefully as he spoke the name. Saw Noah flinch. He filed that away. He was scared of Morrigan. Useful.

'What about Morrigan?'

'Why are you doing this? Whatever Morrigan wants. Surely you set this place up because you wanted an easy life, not to run around after some psycho, doing whatever they tell you to.'

'You know nothing about what I'm doing. Now get out.' He stood up, made for the door.

'I do know what you're doing,' said Tom. 'You're scared, aren't you? Of Morrigan.'

Noah stopped. Froze. Tom could see that his intuitive guess had hit a nerve. He continued.

'Come on, Noah, why? You had a good thing here until you got involved with Morrigan. Or did Morrigan get involved with you?'

Noah turned. 'You know nothing about me, nothing about what I'm doing here. You wouldn't understand what's going on.'

'Oh, I would, Noah. I can see you're scared of Morrigan. That you're doing what you're told because of that. Why? Has Morrigan got something on you, is that it? Blackmail?'

Noah crossed right to him, stood over him. 'I said, you know nothing, nothing . . .'

'OK, Noah, no need to lose your temper. I'm just saying, it doesn't have to be like that. It's not too late to stop this.'

'And you would know, would you?'

'Yeah, I would. You can stop all this. And I can help.'

Noah just stared at him. 'You can help.' A statement of disbelief more than a question. 'And how could you help?'

'By standing with you. By refusing to do what this Morrigan wants.'

Noah sighed. Tom felt he was getting through, but still not convincing him. Whatever power Morrigan had over Noah, it was strong. But, Tom was sure, there was nothing magical about it.

'Morrigan has no power over you, Noah.'

Noah laughed. 'That's where you're wrong. Morrigan has power over everyone round here. Even you.'

'Bullshit. Morrigan has no power at all. It's just fear and mass-manipulation.' He stood up, stood right next to Noah. 'That's all it is. Smoke and mirrors. The emperor's new clothes. It just needs one person to stand up and call it out. You can do that, Noah.'

Tom placed his hand on Noah's shoulder. Noah turned towards him, no longer hiding the fear in his eyes. Tom knew in that moment that Noah could go either way. He just had to say nothing, wait and see.

Noah smiled. 'You think Morrigan doesn't control everyone? Even you? Morrigan doesn't need to do it alone. Morrigan works through others. Like me.'

'Noah, whatever Morrigan's got on you it's not important . . .'

'Not important?' Noah laughed. 'Really.'

He shook off Tom's hand, walked to the door, called in his two men again.

'Take him home,' he said, pointing to Tom. 'And make sure he stays there.'

They crossed to Tom, took one arm each.

'Wait,' said Tom, as they dragged him towards the door. 'Just tell me. Where's Lila being kept? Please, let me know. Just tell me and I can get her out.'

Noah turned his back on him.

'Please . . .'

Tom was dragged out. Noah didn't move.

Tom was driven home. Already there was a reception committee waiting for him. Cars and other vehicles, four-by-fours, quad bikes, ringed the front of his house. Local villagers sat in them or strolled about. They all stood to attention when Tom was driven up.

He was pulled from the car, pushed towards his front door.

'Stay in there,' said one of the travellers, 'until you're told otherwise.'

'And if I don't?'

He smiled. 'Then you'll never leave your house again.'

Tom walked up to the front door.

Locked himself inside.

59

Darkness was falling. The calm of the day gone, the wild of the night to come. It was the wolf hour.

Kai walked through the caves. His injuries still hurt, the pain intensifying the nearer he came to the pit, the source of most of them. He tried not to let it show, certainly not in front of the two men Noah had given him. He wasn't sure whether they were there to enforce Kai's word or to ensure he didn't run. At that moment he didn't care. All he was bothered with was not appearing weak.

And ensuring Lila did as she was told.

It had taken him longer than he thought to reach the pit. His knowledge of the caves wasn't good, as he had demonstrated to himself on his earlier escape. But again, not wanting to lose face before the other two, he had pretended he knew where he was going. And he had found the pit. Eventually.

He didn't catch the smirks that passed between the two men with him.

He reached the edge of the pit, peered down it, torch in hand. He hid his shudders at returning there, swallowed down his nausea on seeing Kyle's body.

'Hi, Lila,' he called.

She looked up. Her face twisted with disgust, hatred. 'Fuck off.'

The two behind him smiled. He was glad for the bad lighting in the cave as they couldn't see his face redden. He tried to ignore her reaction.

'Got something for you,' he called, and threw down a white cotton shift. 'For you to change into.'

'I said, fuck off.'

The two others didn't bother to hide their laughter now. Kai felt himself getting angry.

'Put it on. That's an order.'

'Don't take orders from scum like you. Now, as I've already said, fuck off.'

Kai felt himself start to lose control. 'Put it on. Now.'

'Make me.'

He paused, looked between the other two who shrugged. He looked back down at Lila, incandescent with rage, knowing there was nothing he could do about it. So angry yet so impotent.

'I will. Oh, I will.'

'Go on, then.'

Kai stared at her. 'Or . . . these two here will. Yeah. They'll climb down there and . . . and make you put it on. They'll put it on for you.'

'And I'm sure they'll look very nice in it.'

The two men's laughter increased. Kai was even more enraged.

'You're going to die tonight, Lila. One way or the other. Now put that on. Do as you are told . . .'

Lila picked up the shift. Looked at it.

'Put it on. I'll wait.'

'And watch as well, fucking pervert.'

'You used to be my girlfriend. I can watch if I want to.'

Lila gave a cruel smile, mimicked his words back to him. The other two, all pretence at respect for him gone, laughed even louder. Which just made him all the more angry.

She stared up at him, defiance in her eyes.

'You've got . . . got to take your things off underneath, put it on . . .'

'Make me. Come down here and make me.'

Kai, by this point fuelled by anger and embarrassment, turned to the henchmen. 'Give me the ladder. Now.'

They unfurled a metal segmented ladder they had been carrying, threw it over the rim of the pit. Held the top. Kai, ignoring the pain in his body, went straight over the edge and climbed down. Once there, he tried to ignore Kyle's body, crossed straight to Lila. Grabbed her.

'You . . . will . . . do as . . . you're told . . .'

He grabbed the shift, tried to force it over her head, simultaneously pulling at her clothes.

Lila fought back, scratching, clawing him, punching him. She noticed which points on his body had the most effect, kept hitting them.

Kai began to crumple under the weight of her blows. She delivered one final kick, ran for the ladder. Climbed up. The men grabbed her at the top. She knew it would be pointless to struggle against them. Knew that her rebellion and defiance had been for Kai alone.

'Leave him down there,' she shouted, trying to kick the ladder away. 'Leave him, bastard, lying cowardly bastard . . .'

One of them pulled her away from the edge, the other held the ladder as Kai came back up. He looked in an even worse state than when he had gone down. He moved over to Lila, stared at her. Held up the shift. Triumph in his eyes.

'Now who's won?'

'It's not over yet. Like I said to Morrigan, if I'm going, you're all coming with me.'

Kai tried to hold her gaze, stare unblinking and smiling into her eyes. But he couldn't. He dropped his look, turned to the other two.

'Bring her. It's time.'

Then stomped off to what he hoped was the exit.

60

Pirate John tried once more, turning the key as hard as he could, flooring the pedals, but it was no good. The car was dead.

It was dark, the village deserted. He knew where everyone would be, or at least preparing for. It was, he had decided, the perfect time to make his getaway, so he had loaded up the car with as much stuff as he could and got ready to set off. And now it wouldn't start. Typical. Just his luck.

One last try, one last failure. He rubbed his face, felt sweat on his hands, thought what to do next. If the car doesn't work, he thought, then the bus will. I just have to get out of the village to find one.

Out of the car and straight up the road. He didn't even look back.

'Beware the calling of the dead.'

Pirate John had been walking for nearly an hour and hadn't seen a bus. He had tried to keep off the main roads in case he was seen, but when no buses turned up he abandoned that plan and found himself on the cliff-side path, walking towards the next village, or even town if his feet held up. Anywhere to be away from St Petroc and all its attendant madness.

As he walked he thought of Morrigan's words to Tony Williamson. *'Beware the calling of the dead.'* He tried to laugh it off, but in the darkness, with the sound of the water against the rocks, it all came back to him. He was chilled by something more than the night.

'Walk along the cliffs around here, where there have been lots of shipwrecks off the coast, you can hear the dead calling out their names. And sometimes they call out the names of those about to join them. Take care you don't hear your name . . .'

The wind whipped up around him. He turned up the collar of his coat, a belated and futile gesture as his ears were already frozen and it didn't reach them anyway. It made him lose his footing slightly, stumble over rocks he might otherwise have noticed.

You would think Morrigan had planned this wind, he thought, and laughed to himself. The laugh was stolen away by a sudden gust.

He saw something ahead of him on the cliff edge of the next bay. Something that wasn't usually there. At first he thought that a couple of the stones from the circle had uprooted themselves and gone for a walk. A pair of granite would-be suicides goading each other to jump into the crashing water below. But as he approached he saw that they weren't stones, but men. At least he assumed they were men; bundled in insulated waterproofs they could have been either gender. And they were holding something. Fishing rods.

It wasn't unusual to see night fishers in the area. But they tended to appear when the weather was calmer, the water smoother. Neither looked at him, both intent on what was happening at the ends of their lines.

Then he heard something. Or rather someone. Calling his name.

He stopped walking, listened.

'John . . . John . . .'

He looked round. There was nobody about but the two night fishermen up ahead and himself. And they were ignoring him. There it was again.

'John . . . John . . .'

The call of the dead. He shuddered. Get a grip, he thought. Have a bit of common sense. It was the wind playing tricks on him. Making him believe he had heard something that wasn't there because he was in an agitated state. Projecting whatever fears Morrigan had tried to instil within him onto the wind, an oncoming storm. That was all.

'John . . . John . . .'

He moved quickly, almost running, stumbling over the stones, sharp and misshapen, catching at his feet.

He neared the fishermen. Couldn't make out who they were under all their clothing. All he could see of their faces was a dark shadowed hollow where their hoods took in what moonlight there was and gave nothing out. Blank-faced. Empty inside.

Stop it, he told himself. You're falling for Morrigan's bullshit again. You've avoided the crow warning, you've got away. You don't have to—

'John . . . John . . .'

He moved quicker, stumbling again, falling to his knees this time, the stones piercing his jeans, ripping them, drawing blood. And hurting. He stood up. Saw the two fishermen were barring his way.

'Excuse me, I need to get past . . .'

The path was narrow along the cliff edge, with enough space for one person to pass another but not much else. Move too far to one side and you were in the heather and gorse. Too far in the other direction and you were on your way down to an early death.

'I said I need to . . .'

'John . . .'

'John . . .'

He realised the source of the voice. The night fishermen.

He could see smiles glinting like blades inside their hoods.

'Just move, please. Let me pass and . . . just let me pass.'

But they didn't. They moved towards him. Both at the same time, taking slow, menacing footsteps.

He backed away, stumbling once more, keeping his balance. If he went over now it could be fatal.

A desperate anger rose up within Pirate John. 'Listen, let me past or I'll . . . I'll fight you. Both.'

No reply.

'I . . . I will. Honestly. I will . . .' He struck what he assumed was a boxer's stance.

The two men looked at each other, backed off.

Pirate John smiled. 'That's better. Good. Move and let me pass.'

They did so. Pirate John, wary all the time, shuffled past them. Neither made any attempt to stop him. 'Thank you,' he said once he was safely out of their reach.

He continued walking away from them.

Heart still hammering, he trotted on. He had won. This really was going to turn out all right. He was going to escape. No one would—

'John . . . John . . .'

'Not again . . .'

He turned, ready to argue, but didn't get a chance to move.

The first fishing hook landed on his arm. Penetrated his coat, right through his layers to his skin. It was razor sharp. Embedded. The fisherman pulled. Pirate John, caught off guard, went along with it.

The second barb caught him in the cheek. He yelled. The fisherman pulled. Pirate John tried pulling back but felt the hook ripping his face. He tried to get his arm up, release the barb, but it was no use. He was hooked.

He turned his attention to the other hook in his arm. Tried the same thing there. Nothing. Then felt another barb catch him in the neck. It stung. They pulled. He screamed.

He looked at the fishermen. They had put down their poles and held two reels of wire each. They were drawing him towards them like reeling in a catch. He had no choice but to go along with it. One of them looped the wire around him like a lasso, pulled tighter. Pirate John was trapped now.

He tried to pull away, felt the flesh in his face and neck tear, smelled the coppery smell of blood, felt his face and body become wet and sticky.

'John . . .'

'John . . .'

Laughing now while they said it.

Pirate John felt his body weaken. Another lasso of wire, another pull tight.

Then he felt the ground shift from under him and he was flying over the edge towards the rocks.

No time to think, to feel, to decide whether he had been right or wrong.

Nothing.

A crow wheeled overhead, cawing as it went.

61

Tom had been busy. He hadn't allowed his enforced captivity to get the better of him, to just sit and feel helpless. That wasn't part of his training. Instead he remained calm and rational. Thought. Planned. How to turn the situation to his advantage. He had made several trips to the utility room, the kitchen, the living room and the bedroom, gathering, respectively, bottles on the way to recycling and cans of petrol, tea towels, bottles of spirits and bed linen, ready to implement his plans.

But first, he had to speak to the people outside. Give them a chance.

He loaded everything into the bedroom underneath the big window that opened out on to the front of his house, then went to the door and stepped outside.

The light spilled out behind him. They had been sitting around, some holding shotguns and rifles, waiting, on edge. His sudden appearance brought them all together. Weapons were raised, pointed towards him. He could tell they were scared, nervous. This wasn't what they usually did. Who they usually thought of themselves as.

And that's what he would impress upon them.

'Listen up,' he shouted. He held his hands in the air. 'No weapons, I'm not here to attack you. I just want to talk to you. Yeah?'

No reply. They hadn't elected a spokesperson and no one wanted to take on that role so they collectively fell silent, each person waiting for the next to react first.

'I'm sure you think you're doing the right thing, or the right thing as you see it. I'm sure you all think that going along with the rest of the village, doing what you're told, is right. Holding your guns on me. Why are you doing that? What have you been told about me? I'm an enemy? A dangerous person? What? I'm just a bloke. Trying to live my life. Trying to make sense of what's going on here.'

Again no reply.

Tom continued. 'You might feel that here, now, in the dark, this is right. But tomorrow you won't. Each one of you, all of you, won't be able to face yourselves in the mirror in the morning. Know why? Shame. You'll all be ashamed of what you've done tonight. You won't be able to look at each other either. You'll hate each other because everyone else will remind you of what you did. You're going to hate yourselves. Is that what you want?'

Tom waited, hoped his words were sinking in.

'Fuck off.'

He checked the crowd, tried to see where the lone voice had come from. A young man, features trying to hold anger but badly covering up his fear. He had spoken. Tom recognised him.

'I know you,' he said, pointing at the young man. 'You work in the garage where I got my Land Rover serviced. You might have even done the MOT. Didn't you?'

The youth just studied his feet, suddenly struck dumb.

Tom scanned the crowd, kept trying. 'You.' He pointed at a middle-aged man. 'You eat in the Sail Makers. With your wife. We've chatted about rugby. I brought you and your wife your food. You always have the steak, medium rare. Why are you doing this? How am I suddenly your enemy?'

Again, there was no reply.

'You work in the village shop,' he said, pointing at a stout woman holding a shotgun. 'You've sold me eggs and bread, newspapers. Did you want to shoot me then?'

He didn't expect a reply, but this time he received one.

'Don't try that bullshit on us.'

Tom didn't recognise the speaker but he recognised the fear in his voice.

'Yeah,' said another, suddenly emboldened.

'Yeah, fuck off. We don't need you to tell us . . .'

Others joined in now. The mob had found its voice.

Tom nodded. 'Fair enough. But don't say I didn't warn you. What happens next is your own fault.'

He went back inside, shutting the door hard behind him.

He could still hear their jeering as he walked up the stairs, fear- and rage-fuelled voices, building themselves up to an angry, unstable mob. He went into the front bedroom, took a cheap lighter from the bedside table, picked up a bottle and lit the petrol-soaked rag stuffed in the neck of it.

He opened the window as wide as it would go, flung the bottle out as hard as he could.

It hit a four-by-four, the target he had been aiming for. The bottle broke immediately, spreading liquid fire all over the roof and down the sides.

The crowd scattered, some screaming.

Tom kept up the bombardment, letting the next bottle sail through the air, hitting the front of an estate car, rolling underneath. He knew what would happen next, crouched down to avoid it.

The fire from his makeshift Molotov cocktail hit the petrol tank and the car exploded.

Screams increased as people scattered to find safety.

Tom had expected one or two shots to be fired at him and had ducked down in between raining bottles just in case, but there were none. The four-by-four was the next to blow up. Tom found another bottle, lobbed that one straight into the remaining crowd.

That did it. They piled into what cars were left and drove away as fast as possible.

Tom waited until he was sure they had all gone, then went downstairs, opened the door. The area in front of his house looked like a battlefield. Afghanistan again.

He made sure there was no one left, then went back upstairs, gathered up the remaining bottles and loaded them into the back of his Land Rover. Checking to see that the fires would just naturally burn themselves out, he got behind the wheel, set off for the stone circle.

He just hoped he wasn't too late.

62

The sky was all cloud, heavy and dark, the stars and moon obscured. Like the world had thrown a blanket over itself, keeping everything hidden, especially its secrets.

The stone circle was prepared. The altar stone covered by an old purple velvet sheet. At either side were huge steel milking pails to catch the blood for the second part of the blood ritual; sprinkling it on the land in order to see it symbolically come back to life. Burning torches had been placed at each end. There were others scattered around the stones, held aloft by those in the congregation.

Most of the villagers had dressed for the occasion. Taking inspiration from the land around them, they wore headdresses of woven rowan sticks, masks of oak wood and bark, torsos of wicker. On their woven chest pieces were daubed ancient designs and symbols, curling trees, black toads, bulls' heads. Bare arms were painted with coiled adders. They were no longer individuals, or twenty-first-century villagers. They were the past, reborn.

Among those in the crowd was Pearl, standing with her parents. She seemed to be held there against her will. She looked visibly sickened by what was unfolding in front of her. Her parents both maintained flat, stony expressions. It was impossible to tell if they were enjoying the proceedings, or were appalled by them. Just standing, watching, a means to an end. Most of the other watchers wore the same expression.

As if conjured out of the night, Morrigan, resplendent in crow regalia, appeared, lit by braziers before a shadowed bank of hedgerow. The figure walked to the altar, took up position behind it. The mood of the crowd immediately shifted, became intense, concentrated. Cloak unfurled, flapping like the long, oil-black wings of a crow, the neck a wreath of coal-dark feathers, Morrigan held up a dagger, the blade glinting in the firelight. At first glance it looked sacrificial, but on closer inspection it was revealed as the razor-sharp blade from Grant Jenner's kitchen. Morrigan's acolyte stood alongside watching, face enrapt, frenzied.

At one side the local primary-school music teacher took Morrigan's nodded head as a cue, began to play a slow, monotonous beat on a drum. It was the only sound.

Morrigan gestured. Noah appeared behind the crow figure. He turned, nodded. Kai and his two men brought Lila forward, bound at the wrists and gagged. She still screamed, her actual words muffled and stifled by the gag, the intention behind the words coming through clear enough. They dragged her onwards, forcing her onto the stone altar. She fought them every step of the way. They held her down, one at her shoulders, the other at her feet. And still she fought, refusing to give up or give in.

Even under the costume it was clear that Morrigan was angered by her behaviour, but wasn't about to let it ruin the ceremony. The ritual would still go ahead. It had to.

Morrigan raised the knife above Lila's body. Opened a crow beak to begin an incantation.

The words were never said.

The air was filled by the sound of a revving engine, lights accompanying it. The crowd looked to where the source of this was, saw a Land Rover barrelling towards them as fast as it could.

Some stood dumbstruck, not believing what was happening. Others noticed their predicament, scrambled to get out of the way. Whoever was behind the wheel wasn't slowing down for them.

The Land Rover reached the stone circle, screeched to a halt. Tom got out of the driving seat, lighter and bottle already in hand. He lit the alcohol-soaked rag, hurled it into the centre of the crowd. It smashed on the ground, the liquid fire spreading outwards in a blue-tinged orange blaze. The crowd ran, some with wooden and wicker costumes already aflame.

Tom capitalised on the moment, taking another bottle from the car, lighting it, hurling it. Another crash, another fire, another set of screams. Confusion, running. Some of the crowd dropped their torches as they ran, adding to the flames.

Tom scanned the crowd, trying to see where Lila was. He saw her through the smoke, fighting with two much bigger men. Another lit bottle lobbed, then he ran towards her.

'The ritual must not be stopped ... the ritual most not be stopped ... Hold her ...' Morrigan was screaming, eyes dancing with madness. Still waving the vicious-looking knife. The two travellers tried to hold Lila down but Lila, emboldened by what was happening elsewhere, was making it as difficult as possible for them. Morrigan couldn't get a clear stab at her. Morrigan's acolyte stood at the side wringing his hands, keening at the pleasure being denied him.

Morrigan joined the two travellers, helped to hold Lila down. Tom ran forward, praying that he could reach her in time.

He couldn't.

Morrigan held the blade above Lila, swiftly mouthing an incantation, ready to bring it down, and he was too far away to stop her. He opened his mouth to scream.

And suddenly Pearl was there.

She had left her parents, run straight for the altar. She flung herself at Morrigan, grabbing the crow's blade arm before it could reach its target.

But Morrigan wasn't giving up easily. The two struggled, Pearl younger and supposedly stronger, Morrigan in the all-consuming grip of a powerful madness.

Pearl didn't see Morrigan's acolyte behind her pick up a rock, bring it down on her head. With a cry she fell to the ground. Morrigan thrust the knife at her.

And then Tom was on Morrigan. Struggling to get the blade out of that gloved hand, trying to release the taloned grip on the handle before Morrigan could reach Pearl. Morrigan fought more like a gang youth high on some kind of bulletproofing drug.

'Let it go, you old witch,' he shouted. 'It's over.'

He yanked Morrigan's arm, twisting it over, backwards and up, shaking that wrist, pushing hard. Morrigan cried out, let go of the knife. Tom tried to kick it away with his foot, pulling the crow headpiece off as he did so. He stopped in surprise.

'Jesus Christ. *Isobel* . . .?'

The retired schoolteacher struggled against him, screaming and spitting.

Tom didn't have time to process the surprise. Noah was straight on the knife, trying to grab it. Emlyn, Morrigan's acolyte, saw and brought his rock down on Noah's hand. Even above the shouts, Tom could hear the sound of Noah's knuckles smashing.

Emlyn yelled at him. 'Traitor . . .' Then looked up at Tom. 'You as well . . . All of you . . . Now let her go, you cunt . . .'

Tom pushed Morrigan, by now worn out and deflated, down to the ground. He turned to Emlyn, still standing with his rock.

'Why'd you have to interfere?' Emlyn screamed. 'Why? Who the hell are you to say what we can and can't do?'

'Shut up.'

Tom walked towards him. Emlyn held the rock in what he presumed was a threatening stance. Tom thought he would offer little resistance. He was an old man and whatever commitment was in his eyes couldn't be matched by his limbs. Tom was wrong. Emlyn flung himself at him, no longer an old man but some wiry, screaming imp, eyes ablaze with hatred and madness.

'Kill you . . . I'll kill you . . .'

Emlyn tried repeatedly to bring the rock down on Tom, snarling and spitting as he did so, his stabbing motions aiming for Tom's face, chest.

Tom had no time to think, only react. He grabbed Emlyn's arm, surprised by the old man's strength, and with his other hand pulled him in close to his body. He locked his foot behind Emlyn's leg, pushed him in the chest. Emlyn fell backwards, sprawling on the ground. Tom knelt beside him, took the rock from his hand, threw it away. He pulled his fist back, ready to strike Emlyn in the face, but the old man was struggling to breathe, the wind having been knocked out of him by the fall, and with the shock of hitting the ground had come the realisation that he had lost. The madness in his eyes was gone, replaced by fear, the beginnings of tears. Tom stood up, left him lying there.

He heard Pearl groan from beside him, went to help her up.

'You OK?'

He tried to pull her into a sitting position.

'Steady,' she said. 'Everything's still spinning.'

He moved in close to examine her wound.

'I'll be all right,' she said, touching her head, wincing from the pain. 'Where's Lila?'

Tom looked round.

Morrigan, and her knife, had disappeared.

So had Lila.

63

'Run, just fucking run . . .'

Kai pulled the rope that Lila's hands were attached to, dragging her along behind him. Sometimes she stumbled, fell. He just yanked her upright again, kept going. He had to get away. Had to. And she was coming with him.

For now.

Kai had seen what was happening, guessed which way the tide was turning. The police would eventually be called, he could see that, whether Rachel Bellfair was one of them or not. And there would be plenty of explaining to do. Lots of deals made and a hell of a lot of finger-pointing. If he stayed around he would be singled out more than most, used as a scapegoat. And he wasn't about to let that happen. Not at all.

So he had told the other two to go and help Noah, had grabbed Lila and run. At first just blindly, with no plan. *Just get away.* The words repeating over and over in his mind, a mantra. Just get away. He soon realised that there was nowhere he could get away to. Everywhere would soon be tainted. He had to think. Be cunning.

And it came to him. So simple. So obvious. How to get rid of all his problems in one go.

The caves. Dump Lila in the pit once more, leave her to rot. If the fall didn't kill her first, that is. She had caused all this. She was the one responsible for everything he had done. She deserved her fate.

Then, job done, he could stay in there until it all blew over, find his way out again and be off. Perfect.

Lila tripped, stumbled. Went down again.

Kai looked around, shone his torch. One cave looked the same as another to him. Not for the first time in these caves he wished he hadn't dropped out of university, hadn't stopped studying geology. But if he had stayed at uni none of this would have happened. *If...* He stamped down on those thoughts, knowing no good would come of thinking that way. There was a fork before him. He wondered which way to take.

He turned to Lila. 'Get up, keep moving.'

She still had the gag in, thankfully, or he would never hear the end of this. She stood up, staring at him with undisguised hatred.

'Come on,' he said. 'This way.' He took a tunnel at random and set off once more.

64

'Where's she gone? Where's Lila? Where's Morrigan taken her?' No one answered him. No one knew. For most of them, Lila's whereabouts weren't a priority. He tried again. 'Where's Lila?'

No reply. Everyone moved about in their own, shell-shocked little world.

He was about to shout again, but someone came and stood directly in front of him, drawing his attention so he couldn't look anywhere else but at them.

Rachel.

'Where is she, Rachel? Where's Lila?'

Rachel just stared at him. Anger burned in her eyes.

'Where's she gone? What's that evil old bitch done with her? Tell me.'

'This is all your fault,' said Rachel. Evenly and steadily, her eyes never leaving his. 'This mess. It's all your fault. You'll pay for what you've done. I'll see to that. I'm police.'

'Not after tonight. You're finished in the police force. Now where is she?'

Rachel just smiled. Tom grabbed her by the shoulders, held her tight.

'Ow . . . you're hurting . . .'

'This is nothing to what you're going to get if you don't talk. Now again, where is she?'

Rachel gave no answer so Tom, letting all his frustration and fear build up, shook her. Hard. Harder than he intended, trying desperately to make her talk, get some sense out of her.

'Tom . . . don't . . .'

'Then tell me. *Where* is she?'

Understanding seemed to dawn in Rachel's eyes. Tom stopped shaking her. She looked round as if seeing her surroundings for the first time. Comprehending what had just occurred. She looked back to Tom, spoke as if she was coming out of a heavy anaesthetic.

'Everything's gone. Everything . . .' Her curious look said that she wanted Tom to explain it to her. 'It's all gone . . .'

'Yeah, it's all gone, everything. Now where is she?'

Rachel frowned once more. 'I can't think about . . . her . . . I've got to . . . got to save . . . my career now, my family. My . . . I'm police.' She looked up at him, her eyes becoming clearer, more lucid as she spoke. 'I've got to salvage something, make something good come out of this. What can I do? How do I do that?' A desperate edge of hysteria creeping into her voice now. 'There must be a way, there must be. I just have to think of it . . .'

'You can start by telling me where Lila is.'

She shook her head, wanting to stay in the comfort of her own mind, not wanting to reappear in the real world any time soon.

Tom grabbed her by the shoulders again, shook her. 'Tell me. *Where is she?*'

That finally broke the spell. She stared at him.

'Where's Lila?'

'I saw Kai grab her, pull her away.'

'Kai?' Tom had completely forgotten about him. Didn't think he was even worth considering. 'Not Morrigan or Isobel or whatever she's calling herself?'

She shook her head.

'Where to? Where did he take her?'

She frowned. 'Don't know. Looked like they were heading towards the old mine workings . . .'

Tom let go of her. She kept staring at him.

'We could have had something, couldn't we?'

He turned his back on her.

'*Couldn't* we?'

He ignored her, walked away.

Noah barred his path. He was clearly in pain, cradling his broken hand, face contorted.

'I'm not in the mood,' said Tom, trying to move round him.

'You need help. I know where he's taken her. I can take you there.'

'This some kind of trick? After everything that's happened?'

'No trick.'

'Then why should you bother?'

'Look around,' said Noah. 'It's all turned to shit. You think I'm staying with this lot?'

'Very pragmatic. Come on.'

Noah led the way.

Tom turned, allowed himself one final snapshot.

Pearl was on the phone, calling the police. Rachel was staggering round, completely dazed. The rest of them were trying to put out the fires and leave as quickly as possible. Back to their own lives, desperately trying to give themselves alibis. Emlyn was sitting by the altar, broken. Sobbing.

Tom turned away. Followed Noah.

65

Kai reached another fork in the caves. He paused, deciding which way to take.

Lila looked down at her hands, her wrists. They were red, skinned, where the bindings had worn away at them. But the rope was slack in Kai's hand, looping down to the floor between the two of them. He hadn't noticed. Recognising she might not get another chance, she pulled the rope hard and watched it saw through Kai's hands, making him cry out at the sudden friction burns. She pulled harder until it was free of him. And ran.

He was on her straight away, staggering over the rocks and debris, his desperation at losing her overriding anything else. He grabbed the trailing rope, pulled it tight. Lila collapsed to the floor, body stinging from the rocks beneath her.

'You can't escape,' said Kai, gasping for breath. 'These caves go on for miles in every direction. *Every* direction. Up, down, forward, back. You get lost in them you'll never get out.'

Her gag had loosened. 'I'll take my chances.'

He gave a bitter laugh, pulled her to her feet, tied the rope round his wrist, and kept walking forward, dragging her along behind.

Eventually, more through luck than actual knowledge on Kai's part, Lila thought, they reached the pit once more. Stopped at the rim of it. Kai looked at her. Still that bitter smile on his face. This time triumphant. The triumph of a small man.

'This is where we say goodbye,' he told her.

'I don't think so,' said a voice from the darkness.

Kai swung the torch round. There stood Tom and Noah.

'What the fuck? What . . . How did you get here before me?'

'Because I know the way, Kai,' said Noah. He shook his head. 'You're fucking clueless.'

Any sense of triumph totally disappeared from Kai's features. He looked helplessly between the two of them, then back to Lila, the pit.

Tom moved forwards. 'Let her go, Kai. Let her walk away.' Moving steadily closer all the time. 'I just want Lila. That's all. Just hand her over. She and I will walk away and that'll be that. Yeah?'

Kai kept staring at him, eyes wild. He pushed Lila back towards the rim of the pit.

Tom kept his voice calm and steady. 'Come on, Kai . . . you can do it . . .'

'Get back . . . get back . . .'

Kai moved closer to Lila. Tom stopped moving.

Kai turned his attention to Noah. 'What're you here for? What d'you want?'

'Kai,' said Noah, matching Tom's measured tone, 'it's over, mate. Finished. Everything's gone. We've got to get out of here. Quickly.'

Kai looked between the pair of them. He opened his mouth to reply but the voice that spoke wasn't his.

'You're going to stay just where you are.'

They turned. A huge, crow-like shadow detached itself from the wall, walked forward.

'Isobel,' said Tom.

'Call me by my real name,' she hissed. 'It's Morrigan. Morrigan . . .' The knife glittered in her hand. She moved towards Kai and Lila.

'The girl's mine. The ritual must be completed.'

'Put the knife down, Morrigan,' said Tom, the name coming reluctantly to his lips. 'It's all over. Don't make things even worse.'

She didn't move. No one did.

Tom held out his hand. Began edging towards her. 'Give me the knife. Let it go.'

'Stay where you are . . .' The words spat out, the knife extended.

Tom stopped moving. He glanced at Lila, noticed that behind Kai, unseen by the others, she was slowly doing something with her hands.

Morrigan stared at Noah, eyes wide, red-rimmed. 'Traitor. Traitor . . .'

Noah seemed momentarily conflicted, once again weighing up his options. He shook his head. 'That's it,' he said. 'I've had enough. I'm off.'

Tom reached for him, grabbed his sleeve. 'What you doing?'

'Getting out of here. This shit's just . . .' He laughed, shook his head. 'You're on your own, mate.'

He turned to go. Morrigan moved quickly, slashed him with her knife. He gasped in pain and surprise, looked down at his arm where she had caught him.

'*No*,' she screamed. 'Traitor . . .'

Noah didn't stop to think. He ran. Kai looked after him, wanting to follow, but missing his moment. He stayed where he was, transfixed by the blade in Morrigan's hand.

In the confusion of Noah's exit, Tom tried to move forward against Morrigan. She swung the knife out towards him in a glittering arc. He stopped.

'All of you . . . all of you, letting me down, disappointing me . . .' She swung her gaze at them, spat the words out. 'I did this for you. For the village. For the community. For us . . . for us, all of us . . . for the future . . .'

Tom noticed that Lila had loosened the rope around her wrists, had pulled her hands free while the others were distracted.

Morrigan kept talking. 'Well, it's not too late . . . The sacrifice is still here.' She pointed the knife at Lila. '*She's* worthless. Not one of us. No use to anyone, won't be missed. I'm doing you a favour, my dear . . . You can be part of something wonderful . . .'

She swung the knife at Lila. But Lila wasn't there. She'd jumped out of the way.

'Bitch . . . you're going to suffer, you'll die slowly . . . and I'll enjoy every exquisite minute of it. I'll feed on your fear, your pain . . . I'll make it slow, you'll feel everything . . .'

Another slash forward of the blade.

Lila shifted once more, tried to reach Tom but Kai was in the way. Rooted to the spot by fear and indecision, Lila's movement seemed to wake him. He turned.

'Hey . . .' he shouted, making a grab for her, 'you're . . .'

Morrigan swung the knife again, trying to follow Lila's movements. She was too slow. Lila was no longer in that space.

But Kai was. The knife caught him just below the ribcage. His forward momentum, reaching for Lila, thrust it straight up inside him.

Morrigan stared, face etched in shock, as understanding slowly dawned on Kai's face. He staggered backwards, blood erupting from his chest. He stared at the knife, not believing it was actually there, and though he tried to react his body wouldn't respond. He moved as if to sit down but suddenly disappeared into the darkness of the pit, the only sound that of his body hitting the metal bed frame, the noise reverberating round the chamber.

Morrigan stared after him, fascinated. A voice startled her from her reverie. She looked up, uncomprehendingly.

'Worthless, am I?' Lila was shouting. 'No use to anyone? That's what *he* said. That's what my *mother* said. And you're *liars*, the whole fucking lot of you . . .'

Lila swung her fist, connecting directly with Morrigan's face. The crack of her nose splintering echoed round the cave. Morrigan put her fingers to her face. Blood gushed between them. She slumped to the ground.

Lila moved in, ready to administer another blow.

Tom rushed forward, grabbed her.

'It's OK, I've got you . . . I've got you . . .'

Lila stood rigid, a beacon of trembling anger. Then collapsed sobbing into his arms.

PART FOUR

66

Morrigan hated waiting. Like death before death. Anger-inducing in its stupidity. And Morrigan knew all about anger. Its power, its energy. Its beauty. Morrigan *was* anger.

Here, in this cell, separated from her partner, she had time to think. To plot. To plan. Dissect what she had done wrong. Plan how to improve. For next time . . .

She had always hated her birth name and now she could dispense with it completely. Isobel was a lost girl. A dull girl. An ignored, hurt girl. A weak girl. Morrigan was strong. Powerful. Everything Isobel wasn't.

A long journey from her childhood. That wretched child, born into an illiterate family in a remote Cornish community. A family that created children because they had nothing else to do with their lives. They had neither the education for college, nor the where-withal for social interaction. They'd kept themselves to themselves, in almost complete isolation.

She had brothers and sisters. Father and mother. But she had trouble remembering which was which. She could recall those times only through abstract images and sounds, feelings and emotions rather than concrete memories. Darkness, screams, grunts. Pain on her skin, in her body. Cries in return. Black and grey smudged blurs of faces, eyes small and red, screaming again. Sobbing. Cold. Her body untouched when she wanted it, touched too much when she didn't. Numbness. And when the outside world removed her from her parents, she was neither grateful nor upset. Just accepting.

She soon had a new family. Two foster brothers and a new mother and father. She remembered them smiling at her. Remembered those smiles curdling into fear as they reached her eyes. The wild child. The savage. The other names the two boys called her. Behind their parents' backs at first, then later to her face. She was hurt by them, cried. But recovered and showed them what a real wild child could do.

She was given another set of parents after that. Placed under what they said was supervision. A therapist was brought in. A large, smiling woman swathed in too-bright voluminous clothes and scarves. She asked her questions. Suggested that she play with certain dolls while she watched. Made notes. Blind to what the therapist was doing, she went along with it. The therapist talked lots to her, and she found her voice, talked back. And talked more. And more. And the therapist told her she was a clever little girl and she would do all she could to help her. She didn't think she needed any help so just nodded and said thank you, the way she knew the therapist would like.

Then another family. And attending school. By now she had learned to watch the other children, see how they behaved. She didn't want to be the wild child any more. So she kept those parts silent inside her and copied what the other children did. The more she copied, the more they seemed to like her and let her join in with them. She liked that. It gave her acceptance, made her feel like she could move amongst them unobserved. She felt superior in every way. And that gave her power. The biggest thrill she had experienced in her small life.

She was an exceptional student. The school was proud of her, gave her more work, harder questions to answer. She enjoyed it, devoured it. Felt even more superior to her peers as a result. Her teachers recommended university.

But what and where to study? She had discovered a real and profound passion for history. Especially the history of her land, Cornwall. They suggested Oxford or Cambridge, told her she would definitely get in. She didn't want to go to either of those places. Too far away. She was connected with the land, and it with her. She would wither and die if she was removed from it. So she stayed local, went to Falmouth University.

But her real study took place away from the university. Her quest to understand the history of the land of her birth led her to paganism and witchcraft. That was when she truly came alive, felt herself flowering and blossoming. Like simultaneously coming home and bursting out of it. Like she had found what she had been looking for all her life and would only serve this path from thereon.

Her birth name was now inadequate for the person she was becoming. She needed a real name. A witch name. Morrigan. The crow sighted flying high above wars, the goddess of battle, sovereignty and prophecy. The warrior queen. Perfect.

She started a pagan society at university. It attracted a few like-minded souls but none of them took it as seriously as she did. Except one. And Morrigan knew as soon as she saw him that he was the one for her.

Small and unprepossessing in appearance, but as soon as their hands touched she felt a spark of electricity flow between them. She felt her power rise within. He was to be her perfect partner. And he understood that too, for he had been looking for just such a person as Morrigan to submit himself to. They recognised their need in each other. The perfect mirror image.

They began to pull away from the rest of the group, performing rituals involving only the two of them, more and more extreme as they began to understand each other, and their place in the world. They used their earth magick to pleasure themselves and each other. Morrigan had the power. He was the submissive.

Beatings. Knife work. Scarring. Burning. All part of their self-invented sex-magick rituals. Morrigan also found herself slipping back into her childhood during particularly intense rituals, absorbing the violence inflicted on her, utilising it, acknowledging it and turning it outwards, throwing it onto her new partner. For his part he took it gratefully, understanding his function, gratifying his goddess.

It was their sort of lovemaking. Each fist to the face, each knife wound, each nail hammered into his soft flesh delivered with delicacy and care. The most intense, erotic, beautiful experience either of them had ever known, ever would know.

Morrigan needed the power the rituals gave her. To sublimate one personality allowed the other to soar free. It became a drug to her, wanting it more and more frequently and in more intense measures. Chasing that initial high, never sufficiently recapturing it, always pushing further. Further.

Her partner recognised this. Told her she needed to stop. She would kill herself in pursuit of something she could never attain. And she would kill him too. She listened. But knew she couldn't stop, so what would they do instead? How would they capture that exquisite high?

Involve other people, he said. Exercise our ritual magick on them.

They knew the secret societies where their kind of magick was practised, sought out the most adventurous, or sometimes foolhardy, of them. Brought them into their ambit. Performed rituals.

Morrigan loved the screams. The pain. None of them were as adept as her partner at receiving pain gratefully and graciously, which made the experiences all the more visceral and thrilling. He assisted, enjoying the pain vicariously. Morrigan was in charge. And she discovered something about herself. The pain of her victims, their suffering, was like meat and drink to her. She fed on it, gorged on it, subsumed it into her body. It gave her power she hadn't felt before, strength she couldn't previously have imagined. It gave her life.

But eventually, those highs also passed. They needed more and more extreme rituals, more pain, more suffering. And victims were harder to come by. So it fell to her partner to find a way forward once more.

You've gone as far as you can at this level, he explained. Use your rituals, direct your power towards the outside now. Luxuriate in a world remade in your name, by your hand. As for him, he would have the pleasure of seeing his goddess succeed.

So began the next chapter of Morrigan's life.

What did she want? Control. Power. How would she get it? By following his instructions.

But remember, he told her, operate through fear. They must be scared of you. A scared populace is a pliant populace. A suggestive populace. This is a grand experiment but it needs to be carried out thoroughly to ensure its success. So scare them. The way you scare me . . .

It worked. She used her ritual magick for all who came calling. Asking nothing in return but to speak for her when the time came. And it would come. No doubt.

They accepted her magick, these farmers, these rural folk. Kept their silence, gave no dissent. Complicit through their fear of her and her power. She never doubted her own abilities. That ensured they never doubted them either. Every outcome was the one she wanted, and she always convinced them that it was the one they wanted too. Fearful, they never argued.

Word of her abilities spread. As did her power, her influence. And soon came the challenge her abilities needed.

The marina.

She smiled when she saw the news, understood the implications. Could she get the whole community to support her? Follow her? Use her power, exert her control over all of them? Of course she could. And as for complicity . . . Get a whole village not only to be complicit in, but actively to take part in, the ultimate ritual, the blood sacrifice of another human being? Oh, yes. She had positioned herself perfectly. She could do that. She held the power of life and death over all of them. And she loved it.

That was all in the past now. But Morrigan was still here. She wasn't scared in this cell. It would only be a matter of time before they released her. Her rituals would ensure that. Then she could start again. Not repeating the same mistakes. This time she would get it right. She smiled. This time she would truly fly . . .

67

'So,' said Janet, 'I hear you've had a busy time of late.'

'You could say that.' Tom nodded. Almost smiled. 'Although obviously I wasn't there at all.'

'Obviously. And how did you manage that?'

'Ducked out quickly. Made a few phone calls. Then just kept a low profile. No one else was up for talking about it much. The police are still working through it all now.'

'And what about you?' she said, leaning forward. 'Are you still working through it?'

He was beginning to regard the room as a comforting place that he could retreat to. The sloping ceilings with only glimpses of treetops and sky meant the rest of the world could be miles away. And his therapist's smiling face, calming manner. No, not calming exactly, but encouraging. Creating a space for him to say what he never could anywhere else.

Or thought he never could.

'I'm still . . . I don't know what's changed since the last time. Well, everything, kind of. Lila, the girl, is still staying with me.'

'How long for?'

Tom shrugged. 'I don't know.'

'Is that wise? How d'you feel about that?'

'She needs somewhere to stay. Somewhere to be anchored to.'

'Someone?'

'Maybe.'

'And is that someone you? D'you feel up to it?'

'I don't know. But I can't just throw her out when she's got nowhere else to go.'

She glanced down at her notes, back up to him. 'And what about you? Do you need someone to be anchored to? And if so, is it her?'

He thought long and hard before answering, playing out so many possibilities in his head, running through various ways to explain. 'I don't know,' was all he could eventually come up with. Then before she could say anything he spoke. 'I do know one thing, though.'

'What's that?'

'If she stays, and I mean for any length of time, I'm going to have to tell her.'

'Is that wise? Are you sure?'

Tom smiled. 'Wise? I doubt it. But it's the right thing to do. She needs that honesty from me.'

Janet couldn't argue with that.

Later, he sat in the garden opposite Lila. Spring had announced its presence and people were rushing to make the most of it. Tom had cleared a space in the semi-wilderness of the garden, found furniture for them to sit on. It felt homely. Relaxed. He sipped whiskey. Lila had a Coke.

After the night in the cave Lila had gone home with Tom. Neither talked about it, both expected it. She slept for hours, nearly the whole of the next day. At first she suffered night terrors but they subsided the longer she slept. Tom knew because he had been awake all that time, looking out for her. Ensuring that nothing else happened to her.

He had done the same for her in the aftermath of that night with the police. Shielded her from them, kept her in his house. He had done the same for himself too. Kept out of the ambit of the police. No one was in any hurry to incriminate him in anything because that would mean that they would be incriminating themselves. So his part was, through no special pleading, covered up.

Emlyn and Isobel Chenoweth were in custody. Isobel had been charged with Kai's murder. The body of Pirate John had been found at the base of the cliffs. It was announced as murder but the police didn't know where to begin to look for suspects.

Noah and most of the travellers had disappeared. No one knew where. No one had heard from them. Rachel was also in custody. She had lost her job with the police force. Despite her contacting him several times, Tom had had nothing to do with her.

A lot of people were talking of moving away from the area. Tom wasn't surprised at that.

And St Petroc hadn't won the bid for the marina. Probably just as well, thought Tom.

Then there was Pearl.

He was unsure whether to go in to work the next day. But Pearl hadn't phoned him to say otherwise so he had turned up as usual.

He had made a point of walking through the village. It had the haunted, abandoned feel that he had experienced in villages and settlements in Afghanistan after the collective madness of battle had passed by, leaving only the ghosts, the bereft and the shell-shocked civilians who couldn't believe they had once tried to be insurgents. Had thought they had a point to make, a war to fight.

The few people about kept their distance from each other, from him. He had been right: the village was in collective shock. Shame and disgust stopped them looking at each other and barely at themselves.

He saw that the village shop was open, deliberated, went inside. The same stout, angry-faced woman was behind the till. She usually looked formidable, judgemental but she didn't look like that today. He could understand her impulse, though. Try to go back to normal. Pretend it had never happened.

Tom took a loaf of bread from the shelf, placed it beside the till. Her face reddened. She wouldn't meet his eyes.

'Quiet today,' he said.

She stated the price of the bread, waited for his money.

'Was yours one of the cars destroyed last night?'

She looked like she didn't know how to respond. Tom stayed where he was, gave her no choice but to address him.

She nodded.

'The four-by-four or the estate?'

'Estate.'

'Insurance cover it?'

'I don't know.'

'It's still in front of my house so give me a call when you want to come and get it. Maybe I can give you a tow with my Land Rover.'

She nodded once more, her face now beetroot.

He studied her, this woman who usually had an opinion on everyone and everything, now struck silent. Whatever rage he had felt towards her – and the rest of them – had dissipated with the new day. He remembered Afghanistan once more, would-be insurgents in tears as they realised what they had done. Just normal citizens doing what they had believed in, thought was right. Confronted with the enormity of their crimes they had always crumpled. Begged for forgiveness from Tom and his team when it wasn't theirs to give.

'We've all got to rebuild,' Tom told her. 'Move forward. Haven't we?'

She didn't reply.

He left the shop.

He found Pearl sitting by herself in the bar. It looked dusty and old, light slanting in through the ancient windows, stray beams of illumination that just showed up how dark everywhere else was.

'Closed.'

She looked up as he entered.

'Oh. It's you.' She looked down again, unsure what to say to him.

'Yeah, it's me.'

He pulled up a chair, sat next to her.

'You not opening today? The place'll be overrun with journalists and news crews. You're missing out on a small fortune.'

She shrugged. 'Not bothered.'

'Fair enough.'

'I'm sorry. I was wrong. I was ... I don't know why I ...' Long-dammed tears began to flow.

Tom put his arm round her. She sank into him.

'It's OK,' he said. 'Your parents were there, this is your village, you ... I don't know, did what you felt was the right thing to do.'

She said nothing, just cried.

Eventually she looked up, wiped her wet face with a tissue. 'Thank you.'

'For what?'

'Just ... being understanding. My parents have left the village. Don't know if they'll ever be back again. Don't know what I should do ...'

'Run this place.'

She shook her head. 'I can't ...'

'Course you can. Take over from what they did. I bet you've been turning away bookings already, haven't you?'

She nodded.

'Place'll be rammed soon. Just wait till the tourists get a hold of the story. Proper little goldmine, this'll be.'

'I'll need someone to run it with me.' She looked up at Tom.

'Me?' He thought. 'I should ... keep a low profile.'

'Why? Who are you really, Tom?'

He almost told her. 'Just a friend. That's all. Hopefully your friend.' He changed the subject. 'What would that involve if I did it?'

365

'I'll have to run the whole lot, hotel and everything. You can have my old job, bar manager. That's if you're not going to disappear. You always said you never knew how long you'd be around for.'

Tom's turn to shrug. 'I've got nowhere else to go. Here's as good as anywhere.'

'So what d'you think?'

'I think you'd better open those doors. There'll be a lot of thirsty and hungry journalists looking for somewhere to set up shop. Mostly thirsty.'

She smiled at him.

The Sail Makers had been busy every day since then. Tom had taken on extra shifts and would do even more in his new role. But there was one more thing – the most important thing – he still had to do.

He looked across at Lila sitting in the garden, drinking her Coke.

Now or never, he thought.

'So,' he said, 'what d'you want to do now?'

She shrugged. 'Drink this. Maybe have another. See what's on telly later. Why?'

'That's not what I meant.'

Lila nodded. Looked away. 'I know what you meant.'

'Right. Well, I just wanted to say, you're welcome to stay here. As far as I'm concerned, this is your house as well as mine.'

She tried to hide how pleased his words made her.

'Thanks.'

'I mean, it won't make everything perfect overnight, but it's a start. You can get yourself sorted out from here. This can be your home. For as long as you want it.'

'OK, then.' She nodded. Then looked up. 'Just one thing.'

Tom braced himself. He knew what she was going to ask. And he knew he had to be honest with her in his reply.

'Fire away.' He regretted his choice of words immediately.

'Who are you?'

He smiled. Just what he had expected.

'I mean, I know your name, Tom Killgannon, but I know nothing about you. I know there's something gone on in your past and you're here for a reason, but if I'm going to be living here with you then I need to know who you are. You know everything about me.'

'That's fair enough. I'll tell you. And once I've told you, I hope you'll still want to stay.'

Lila looked apprehensive. Tom began.

'First thing you should know, Tom Killgannon's not my real name.'

'What is it, then?'

'Doesn't matter. Really, it doesn't matter. I don't use it any more, I doubt I ever will again.'

'How did you come to be here?'

He poured himself a whisky.

'I told you I was ex-army and that I joined the police force. Right?'

She nodded.

'And that I got sent up to Moss Side undercover?'

She nodded again.

'Right. Well, the area had changed so much when I got back. Didn't recognise it, hardly. I mean, it had always been rough, that's where I'm from, but it was so bad. Poverty was really biting, no jobs, nothing. No hope. And the place was divided up between the gangs. They were the only growth industry. Gangs and drugs. And people living in fear. Community? All gone.

'Julie, my sister, was separated from the bloke she'd had a daughter with. And Hayley, her daughter, my niece, was doing her full-on teenage rebellion thing. Driving her mother mad. No one could reach her.'

Lila smiled. 'Yeah, recognise that.'

'I doubt it. Not like her. She was really full on. Fifteen and running with the drug gangs and using as well. Horrible to see.'

'So what did you do?'

'Went undercover. That's what I was there for. No one knew I was from round there. They just thought I was ex-army, home after the Middle East. It worked as a cover story, got me in with them. I mean, it took a while, didn't just happen overnight, but they eventually accepted me, came to trust me, even. I ended up being thought of as one of their own.

'But obviously I wasn't. There I was, working my way up in the organisation, but really gathering as much evidence as I could on them. Getting closer to the top guys. And I did some ... shall we say, morally questionable things on the way. Things I'm not proud of, but that were necessary to get me trusted, to be convincing.'

'Like what?'

'Oh, you don't want to know.'

'I do. If I'm living here under the same roof as you, I want to know.'

Tom sighed. Told her the truth. 'Punishment beatings. Drug distribution. Even arranging arson against potential enemies and competitors. All sorts of shit.' He looked up at her. 'Sorry.'

'Go on.'

'Well, that made them trust me. I got a reputation as muscle. Intelligent muscle, though. And I was there for nearly two years.'

'So what happened? I'm assuming something happened.'

'Oh, yeah, it happened all right.' Tom paused, blinked away a mental image that came fleetingly to mind. Continued. 'There was a shipment due. They needed my help with it. A big shipment. The kind that could break the whole gang, if they had someone on the inside that knew what was happening. Which they did, of course. So I informed my handlers and when it arrived, the police were waiting. But of course, nothing ever goes right.'

He paused, took a mouthful of whisky. Another one. Lila said nothing, waited for him to continue.

'There were more people around that night than I'd expected. Many more. One in particular.'

'Hayley?'

Tom gave a sad smile. 'Yeah, Hayley. And more guns than anyone was expecting. The whole thing was a bloodbath. And I contributed to it as well.'

Another sigh. Another mouthful of whisky.

'And when all the smoke cleared and the bodies were counted, Hayley was one of them.'

He stopped, his mind right back in that night. He had never forgotten it. Never would.

'I don't know who did it, I never found out. There was crossfire . . .' He stopped, wiped back tears. 'Crossfire. And . . . she was dead . . .'

'But you didn't kill her.'

He looked up, fresh tears in his eyes. 'I might have done . . .'

'I don't think you did. And you can't blame yourself for it.'

Another sigh. 'But I do. I could have got her out of there. Told her who I was, what I was doing. Got her out. But I didn't.'

'You couldn't,' said Lila. 'You had a job to do.'

'Yeah, some job. Took some drugs off the streets, some gangsters, so what? A new batch of drugs arrived after that, a new load of gangs to distribute them. But Hayley was gone for ever . . .'

Lila looked at him, understanding something for the first time.

'Anyway,' said Tom, keeping going, 'my work was commended. I'd amassed enough evidence against the gang to put them away. And then I was given a way out, because I'd burned all my bridges in Manchester. Give evidence anonymously, be seen as striking a deal, let them take all the blame. Ghost away. I said yes. But there was a catch. I'd have to go into witness protection. Or UK Protected Person Service, to give it its full title. Get a new identity, leave the

369

police force, move somewhere where I was completely unknown. Here seemed as good as anywhere.'

'You told me you were from Middlesbrough the other night.'

Tom smiled. 'Yeah, that's what I have to tell people. Tom Killgannon is from Middlesbrough, to all intents and purposes. They sent me there after Manchester to get used to the place for a few months, so if anyone asked me anything about it I'd know what I was talking about. But there was one other thing.'

'Yeah?'

'They thought I was too good at my job to let me go completely. A plausibly deniable asset. So I had to agree to what they wanted if they were to leave me alone. If I wanted to come to terms with what I'd done, what had happened to Hayley, have any chance at a new future, all that.'

'What?'

'I have to be here when they want me. Ready and willing to be recalled. Push a button and up jumps Action Man.'

'Did you agree?'

'I had no choice. So here I am.'

'Did you talk to your sister?'

'I tried. Sent her a message explaining that I'd been working undercover, that I did what I'd done because I was police. And that I was genuinely sorry for Hayley's death, for the grief and anguish I'd caused her and if I'd contributed to it I hoped that she could find it in her heart to forgive me. All of that.'

'And did she?'

He sniffed, drank more whisky. 'Never heard back.'

He looked up, directly at Lila. 'So there you go. That's who I am.'

She returned his stare, unblinking. Nodding. Eventually she spoke.

'So I remind you of her, is that it? Your dead niece.'

'Well, no . . .'

'You couldn't save her so you'll save me instead? Is that it?'

'It's not like that.'

Anger rose within her. 'Well, it sounds like that to me. I'm just some . . . I don't know what I am, what you think of me.'

'*No*, it's not like that,' said Tom, raising his own voice. Then softening it again, thinking. 'Well, I don't know. Maybe. Partly. But I couldn't just stand by and not help you, could I? Everything you've been through. You didn't deserve all that.'

'Really? Didn't I? Sometimes I think I do. I've done some bad things. Look what I did to Danny.'

'Self-defence. And you didn't kill him.'

'But I helped to get that student killed.'

'No, you didn't. But when you realised you'd done something wrong, you tried to put it right. That's the act of a good person. You don't deserve what you got, Lila. And I would hate to see anything more happen to you.'

She kept staring at him, took her time to reply. 'Well, if anything did happen to me, it would be my fault, right?'

'Yeah, of course.'

'Not yours, mine.'

'Absolutely.' He sighed. 'I meant what I said, though: this is your home as well as mine. For as long as you want it. No strings, no questions. OK?'

Lila thought. 'OK,' she said after a while. Then she thought some more, smiled.

'What?'

'You. You look like this big strong bloke, but you're not, are you? You're as much of a fuck-up as I am.'

'You reckon?' Tom smiled.

'I reckon. I don't think it's you looking after me – I think I'll have to look after you.'

He laughed.

Lila looked round at the garden. 'You know, you could really make something of this. Something really decent here.'

'You think? Maybe. I'd need help, though. Couldn't do it on my own.'

She smiled at him.

'OK, then. Deal.'

A crow sailed overhead, cawing. They ignored it.

They sat in silence. Both drinking, both smiling.

Acknowledgements

Firstly, thanks to Jade Chapman for suggesting that I might like to look westwards for inspiration.

To my agent Jane Gregory and everyone at Gregory and Company for getting in the ring and going the full ten rounds on my behalf.

To everyone at Bonnier Zaffre for making me feel so welcome and doing such a great job on this book. With special and huge thanks to my wonderful editor Katherine Armstrong for giving so much and making me up my game to match her vision. If you enjoy this book, you've got her to thank.

And to my wife, Jamie-Lee. You turn research trips into adventures. You turn everything into an adventure.

Read on for a conversation with
Martyn Waites . . .

Where did the character of Tom Killgannon come from? Is he based on anyone you know?

Not really. I suppose, as someone once said, your series character is always a version of yourself but five years younger. As I've got older it might be ten. Or twenty . . .

But no. I knew for this new book that I needed a new central character and I had to make him interesting enough to base a whole series on, if readers wanted to stick around for that. I'd just moved to the south-west after spending most of my adult life in and around London so it was quite a change. I decided to create a character who could mirror that sense of dislocation I was experiencing. Looking at a place with an outsider's eye. Although, it must be stressed, my background is very different to Tom's.

You wrote eight successful books under the pseudonym Tania Carver. How's it been writing as Martyn Waites again? Do you miss Tania?

Not yet. I'm just enjoying being Martyn again and writing about Tom Killgannon. Being Tania for such a sustained length of time was an interesting experience. At first the publisher kept my identity quiet which was difficult for me as I have a natural tendency to talk about myself as much as possible, especially when I've had a drink. The first book, *The Surrogate*, was a bestseller, nominated for the Theakston's Award, and WHSmith's book of the week. It was difficult to stand there in Smith's watching people pick my book up and buy it and not be able to tell them that Tania was really me. And yes, I did stand in bookshops and watch people buy it. It was the first book of mine to have that kind of success. And it didn't have my name on it!

When I was writing as Tania I always knew the difference between a Tania story idea and a Martyn one. If I had a Martyn idea I'd have to file it away to use later. Well, now it is later. After nearly a decade writing only Tania stories it's great to come back and write as myself again. I wouldn't rule out another pseudonym in the future, though, especially if I had an idea that was miles away from my usual stuff.

You're well known for your love of gothic horror, having penned the sequel to *The Woman in Black*, *Angel of Death*. What first got you interested in that genre?

That came before crime fiction. It came before most things, really. *Doctor Who*, horror movies and comics. That was my childhood. Actually, it's been my adulthood too . . .

Growing up in the seventies, there was always a late-night horror movie on Friday nights. It was kind of a rite of passage to be able to stay up late and watch that. Then BBC2 started running summer double bills of old Universal and Hammer movies on Saturday nights. I couldn't have been happier. It was often the highlight of my week. Yes, I was a sad child. I didn't just watch the films, though. I bought books, magazines, model kits, posters, comics, the lot. And it grew from there. I still have most of the things from that time. And now I've added to that collection with DVDs and Blu-rays. And books, of course. Too many to list.

My latest passion – which really informs the novel – is the folk horror revival. I'm very much a part of that. For years it was thought that urban landscapes held the most potential for horror. Obviously that's not right. Hopefully books like mine will go some way towards correcting that. Also, a great read is Adam Scovell's *Folk Horror: Hours Dreadful and Things Strange*.

St Petroc is a fictional town in Cornwall, but the 'old religion' is very much a reality of Cornish history. When did you first come across it and are you a believer?

Of paganism? No. I'm not a believer in any religion, especially not organised ones, I've got no time for them. But I do think paganism as an abstract idea makes sense and seems fun. I do love the whole mythology and ritual aspect that comes with it but I would never partake myself. I could never be a believer.

Paganism in the novel is kind of a means to an end. It's just playing on a community's fear and beliefs. It's about what would happen if a convincing, charismatic fanatic took hold of a scared and impressionable populace. What could you get people to do? How far could you take it? That's kind of how I see most organised religions. Systems of control. And then they're taken to extremes: If you do something horrible in another's name – God's name – then you can lie and convince yourself you're doing it for a higher reason, for some kind of greater good, you're not just some shabby little murderer. Religion is a great justifier.

There's also a true story behind the novel. Charles Walton, a seventy-four-year-old labourer, was murdered in the village of Lower Quinton in Warwickshire in February 1945. Despite suspicions his killer was never prosecuted although it was strongly suspected Walton had been murdered as part of a blood ritual for the land or in a witchcraft ceremony. 1945 isn't that long ago. Especially in remote rural areas . . .

Crime fiction is often described as taking events of the day and exploring the ramifications, both the good and the bad, of some difficult subjects. *The Old Religion* can be read as an exploration on Brexit and what could happen – and in some cases, already is happening – to

those areas that have benefited substantially from EU support, but whose people voted to leave the EU. Why did you choose this location to tell this particular story?

Just for that reason. That was a big part of it. Cornwall is one of the areas, if not the area, most heavily reliant on EU subsidy and grants in the UK. They all voted to leave the EU. But expected to still get the same amount of money from . . . somewhere. Obviously this won't happen. Farmers were the same. I think it's just dawning on the leavers that they've been lied to, or at least I hope it is, and all the things they've been promised won't be happening. In fact, their lives will be substantially worse than before. Normally I would say they deserve it for what they've done, but unfortunately they're dragging the rest of us down too.

So this question kind of follows on from the last one, really. The Brexit referendum was hijacked by the odious Farage and the far right. Johnson and Gove blatantly lied to the country. No one thought the leavers would win, especially not the leavers. But they did. Their lies were believed, unfortunately. And now St Petroc is kind of the UK in microcosm. A dangerous fantasist has taken hold of a scared populace and is insisting they do something that would make them palpably worse off. I quote Chesterton in the novel: When people stop believing in something they don't believe in nothing, they'll believe in anything. That's our country at the moment. Brexit is the worst thing to happen to this country in my lifetime. And crime fiction should absolutely be discussing it.

Who are the people – writers or otherwise – who have most influenced you and your writing?

How long have you got? I'll keep the novelists separate as much as possible (I've seen the next question) so here goes. What I love most is a distinctive voice and a restless spirit for an artist. I hate it when some people say, 'This is my era' about things they were watching/listening to/reading in their twenties as if everything they experience subsequently isn't worth bothering with. Not me. It's my era till the coffin lid gets nailed down. And those are the kinds of people who inspire me.

In music I guess my main guy is Tom Waits. He's been through so many different styles of music yet his true persona, his voice, has shone through every time. Scott Walker is another. I know people say they hate his new avant-garde stuff but I don't. I wouldn't say I love it as much as *Scott 4*, but then there are very few things I love as much as *Scott 4*. I have a massive love of sixties Southern soul too. Get me drunk and I'll tell you the whole history of Stax Records. Or if you're really unlucky, I'll sing it to you.

Again, comics have been a huge influence. Jack Kirby, Steve Ditko and Stan Lee are the holy trinity. Kirby's *Fourth World* series are among the greatest works of twentieth-century art and I'll fight anyone who says they're not. There are loads more since then, but everything stems from those three.

Doctor Who is still the perfect TV series. I never get tired of watching and rewatching it. Same with *The Outer Limits*, *The Avengers*, *The Prisoner*, film noir, old horror movies . . .

There's so much more stuff I could mention. I have a huge collection of old pulp horror and crime paperbacks that I still read and reread.

It's all there in my writing to lesser and greater degrees, because it's all in my head and heart.

Who are your favourite authors?

My all-time favourite is Graham Greene. He did everything from literary to genre, serious to comic and he did it superbly. I still reread him and still find more and more things in his books.

I have a passion for seemingly neglected twentieth-century British writers. I love Patrick Hamilton. He should be huge. James Curtis. Gerald Kersh. Julian MacLaren-Ross. All those guys.

As far as crime goes, there's the holy trinity of Dashiell Hammett, Raymond Chandler and Ross MacDonald. Massive influences, all, especially Chandler. But beyond them there's Cornell Woolrich, David Goodis, Jim Thompson . . . And plenty more besides. I tend to read older stuff for fun.

As for current authors, if I name them all I'll probably miss someone out. I will say I particularly love what Laura Lippman, Megan Abbott, Alison Gaylin and Christa Faust are doing with the contemporary crime novel. Damned exciting.

Have you any advice for aspiring writers?

I could teach a course on it! In fact, I have done . . .

The main thing to say is to keep going. Don't be put off by rejection, learn from it. If you write a novel and try for six months to get it published or to find an agent then decide to give up or publish it yourself, you're not a real writer. You need to work at it. Constantly, day and night. It has to be in your head at all times. If it doesn't feel like hard work you're not doing it right. If you can walk away and leave it, you're not a real writer.

But if you can keep going, not take no for an answer, ask why someone who read your work didn't like it and learn from it, then you've got a chance. Go on a course, get your work properly critiqued. Be prepared to put in the effort.

And read. Constantly. Obsessively. If you don't read other people's books, then no one will want to read yours. And nor should they.

What are you reading at the moment?

I've just finished *Prelude to a Certain Midnight* by the aforementioned and brilliant Gerald Kersh. It's kind of a crime novel but, being Kersh, so much more than that. I've also got a collection of Arthur Machen short stories on the go that I dip into when I need a bit more weirdness in my life. I'm about to start rereading the great Ted Lewis and I'm also rereading Ed Brubaker and Darwyn Cooke's run on *Catwoman*.

What next for Tom Killgannon?

Well, he's coming back. Definitely. That's the first thing. The new novel is called *Cage City* and it's quite different to *The Old Religion*. Tom's in prison. Why? What for? I'm not saying. You'll have to read the book. I'll only say one thing and it's a quote from the great Jim Thompson: 'There is only one plot – Things are not what they seem . . .'

If you enjoyed *The Old Religion* why not join
the Martyn Waites Readers' Club by visiting
www.bit.ly/MartynWaitesClub?

**Turn over for a message from
Martyn Waites . . .**

Dear Reader,

Wow. Writing those two words makes me feel like I'm a character in a Jane Austen novel. Or even Jane Austen herself. I have a history of literary crossdressing (I've written eight thrillers under the name Tania Carver). But there, I'm afraid, the similarity ends. I'm here to talk about my new novel, *The Old Religion*. My editor describes it as a cross between Peter May and *The Wicker Man* and who am I to argue?

It's a series of firsts for me. My first novel with a totally rural, as opposed to urban setting. My first novel set in Cornwall. And my first to explicitly acknowledge the result of the Brexit referrendum. I'm primarily known as a crime writer having written the above mentioned Tania Carver novels as well as another ten under my own name (and co-authored along with Mark Billingham, Stav Sherez and David Quantick *Great Lost Albums*, the funniest music book ever written, but that's for another time). But one of those ten was the official sequel to Susan Hill's *The Woman in Black*. Definitely not crime. Horror. Ghosts. Gothic.

I had a great time writing it. Every gothic urge that I've suppressed when writing urban crime novels came out. Thinking it would be my only chance to write anything like that I threw the kitchen sink at it. All my influences from Poe onwards showed. And I didn't care. It also got me interested in a nascent movement that's since gained quite a bit of traction. Folk Horror. It explores rurality not as any-thing idyllic but more as an uneasy, terrifying place that can't be tamed by humanity and retains its own secrets and powers. A place where superstitions and rituals still take precedence.

I had all this in mind when I started on *The Old Religion*. I wanted to write a noir novel that not only explored what contemporary rural communities are like – and how they are suffering – after the referrendum, but also incorporate strong folk horror themes of fear and superstition. I hope I've succeeded. I've certainly given it my best shot.

With that in mind, there's a little something extra here for you. Originally I had sections in the novel showing rituals and their outcomes. These were cut for various reasons and their stories subsumed into the larger narrative but I kept the original pieces and think they work well as short stories or vignettes, expanding the wider world of the novel. Here's one of those pieces.

If you would like to hear more from me about *The Old Religion* and my other future books, you can visit www.bit.ly/MartynWaites Club where you can join the Martyn Waites Readers' Club. It only takes a moment, there is no catch and new members will automatically receive an exclusive ebook extract from *The Old Religion*. Your data is private and confidential and will never be passed on to a third party and I promise that I will only be in touch now and again with book news. If you want to unsubscribe, you can of course do that at any time.

However, if you like what you read then please let people know. Social media (I'm on Twitter as @MartynWaites and on Facebook, but I rarely go there), Amazon, GoodReads, all of that. It really does make a difference for writers.

But enough of my yakkin'. It's time to enter the world of *The Old Religion*. Enjoy, dear reader . . .

All the best,

Martyn Waites

Want to read
NEW BOOKS
before anyone else?

Like getting
FREE BOOKS?

Enjoy sharing your
OPINIONS?

Discover

READERS FIRST

Read. Love. Share.

Sign up today to win your first free book:
readersfirst.co.uk